Mission
of the
Artist

Barbara Joy Cordova

To Mary,
Have a great year
Love Barbara Cordova

An Artists for a Better World Publication

This book is dedicated to L Ron Hubbard, a writer and philosopher who has been my greatest source of inspiration.

* * * *

Many people helped me on the long and rewarding journey of writing this book. Their assistance is very much appreciated. I'd like to personally thank some of my key supporters:

Thomas Lane
Sunja Ackerman
Gen Whitt
JoAnne Childress
Kent Davis
Marti Marshall
Robin Farrow
Mike Mendelshon

* * * *

My special thanks to Bruce Wiseman, president of the Citizens Commission on Human Rights and author of the book "Psychiatry, the Ultimate Betrayal."
                    http://www.cchr.org

Cover artwork by Kathy Yaude ©1998

Part I - The Mission

Chapter 1

The Empress Zeena stood in front of a large arched window in her planning room. She gingerly ran her fingers along the window's stone ledge, as if to remind herself of the fact that her empire was still standing. Zeena sighed a deep breath of relief as she looked out upon the beautiful lands of Athena. The planet full of artists was once again united as a team. "It will never happen again!" she thought, practically aloud, as she remembered the tragedy that had threatened her beautiful homeland several hundred years ago. Some of the pride and honor that she'd worn before the catastrophe had slightly faded from her majestic countenance. Zeena still blamed herself for what had occurred. Although the planetary healing process was nearly complete, remnant scars still remained from the battle. She thought it unfortunate that some of the artists continued to hold back on their true powers, and that many team members were now gone. Even though the new foundation wasn't quite as strong as the old one, the Empress hoped that her hindsight, and that of her people, would help them not to make the same errors again.

Zeena's thoughts were suddenly interrupted by a flash of brilliant whiteness that she saw out of the corner of her eye. She was dazzled by the sight of a winged horse that soared into view, gracing the skies with his elegance. A playful young man sat astride the horse. He drew an image of a rainbow in the sky, not knowing that he was also drawing the Empress into a less serious mood. She waved to the rider and smiled warmly at him as he flew by.

A splash of sound hit Zeena's ears as she was taken in by a sudden musical performance taking place beneath the window. Two men magically plucked the strings of their instruments, while a vocalist poured an enchanting song from her heart. Zeena's smile widened with pleasure as she bathed in the artists' creations. As her spirits lifted upwards, she reminded herself of the potential power of this planet, full of creative beings. "Art, like a laser beam, cutting through the despair and awakening lost dreams," she thought, while noting how she herself was being uplifted by the entertainers outside.

As the music intensified, a dancer emerged, as if from nowhere, and started leaping in harmony with the song. He stepped into the air and twirled like a top, until he was several feet above the ground. Higher and higher he rose, until suspended, parallel with the fifth story window where the empress stood. Zeena smiled, and applauded approvingly. Then she playfully climbed upon her window ledge and held out a welcoming hand. The agile dancer saw this as a signal that she wanted to join him. He took her hand and pulled her from her perch. Zeena's long silver hair added an embellishing, rhythmic motion to the sky dance, as it whipped around her. She couldn't remember having this much fun for a long time. In fact, she almost felt guilty. While she danced with pleasure, enjoying the new freedom, something tugged at her heartstrings. As the music crescendoed, she slowed down. Her smile turned to a frown. "Thank you for this dance," she said to the dancer, as she quickly kissed him on the cheek.

"You're welcome, my Empress," he said. He gave her a look of both respect and puzzlement as she scurried back through the arched window, stumbling upon the planning room floor. The dancer floated downward, back to where the musicians stood.

The surge of song emanating from the singer ebbed into silence, as she noticed the swiftness of Zeena's departure. For a moment, she caught herself worrying that perhaps her singing had displeased the Empress. As the small concert of song ended, one of the musicians put his arm around the girl. "Kareva, what is the matter?" he said, sensing her withdrawal.

"I don't know if the Empress..." Before she could complete her sentence, a small white bird with blue-tipped wings, sent by the Empress, circled nearby. Kareva smiled as she snapped out of her self-abasing thoughts, "nothing, never mind," she said, watching the little winged messenger, which she knew to be a symbol from the Empress to acknowledge them for a performance well done. Kareva then realized how silly it was for her to ever think the Empress would insult an artist. It was just something that Zeena would never do. Kareva thought about the fact that such an idea must have simply lodged itself into her mind like a piece of residue from the past, an aftermath of the tragedy. She was merely equating Zeena with someone else!

The little white bird knew his job was done, and flew back into the palace planning room, where Zeena tensely paced around. Some of her stiffness momentarily abated as the little creature landed upon her shoulder and nuzzled her cheek. She stroked the head of the bird and then opened the door to a large gilded cage. The bird obediently flew inside.

Now that the problems on Athena were under control, one might presume this was enough to make Zeena happy, but she was nevertheless quite worried. The salvaging of Athena had been a true test of strength, even for her. All her attention had been averted from other pressing matters in the galaxy. She had tapped deeply into her own well of power in order to keep her homeland from going down altogether. It was only moments ago, while dancing in the sky, indulging in a brief moment of pleasure, that she had perceived that there were troubles with other planets in the Milky Way galaxy.

Zeena grew tired and lay down on a pink satin resting couch, her body sinking into a comfortable position. "Be damned you Black Knights!" Zeena said aloud as she slammed her fist into a couch pillow. "You're still at it!" she said, relying on her keen perceptions which told her that the Knights were still actively wreaking havoc in many sectors. It always disgusted her that such

3

creatures dubbed themselves with a name that implied they were doing noble deeds. She knew that in their twisted way, they actually believed they were right in their actions. The Athenians, however, took their name to heart as merely a pun that really meant "Black Nights," as this is what they attempted to bring to many a civilization.

Zeena silently regretted the fact that she'd been so out of touch with leaders of some of the other planets. They had normally informed her of their exact troubles.

As she closed her translucent eyelids, she started to recall some of the missions she'd sent her people on long ago. She saddened as she remembered some of the great artists, many of whom were no longer around. They used to go to other civilizations that had suffered attacks from the Knights. The Athenians used their artistic talents to help others revitalize their hopes and dreams, and got them to work together after being torn apart. If only Athena herself hadn't been a victim of the insidious attack by the Black Knights, Zeena knew she could have spent the last several hundred years sending her artists out to help fight the decay of many a civilization.

As Zeena lay on the couch, she drifted out beyond the bounds of her physical body. She was getting a spiritual perception of something that puzzled and disturbed her and she couldn't quite put her finger on its point of origin. "What is it? Where?" She was being drawn to something, and she wondered what it was. Several questions begged for attention in her mind, and she tried to zero in on the one that was the most prominent, the one that was causing her to reach out and seek an immediate answer.

Like a boomerang, thoughts about the tragedy kept coming back to her. "But why?" She wondered. She thought she'd filed these memories in the archives of her mind labeled "Athenian history." She knew she was now ready to carry on and face the future, but there was a piece of the past she couldn't ignore. "Why? Oh, I see, it's a clue. That's it, a clue," she gaped as a hazy image started to form in her mind. Then the picture got clearer and clearer as she adjusted the tuning on the scene she was looking at. There, before her, emerged a lifelike image of a beautiful Athenian woman with long blond hair and bright turquoise eyes. "Rhianna," the Empress said, sitting up as if being propelled by this picture. Zeena shuddered with both fear and relief, as she recalled the fateful moment when Rhianna's courage had helped to keep Athena from going down altogether. Unfortunately, although Rhianna's heroic act had helped save Athena from total doom, she herself was not saved from the clutches of the Knights. After a sad encounter with the gods of darkness, hundreds of years ago, Rhianna had left Athena, and had not since returned. The Empress suddenly realized how much she missed this being of whom she was very fond. Zeena now sensed that something was wrong with Rhianna. "My dear Rhianna, where are you? After what you did for Athena, I owe you my assistance. But I must locate..." she said aloud, as she was interrupted by the sound of desperate knocking on her door. Zeena jumped up and went to see who the urgent caller was. Opening the golden door, she was greeted by the face of her assistant, Gilmar, a tall man of nearly five hundred years in age. He was somewhat frantic.

"Gilmar, what is the urgency?"

"I'm sorry to disturb you my dear Empress."

"There's no need for apology. Come have a seat," Zeena said warmly, while putting her arm around her assistant.

Zeena could almost perceive what Gilmar was going to say, before the words tumbled out of his mouth.

"I was in the galactic map room a few moments ago, when I noticed a red 'danger' signal coming from one of the solar systems on the chart. When I saw this I thought I should warn you."

"This could be one of the answers I'm looking for. You are one step ahead of me, observing the map before I finished my perceptic search."

"I'm sorry, I just thought you might want to see what was going on."

"I'm the one who should be sorry for having neglected the map for so long," said Zeena, as both of them left the planning room and flew down a long palace hallway toward a huge, dome-shaped room. Zeena and Gilmar lifted their robes as they climbed the small stairway that led to the door of the room.

There, in the center of the room, laid out on a round table, was an enormous map. Each solar system had colored lights on top of the individual planets. The colors were used to signify degrees of danger. Zeena moved around to a section where a bright red light fiercely blinked on and off several times per second. Her eyes zeroed in on a tiny planet in the outer rim of the galaxy. She pushed a button that made the planet grow larger. "Earth, my god, that's where she is!" she said while tightly holding onto the edge of the table. "Red. Not a good sign at all."

"Nearly the highest level danger code there is. If this were two shades brighter, wouldn't it mean that the planet would be...?" Gilmar paused, knowing he didn't need to go on. He looked straight into Zeena's fiery eyes; both of them growing more and more concerned over this sight.

"Gilmar, please excuse me, I need to be alone in here for awhile," Zeena said, while hot and cold waves ran through her body. "I am not quite done with my perceptic search."

Gilmar quietly closed the door on his way out. Zeena gently ran her hand over the small red bulb. Then, feeling like a laser beam had cut to the core of her being, she suddenly became awakened to the fact that a number of her old teammates were now on Earth. "That's where they are! Lost their magic and power; and such short lifetimes. Barely enough time to get anything done."

Zeena sensed that many of her old friends had been born and died a number of times. They didn't even have the chance to live a decent life span. A typical Athenian often lived up to six hundred of those Earth years, and one still looked young up until around the age of five hundred. The Empress herself was an exception in that she had been able to preserve her body fifteen hundred years now.

Zeena wanted to get a general picture of the state of affairs on Earth, and her intentions were so strong that she stirred up the air and caused a warm wind to come whistling in through a small, round window. Closing her eyes, she got a perception of some of the general conditions on the planet, and sensed that the Knights had infiltrated long ago, but were wearing a guise that she couldn't quite make out. She just perceived that the damage they had inflicted had created a disaster on that planet.

Once again, like a boomerang returning, she was hit with a picture of Rhianna. She opened her eyes and started slowly pacing around the large, round map. "Rhianna, what is it?" she said aloud and then went back over to where the little red light blinked, as if being summoned by it to take a better look at something.

"Trouble. I know you are in trouble." It was easier for Zeena to perceive specifically what was happening with her fellow Athenians than with other beings in the galaxy.

The picture of the radiant Athenian she once knew transformed into an image of another female. It was Rhianna, wearing her current Earth body. The dynamic glow around her had faded; the one that used to shine brightly with a strong sense of purpose and vision. The Empress sensed, however, that underneath her troubles, she still harbored a bright illuminating presence. Somehow, this would have to be rekindled so that she could carry on with the crusade she had embarked upon. Zeena sensed that the mission Rhianna was now on was very similar to others she'd taken on in the past, but this time she was on her own and had gotten into some grave danger. Her mission was vital in helping to salvage this sad little planet.

The last thing Zeena needed to know was the whereabouts of Rhianna. Although she knew she was on Earth, this was not good enough. She had to get a closer estimation of where to find her. This was the hardest feat of all, and it took a much sharper degree of concentration, as she was now dealing with a completely unknown and distant location.

Continuing with her ritual, she focused on her target on the map. Like the eyes of a bird hovering over a field in search of its prey, Zeena zeroed in on the distant planet in the galaxy in search for her old friend.

"Rhianna, give me your physical location," she thought loudly. At that moment, she saw something happening on the map. When the Empress gave her command, a golden light appeared. In compliance with Zeena's wishes, the magic light scanned the planet. Then it pinpointed a particular area of planet Earth and flashed on and off several times.

"So that's the area you're in. I need to know more," she thought, as she worked on getting the exact name of the area where Rhianna was, as well as more facts about her current life on Earth.

The Empress knew what her next move had to be.

Chapter 2

Zeena sat at a desk in her planning room and looked pensively at the screen of a small computer-like machine, known as a telecomm. This machine was used to communicate with residents on Athena, as well as beings on nearby planets. Zeena placed her hand on a knob and adjusted it so that names and descriptions of various Athenians came into view. She quickly scanned over characteristics of many Athenians until she came across the one who would be right for the job.

"Devon, yes, this is who I will use," she said to herself, and punched in code numbers that hooked her up with Devon's telecomm, allowing instant communication.

The Empress reached Devon immediately and summoned her to the palace to get briefed on her mission.

Devon, a young inquisitive Athenian, hated mystery and wondered what her task would be. Although she knew it was official policy never to reveal the nature of missions over telecomm, Devon could hardly stand the suspense.

It had been awhile since she'd been on a mission, and she was looking forward to a good adventure. Around her home were various viewing discs of other civilizations, including Earth, which she studied from time to time. She hoped to someday visit these places that were so different from her home.

Devon rapidly walked over to her beam glider, a vehicle used for local travel around the planet. She flew as fast as she could until she came to the landing ramp near the palace. She got out of the glider and made her way to a couple of large golden doors that stood like guards at the entranceway to the castle. Devon punched a special code into a small box on a wall, letting Zeena know she had arrived. The doors welcomed her by opening and letting her inside. She dashed up a winding flight of stairs to the planning room where the Empress received her. It had been a long time since Devon had been in this chamber. When she arrived she was practically out of breath as she greeted the Empress.

"Devon, please have a seat," Zeena said, motioning toward a large chair in front of a stone desk. The Empress sat behind the desk facing Devon.

"Your promptness is appreciated. Would you like some liquid?" she asked.

"Yes, please my Empress," replied Devon as Zeena handed her a silver goblet full of green juice from a local plant. Devon gulped down the sweet fluid and put the cup on the desk.

Some of Devon's excitement turned to worry as she saw the solemn look that caused Zeena's brow to wrinkle excessively. The Empress' piercing eyes gazed right at Devon.

"Devon, I now want to inform you of your special mission. You will be going to planet Earth. It is there that a great Athenian who once went by the name of Rhianna now resides."

Devon was shocked to find out that this being whom she had studied about on Athena history discs was on such a backward planet. "Earth? What a sad fate! From my understanding this place is not very technologically advanced. Many of the people there do menial jobs, not very creative ones either. What would a powerful artist like Rhianna be doing on such a backward planet?"

"Apparently she's been trying to help make it a better place to live. She was doing well for some time, but unfortunately she ran into problems recently. Rhianna has backed off from her mission." The Empress paused, gathered her thoughts, and then went on. "Yes, my dear Devon," the Empress said as she closed her eyes while Devon's stayed wide open, focused fully on Zeena as if nothing else around her mattered. "I will give you some more data on Rhianna. I perceive that she got herself into a position on Earth where she became a well-known artist in the music field. She was using her position to speak out against some of the immoral activities there."

The Empress opened her eyes and hesitated for a moment. Devon could hardly stand the suspense. "I had a problem getting the full vision, but there's something I picked up on. There's an evil force that Rhianna has run up against in the city where she lives." The Empress tried to hold back the grief that came over her once again. She settled back in her body and opened her eyes and looked at Devon. "Rhianna was creating a good impact. Then something happened. I can't get a clear picture, but I know she's in danger. To make matters worse, I don't think she knows who the true enemy is. Earth is not a safe place to be doing great things without a team."

Devon sat on the edge of her seat, having some apprehension about what she knew the empress was going to say next. She knew Rhianna was special, but why all the fuss over such a backward place?

The Empress continued, and answered the question in Devon's thoughts as she went on. "I want you to go to Earth and find Rhianna and give her a message from me that will help her to succeed. You see, my concern about this chaotic planet, in spite of all the madness there, is that it is special. There are a lot of artists there, many of whom were once Athenians. Some of them are doing good things. Although they have tumbled down the track of time and aren't using the powers they once had on Athena, they still have tremendous potential. A number of them, however, are leading lives of false complacency and have come to believe that their artistic goals are just too impractical. Many of them are suffering from chronic cases of the deadly disease you and I know as 'Dream Demise.' I sense that there is a sweeping influence of evil that has been hypnotically commanding the lives of many artists and others on Earth." The Empress paused as her anger permeated the space, sparking a comment from Devon.

"It's the Knights!"

"I believe so."

"Do you think that Rhianna may have fallen prey to their schemes again?"

The Empress looked downcast for a moment, "Yes."

Starting to dwell on Rhianna, she briefly paused, then pulled herself out of her contemplation and continued. "I have determined that Rhianna is known on Earth as Nicole Jensen. Her art form is songwriting and singing and she has imprints of her songs on plastic-like discs. She is somewhere in Los Angeles, which in Earth terms means "the angels." Unfortunately, I am not able to get you her precise spatial coordinates, but I would suggest trying to locate her through an Earth residence directory. You can also find out where you can get one of her discs, and use this as a clue to try and track her down. There is a place known as Hollywood, in the angel city, one of the main headquarters for Earth artists. This would be a good place to start your search."

The Empress then opened a desk drawer engraved with small flowers and pulled out a small coin. She pulled out a golden chain and attached the coin to it. She told Devon to come over to her and had her bend down as she proceeded to place the chain around her neck, where it rested with a few other chains that Devon wore. Zeena gave Devon instructions as to what to do with it once she found Nicole. She also told her that the coin had certain powers. Once in Nicole's possession its magic would allow Zeena to better connect with Nicole in order to perceive the effects that she was creating on others in her area. Fondling the special coin, Devon sat down.

Some of Devon's excitement slipped out of her face and Zeena could see this. "Devon, what is the matter?"

"Well, this sounds like such a short mission. I was really hoping that I could do more than just deliver the coin. Perhaps I could remain on Earth for a while and help Rhianna, I mean Nicole. I have a lot I can contribute to the Earth people."

Zeena smiled at Devon's good-natured desires. "My dear Devon, I would love for you to be able to stay and help, but I'm afraid there is something you do not know yet."

"What's that?

"Although your body looks deceivingly similar to an Earthling's, it will not be able to endure the toxic level of the atmosphere for any length of time. You see, there are so many harmful substances in the air that your system will be vastly harmed if you should keep your physical form for too long. Your body simply will not hold up. The radiation from the Earth's sun will weaken you tremendously, too," the Empress said.

Devon's disappointment at not being able to experience the degree of adventure that she'd hoped for was keen, but then her interest perked up as Zeena continued with further mission instructions.

"I know you thirst for something to do that is more eventful than the mere deliverance of a coin, and I want to let you know that there is one thing more to your outing on Earth than what I have just told you."

Devon shared a smile with the Empress. "As you set out to contact Nicole, I want you to do an inspection in the Los Angeles city, and take note of any degraded conditions you run across with the artists there. Who is influencing them, as well as their society in general?

What are the identities of these Knights in disguise that are getting people to agree with their wicked ways? You may have to get several clues, which will lead you to the source of evil. Hopefully, you will be able to uncover the one true guise that these scoundrels are wearing before your time is up," Zeena said, as Devon recalled an old mission she went on where she had needed to do some very swift spy work.

"If you determine who the culprits are, I want you to relay this data to Nicole. She has been tricked unwittingly by the ways of the black warriors, and so have many others on Earth. The truth must be known before it is too late. Do your best, but don't delay," Zeena said, glancing at the shiny gold piece which rested obediently upon Devon's white gown. "Remember that the most important part of your mission is getting the coin to Nicole."

Devon was glad that her thirst for excitement would soon be quenched. "So, I am going to get to be a spy!"

"Yes, but you are going to have to be an invisible spy. As I have warned you, your body will suffer greatly if you remain too long in physical form on Earth."

Devon knew exactly what the Empress was going to say next, and in unison they both spoke the word, "De-molecularization."

"Yes, Devon, this is one of the reasons I have chosen you for the mission," the Empress said as Devon reminded herself of her ability to disassemble all of the molecules in her body, as well as any clothing and material objects she had with her, making them temporarily invisible.

"Well, now that I know I can de-molecularize, I can spend plenty of time on the Earth planet."

"Not exactly," said the Empress, kindly trying to buffer what she sensed might be a disappointment to Devon. "You see, it is because of the factors that I had previously mentioned that there is a time limit on your mission. You will have ten Earth days from the time you first utilize your body. While spying, you may have to use your body from time to time, to get information from Earthlings. However, even using it on and off will tire you. I'm afraid that after nine days you will feel very ill, barely able to go on, but you will have one more day to put it on briefly and get back into your space ship. After that point you'll become too weakened to use it at all."

Devon swallowed, "Oh, I see." Then she changed her tune, and brightened up again, realizing that it was her special ability to become invisible that had gotten her the mission in the first place. "So, how are we going to know if Nicole succeeds once I give her the message?"

"We will be able to detect any changes in Nicole's area of influence via the light signals in the galactic map room. If she succeeds, the impending danger should begin to ease, and the red light will fade. I will also be able to do a perceptic search, and tune in on Nicole and other Athenians to get a feel for any positive changes," Zeena said. Devon nodded with understanding. Zeena then reached into the same drawer where she got the coin, and this time pulled out a small black box. "Here is a language assimilation box. You will need it to become versed in the language called 'English'. I have programmed the box for you so that all you have to do is wear this attached headset for a short period of time. You will then be quickly taught this new language. Though you won't be perfect at it, you will at least be skilled enough to communicate with the people where you are going. You will also have to study some of the customs of the Los Angeles people. I regret that you won't have more time to do your learning, but there is a need to hurry, as neither Rhianna or planet Earth are doing very well right now."

The Empress contemplated something else that she felt might be necessary for Devon's quest. "Since Nicole has been harmed, she may not be very willing to meet with a perfect stranger. Humans often have fear of being betrayed by others. So there is one more thing that you need to be armed with," she hesitated.

Devon's eyebrows raised inquisitively. "What's that my Empress?"

"Something that will melt down any defenses Nicole could put up to bar your way into her life." Zeena closed her eyes. "This part isn't easy. I must now do an intense perceptic search of Nicole, in order to feed my suspicions about something, and give you a weapon that could help you to get through to her."

As Zeena's eyelids shut tightly, wind came whipping in through the large arched window. She placed her two slender, outstretched hands upon the desk in front of her, pressing them onto the marble top as Devon sat wide-eyed.

After several moments, Zeena opened her eyes. A smile alighted upon her face. The wind stopped as Zeena sat silently gazing into Devon's questioning eyes.

"You look as if you have good news, my Empress."

"I do," she said and paused, "She remembers Athena. But because of all the deliberate obliteration of full memory that occurs between lifetimes, she only has a vague notion of us. There is, however, a strong spiritual bond that she is aware of. You can use 'Athena' as a way to get to her heart."

The next day, Devon eagerly awaited her time of departure to the little planet in a far corner of the Milky Way galaxy. She looked forward to riding in a space rider, a small space-ship used to travel to other planets. She knew it would be easy to navigate with the use of her universal grid, a map and a direction finder.

Chapter 3

evon's arrival in Hollywood occurred on a warm Sunday night in April, when darkness blanketed the sky. She parked her space ship in a secluded area away from the main city, and then put up a special shield, which rendered it invisible. She then de-molecularized, making herself invisible. She tried to get familiar with these new and strange surroundings that engulfed her. Devon didn't know exactly where to go, so just floated around aimlessly until she noticed a couple of large beams of light dancing back and forth in the sky. Intrigued by them, she followed them to their emanation point. She saw that a round, white machine with a bright light in the center of it was the source of the lights. The machine was in front of a building that had a large reptile on its roof. Devon knew from her studies that these creatures were part of Earth's Jurassic period. At first she was confused as to whether she had perhaps accidentally gotten into some sort of time warp, but as she got closer to the dinosaur she saw it was fake. Breathing a sigh of relief she made her way down to the roadway labeled Hollywood Boulevard. Excited by the stars embedded in the pavement, and the large variety of people scurrying down the street, Devon figured this would be a good place to start her adventures.

As she hovered slightly above the street she could see a parade of vehicles slowly following one another for what seemed like miles. They moved at a leisurely pace, but the people inside didn't seem to care, for they were busy amusing themselves by talking to one another. She noticed red, green and yellow lights beaming on and off which regulated the motion of the vehicles.

Devon's curiosity drew her closer to the action below her. She saw a shiny black vehicle full of young males, who were driving along as loud electronic blasts of music were being emitted from small speakers within the car. A vehicle full of females pulled up beside them, which caused the males to protrude their heads out of the car. The female driver had on thick, black eyelash coverings and red lip paint. She was wearing a piece of material that barely covered her breasts. One of the males said, "Hey babe, nice bra, looks just like the one worn in concert by..."

Devon didn't catch the name of the person who wore the underwear in concert. She just heard the girls giggling and could tell there was more interchange between the people in the cars. This intrigued her and made her wonder what it was about, but she continued on with her mission.

She was shaken up by all this new and unusual activity, as it had been ages since she'd been away from her homeland to see anything other than the beauty of Athena. She was not used to all the noise and commotion. Her attention was drawn to a dark side street that veered off to her left. Devon decided to see what was there. Down the alley were people who didn't seem as happy as all the humans on the main boulevard who were enjoying their night out. A man with a torn, dirty shirt and matted brown hair was busy at work selling small tablets to a few others that were gathered around him. They were arguing about the price of pills while disagreeing on the quality.

"Better be the real shit, man. I want a good high," said a customer of the man selling the pills.

She had enough of this sad sight and her attention was now yanked by a couple of bodies walking down a street in front of her. Confused as to whether they were of the male or female sex, she followed them from behind to solve her dilemma. One had long, blond, curly hair that was nearly waist length, and wore tight, spotted animal skin pants and a sleeveless cowhide top with holes in it. There was a rope around his, or her, hips and several fake skull and crossbones dangled from it, making dull, clanking sounds with each step. The other person was similarly dressed but had long, shiny, black hair. Devon's curiosity drew her closer so she could listen in on their conversation. At first she felt a little guilty being taken in by this sight, as it wasn't particularly on her mission orders to be looking at all the strange humans in Hollywood. As she got nearer, not only did she find out that the voices were both male, but also that they were part of a music band called "Rodney and the Gutter Rats." As she listened to them it seemed that their band was getting more and more popular, even very close to getting a thing called a "record deal." There were a couple of guys in the "Artists and Repertoire" department at some place called "Twisted Records" in Hollywood who were going to make a decision tomorrow evening at five as to whether they'd be signed to this label or not.

After finding out that they were musicians, she figured that the Empress wouldn't mind if she inspected them further. She decided to visit this "Twisted" place the next day, which was a Monday.

Monday arrived and it was time to find out where "Twisted" was. Devon was hesitant, as she knew that she had to make her first physical appearance in order to get directions there, and this would be the start of her mission "time clock" where, wearing the body or not, she was then on the big countdown.

She awkwardly looked for an inconspicuous place to reassemble her body, hoping no one would see. She found a large, empty, garbage receptacle and decided this was the best place she could currently find to make her transition. Besides, she'd seen some people in the city that seemed to reside in these containers. She didn't worry about looking too out of place climbing out of one, which is exactly what she did. However she did get some funny looks from a few people. One person made an amusing comment about the "dress" she was wearing. Devon knew she must have looked pretty out of place with her Athenian gown on.

After asking a few people where the record company place was and getting nothing but strange looks and no answers, Devon decided to do what one person suggested; go to a phoning cubicle and look in the "Yellow Pages." She found nothing in the yellow part of the book, but then noticed half of the book was white so she quickly went to the "T" section until she came to what she was looking for. She got the exact address. Her next task was to find out how to get there.

She walked down the street and coughed a little, realizing how right the Empress was about the air quality here. Looking up, she noticed a thick gray sky covering and figured this must be what the Earth people refer to as smog. Devon wondered what they did to get such a dirty sky cover. She felt like asking someone, but decided to save this bit of curiosity for later, if she had time. She left the cubicle while two people pointed at her from a distance and made her feel somewhat self-conscious. Devon ignored them and approached a female who was walking in her direction. She asked her if she could direct her to Highland.

The female said "Why, yes, dear. I can tell you. Just take Sunset and go west about six blocks."

"Where's Sunset?" asked Devon.

Laughing, and looking at Devon's dress, the woman replied, "Where's Sunset? That's the street you're on. You from a foreign country or something?"

Devon replied, "I guess you could say that. Thank you very much."

"You're welcome."

Devon started to get dizzy. She went to find a place to de-molecularize her body and clothes again. Then she headed for her destination. While quickly strolling down the street, Devon's attention was yanked to a large sign on the top of a tall building. There in front of her she noticed a picture of a woman in tight pink pants and a top that barely covered her extremely large breasts. Devon spent a few seconds wondering what the purpose of this picture was.

She arrived at the record company, went inside the building, and located the "Artists and Repertoire" department. Inside the room there was a long table with piles of small discs on it. Two men were seated at the table smoking cigars. One said, "Well, Ralph, now that we've heard them all it's time to make some decisions."

Ralph replied, "Yeah Marvin, and who will the lucky winners be?"

"Well I sure know who it ain't gonna be." Marvin snickered, picked up a disc in front of him, and handed it to Ralph. They both laughed snidely as Devon cringed to herself.

Then Ralph said, "Yeah Marv, those guys are on some weird kind of Utopian 'save the world' kick." He looked at the disc. "They're starting out on the wrong foot already. C'mon, look at these titles. 'Vision of Peace', 'A Brighter Day', 'World in

Harmony'? Why did they even bother to send a tape to us? They must be real desperate," he said, trying to appease Marvin who was his boss.

Devon noticed that his comment sounded stiff and insincere. She questioned his belief in what he had said.

Marvin spoke, "Yeah, tell 'em to get real. Why don't you toss it in the reject pile?"

Ralph gently flung the disc, then Marvin picked up another one, saying, "Now we're talking. 'Rodney and the Gutter Rats,' You're talking big bucks now. Can't miss with songs like 'Sleazy Lady', 'Let's do it', and 'You Get Me Hot.' They know sex sells. Got the following to prove it too. Yeah, good ol' Rodney. He'll do whatever it takes to become famous. His manager, Jim Scott, has got him well trained. He's like putty in Jim's hands. Been able to mold him into an image of the rock idol that the kids want. You name it: lewd, crude, obscene, he'll do it. What a spirit! By the way, you ever seen 'em perform?" Marvin asked.

"Nope, can't say I have."

"Well, Ralph ol' pal, now's your chance. Rodney happens to be doing a set tonight at the Outhouse. Since we're pretty well wrapped up, what do you say we catch the show?"

"Sounds like a plan. Let's go," Ralph replied.

Devon looked around in astonishment at the number of discs that ended up in the reject pile, and thought it was odd to see so many artists just tossed aside like waste matter. Rodney was one of the few that didn't end up in this "Outhouse." "Why not make room for more of them?" she wondered.

Ralph and Marvin headed out of their office and down the hall. Ralph paused for a second.

"What's the matter, buddy?" asked Marvin.

"Oh, I think I forgot something. Why don't you go on down and I'll meet you at the car," Ralph said, then mumbled something to himself.

Marvin continued down a stairway while Ralph, accompanied by Devon, went back to the office. She was curious about his move. Ralph couldn't stand the facade he had to wear to keep his job sometimes.

Ralph walked over to the reject pile and picked up the disc of the group with the "Utopian" songs on it that he had pretended to detest. He stuck it in an envelope and addressed it to another record company with a note inside saying, "Although we are not signing this group at Twisted Records, perhaps you might want to listen to them. They do have some worthwhile messages." Then he signed it "Ralph Carson, A&R." He sealed and stamped the envelope then stuck it in a mail chute on his way out, as Devon followed. Devon smiled to herself, happy to see that Ralph still had a heart, unlike his cohort.

Ralph had always been afraid of losing his job if he spoke up and stated how he really felt, so he made a habit of placing money ahead of his integrity. He didn't have the guts to just quit, as jobs were scarce.

Meanwhile, Marvin was in the car, arrogantly puffing on a fat cigar, while engrossed in a newspaper. As Ralph got into the car he said, "Ralph, take a look at this article in the 'LA Slime.' Looks like the Gutter Rats got some rave reviews. All those lonely teenage girls looking for a sex god to drool over ensure that every concert those guys do is a real sellout." Marvin went on, "Yep, I figure our personal profits should be pretty damn high once we get the Rats on the label. Remember that red Porsche you wanted?"

Ralph put back on his facade. "Hey, I could have it for Christmas the way things are going, thanks to stupid teenagers who have daddy's money in their pockets."

"Yep, that's what matters. Keep those dollars rolling in and I don't care what kind of crap we have to press into plastic."

Marvin and Ralph arrived at the Outhouse, parked their car, and went in. Devon was glad she wasn't wearing her body because she knew she would really have felt sick at this point.

The three of them went to a table for two in the back of the room as dissonant music blared. Many of the clientele of the club were mimicking the Gutter Rats' style of dress, even down to their pierced noses and bellies. It was very obvious to Devon that the Rats were a strong influence in the lives of others.

To Devon, the song that was being performed when they arrived seemed to go on forever. When it ended she saw the singer step to the front of the stage. He had a microphone in one hand and a container labeled "beer" in the other. Marvin gave Ralph a sly look and nudged him with an elbow. "That's our boy."

Rodney guzzled the last of the beer in the container, squeezed it and threw it down. He belched, then held the mic up to his mouth. "Hope you're all getting ripped tonight. Only way to do the Rats. This next song is called "You Get Me Hot.""

He proceeded to sing while shaking his hips and pelvis around. One intoxicated girl in the front row shouted, "Ooh, baby, I want it." Then a few others joined in the chorus, making similar comments.

Devon wasn't sure what they were talking about until she saw Rodney grab his crotch area and move his hand up and down. The girls squealed as he sang these words:

"You get me hot!
Oh what have you got?
One look and I was through,
I knew I must have you.
Let me take you for a ride.
I'm going into overdrive.
I'll take you to my home.
My wife ain't there. We'll be all alone.
You can do me all night long.
Being with you I can't go wrong."

Rodney stopped singing as one girl nearly fainted from infatuation, not to mention a fair amount of drugs.

Ralph and Devon silently sneered.

Rodney was dripping with sweat as he introduced the musicians to the crowd. "On bass, Joe Stud," Joe took a bow and there were more squeals. "On guitar, Jimmy Tight-Ass. On keyboards, Vick the Viper. And our drummer, Spike the Slammer."

"And our fearless leader, Rodney," Vick said while looking through a drug fog, getting a fuzzy picture of the audience.

The crowd went wild for some time and when the screaming finally died down, the Rats exited.

Ralph and Marvin got up and started to walk out.

Marvin said, "Yeah, I'll give their attorney a call tomorrow and work out the details. Don't want to spring the news on 'em tonight. Got to use a more formal business approach."

"Good idea, pal," said Ralph as he gave him an insincere pat on the back, wondering when he was going to stop acting like such a rat himself, and just get brave enough to leave his job.

Devon decided to let Ralph and Marvin depart without her. Being repulsed, yet at the same time intrigued, she decided to stick around and observe what happened next in this scenario. She made her way backstage, where the Rats were conversing with one another about how the show had gone. A few young females also managed to sneak backstage, but had a much harder time of it than Devon. One of the girls held out her hand, as if to show her friends something of value, and said "Oooh, I just touched Vick on the arm."

The other girls were awed. Rodney was drinking a bottle of beer when a man with greased back dark hair, wearing a black leather jacket and flashy gold watch, walked up to him. "Hey Rod, aren't you gonna say hello to your ol' manager?"

Rodney replied, "Scott, how's it goin' man?" Putting his arm around him, he asked, "Say, did we kick ass tonight?"

"As usual Rod, the cock bit went over well with the babes, but I'd still like to see you work a little more on that pelvic punch. Don't hold back as much next time. Just let those hips fly. We need even more girls squealing. It's better publicity," said Jim Scott with a wink.

"Yeah, I know. I know." Rodney put the beer bottle down on a table and ran his right hand through his stringy hair. "I tell you man, sometimes I just don't know about this act."

Scott looked puzzled. "Don't know? What don't ya know? You're a natural at this stuff. Don't start givin me shit again Rod. I told you, once we get the deal you can make some changes in the show, do some more of those other songs of yours, but for now, it's what sells. And you and I both need the bucks," Jim said, giving Rodney a friendly shoulder punch.

"Okay man, okay." said Rodney, suddenly looking downcast. Sometimes he wished he'd never sold his soul for fame. It was too late now.

"What's the matter now? Where's the spirit? Is the job too demanding?" Jim asked snidely.

Rodney paused before answering, "Nah, it's not that."
"By the way, you and the old lady still fighting?"

"Yeah," Rodney replied.

"Eh, forget it. You know women. They get so damn over-emotional over nothing. By the way, I've been holding onto these for you," Jim said as he put his hand in the left pocket of his leather jacket and pulled out two tablets, which Rodney took and instantly swallowed.

"Good ol Prozac, the only thing that might make me forget my miseries," he mumbled.

"Now go over there," Jim said, pointing toward the females standing around backstage. "Grab one of them young ripe ones, go out and live it up. Just forget about the old bitch at home." Rodney looked a bit confused, so Jim said, "Hey, remember, our friendly shrink not only recommends pills, but also a good affair every now and then to keep your interest aroused in the opposite sex. Do you remember the motto?"

"Rodney mumbled in acknowledgment, "Yeah I know, "if your love life ain't heatin', there's nothin' wrong with a little cheatin'.""

"You got it. Besides, you can practice the pelvic punch." Trying to humor him, Jim patted Rodney on the back, then left.

Rodney picked up his beer and took another swig, then put it back on the shaky brown table. He decided that Scott was right. Rodney remembered a time when he went for counseling and was told that his depression was caused by some chemical imbalance in his brain. Although he often wondered if it wasn't simply caused because he was so unhappy, he went along with these words of wisdom. Rodney buried his head in his hands, anxiously waiting for the Prozac to numb his miseries. He blocked out the fact that his true creative urges had been on a downward landslide ever since he'd started taking this drug. Several minutes later, one of the young girls looked over at him, bewildered, as he lifted his head and started writing around like some sort of distraught serpent. He knew he was losing control, but did his best to "maintain."

Then he heeded Scott's advice and walked toward the young female groupies. Jimmy Tight Ass stood in his path as he strutted along.

"Hey man, you look like hell," said Jimmy, noticing Rodney's crazed look.

This was enough of a stimulus to cause an instant response from Rodney's drugged mind. Without analytical thought, Rodney punched Tight Ass in the stomach and watched him nearly keel over in pain. Jimmy Tight Ass stood and held his stomach. Just as he was about to retaliate, Rodney moved out of reach. He had nearly approached the girls.

One of them said, "Look who's coming our way." They all made an effort to stand provocatively.

Rodney cast aside any hidden guilt and put his arms around a couple of the girls. "You ladies enjoy the concert tonight?" he asked.

"Oh, did we ever," one of them said.

"Well, tell you what. Ol' Rodney would like to take one of you lucky gals out on the town and show you a real good time."

One girl couldn't control herself. Clinging tightly to his arm, she said, "Take me, take me."

Another girl said jealously, "No, take me, me."

Rodney replied, "Okay ladies, calm down. Let's do this fairly."

He had the three of them line up next to each other, then closed his eyes, put his right index finger out, spun around and said some words that sounded strange to Devon. "Eeny, meeny, miny, mo, you're the babe that gets to go." As he opened his eyes, his vision was so blurred that even though his finger was pointed at one of the girls, there appeared to be six of them. The winner squealed, then ran up and pawed him. Rodney shut his eyes tightly, trying to obliterate the illusion he had just seen. Then he opened them and clumsily put his arm around the winner. The girls were so caught up in the game that they didn't notice Rodney's dizziness.

25

The two losers just looked at each other in disappointment and then one said to the "babe" that got to go out with Rodney, "Hey Cheryl, hon, you have a great time. Call us tomorrow and tell us about it."

"I will," Cheryl said and winked at her friends.

As the two girls left, Rodney impulsively grabbed a clump of Cheryl's long hair from its roots, pulled her head back and said, "What do you say you and I hit my favorite pub, 'Belchers' and then head for a hotel?" This hurt and shocked Cheryl, but she just figured he was being playful. She gazed into his foggy eyes and replied, "Sure, anything you want Rodney. I've always wanted to make it with a Rat. This is a dream come true."

Devon thought to herself, "Yeah, he's a rat alright," then felt sorry for him. From the way he carried himself and by his far from genuinely happy smile, Devon could see that Rodney was suffering. She got the idea that he probably wasn't leading the life he'd originally planned. Devon thought that perhaps the real rat was his manager, the one who seemed to be influencing him. She saw the cold, manipulative ways of Jim Scott, and wondered whether he was a Knight in disguise. "Could it be the music managers? Is this their costume?" she thought, using this as her first piece of possible evidence.

After Cheryl and Rodney had departed, Devon wandered back to the part of the club where she had been entertained by Rodney's stage antics. She overheard that the club was getting ready to close soon. There was only a small handful of people left inside. A female wearing a short blue dress was standing at a table picking up empty bottles of beer and placing them on a tray. The clouds of smoke that had filled the room were slowly dispersing. Up on the stage was a male dressed similarly to Rodney. He was holding a mike and parading around, singing and shaking his hips. The mike was turned off, but he didn't seem to care, as he was just concerned with how he looked and how interesting he appeared to three guys and four girls who sat at a table near the stage watching him. They were all wearing attire that was similar to the guy on stage. As he sang, one of the girls whistled at him. Some of the people at the table were engaged in conversation with one another and their eyes were occasionally drawn to the guy on stage. A couple of the girls sat in admiration as they watched the Rodney imitation.

A tall man walking toward the singer interrupted the performance. He stopped near the stage and said, "Come on Jake. I've got to shut down now. Let's go." The man walked away and Jake resentfully complied. He got off the stage and walked over to his friends. "Keep it up and someday you and your band will pack the place just like the Gutter Rats. You'll be a big hit with all the babes too," said one of the guys at the table.

Jake replied. "Yeah, it's nice to have a model like Rodney to follow. I know I'm not the only one who's trying to be like him, but you know man, I think I got a lot of potential."

One of the girls who was listening to him stood up. She went over to him and ran her hand through his long stringy hair and said, "I think you're hot like Rod, and you're probably just as good in bed too. All you need are some good drugs, like the shit that Rodney gets, and ooh babe..."

Just as Jake was soaking up this compliment there was a loud interruption.

"Come on guys, wrap it up," the man trying to close the club said.

"Okay Dan, we're going," Jake said as the group of Gutter Rat look-a-likes got up and started walking out of the Outhouse.

Chapter 4

Devon found her thirst for more clues was nagging at her the day after her first Earth concert at the Outhouse. Although "a manager's suit" looked like a cunning outfit for a Knight to wear, while doing sleuth-work one never just took one piece of a puzzle to solve an investigation. All the pieces had to fit together, and there had to be a common thread that ran through the whole picture. There were other art forms she'd yet to inspect. She laughed to herself, as she entertained the thought that an Earth movie producer would probably love to write a script based on her adventures as an undercover, or better yet "uncovered," agent from another planet. While indulging in this comical thought, but not knowing where to go next in this strange new land, she realized she'd just given herself the next clue to trace.

"Movies," she thought, while aimlessly wandering down Hollywood Boulevard, observing the various theaters that sporadically lined the street. It was there that she was drawn to a cinema, where a line composed strictly of males waited to go inside. Her curiosity was sidetracked a bit from her main purpose. She had to find out why there were no females attending the showing of this movie entitled "The Outcast."

Once inside, Devon noticed that several men were sitting in pairs. She noticed an unusual bond of affection between many of them, as they held hands, or put their arms around one another. She was glad she wasn't present in her female body, as she thought that perhaps she would have been treated like some sort of unwanted guest.

The lights soon dimmed out the sight of all the cozy men around her as a curtain opened revealing a large, white screen. As the movie started, a mother and father were sitting on a couch in a living room. They looked at each other in a mournful way after having just found out that their son Joey was gay. Devon was puzzled as to why they weren't cheerful. It seemed to her that they should have been glad their son was having fun in life.

As the movie continued, Devon's question about why the parents weren't happy was answered. There, before her eyes, was a scene with Joey in a club filled with men. Joey was up on stage dancing around in nothing but a pair of underpants. Several men sat at small tables drinking liquor and smoking cigarettes. Devon noticed that Joey was doing the "pelvic punch" just like Rodney. The only difference was that this time it was the males that were shouting, "Ooh, I want some." Soon the scene changed to show the outside of the club, which had a big flashing sign that read "Gay Dancing." It was then that the gears in Devon's mind started turning, concluding that "gay" was just another term the Earth people had for the word "homosexual."

Although Devon was quite tough, she knew that if she'd had her body on, her stomach would probably have been doing somersaults after observing the next scene in the movie where four men were frolicking around in bed together. She forced herself to stay and tolerate the rest of the movie for research purposes.

Joey was at his parents' home sitting contentedly on a couch with his boyfriend. His parents admitted they were wrong in not accepting the lifestyle he'd chosen for himself, and to make amends, decided to have a big wedding for their son and his male partner.

Leaving the theater, Devon took note of another element that could possibly be insidiously destroying the Earth culture. "Gays." Could it be that the Knights are homosexuals who are trying to promote the acceptance of such abnormal acts in order to cause the race here to cease? Another puzzle piece, but still much missing.

On she went, unhappy with her incomplete findings. She'd only been in these alien surroundings a short period of time, but Devon was very impatient. She hated to work under such tight time constraints, but was determined to find the answer.

Devon floated back down the boulevard of stars, flitting by various sights that were starting to become familiar. Movies seemed to be the most accessible form of amusement and enlightenment, so she decided to allow herself one more showing for the day. An array of choices presented itself to her. Having no idea on Earth as to what any of the movies were about, she somehow had to make a choice. She decided to do the "eeny, meeny, miny, mo," routine which she'd learned from Rodney. "Mo" turned out to be a film called "Night Fire." Devon started having second thoughts about this movie, thinking that a show about campfires, or some such thing, might not give her the information she needed. Fortunately, her prediction was wrong.

Devon was greeted by a man with a large gun running down a city street shooting down everyone that stood in his path. Streams of blood oozing from bullet wounds painted the street and sidewalk. The movie went on. A man. A gun. An attempt to escape from a city where he'd had a bad childhood and was taking it out on the people around him.

A teen in the audience adopted the main character as a role model, and was inspired when the character spoke these words of encouragement; "Yeah, when people get in your way you've just got to take out your gun and shoot them down. Doesn't matter if they're a friend or an enemy. It's the only way." The character then shot his friend.

Near the end of the movie, there was a scene in a courtroom where the man with the gun was on trial. After a verbal barrage of testimony flying about between defense and prosecution attorneys, the judge came to his final conclusion, "Not guilty due to an uncontrollable impulse."

"Judges," Devon thought to herself, inspecting another prospective influence responsible for allowing evil to permeate their society.

As Devon left the theater, her attention was drawn to a conversation in front of her. The teenager, Pete, who had adopted the words of wisdom of the killer in the movie, was talking to another kid. They stood on the edge of a sidewalk. Both wore short baggy pants that fit like large grocery bags. Pete scratched a short tuft of black hair that barely covered the top of his otherwise shaved head. Then he spoke to his friend, Al. "Man, I'm gonna do it now. I was thinking about getting a gun after that show I saw on TV, but wasn't sure. Now I'm convinced I've gotta do it. Guns give you power."

Shot with a new idea that she hadn't previously considered, Devon wandered away from the scene of yet to be committed crimes. She knew that Knights were good actors, but hadn't actually pondered the idea that they might actually be playing parts in movies or on TV.

The next morning, day three, Devon's journey led her to yet unexplored territory in this new and strange land. Sailing past a bus stop, something caught her invisible eye. She backtracked to see what it was. There on a bench was a picture of a pig that had been cut in half with its internal organs exposed, and blood dripping from them. The heading above the pig read "Contemporary Analytical Art Concepts," and underneath was the address of a nearby art museum where the piece was proudly displayed.

Devon made this downtown Los Angeles museum her next destination. She got a cold, empty feeling as she penetrated the walls of the building that housed the artwork. Devon looked at the walls and saw many of them adorned with what looked like leftover paint drippings from wet brushes. Other canvasses, she assumed, were probably the scrawlings of children. The sliced pig was nowhere in sight, but this didn't exactly bother her.

As she looked around the room for pictures of something she could identify, she overheard one man talking to another. "Things aren't what they used to be. To see real art these days you have to go to a museum where you can see works of the old masters."

Devon wondered who this "old master" person was, and wished she'd gone to see his art instead, just out of the desire for some aesthetic relief.

Desperately trying to find some meaning in the paintings, Devon spied a female who was explaining the hidden message in one of the pieces to an attentive male. She said, "You see, the red splotch covering the black splotch means that the artist felt hostile toward another person in his life, which is represented by the black. He used the red to represent his feelings, for we all know that red is the color of anger." She pointed and continued on in an erudite manner, "Down here you see yellow dripping onto the black. This means that he then got over his hostilities and is now feeling bright and sunny again toward the person who was the target of his fiery emotions."

The male was puzzled, but at the same time looked like he wanted to please the female, so hid any sign of ignorance, "That's very fascinating, Dana," he said. "How did you learn to decipher all of that?"

"Oh, well I took a class in psychological art analysis," she boasted, then went on to explain the true meaning of the other paintings to her captive audience. Dana led her male friend to a picture which was a collage of various overlapping genitals, both animal and human, and went on to explain about how sexuality should be expressed in whatever way one desires. Devon overheard her say that art is a great medium to express this message, as she had learned in her art analysis course.

The male put on a pretentious smile.

After the lesson in art analysis, Devon went off to observe some of the other works to see if she could figure them out for herself. No matter how hard she tried to decipher what the artists meant, she just became more perplexed.

One painting had writing below it that she assumed was a description of the splotches of paint that hung above it. She read these words: "Night rode on the wicker square. Splattered breezes ate the sparrow, awaiting the blue sun tomorrow."

This piece of poetry just whirled Devon into more confusion.

After deciding she'd had enough, she was about to leave, when she caught a glimpse of the picture that had drawn her into the museum in the first place. There near a back exit was the pig, organs and all.

Devon left, starting to feel homesick. She had been inundated with enough for now, and decided it was time to try to organize her observations, in order to deliver them to the Empress via thoughtscriber. She looked forward to the peace and quiet she hoped to find in an Earth hotel room. Devon thought of locating a vacant room and just materializing there, but knew this could cause a problem, as the hotel staff might let some humans occupy the space, not knowing she'd already checked herself in. This left her no choice but to put on her body and come up with some Earth money to pay for the room. She reluctantly decided to sell one of the golden chains around her neck, which was made of Athenian gold, abundant in the sands of Athena. Anyone could collect it in nugget form, melt it down, and make their own jewelry. She knew that gold was not so plentiful on Earth, and could be sold in exchange for money as it was highly prized.

Using what had come to be her "changing room," a garbage dumpster, she remolecularized and removed a chain from around her neck. It was roughly equivalent to a twenty-four karat gold chain except for slight compositional differences that she knew an Earth jeweler's equipment couldn't detect.

Devon located a place where gold could be traded for cash, and arrived just before closing time. After getting the money, she headed down the street to find a hotel.

As Devon strolled down the pavement, she heard a jumbled vocal chorus of many loud voices. It grew louder and louder as she walked on. She wasn't sure where it was coming from, but her curiosity was aroused. Not paying attention to other pedestrians on the sidewalk, she collided with a woman walking in the opposite direction of her.

"Oh, excuse myself," Devon said.

The woman gave her a funny look, and said, "It's okay."

Before the woman skirted away, Devon questioned her, "Do you know what all the noise is?"

"Yeah, sure. It's the parade over on Highland," she said, pointing toward the commotion.

Devon thanked the woman, and then went over to inspect the source of the chorus.

She stopped and watched as throngs of people marched down the street. It was mostly men hand in hand with men, and women with women. Overhead was a banner that read "Gay and Lesbian Esteem March." Leading the way, were some of the characters from the movie "The Outcast."

The marchers came to a halt, and Devon noticed a couple of women affectionately exchanging a big wet kiss.

A speaker got up on a wooden platform, and Devon saw a short, balding man who stood and held a microphone.

The man warmly welcomed the crowd, then spoke. He acknowledged the gay and lesbian artists who were responsible for helping to popularize the expansion of their growing community. He gave special thanks to those involved with "The Outcast," as this recent box office hit had now crossed the borders of the gay community and was starting to be played in mainstream theaters.

The warm spring heat beat down on the speaker's head, causing a bead of sweat to run down his shiny forehead. After wiping the salty perspiration from it with a handkerchief, he continued, "We are now starting to get much more support from the straight community, due in great part to "The Outcast." In fact, here today I have a few supporters I'd like to bring up, to say a few words to you. The first one is Bertha Homer. She was anti-gay until she saw the movie."

"Pardon me boys," Bertha said, trying to pass by a couple of men, one of whom had his hand on his partner's butt and was squeezing it. She made her way to the platform.

"Miss Homer, can you please tell us what swayed you to see the importance of our crusade?"

Bertha cleared her throat and spoke, "Well, I must say, I never thought I'd be up here talking to any of you today. Years ago I was a bible believer, only swearing by traditional relations between a man and a woman." She paused as quiet hisses and boos emanated from the audience. Then she went on, "but not anymore."

The audience cheered.

"'The Outcast' was the final straw that helped me turn the other cheek on this old prejudice. I was so touched by the struggles of Joey and his partner to be accepted, that I couldn't help but shed my own biased views."

Bertha spoke a little longer, and then the emcee brought up the next guest, a well-known psycho-therapist named Dr. Muriel Galick. As Muriel approached the platform, several newsmen with cameras encircled the stage, ready to pounce upon her upcoming words.

Muriel waved at the audience cheerfully, and a loose layer of skin from her overly pudgy arm flapped back and forth. Then she spoke, "My good friends, it is so good to see that your numbers have doubled since last year's event. Good sign, real good sign."

Devon was thinking to herself, "Bad sign. Their race won't continue if this keeps up."

"Now I realize that there is still some public aversion to your sexual preference, and this is what I want to address. Since we are getting coverage on major TV channels today, I thought I'd use my position of authority to inform the public of the true reasons for the validity of your lifestyle," she said. She cleared her throat, then continued in a sympathetic tone, "My dear people, the gay community has suffered much defamation over the years. Fortunately, however, there is now much more acceptance than in the past. But there are still those who seek to ridicule gays. This is sad, as the reason for their condition is one that cannot be helped."

As Muriel spoke, Devon happened to glance at a woman who had her arm around her partner and managed to sneak a quick feel of her breast, thinking that no one was watching.

"You see, it all goes back to childhood. This is often instigated because of abuse from a parent of the opposite sex. This validly justifies the desire to seek out same sex partners later in life. A woman finds comfort and understanding with another woman that she feels she cannot attain with a man. And men, well, they just feel more secure with other males.

It all comes down to "feelings." If it feels good, do it. One must trust his innermost emotions, the ones that come from the "id." Too many people try to rationalize and fit into a publicly accepted mold, but this can be detrimental, and is the source of depression. Same sex relationships can be perfectly healthy, and should be guilt free," she said emphatically. The audience went wild with applause.

"Now, in closing, I must say that with the rapid spreading of AIDS, I have much sympathy for all of you, and don't want any more funeral invitations. I suggest that you remain with one partner, and do your best not to engage in sexual group encounters, or promiscuity."

Devon was so taken in by all the unusual festivities that she nearly forgot that she was wearing a body, until her lungs reminded her. She started coughing wildly. The sound of whistles and clapping faded into the background as Devon departed. She filed the memories of the gay festival into the recesses of her mind, along with her other adventures.

Chapter 5

*D*evon anxiously walked into the reception area of a local hotel. She stepped up to a desk and was greeted by a woman who tried to hold back from giving her a funny look. Devon's attention was on the pictures in her mind of sexual acts between males, and guns being shot off in all directions.

"And how long will you be here?" the woman asked. Devon put her attention back on the lady.

"About one Earth...uh one week."

"Okay, please fill this out," the woman said. She handed Devon a card with spaces for names and addresses. Devon knew she had to be clever and think of some place where she was from, so she got an idea by listening in on what some others nearby were saying. She then filled in the information.

"Please put your last name here and sign the bottom," said the woman.

Devon did as she was asked, and then gave it to her. The woman looked at it rather oddly. Devon was sure that it was the signature she was puzzled about.

"I see you're from San Francisco, just like those people who were next to you. Small world isn't it."

"Yes, it is," Devon replied, and handed her the currency required.

"I see you don't have any bags with you. Do you need some help bringing them in from outside?"

"Oh, no, no that's okay. Thank you for your offer, though," Devon said, not quite understanding why she should have paper bags. The other people she saw had clothing carriers that she learned were called "suitcases." As she walked away from the reception area she heard someone behind the desk say, "She looks like a flower child from the sixties. We get all kinds here in Hollyweird." This was enough to make Devon decide to buy some clothes that would be more acceptable.

Devon opened the door to her room, trying hard not to cough from the Los Angeles air. She held her breath for a moment, then went inside and collapsed into a comfortable chair. Just as visions of her experiences started to swim to the surface of her mind, she noticed a square monitor with a couple of knobs on it. It was embedded into a wall.

"Must be one of those television things I remember learning about," she thought, as her curious nature compelled her to turn it on.

The first thing she saw was a newscaster sitting behind a desk, with the letters KWRP posted up on a wall behind the desk. The newsman was talking in a serious and sullen tone.

"A local teenage boy has been accused of murdering another youth. Sixteen-year-old Pete McNeel told his mother that after seeing the movie "Night Fire," he was going to model himself after the lead character, Burt Bullitt, and start shooting those who stood in his way. Mrs. McNeel hadn't believed her son until he had actually gone out and shot another boy. Mrs. McNeel said she knew that her son had a lot of stress and anxiety in life, but never thought he would go to this extreme."

Devon watched as a picture of Pete was displayed on the TV. She sat forward in her chair as she noticed it was the same boy she had overheard talking after the showing of the movie!

"Although Pete may have committed this crime, it is almost certain that he will be acquitted due to his personal psychiatrist testifying that he has been suffering from adolescent stress syndrome," the newsman said, and then went on talking about something else. Devon tuned out as the gears in her detective-like mind started turning in an effort to fit the pieces of the puzzle together. Her attention was soon distracted by a barrage of bullet shots emanating from the TV set. She looked at it and saw several bodies lying on the ground, dead. "Enough of this Burt and his bullet type stuff," she thought, and turned off the TV.

"What guise are you wearing?" she thought. "Who was the destructive force in this scene, Rodney? Ralph, Marvin, record company, promoting twisted music? Hmm. Record companies? Manager Jim Scott? Evil? Movies? Producers? The Outcast? Homosexuals? Are they the ones? They are stopping the race from continuing? Are the producers behind this? Night Fire? Violence?

Movie producers again? Are they out to destroy Earthlings? Art museum? Splotches, guts? Art museum owners? Degraded art?"

Devon stopped in her mental tracks, as she whirled in a slight sea of dizziness. She ignored her body's reactions as best she could, contemplating whether she should go out and do more observing before trying to draw conclusions. Yes or no, back and forth, she bounced this idea around. Time. She wished she had more time to get more clues, but this would give her less time to find Nicole. She'd have to do her best with the data she had. As much as sleuthwork frustrated her, Devon loved the intense challenge that was inherent in this type of task.

Devon mentally reviewed her adventures again. There was one she'd almost forgotten to include. "The Gay and Lesbian March." There they are again. Homosexuals. The words of Muriel Galick echoed inside her mind, as a vivid picture of two women kissing flashed before her eyes. "Same sex relationships can be perfectly healthy and should be guilt free."

"How can she say this? Doesn't she see the detriment of..." Devon hesitated. "Muriel, psycho, what was it? Pshycho-something...Hmm. She's in favor of this unnatural behavior. Another clue, but still not enough consistency. Too many variables. No. There's got to be one main guise. That's how they usually do it. This is a tricky one. I have to dig deeper. Who is it? Do I really have enough evidence? Johnny Bullitt. Violence. The newsman. What was he saying again? A murder, after a movie. But may not be guilty. Why? Oh, yes, there it is. Because of adolescent stress syndrome. Adolescent anxiety. What does this have to do with it? Not his fault. Psychiatrist?"

The wheels kept turning, as Devon scoured back over the ground she'd covered, "Psych... Where else did I hear? Oh, yes, that was it. The art museum. The analysis. Psychological. There's that word again."

The picture was becoming somewhat clearer. "Oh, wait a minute. Rodney. Jim Scott mentioned a shrink. Now I'm getting puzzled by this again. A shrink told him that cheating and drugs were good things. What is a shrink?"

Devon was onto something, but she needed to get a question answered. "Someone in this hotel would know," she thought, as she picked up a phone and dialed the hotel operator. Forgetting that speaking took more energy than she currently had, not having been out of her body for awhile, she nearly choked on her words. "Hello, can..you tell me wha..t is a shrink?"

The operator paused, as if surprised by such an idiotic question.

"Hello, are you there?"

"Yes. Is this a joke?"

"No, I'm j..ust new..here in this part of country and I've heard this word men..tioned and I want to find out what one is."

"Oh, I see. Well, shrink. You know, a psychiatrist."

Devon's eyes lit up, "Thank you," she said and hung up the phone, while the operator held the receiver out and gave it a strange look.

"The thread. I'm starting to see it. This is good, but have I observed enough? If only I could stay longer, I could get more clues," she thought. She was concerned about doing a thorough enough job. Needing some relief, she de-molecularized for a while.

Time swiftly ticked away on a clock on the nightstand. Devon was down to six days left on her mission. It was time to start seeking out Nicole. She put her body back on, and as she walked by a full-length mirror she caught a glimpse of herself. She backed up and looked at her appearance. She knew that soon she'd have to be using her body more often, so it was time to clothe it in more acceptable attire. She'd have to locate a place to get some Earth garments. Devon walked out of her hotel room, more self-conscious than before. She rode in the elevator, going down to the lobby, and received the usual strange looks from others. They noticed her silky white gown and golden sandals with straps that crisscrossed around her calves. Devon observed that it seemed to be some sort of ritual that people didn't speak to others in elevators. She noticed that a few people kept staring at her when she appeared not to be looking at them. Then as soon as her eyes caught theirs they would quickly look up at the numbers lit up above the door, pretending to be interested in them.

The elevator stopped and Devon walked out and started coughing. The air quality was especially bad that day. She realized that she shouldn't have put her body on that morning, but should have just traveled to a nearby shopping center and found a place to reappear indoors. Devon knew she couldn't go back to her room to take off her body as this was the time the maid would be cleaning up. She decided to correct her error and chose a place across the street from the hotel to de-molecularize again. She saw an area where some men were pounding nails in wooden beams. There was a sign that said "Murphy's Construction Company," and right near the sign were four plastic, portable boxes which some men were walking in and out of. She got closer to one of the boxes and saw that they were private little rooms with lettering saying "In Use."

"Perfect."

She waited until one man left, then entered. She quickly de-molecularized her body and possessions, thinking no one had noticed her. Then as she left she heard one worker say to another, "Joe, I saw some lady go in there. I'd wait a few minutes before you use that one."

The other worker replied, "But Mack, the sign says 'Vacant'. She must have left."

Joe scratched his head, "I don't know. I never saw her come out."

"Okay Mack. You been hitting the bottle again? Tell you what, just in case you might be right, I'll be a gentleman and knock," said Joe, and proceeded to knock, getting no reply.

Mack was very puzzled.

"There. Ya satisfied?" Joe asked, as he smiled and shook his head. "Why don't you take an early break this morning. Get some good strong coffee. You been working too hard, ol' pal." He patted Mack on the back and went into the stall. Mack looked very confused.

Devon laughed to herself while realizing that she'd have to be more careful. All she needed was to be discovered. She knew that here in Los Angeles something called "gossip" traveled swiftly

41

and news reporters had a reputation of seeking out bizarre things, whether real or fictional.

Devon went to a shopping center which she'd heard people refer to as a "maul." She wondered if this was because of their actions around tables with "SALE" signs. After observing people deeply engrossed in looking at various clothing pieces, Devon decided to find a spot to put her body on.

Devon walked around the crowded shopping center observing how other females were dressed. She saw many in pants, but didn't like the idea of wearing them. She noticed that there were some women wearing skirts and tops. She thought she'd pick some of these as they looked like they'd be more comfortable.

After purchasing some nice clothes, she wore one of her new outfits out of the store. She was still getting funny looks, directed at her feet. She went to a shoe store and purchased the kind of shoes that seemed popular for women to wear. She got a pair of heavy black lace-up boots with thick rubber platform soles and chunky heels. As weird as she felt, she knew that she must finally fit in, as she no longer got strange looks. She smiled to herself, thinking how funny she would look on Athena.

Chapter 6

Devon cautiously walked through the shopping center trying to get used to wearing heels, something she'd never experienced before. She had so much concentration on this that she almost didn't realize something was missing, until she nearly slipped on the smooth floor. As she fell forward, she didn't feel the chain on her neck swing out and then back to her chest.

"The coin!" she gasped. She spoke aloud, catching the attention of two ladies walking by with shopping bags. Devon knew she had had so much attention on the way she looked that she hadn't noticed the chain had fallen from her neck, most likely while trying on clothes.

Devon abandoned all thoughts of the awkwardness of her new shoes and proceeded to make a fast turnabout, running toward the clothing store where had she purchased her skirt. Suddenly she tripped and fell to the ground, dropping the bag that carried her Athenian gown and shoes. She made her way to a bench where she sat next to a young boy eating an ice cream. The boy stared at Devon as she quickly took off her new shoes and dumped them into the bag. Then she ran, barefooted, in the direction of the store, desperately hoping to find the chained coin in the dressing room.

She got to the store, but couldn't remember exactly which room she had been in so did a rapid search, starting with the first dressing room she came to. No one was in it, and neither was the chain. She tried two more rooms. The next one was closed and someone was in it, so she knocked. A lady opened the door. "Excuse me, do you see a gold chain in there?" she asked an oversized woman who was trying on an undersized dress.

"No ma'am, don't see one," the woman said, barely searching the room. Devon saw that most of her interest was absorbed in trying to zip up a tight dress that gave her a thinner look.

Devon's frustration mounted as she went to the next room, and the next. Finally she'd covered them all, and still no coin!

Devon walked out of the dressing room with thoughts of what the Empress would do if she knew what had happened. Just as she was thinking of how to explain this to Zeena, her ears were drawn to one of the sales girls behind a counter. "It's really pretty. Wonder what all this weird writing is. Never seen anything like it. I think I'll keep it if no one claims it," the girl said to another sales girl.

The other girl spoke. "Yeah, maybe it has magic powers." They both giggled.

Devon went from terror to enthusiasm in a few split seconds as she turned and saw the sales girl wearing the "key" to her mission. She dashed over to the counter and calmed herself down. "Excuse me, I just overheard what you said and I came to tell you that the coin is mine. I have been looking everywhere for it." She tried to be polite and not just grab it from her.

The sales girl looked down at Devon's feet. "You know you aren't allowed to be in here without shoes."

Devon's feet were the last thing on her mind. "Oh, I'm sorry. I'll put them on, but can I please have my chain and coin back first."

The girl gave Devon a suspicious look. "All right, you can put them on later, but how do I know it's yours. You can't always trust people these days, not that you are dishonest, but suppose someone else comes along after you leave and says it's theirs?"

"Believe me, this won't happen. No one on Earth knows about it," Devon said, getting desperate again. The second sales girl went on to help a customer as the one with the coin talked to Devon.

"Can you prove to me that it's yours? What's engraved on it?" the girl asked as she looked at the strange lettering on the coin. Devon tried hard to recall what the coin said exactly. "Yes, I can tell you." She knew she'd have to translate the Athenian language into a description in English words. "There is a small triangle followed by a square with a line through it. Then there is a circle, no a squiggle, and after that there is a circle. Then after that I think there are three dots, or four, then there is an octagon with two z's inside of it."

As Devon spoke, the girl's eyes were glued to the coin. "That's astounding. Must be yours if you can remember all that. What in the world does it mean?"

"It doesn't mean anything in this world," Devon said.

"Okay, you can have it back," the girl said, handing it to Devon, who intently clutched it in her hand and then secured it around her neck again.

"Thank you very much. You have done a very good deed for your planet." Devon said. The girl gave her a very puzzled look.

"Remember to put your shoes on," she said as Devon walked away.

"I will."

Devon sat on a bench and sighed a big breath of relief as she placed the shoes on her cold feet. She figured out how to re-lace them, but was having trouble tying the laces in a bow as the shoe salesman had done when he put them on her feet. One thing Devon always hated about visiting other planets was the little idiosyncrasies that were native to the inhabitants. After struggling with the bow attempt, she just gave up, and tucked the laces into the shoes. Then she got up and started walking, getting a little more used to her new height.

It was time to get on with her mission. She remembered the Empress telling her that Nicole had her music on discs. She had also told Devon to try an Earth directory to see if Nicole's location could be found. She found a phone booth and looked through the yellow pages, then the white ones. She found nothing under Nicole Jensen, so went on to the only other clue she had, thinking that perhaps Nicole's address might be on one of her music discs.

Devon didn't really know where to start looking. She asked an old man in the mall. "Excuse me, could you inform me as to where music discs might be found?"

"Do you mean a record store?" he asked.

Devon hesitated, hoping that's what she was supposed to be looking for. "Yes, I believe so."

"Well, there's one right over there," the man said, pointing to a nearby store to their left that said "Records of the Good Days."

"Thank you, sir. I will try this out." Devon left the man and headed to the store.

She walked into the store and was greeted by an Elvis Presley song. She assumed it was a current tune of the nineties. She looked around the store and noticed several rows of bins with records in them. She saw that they were grouped in alphabetical order and quickly made her way to the "J" section. Devon anxiously dug through, trying to find "Jensen" on the covers. "Nothing," she said aloud as she looked a second and then a third time to make sure she hadn't missed anything. Then she started taking out the records one by one and examining them carefully to see if perhaps Nicole Jensen's name was somewhere else on there. She took out the entire "J" section and checked front and back, piling them up in a stack on the bin in the section next to her.

A tall, skinny salesman with red hair noticed Devon and went over to her, trying not to act irritated. "Hi. Can I help you find something?" he asked with enforced politeness.

Devon jumped, as she hadn't noticed him. "Oh, yes, thank you. Where are the discs of Nicole Jensen?"

The salesman replied, "Sorry, lady, I don't think we carry her stuff here. She's not an oldie. We only carry records here."

Devon was confused, "Records. Oh. These are records," she said, partially asking, and partly acting as though she knew what he was talking about. She hated not having a full understanding of things.

The salesman laughed. "That's funny. You act like you've never seen one before. Maybe that's why you're not finding stuff by Nicole Jensen. Looks like you're in the wrong kind of store."

The salesman told her that Nicole's music would be on something called compact discs. Devon was relieved he'd saved her from having to ask another dumb question. "So do you know where there might be another store around here that carries these compact discs?"

He scratched his head and looked around. "Hmm, not sure how many stores still have much of a selection by her. She was real popular about a year ago, but then she kind of faded out; stopped getting radio air play. I'm trying to think," he said, as his attention was suddenly drawn to Devon's eyes. As he focused on her, he almost lost his thoughts as he was taken by her incredible beauty. He'd never seen anyone with such sparkling turquoise eyes and such a perfect complexion.

"Say, by the way, you've got great eyes. I couldn't help but notice how great that color of contact lenses looks on you." Devon pretended she knew what he was talking about. She was hoping he wouldn't get too sidetracked. He was looking at her in a way that males do when they are attracted to females. "Thank you."

"Now, let's see. Oh, Nicole Jensen," the salesman said, noticing he was getting a sort of aggravated look from his boss as if to tell him that he needed to sell some records. His sales were down that week. "Sure you wouldn't rather have something by Joni Mitchell? She wrote some good lyrics too."

Devon started to get frustrated with the detour he was taking her on. "No, I came to find something by Nicole and I will do whatever it takes to find it."

"Hey, I admire your persistence. Tell you what, I'd like to help you out, but there's nothing here of Nicole's," he said, while starting to put back the whole "J" section that Devon had taken out. "I know of a place that I think still carries her CDs. It is about three miles from here. I'm off work in about fifteen minutes and I'd be willing to go there with you. In fact, I wouldn't mind checking some discs out myself. I really like this "old fogy" stuff, but I've got a CD player at home and sometimes I like to get them instead of records."

He looked at her with a gleam in his eyes. Devon quickly tossed his offer back and forth. She knew he could help her trace down Nicole's discs faster than she could do it herself. She was a bit worried about that look he was giving her, though. All she needed was for him to start thinking of her as a mating prospect. On the other hand, she thought, it would be nice to have an Earth friend to talk to for a little while. She was starting to get lonely. But, then again, she would have to leave her new friend behind once she found Nicole's discs.

Seeing her hesitation, he asked, "Well, what do you think?"

"Yes, I would like your kind assistance," she concluded. "What are you called?"

"What am I called? Wow, you have such a cool way of putting things. The way you act. Almost seems like you're not from this area. What am I called? Well that depends who you're talking to about me. When my mother gets mad at me she still calls me Timothy Daniel Wakowski, but most people just call me Tim."

"Tim, I am pleased to be acquainted with you. I am simply called Devon."

Tim reached his right hand out for hers. She stood there for a couple of seconds, confused. Then she remembered seeing other Earth people grasp hands and move them up and down in a ritual greeting. She put her hand out and they shook.

"Devon, how old are you? If you don't mind me asking." he said.

"Oh, no, I don't mind. My body's age is a lot older than you think."

"What, thirty something?"

"Oh no, would you believe two hundred and something?"

Tim started to laugh. "You are a riot. I've never met anyone like you, but it's okay. Some girls are sensitive about their age, so you don't have to tell me. I still think you're cute, even if you are a lot older than me."

Devon started to loosen up and stopped feeling uncomfortable as she had before. She asked, "What is the age of your body?"

"Me, oh I'm going to be twenty-four next week. I'm getting up there. Before you know it, I'll hit the big "three-o" and start going over the hill. But I'm not too worried about it. I'm sure I'll live long, just like most of my family. In fact I have a grandfather who made it all the way to ninety-five. I know many people who don't get past seventy-five," he boasted.

Devon grew sad at the fact that Earthlings lost their bodies at such early ages. When she was ninety-five she had been like a young Athenian child.

Devon's thoughts were interrupted when Tim's boss, walked over to Devon and politely said, "Excuse me." Then he turned to Tim. "Can I see you for a moment in my office?"

Tim looked at Devon. "I'll be back soon. I'm off in five minutes. Don't go anywhere."

"Okay," she obediently replied.

Tim went to his boss' office where he got a lecture on how poorly his sales were doing and how if he didn't shape up, he'd be out of a job. Tim hardly heard what was being said. His attention was on Devon, hoping she wouldn't leave. Tim acknowledged his boss and figured he'd handle the problem tomorrow, but for now he was about to take a pretty girl on a date to another store.

Tim hurried back to where he had left Devon standing, and to his pleasant surprise saw that she hadn't moved. "Oh good, you waited. Sorry for the delay. He just gets too grumpy sometimes. I handled it okay though. So where is your car parked, Devon?"

"I do not have one of those," she replied.

"Oh, so you took the bus?"

"Yes."

"Must be tough to live in this city without one. Takes so long to get anywhere without your own wheels."

Here was her chance to let him know she wasn't going to be a permanent part of his life. "Oh, it doesn't matter, because I don't live here. I'm just visiting."

"Where are you from?"

"Uh, San Francisco."

"That's a cool city. Lots of nuts there just like LA."

"Yes. I know," Devon said, thinking about how well she'd fit in there too.

They got in Tim's car. As they drove along, Tim fiddled with the radio. Devon looked out of the window and there in front of her on a big sign was another picture of that same woman she'd seen before, with the overly large breasts and tight stretch pants. She strained to see the small letters above the sign. There appeared to be a name and someone's phone number. Tim said something, but she didn't hear.

He asked, "What are you looking at?"

"Oh, that woman up there," she replied as they came to a stoplight and he saw the billboard.

Tim laughed. "Oh, yeah, that's Dingalene. I guess you've never seen her, being from Frisco. A local band named themselves after her. Of course it's just a nickname. But anyway, she's the dancer for the band. They put her up on the sign to draw attention. You call the number on the sign and it gives the dates and times of their gigs. She's kinda sexy, but I think some doctor went overboard on the boob job. I read that the band wasn't doing too well for a while, before they had Dingalene."

"How did she help them?"

"The band consulted a PR firm and were told to get a sex kitten in their act, something that was recommended to the firm by some shrink. You know, sex equals sales. A dumb blonde like that isn't good for much. So this is a big break for her. There are other uneducated girls I know who don't know what to do, so resort to sleaze dancing, sometimes even topless. Anyway, I guess the Dingalene band gets a bunch of horny old men at their shows now."

Devon was laughing to herself at how ridiculous Dingalene's career seemed.

Tim continued to play with the radio as he drove along. "This song again. I get tired of the same old stuff. Wish there was more variety."

"Tim, why is it that so many musicians get rejected at record companies?"

"Hey, I sure wish there was more diversity, but there are these stupid corporation rules. I think the guys running the show are afraid to vary the selection of tunes too much. The music biz these days is run by businessmen who market music like it's some new sort of material object to make a big buck with."

As Tim spoke, Devon flashed back to a picture of Ralph and Marvin and the big pile of discs they had rejected.

Tim went on, "It's not like it used to be back in the sixties and seventies when good musicians and songwriters had a better chance of making it here in LA just on sheer talent. I mean I like some of the new metal and stuff, but it's lacking something for me." He turned a corner.

"Too bad Nicole didn't last long. She was a chick with balls. I think it's great the way she went out and knocked on doors to get people to come to her concerts. She got so many people to her shows that some record company guys started flocking around her. You know; the only reason they did this is because she had such a big following.

"This isn't the usual way it is done?"

"You aren't too hip to this stuff are you?"

"No."

"Not many performers are that ambitious. Artists usually wait for someone else to do all the work, but not Nicole. It was amazing she made it big doing the type of songs she had. Takes a lot of guts in this society to be alone and sing out against things like the media, drugs and crime and stuff. I remember seeing her on TV talk shows looking kind of nervous, but this didn't stop her from being a rebel. It's a drag that her record company canned her after such a short career, and such hard work.

"Yeah, it's too bad," Devon said, noticing that Tim liked to talk a lot. She didn't mind in this case because she was fascinated by what he was telling her. "Hey, I bet you listen to oldies, being two hundred years old and all. Oldies to you are probably Bach and Beethoven. Did you ever see those guys live?"

"No, can't say I have."

"Yeah, so what kind of tunes do you like?"

"Oh, let's just say that the kind of music I listen to is out of this world. Very spiritual."

Tim replied with strong interest, "Cool. Do you have a tape of this music, maybe where you are staying, that I could listen to?"

"No, I left all my music at home in Ath... in San Francisco."

"Well, you got me curious. Maybe sometime I can visit you there and you can play it for me."

"Maybe."

Chapter 7

Devon had no idea what to expect as she followed Tim into a store called "Newies but Goodies." She was welcomed by loud, dissonant, electronic sounds. Tim told her that the band they were playing was called the "Noise Machine" and that it was a new grundge metal group. The harsh sounds of the "Noise" scratched Devon's ears as she anxiously followed Tim to the "J" section. Then the "Noise Machine" ended and another song came on, from an entirely different group. This instrumental music was more pleasing to her.

Devon noticed that many of the artists she inspected were technically skilled, but she couldn't understand how they let their messages get so deranged.

Just as she was deep in thought, Tim spoke. "Well, here we are. Hope we're in luck." Tim started thumbing through the CD's.

As he got to the point in the "J's" where the discs should have been, he said, "Nothing. I don't see one single CD of hers. Let me start from the beginning. Maybe they're misfiled." He started at the first one and carefully looked at every disc. His long, freckled fingers moved from one to the next. Devon could hardly stand the suspense. She knew that each minute counted. With these discs as her only real clue, she began to worry.

"Damn. I don't see a thing. We may not find anything here. How about checking out one of the more popular groups, like these guys?" Tim asked, pulling out a disc by a group called 'Bloody Lizards,' the last one in the row. "We could go back to my place and listen to them."

Devon ignored the gleam in Tim's eyes and his last comment. "I'm not giving up, Tim. I came to find Nicole's disc and won't leave this store until I do. There's got to be one here!" Devon said with a fiery look that surprised Tim.

Tim's thoughts leaped back from wondering how to get Devon into bed to trying to find Nicole's CDs.

Devon noticed a few bins in front of her that contained square plastic containers. Some people were pulling them out and examining them. "Maybe we should check over there."

"Oh, yeah, I suppose we could inspect the cassette section, but I doubt if they'd have anything over there if they didn't have any CD's."

Devon walked toward the tapes, as if she knew her way around better than Tim. She went to the "J" section and Tim stood next to her as she looked at every single tape, starting from the beginning.

"Good luck," Tim thought, as he folded his arms and waited for Devon's overzealous search to end.

As Devon thumbed through the cassettes, a teenage girl, with purple hair and a nose ring, approached. She stood nearby, silently waiting for Devon to get through. She held two cassettes that she wanted to put back into the "J" section so she could then look for something else. Devon, engrossed in her search, suddenly felt compelled to turn and look at the girl.

Tim, noticing the girl had a nice figure and was fairly attractive, looked her up and down. Devon caught a glimpse of the two cassettes she held. Out of the corner of her eye she saw the letters "Nic." The girl's thumb covered the rest of the name.

"Excuse me, what tape is that?" Devon asked as she turned to the girl.

She lifted her thumb off of the top tape and held them both out for Devon to see. "Oh, this one or that one?" she asked as Devon stared at the clue she came to find! Tim got wide eyed; impressed that Devon's determination had paid off. He was pleased to discover that his trip to this store had not been totally in vain.

"Do you know if there are any more of those tapes by Nicole? If not, I'd be willing to pay you for that one. How much do you want? I have some dollars," Devon said, pulling a fifty-dollar bill out of her skirt pocket.

The girl couldn't understand why she so urgently wanted the tape and seriously contemplated the offer, but she just didn't feel right about it. "Hey, I'd love to take it, but I haven't even paid for it yet. Besides, what's the big deal about Nicole Jensen?"

"She's more of a big deal than you think, but I haven't got time to explain all that. What can I do to get the tape from you?"

"Well, I was going to put it back and try and find something else, but maybe there's some reason I should hold onto it that I don't know about."

Tim and Devon looked at each other as the girl with the purple hair examined the tape, still confused as to what the fuss was over it. "I know she's a pretty good songwriter, but to be honest her music isn't exactly what I was looking for. I changed my mind and decided I wanted more of a metal sound. I was going to see what else I could find."

As the girl said this, Tim went to the "S" section of the cassette rack and quickly pulled a tape out and walked over to the girl. "These guys are hot."

The girl instantly showed more interest in what Tim was holding than in Nicole's tape.

"The Screaming Weasels, where did you find that?"

"Right there in the "S" section."

"That's great. They were out of them last time I checked," she said.

Tim spoke, "Well it looks like we've got what you want and you've got what we want, so how about making a switch?"

"I can go for that," the girl said as she handed Nicole's tape to Tim and took the Weasels from him. She put the other tape back in the "J" section, and went to pay for her merchandise.

At this point Devon put aside any regrets of having Tim as a companion.

Tim proudly held the tape in his hands, "So how much is this worth to you?" he joked, expecting her to go along with it and take out the fifty-dollar bill again.

"How much do you want?" she replied seriously.

He put his arm around her, "How about the pleasure of your company at my apartment while we listen to Nicole's tape together."

Devon hesitated but didn't know how else she was going to get to hear it, so she agreed.

On the way to Tim's place, Devon studied the cassette cover. She was drawn to the picture of Nicole on the front. She finally got to see what her body looked like. Nicole was quite attractive with her straight, shoulder-length brown hair and sparkly blue eyes. She had a slender figure and a clear complexion. Devon had no idea what her exact age was, but could see a slight wrinkle in her forehead and a small amount of gray hair, so figured that for an Earthling she was probably somewhere near middle age, perhaps mid-thirties. She was wearing a long blue dress that fell to her calves. Her shoes were similar to those that Devon wore, which made Devon smile, seeing that they had something in common. Taken in by her strong interest in Nicole, Devon hadn't even noticed that Tim had arrived at his apartment and was parking the car in the back of the building.

Tim's eyes were on Devon, with the same amount of interest as hers were focused on Nicole. "Here we are. You were so engrossed in that thing, I bet you hardly noticed I stopped the car."

"Yes, you are correct."

They arrived at apartment 2D, where Tim resided. He unlocked the door that led to his one-bedroom home. Devon looked around at a variety of wall decorations. She saw a poster of a blond girl in a bathing suit, a picture of four guys in a band that looked similar to Rodney and the Gutter Rats, and another picture of a band that said "The Moody Blues" on it.

Tim told Devon to have a seat on an old, brown leather couch, while he excused himself for a few minutes so he could change out of his work clothes into something more comfortable

Devon was glad he left her alone so she could resume her study of Nicole. This time she widened her vision and gazed at more of the picture on the cover. Nicole stood on a dirt path leading to a large globe in the background. The globe was lit up and the name of the cassette, printed right above it was "Road to a Better World." Devon's intrigue was interrupted by her sudden concern about locating Nicole's address on the tape. She didn't see anything on the front, so she turned it over and tried to make out the writing on the back. There was a list of songs and the names of the musicians who performed them along with Nicole. At the very bottom of the cassette, Devon discovered an address that she assumed to be Nicole's. It said "Recorded at Homebound Studios - 2365 Apple Drive, Los Angeles."

A few seconds later, Tim came out dressed in torn blue jeans, a white T-shirt, and tennis shoes with overly large tongues that protruded from them. He sat on the couch close to Devon, but not overly near. "You sure are fascinated by that tape. I mean, I know she's good, but is there some special reason it was so important for you to get this thing? You were really shaken up when you thought we might not find it."

Devon said, "Oh, well, a very dear friend of mine strongly recommended her music for certain reasons."

"Mind if I see that?" Tim asked as Devon handed it to him. He looked it over. "So that's where they recorded? Homebound. I know of a couple of other groups that recorded there."

Puzzled by this comment, Devon asked, "You mean other bands used Nicole's home to imprint their music on tapes?"

Tim smiled, "Yeah, I'm sure Nicole and a whole bunch of other artists felt like they were living at Homebound Studios when they had to spend all that time recording. But I know Nicole probably has a nice home somewhere else too. I don't think she'd like to live in a studio forever."

Devon tried to hide her new frustration, as she would now have to try and find out where Nicole lived. Her only clue was still the studio.

"Can I play this now?" Tim asked.

"Sure."

Tim put it in a tape deck and went back and sat next to Devon. Tim, whose attention had primarily been on Devon, found himself getting strongly interested in the songs. When the first side ended, Tim got up and turned it over. They both sat still while indulging in the second side.

The last song came on, and Nicole spilled her heart out while singing these words:

"It's time for making changes, changing it right away.

It's time for making changes, making some changes today, change today.

In a world of madness where madmen rule the masses,
they don't care about the consequences they create.
No responsibility for their deeds.
And helping spread the insanity is the media where what
we see is the bad side of humanity.
It's not necessary, and I say; It's time for making changes,
changing it right away.
Time for making changes, making some changes today,
change today....."

Tim got up and turned off the tape, hardly realizing that a half-hour had gone by without his having felt compelled to try touching Devon. He took the tape out of the cassette player, put it in its plastic case, and brought it back to Devon. As he sat on the couch, he said, "Wow! Listening to her makes me want to go out and 'make some changes' in society. She was a pretty brave babe. I mean, she would find something wrong and attack it through her protest songs. The only problem with her lyrics is that I recently heard that some of her songs painted false pictures."

"What do you mean?" Devon asked, puzzled.

Well, I know there were a couple tunes, not on this tape, but on another one, that had strong messages against drugs. She tried to say that these street drugs caused kids to do worse in school, sometimes even get pretty violent. Apparently lots of parents were upset, and worked hard to stop their kids from taking them. Then some articles were written stating that Nicole had exaggerated her claims. One of the articles said that some doctor had discovered a 'drug drive', which was inherent in all beings and was just as natural as urges towards hunger, thirst and sex, and that this drive shouldn't be suppressed.

"It was also said that Nicole was delusive, and her songs in general often contained lies about various subjects."

"And then what happened?"

"Well her record sales dropped a little, but she was still pretty popular. I heard that the articles upset her but she refused to give in, and she continued to do concerts for her loyal fans. Then one night at one of her shows, something happened."

57

At that point Tim's phone rang, "Excuse me," he said as he went to answer it, leaving Devon in suspense.

When he returned he continued his story. "Where was I? Oh yeah. So after this concert, Nicole went backstage, and somehow she slipped and injured her back. Because of some object she fell on, she messed up part of her spinal chord and hasn't been able to stand up straight ever since. She was so shaken up by what was happening to her that she hasn't made any public appearances for the past year. I hear she just hangs out at home and makes tapestries, or something like that."

Devon felt empathy for Nicole and started to see what Nicole faced on this planet. A wave of dizziness suddenly hit Devon as she realized she had overstayed her visit in her own body. She now had to contend with Tim's efforts to get her to stay longer.

"Did you want to hear some other tapes I have?"

"I'd love to, but I really don't have time right now. I've got to get back to the hotel I'm staying at so I can change into different clothes for an event tonight."

A look of disappointment came over Tim's face. "Oh, that's too bad. I've really enjoyed being with you today, and I thought you could stick around and maybe even do something fun later, like watch a movie."

"That would be a good thing, but I already had these other plans," Devon said, knowing that she didn't, but she thought she'd try doing what Earth people sometimes do when they want to get out of things, which was to lie. Oddly, it seemed to her, that the more she backed off from Tim's approach, the more he reached for her. He even put his arm around her as they sat there.

"You are very special Devon. I don't know exactly what it is about you, but you're not like other girls I've met. Can I see you again before you go back to Frisco?" he pleaded.

"I apologize, but I don't think I will have time. My schedule is very filled with activity, and I can't make any promise to you," she said, feeling bad that Tim was so obsessed with her.

"Oh, so you're going to make yourself invisible, huh." Tim said as Devon went into shock for a second, knowing there was no way he could have known about de-molecularization and then realized he must have just meant that she wasn't going to be around for him to see.

"I have to," Devon said, thanking him for the time he spent helping her with her search.

"How are you going to get back? You don't have wheels. Can I give you a ride?"

"That's very kind of you, but I don't want to trouble you. I will take public wheels. You have been overly nice."

"It's no bother," he said as he looked a little resentful, "Hey, you don't like me do you?"

Devon closed her eyes for a couple of seconds as the dizziness hit again. She had to get out of there before she fainted, "No, no. It's not that. You are a good human, but I..."

"'A good human.' Oh, I bet I know what it is. You have a boyfriend. Is that it?"

"Yes, I have one at home."

Tim brightened up, as the rejection he felt was lessening, "Oh well, I guess I should have asked you that in the beginning. Sorry to come on so strong. I just thought since you were so willing to come to my apartment that maybe you were interested in me too." Tim withdrew any further aggressive type comments and stood up and walked her to the door. She coughed and put her head in her hands for a moment.

"You feeling okay?" Tim asked, concerned.

"Yes. I'll be fine."

Devon asked Tim where she could find a bus that went to the hotel where she was staying. After he told her, she parted from her temporary friend and rushed to the bus stop. She got back to her room and quickly took her body off and relaxed in her naked state for several hours before attempting to locate Nicole.

Chapter 8

ay five quickly rolled around. After a rejuvenating rest, it was time for Devon to clothe herself in her human disguise. She adjusted her long skirt, making sure the zipper was in the correct place in the back. Then she stood in front of a mirror, gazing at her humorous appearance. She made sure the chain with the coin was secured around her neck, then tucked it underneath her top. Picking up Nicole's tape, which had spent the evening on a small nightstand, she placed it in one of her skirt pockets.

Devon arrived at Homebound studios at two in the afternoon. She was greeted by a girl at a desk with thick black framed glasses and short, jet black hair, who was blowing bubbles with a piece of gum. The girl quickly put a bubble back in her mouth and smiled at Devon, "Hi. Do you have an appointment?"

"Well, no, not exactly. I would like your assistance though. I am trying to find Nicole Jensen," Devon said as she pulled the tape out of her skirt pocket. The girl looked at the cassette with little interest as Devon held it.

"Nicole, yeah, I heard she recorded here a couple of years ago. I wasn't working at Homebound then. You actually expected to find her here or something?"

"Well, not necessarily. I figured you could tell me where she lived."

"Oh, I don't know that. Besides, even if I did, I couldn't give out that information. I mean it's not that I don't trust you or anything, but hey, some weirdo may be trying to get hold of her so they could go murder her or something. She got herself in trouble a while ago, and I sure wouldn't want to find out that someone who was still after her went and killed her. I couldn't give her address to you or anyone else who walked in off the street."

Devon's hopes sank. She now had two more blows against her: no address for Nicole, and even if there was one she couldn't get it. However, Devon's determination would not allow her to give up. In the moment of silence between her and the receptionist, Devon looked at the wall in front of her that housed photos of various musicians. Devon asked, "Do you think any of those people would know how I can find Nicole?"

The receptionist glanced over at the photos, and although she was getting a little irritated, tried to sound polite, "Look, I wish I could help you, but I have no idea if they would know where she hangs out. You'll just have to try somewhere else."

"There's got to be someone here who can help me find her. If I can't get to Nicole Jensen soon, things will only get worse, and so will she."

A man who walked by them, and was about to go out the front door, stopped short in his tracks.

"Excuse me, I didn't mean to eavesdrop. I couldn't help but overhear your last remark to Jan. What's this about Nicole?"

"Oh, it's that she hasn't been well. She needs help so that she can get back into the music world and carry on with her mission to create betterment in society," Devon said, trying to say as little as possible, but enough to get through to someone who could possibly help. She could tell the man wanted to say something, but she wanted to get her questions answered first, so she just continued, "Do you know Nicole personally?"

"Yes, I do. By the way, my name is Dale," he said as he held out his right hand.

This time she knew what this motion meant. She clasped his large palm in hers and shook it while her hopes came back up again. "I'm Devon. How do you know Nicole?"

The phone had been ringing for a few seconds and Jan reluctantly answered it. She would rather have listened in on the conversation between Devon and Dale, but knew she had to get back to work.

"I'm a good friend of Nicky's. I engineered a couple of her albums."

"Oh, so you know where she is?"

"Well, I might, but I can't just go handing out her address. I don't even know who you are. What do you want with Nicole anyway?"

Now Devon knew she was going to have to get very clever in order to get past the protective barrier that was being put up in front of her. She paused a second, as her attention was drawn to the loud music that suddenly emanated through an open door. Jan lifted her eyes from a phone message she was writing.

"Is there a place we can talk with privacy?" Devon asked Dale, purposely delaying answering his question.

Dale led her up a flight of stairs to a small room in the back of the top floor of the studio. They sat down in a couple of folding chairs. The room was filled with shelves that housed a collection of various tapes. The music sounded much dimmer up here and Devon was glad, as she could now hear herself think.

"I need to speak with Nicole. It has to do with her career. There is a message I must get to her that could help revitalize her. It's very important. I can't say too much. You must trust that my intentions are only to help."

"Yes I see, but you have to understand my position. I must insure that no harm is done to her, and it's not that I suspect you necessarily, but because of her past I have to be careful. Do you have any connection with Nicole, other than the fact that you've just heard her music?" Dale was still slightly dubious of her, mainly because this is how he felt he had to be.

Devon remembered the secret the Empress had revealed to her. Since she was being backed into a corner, she figured she needed all the ammunition she could get right now.

Devon said, "I don't expect you to understand this, but it will make sense to Nicole. You see, the reason I need to meet with her so badly has to do with, with...," Devon hesitated, trying not to say too much, "Athena."

"Huh?"

"Trust me, she will know. I can't say much more. What I have to relay to her is confidential, but I can say that there is some information she badly needs. Please, if you can help me out, I promise you won't regret it."

Dale sat forward in his chair. He was a large man, over six feet tall, and on the heavy side. He barely fit in the small chair. His defenses melted a bit as he gazed into Devon's sweet, pleading eyes. "Well, I might be willing to call her, but I can't guarantee that she'll see you."

Devon tried to hide any slight worry she had. She reached out a gentle hand to Dale's shoulder. She knew that it was an inherent trait for people to like to help others. She tried to appeal to this positive characteristic. "Thank you so much for considering assisting me. You have no idea how much this means. Your help is far more valuable than you could imagine. I know you don't have to do this, but there are a lot of people who will be very grateful."

Dale picked up a phone in the room and dialed Nicole's unlisted number. Devon waited with wide-eyed anticipation. Dale got an answering machine, and after the message ended he spoke, "Nicky. It's Dale. You there? Pick up the phone, hon. Nicky."

Devon counted the seconds flying by and knew every moment counted more and more.

"Hello," Nicole's voice said on the other end.

"Hi, Nicky, it's Dale. I have someone who needs to meet with you. Her name is Devon. She had one of your tapes and read the back and found out that this was where you did your last recording. She came here to track you down. Says it's confidential. Has to do with something called 'Athena'," Dale said. He paused, waiting for a reply, "Nicky, are you there?"

Devon could feel the jaw-dropping silence that permeated from the other end of the phone line at the mention of Athena. Dale glanced at Devon, not understanding what all of this was about.

"Dale, please put her on immediately."

Dale complied.

"Hello Nicole."

"How in the world did you know about my recollection of Athena? I haven't told this to anyone. Is telepathy involved or something?"

Devon looked at Dale, and knew she couldn't go blurting out the truth with a captive audience listening.

"You could say that. But there's more to it. I, uh, just can't go into it now. It's confidential. It's vital that I meet with you in person right away."

There was a moment of silence. Devon's eyes widened with intensity.

"Devon, under normal circumstances, I wouldn't consent to meet a perfect stranger. For some reason, I feel different about you and would like to see you."

"Where do you desire to meet?"

Dale leaned forward in the small chair, raising his eyebrows in surprise.

"My house, ten o'clock tonight. Can you make it?"

"Yes, of course."

"Have Dale give you my address and phone number. Do promise me one thing, though."

"Whatever you wish."

"Don't ever give this information to anyone," Nicole said.

"Sure." Devon hung up the phone.

"You're amazing," Dale said. "Been ages since Nicky has had anyone over, not even many close friends or family."

Devon smiled.

Just as Dale walked her toward the lobby exit, the phone rang and Jan picked it up and looked at Devon. She motioned her with her finger not to leave. "It's for you, it's Nicole."

Devon rushed to the phone and both Jan and Dale saw the smile on her face turn into a look of worry.

"So I'm sorry Devon, but I was so excited about meeting with you, that I totally forgot that I had an appointment at four."

"I understand, but how about after your appointment. Couldn't we meet then?"

"I can't. When I get back, I have some other business to take care of. I'd ask you to come tonight, but my boyfriend is coming over. We're leaving tomorrow morning to go up to Big Sur."

Devon tried to remain calm, "When will you return?"

We haven't decided, but I might talk to Tom about this tonight. You see, I haven't been physically well for the past year, and every now and then I just need to go to a new environment. Helps me feel better. You can try calling me in a few days. Please don't think I'm putting you off. I do want to see you." Devon left the studio with a feeling of being one step forward and two steps back.

Chapter 9

evon could hardly stand the suspense. With only five days to spare, and not knowing when Nicole would be home, she got nervous. At least she wouldn't have to feel the agony of being in her body for a while, and could remain painlessly de-molecularized. She thought about taking advantage of this waiting period, and going out and getting more clues to confirm she was on the right trail that led to the Knights. However she quickly laid that idea to rest. She had too much anxiety about finding out when Nicole was coming back, and knew the only possible way of getting an answer was to spy on her.

Nicole lived in the city of Brentwood, near Beverly Hills, in a large townhouse that sat on a hill. Large, green trees guarded her home making it almost invisible from the street.

Devon arrived and gazed around the living room. The bright floral print couches and potted plants didn't seem to cover up the somewhat somber air that decorated the room. Devon contemplated the sadness for a few moments, and then her attention was drawn to a large, curved window, nearly as tall as the wall that supported it, which created a view of a private yard. She flashed back to a picture of the arched window in the Empress' planning room, and thought of Zeena's words, "Rhianna was creating a good impact, then something happened."

After gazing out the window, she went back to her inspection of the living room. Some plaques on a wall caught her attention. She got closer in order to examine them. Devon noticed they were some sort of awards that Nicole had gotten for her music and her contributions to humanity. The room was silent, except for the singing of a couple of small birds housed in a large silver cage.

A dim light emanated from another room. Devon followed the faint light trail, and there before her was Nicole. She gazed at her and noticed that she definitely looked like the picture on the cassette cover, except, like the dim light in her room, she had lost some of the glow that was in her eyes when the sun was shining more brightly upon her life.

Nicole was on the phone talking to her boyfriend, Tom. "All right, if you need to. Then I'll see you in about an hour," Nicole said, then hung up the phone and attempted to get herself up from a chair. Devon saw that, as she walked, she held onto her lower back in a hunched over fashion, just like Tim had said. Nicole went to the kitchen and fixed herself a meal.

After eating, she walked over to a desk in the living room. She sat down, took a tapestry out of a drawer and started sewing a purple flower, while waiting for Tom. Devon watched with strong interest, finally able to feed her curiosity of what Nicole was really like. It saddened Devon to see someone so powerful hibernating because of fears from the past.

The waiting went by much slower for Devon than it did for Nicole. Devon reasoned about how she could have been there in her body right at that moment giving Nicole the message. However Nicole might not like the idea of an uninvited intrusion.

Finally the doorbell rang just as Nicole finished a flower petal. She tucked the tapestry away in a drawer along with some residual feelings of sadness, and went to answer the door. She greeted Tom with a kiss and then they both went and sat on a couch.

Devon noticed that Tom was a good-looking male, about four inches taller than Nicole. He had short, blonde hair, and a fairly muscular body. Tom's eyes focused on a book lying open in front of him, resting on a long wooden coffee table. The picture he looked at said "Sistine Chapel" under it.

"Amazing. The detail and quality of artwork back in those days," he said, as he sat on a couch.

Devon gazed at the picture as he said this. She was impressed with the beauty and wondered why she didn't see any places like that in LA. The photo made her a little homesick.

"Yeah, I know. It's too bad you don't see this type of beauty here in LA," said Nicole, focusing on the picture instead of her ailments.

Tom looked at the picture for another minute and then flipped the pages in the book, "Must be an art history book."

"How did you guess?" replied Nicole.

"Well, I'm just smart," said Tom as he started turning pages until he got back to the beginning of the book and came to a picture of two men with long pointed sticks chasing an animal. The top of the page said "Stone Ages" Under the picture was the caption, "Deer Hunt."

"Interesting. Talks about how these pictures are one of the main ways people communicated to each other back then," Tom said as he held his hand to his stomach that protruded slightly. "Cave man hungry. Me go on deer hunt. Bring dinner home to family. Yum. Yum. Almost as good as McDonald's. Real beef." He licked his lips.

Nicole laughed and so did Devon. But while Tom pretended to be one of those cave humans, Devon kept worrying how long he'd keep Nicole away from her cave.

"Cave woman, get coals ready for feast," ordered Tom as he got up and went to the refrigerator in the kitchen, then came back to Nicole holding a piece of raw meat. "Me slayum cow instead of deer. Easier to find in these parts of the city."

Nicole still laughed, "Sometimes you're so funny that I forget I'm not well."

Glad to hear this, Devon thought maybe she wouldn't have to stay out of town as long now. She hoped that Tom would continue to distract her from her ailments.

"Did you get coals ready for cooking, woman?"

"Cave woman will use fire in cave kitchen to cook cow on. Follow me," Nicole said and went to the kitchen as Tom walked behind her grunting.

"Instant fire," she said while turning on the stove.

"Very good woman. You may go back outside now."

Nicole went back to the couch and sat down. Tom put the meat back in the refrigerator and turned off the heat. He came out to where she sat and pat his belly. "Yum, yum. Good cow. Next time I save some for woman."

"Gee thanks," said Nicole.

"Now me takes woman and go into cave." He lifted her up and threw her over his shoulder.

"Ow, my back. Put me down you beast," Nicole said as she got down and went behind the couch to hide.

"Sorry, you okay?" Tom said in his normal tone of voice.

"Yeah, I'm all right," she replied.

"Where is woman?" Tom looked around.

Nicole popped up. "Boo," she said as he came over and grabbed her lightly by the hair.

"Woman with long hair convenient for dragging around."

"Woman go to Bedrock beauty parlor and have long hair cut off so she can escape easier," said Nicole.

"Me no let cave woman slip away to hairdresser. Me locks cave door and keep woman here. Tie her down," Tom said as if he was trying to hold her captive.

"Cave man forget one thing. This is woman's cave."

"Oh uh yeah." He scratched his head with a dumb look on his face.

"This means cave woman gets privilege of tying cave man to sofa." Nicole hobbled over to a closet in the room and took out a rope. Then she went over to Tom and put it around his waist and pulled him toward the couch.

"Help," he yelped.

"Come with woman to stone sofa." She dragged him to the couch and forced him to sit down. Then she tied the rope around his legs and attached it to the legs of the sofa. "If cave man promises not to be a beast, woman will untie him."

"Ugh," said Tom. "Translated, that means 'I promise.'"

Nicole unfastened the rope and let him go. As soon as she untied him, he grabbed her around the waist and gently pinned her to the couch, trying not to hurt her back.

"You lied," she yelped while laughing.

"Cave man sneaky," Tom said as he climbed on top of her. They both laughed and embraced and then went back to behaving like modern day humans.

Nicole started coughing when the playfulness ended, and a spell of dizziness hit her. "Okay Tommy, I think it's time to get some rest," she said as he got up off of her. They both went to the bedroom, while Devon politely waited all night in the living room.

She wasn't about to leave without somehow getting an answer as to when they'd be back in town. The worst thing that could happen is she'd have to follow them to wherever they were going, and try and get the message to Nicole while she was away. Devon didn't think this was such a good idea, as Nicole might feel she was being followed.

Nicole came out of the bedroom the next morning, which was Friday, and took some food out and put it on the table for the two of them. They both sat down and ate breakfast.

Nicole continued an earlier conversation she started having with Tom that morning. "So this dream I was telling you about, it was incredible. There were beautiful buildings that looked like something out of my art history book. And there were these fragrant smelling flowers. Then, right before you woke me up I was listening to this incredible music. There was a harpist playing. She had a touch as gentle as a mother stroking a newborn baby's fragile body. I just wanted to stay and listen. It's as if I was in another world, somewhere far from Earth, so that's why I was grumpy when you woke me. I'm sorry."

"Hey, it's all right."

"You know, at times I think about where I've been other lifetimes. I have a strong feeling that Earth is not the only place I've lived. There's this one place that especially seems to haunt me with a vague memory. You ever feel that way?" she asked, while having a fleeting thought about Devon. What could she possibly know about Athena?

"Me, come on. You know I don't believe in that past life stuff. You probably had that dream because we were looking at your art history book last night and you saw pictures of castles. Dreams usually come from real things we see. Then the imagination goes wild with them at night," Tom replied.

"Yeah, that may be, and I don't have proof about other lives, but sometimes I just look at the fact that there's so many planets out there. There must be life on some of them. I mean we can't be the only living creatures in all the galaxies. And if there's life out there, well you never know, maybe we lived elsewhere at one time. I know it sounds a little far out, but I think there's something to this."

"Nicky, you need some good black coffee," Tom said as he rolled his eyes.

Devon wished she could pop up right then and there and confirm Nicole's correctness.

"I don't drink coffee. You know that!" snapped Nicole. "Come on, I know we don't always agree on things, but you don't have to be so sarcastic when I tell you my thoughts." Nicole took a bite out of a waffle and looked out a window having doubts about Tom again. Nicole usually had fun with him, and was glad that she met him during the downfall of her career. He was a professional director, as well as an actor, specializing in comedy. He had a way of cheering her up with his humor, but when it came to philosophical ideas, there were definite clashes. Although tired of having her points of view insulted, she felt she just couldn't let go of him. For some reason she lacked confidence that she could find the right man.

"Okay, okay Let's finish up and get going. I have to stop by my place on the way. I forgot a few things. I left in such a hurry so I could get out of there last night before Fred's baseball buddies came over," Tom said, referring to his brother who lived with him in a house that they both owned.

Devon still didn't have an answer as to the time of their return, so she tagged along in anticipation. If they didn't come back in four days, Devon had no choice but to show up at Big Sur unannounced. She dreaded this idea, as Nicole could really become suspicious of her and maybe react unfavorably.

They arrived at Tom's house and were greeted by a floor covered with beer cans and the scent of stale cigarette smoke.

"Typical of Fred to go and crash out and not clean up his mess. He must still be sleeping," said Tom.

Nicole sat on a couch while Tom started to go to his room. He stopped short and put his hand to his head and said aloud, "I forgot to call Alex and say good-bye."

Alex was his ten-year-old son, who mainly stayed with his ex-wife, Diane, except for some weekends when he visited Tom.

Tom separated from her during a time when Diane took up drinking and then had an affair with another man. He never wanted to break up the marriage, but felt justified in his actions at the time. Tom went over to a phone in the kitchen. "Hi Diane, where's my son? I want to say good-bye since I won't be seeing him this weekend."

"When will you be back?" came a concerned voice on the other end.

"I don't know. Three, four, five days, not sure. Where's Alex?" Tom said as Devon listened in and felt another rush of anxiety come over her.

"Alex is at Joey's house. I'd really like if you could be back by noon on Monday, so you can watch him for me. He keeps nagging me about seeing you. Since you've been working on weekends so much lately, I think it's only fair that you take him on Monday."

"Why, where are you going all of a sudden?"

"It was not so suddenly. I tried calling you last night but you weren't home. If you must know, I am going to get some tests done by a doctor. I've cut way down on the drinking, almost quit, and decided to see what horrible condition my body is in so I could start healing it."

A moment of silence hung in the air after she spoke. Tom had been wanting her to handle her drinking problem for ages. He nearly put aside his feelings for Nicole right then and there, and thought of asking Diane to come back to him. He held back, however, as he didn't know if she'd want to leave her boyfriend. He also didn't know if she'd readily forgive him for the times he'd physically abused her in the past.

"Hello, are you there? Earth to Tom," Diane said.

"That's great Diane. Let me ask Nicole. What time do you need me here?"

"By noon on Monday."

Tom got off the phone with Diane and told her he'd call her back with an answer. Nicole reluctantly agreed to this decision to be back Monday. Devon's roller coaster of high and low anxiety, was now on the down side as she now had a response to her silent question. She stuck around a while longer getting to know Nicole and Tom better.

Tom called Diane back, confirming Nicole's approval. He finished his conversation with Diane, and just as he was about to go to his room to gather up some items that he wanted to take along on the trip, the phone rang again. He started talking to a friend of his.

While Tom was engaged in conversation, his brother Fred walked into the living room dressed in a yellow terry cloth robe. He ran his fingers through his short unkempt hair, attempting to make it neater, as he approached Nicole, "Hey Nicky. What's happening?"

"Oh, Tom and I are going to Big Sur for the weekend to revel in the natural surroundings."

"Sounds cool. Can I come along and be your chaperone? I could drive you around sightseeing during the day and then at night take you to your hotel, two separate rooms, of course, just like in that Dating Game show."

At that point Nicole threw a pillow at Fred.

"Fred I think it's time you got yourself a new woman."

"Hey, if I could find anyone out there with an IQ above 75, maybe I would do that," Fred said as he started picking up some of the Budweiser cans on the floor, "Boy, what a mess. My friends are such slobs. I gotta clean up after them and then go and do their dirty dishes."

Nicole smiled at him. Then she practically forgot Fred was there as she suddenly became absorbed with some news on the radio. The announcer said, "Funds for artistic programs have been cut from many local schools. There has been a conflict with children who are approaching their teen years in that their overly creative side has been seen to prevent them from facing the realities of life. This was a conclusion drawn by leading experts in the mental health field who have studied this left brain/right brain imbalance. Dr. Shifter states, 'Instead of placing a primary importance on practical studies which will be of use in their adult years, they are overindulged with desires to become great artists of some kind. Choosing a strictly creative path could lead to future disappointments, as we have an abundance of artists in the society already, and there is enough competition as it is. It is speculated that these children can be made to adjust to a more functional position in life, once their creative urges are modified by more pragmatic studies. These children have yet to realize that they can gain more stability by taking on positions in the corporate structure of society.'"

The announcer went on to another subject and Nicole felt a flush of heat come over her as she experienced a rush of rage. "Did you hear that, Fred?" she asked, as he held a rag and wiped cigarette ashes and spilled beer off of a table.

"Yeah, most of it," he said with mild interest.

"I can't stand it. I think it's highly detrimental to cut funds for the arts," she said, starting to feel lightheaded.

"Yeah, well what can you do? I mean the guy does have a point about one thing. Here we are in the nineties, and there are an awful lot of starving actors and musicians out there. If kids didn't have their heads up in the clouds, maybe they wouldn't try to bother with such risky careers. Look at the hard time my brother has had when he's been out of jobs. Comes to me to borrow money. Would he go out and get a real job? No."

Everything she was hearing was enough to make Nicole want to go back out on her crusade, but she stopped cold in her thoughts of seriously pursuing this idea. Devon saw the fiery power that began to surface in Nicole. "You have false information Fred. It's the arts that keep the world alive! Yeah, it's a tough business, and I know there's lots of craziness connected to it, but think of what life would be like without it. Think of a day going by without listening to any music."

Fred practically fell down in a nearby chair, after the blast from Nicole. While finishing his phone conversation, Tom heard them arguing. He left the kitchen and walked over to the two of them and made a "time out" sign with his arms, "Okay, knock it off." He looked at Fred. "Nicky and I better get going now, before you guys end up in the boxing ring all day."

Nicole calmed down and just accepted the fact that they had very different points of view. She didn't want to spend hours trying to change Fred.

Tom went to his room and grabbed the items he'd intended to get when they first arrived at his house. Then he and Nicole headed for his car and finally made their way toward the forest by the sea. Devon left them alone and went off and waited in anticipation of their return.

As Tom drove, he grabbed Nicole's left knee and spoke to her. "I see your old passion hasn't died. Maybe it's time you went back to try and fulfill your purpose in life."

Nicole stiffened up, and instantly experienced a shooting pain in her back. "Not yet Tom. I need more time. I'm still weak."
"Yeah, but it's been about a year and you're not getting any younger. In the next few years you'll be forty."

"You don't have to remind me." They drove along while Nicole looked out at the passing cars, feeling a gnawing helplessness inside.

Chapter 10

Monday morning, after a long unwanted rest, Devon anxiously put her body back on. She looked at the clock on the ninth day of her mission. The hands slowly reached for the twelve o'clock hour. Devon hoped that Tom had dropped Nicole off at home and was busy with his son Alex. Devon took a piece of paper out of a hotel desk drawer and sat on the queen-sized bed where her feet dangled off the side. She picked up a phone on a nightstand and dialed Nicole's number. Expecting the worst, but hoping for the best, she let the phone ring several times. After the fifth ring she heard Nicole's voice saying "Hello." Then there was a pause. Devon jumped in, "Nicole, this is Devon." Devon was puzzled. While she spoke she heard Nicole interrupting her, and stopped talking. She heard her say something about "not being home right now," and it took her a few seconds to become aware of the fact that she was talking to a message recording device. She waited for Nicole's voice to end so she could leave a message. Just as she was about to leave the hotel's phone number on the machine, she was cut off and interrupted by the word "hello" again, and wondered if the machine was operating improperly. Fortunately, this time, Nicole came on the line.

"Devon, sorry for the delay. I just walked in the door when I heard your voice."

Devon breathed a sigh of relief.

Nicole went on, "So you wanted to get together. You had something important to tell me, which I have been thinking about ever since I first talked to you," she said as she looked at a calendar on the wall in front of her. "How about tomorrow morning? I'd love to see you today, but I have some things I have to do."

Devon gulped, "Oh, well, that wouldn't quite work. You see, I'll be leaving Los Angeles to go back home then."

"Will you be back any time soon?"

"Oh, I'm not planning to be back for quite a while. See, I live far away, and I really wanted to meet with you while I was in your area. Is there any way we could do it today? I know this is fast notice, but it's critical, and you won't regret it," Devon insisted.

"Well, if there's no other choice, then I suppose we could meet tonight. How about nine? I'd ask you to come earlier, but I have these other obligations. Can you be at my place by then?"

"Sure, I can be there."

"Do you need directions?"

"No, uh I mean yes, please," she said, catching herself.

After Devon got off the phone she wondered if she shouldn't have been so pushy. She didn't spend much time worrying about this. She was just pleased to have an official appointment at last. She took her body off and rested, this time a little more peacefully, until it was time to go to Nicole's house.

When Devon arrived at Nicole's door, the first thing she did was to reassure herself that the chain with the coin was around her neck. She quickly tucked it under her shirt. Then she cleared her throat and knocked on the door of house number nine, where Nicole lived. She waited for a few minutes and got no answer, then pounded harder. Still no answer. Spying a familiar window, she courageously went up to it and tried to look inside. She couldn't see anything, as the drawn curtains forbade any inspection of Nicole's home. Devon could tell there was a light on.

She made her next move and cried out, "Nicole, Nicole," but still got no reply. Her palms were starting to sweat. She went around to another small window and tried to look through it, but couldn't see anything. Then suddenly she felt a light tap on her back. When she turned around she saw an old man.

"You looking for Nicole?"

"Yes. We had an appointment. Do you know where she is?"

"Don't know for sure, but I saw her leave in a big rush sometime this afternoon. I don't think she's been home yet," said the man who lived in the twin house next door. He had just finished watering his lawn when he spotted Devon.

"Would you like to come over to my house and wait for her? My wife made an extra batch of cookies, and you're welcome to have some," he said kindly.

Devon didn't know what would happen if she ate a cookie. She thought she'd probably get very ill. "Thank you for your polite offer, but I will just wait here."

The man left and went and wound up the long green hose in front of his house, glanced over at Devon, then went inside his home.

Devon paced back and forth on the well-lit front porch, like a dog waiting for her master to arrive and open the door so she could rush into the house. The time slowly ticked by and Devon was feeling a little dizzy. She sat on an upper stair and placed her head in her hands. After ten minutes, which seemed like ten hours, she saw a red sports car pull into the driveway to her right. Sure enough it was Nicole! She parked the car and got out of it. Clutching a cane in her right hand, and holding onto her lower back with her left hand, she looked like an old lady as she walked toward Devon. As she approached, Devon could see that her eyes were red and her cheeks were stained with tears.

She wiped her eyes, and then stopped in front of Devon, "Sorry I'm late. I was at my sister's and would have called you, but didn't have your number. There's been a death in my family. I wouldn't have come back here, but I knew you'd be here waiting for me. This is really a bad time to meet with you. I know you're going home tomorrow, but is there any way you could just call me from where you live?"

"I wish I could, but I just can't. There's something I need to give you. I know this is the wrong time, but I don't have to stay long."

Nicole was silent, tossed between the desire to satiate her curiosity about Devon and her duty to her family. "Okay, come in. I feel bad. I know how much you want to see me, and I've been dying to find out how you know about Athena."

Nicole opened the door to her home, excused herself and went into the bathroom, as Devon waited on a couch. The two birds sat quietly on a perch in their cage. They sensed something was wrong, and were silently respectful of Nicole's mourning.

Several moments ticked by, as Devon listened to the sound of running water coming from the bathroom. Nicole tried to wash away some of the grief she was feeling at the loss of her favorite niece, Jenny, who was thirteen. She kept replaying the scene that had occurred earlier that afternoon when she got a phone call from Jenny's best friend, Cara.

"Nicole," Cara had said frantically.

"It's Cara."

"What's the matter? You sound horrified."

"It's Jenny," she cried. "She's dead!"

"No!"

"I, I tried to call her mom, but, she, she wasn't home."

"What the hell happened?"

"We, she, was. The drugs. She jumped from the balcony at my house."

"I'm coming right over! Are you sure she's dead?! Are you really sure!?"

"Y..yes," Cara cried.

"Aren't your parents there?"

"No."

On the way to Cara's, Nicole saw nothing but Jenny's bright, shining face. She remembered Jenny telling her she wanted to be a politician someday so that she could help the people in America get the freedoms they deserved. She flashed back to a time she had had Jenny get up on stage at one of her concerts and speak out against violence in schools. "She would have been a great leader, damn it!" Nicole said aloud.

Nicole swerved into the driveway of Cara's home and came to a screeching halt. A bunch of concerned neighbors gathered around Jenny's body. Nicole hobbled along, pushing her way through the crowd. She ignored her back pain and leaned down to her niece on the pavement. "Jenny, Jenny!" she yelled to the lifeless body.

Nicole went in the house and called an ambulance. Then she talked with Cara.

"Cara, what happened to her? She was never a druggie."

"She was. She just didn't tell you. You haven't seen her for months. You've been secluded most of the time."

Nicole instantly started blaming herself for being so out of touch with her family. "I failed her! I could have done something to stop her. She always listened to me."

"I don't know," Cara mourned. "She got real bad. Jenny was experimenting with different drugs as if she was sampling chocolates from a See's candy box."

"Why didn't you stop her from jumping?" Nicole asked as she felt a flash of heat well up inside of her, forgetting that she was over exerting herself.

"I would have! I was downstairs. Do you think I would have let her do it? I feel so bad," Cara cried.

Nicole held Cara as they both wept together.

Devon patiently watched the hands on the clock strike nine thirty, while Nicole turned off the memory, along with the water in the bathroom. She then joined Devon, feeling a bit more under control.

"I'm sorry to keep you waiting. I just never expected my niece to be a druggie, and then to take her own life!"

"I understand how you feel. You were right to have spoken out against such a deadly disease," Devon said, trying to console her.

"Yeah, but I also didn't get hit until I started heavily confronting this particular social illness. That's what I get for being too idealistic."

"Nicole, I know there are those who would like you to believe your lyrics are filled with false information. They are wrong. I know you have suffered, and somehow managed to damage yourself physically and spiritually," Devon paused and coughed. She started to get dizzy, and her attention went to her own condition for a few seconds.

Nicole tensed up as she heard Devon's words.
"Devon, thank you for your support. There is something that I have to correct you on, though," she said as she closed her eyes, almost reluctant to bring up a memory that was as difficult to confront as Jenny's death.

Devon forced herself to withhold any coughing, as she didn't want to interrupt Nicole.

79

"I didn't bring the damage onto myself. I was practically killed!" She opened her eyes and was shaking as she said this.

"I didn't know that."

"It's true."

"What happened?"

"You really want the whole story?"

"Yes I do," Devon said with such intensity that Nicole was compelled to put thoughts of Jenny aside and answer her question.

Nicole hesitated, realizing she was talking to a complete stranger. However something about Devon comforted her, and made her feel safe. She felt compelled to confide in Devon as if she were an old friend, "I had been doing lots of anti-drug concerts. Parents brought their kids, hoping they'd get the message of how bad drugs were. I was effective in getting hundreds of kids to take vows to get off drugs and getting others never to start taking them in the first place. Then suddenly, just as I was creating a big impact, I started getting threatening letters from some anonymous person. I was told that if I didn't stop my campaign, I'd be killed. I ignored these warnings and continued my crusade until, one night someone pursued me after a concert.

"I went backstage and walked toward my dressing room. Just as I was about to open the door, a man came out of nowhere and grabbed me. He put his hand over my mouth and stuffed a cloth gag in it. Then he hit me in the back and I fell to the floor, while he dug his heel into my back. The pain was excruciating. I turned my head and saw him pull a knife out of his pocket. Then I squirmed around and tried to get away, but the best I could do was to loosen the gag and let out a scream just as he started to come at me with the knife. I yelled so loud that I got the attention of my keyboard player. I heard John say, 'It's Nicole!' This scared the attacker away." Nicole could feel the pain in her back throbbing as she told this to Devon.

When Nicole had finished speaking, Devon started coughing, finding it hard for her to control her hacking any longer. Nicole was so wrapped up in her story that she hardly noticed the coughing.

"Was the man ever caught?" Devon asked.

"No. He got away. To this day I don't know who it was. I can only guess that he was someone who was hooked up with the people who libeled me in the newspapers. I figure that someday, when I get better, I may pursue this attacker, as well as those who assaulted me with libel and slander. But on the other hand, I'm not sure how hard I want to try. I may just end up getting myself killed."

"Have you thought of performing again?"

"Sure I have, but I've got fears of having a replay of the past. I don't know exactly what I'll do. I just know I had a dream that was very alive years ago. A flame was shining bright in my heart. Ever since I was young I had wanted a better world and idealistically set about to help create one. I just didn't think that it would be such a difficult task.

"After my assault, I began to have doubts that I could do much for this planet without getting shot. I want to help, but I just don't know how anymore." Nicole put her head in her hands for a moment. "Now I'm just rambling on. Are you sure you want to hear all of this, Devon?"

"Yes, Nicole. I'm very interested. I am here to help."

"I feel like such a failure. I'm afraid to try and do a concert again. I tried once, but I just ended up letting everyone down."

"How so?"

"After my attack, my agent Carl booked me for a show, had tickets sold and everything, but I just couldn't bring myself to do it. I just flat out refused to perform. Even though I was promised better backstage security, something just told me to quit altogether. My fans were upset, but this didn't matter as much as protecting myself. I just didn't have the energy to fight my attackers. I got very ill, and never felt worse in my life. My record company tried to get me to go back out and perform, telling me that if I didn't continue to do concerts, this would affect the sales of my CD's. I didn't care. Then, finally, they just dropped me altogether. Ever since this happened, I've substituted tapestry for my true creative urges."

There was a moment of silence as Nicole pulled herself out of her past and turned and looked at Devon, whose eyes were glued to her. "Thanks for listening to all my horrible fates. It's nice to hear that you appreciate my art, but who are you, and..."

Before she could finish her sentence the phone rang and startled Nicole.

"Excuse me," she said, and went to answer it. "Hello."

Devon coughed as a wave of dizziness hit her again. She held her breath for a moment as Nicole finished her conversation, then came back to join her.

"That was my sister Cheryl. She and her husband want to be alone and don't need me to come back tonight."

Devon tried to acknowledge her calmly, but instead started coughing wildly.

"Are you all right? I hope that my story didn't disturb you so much that I made you sick."

"No, of course not. I have my own ailments. Please don't worry about me. It is you that I have concern for, and this is why I came. You see I know what you were up against. I admire the fact that you got as far as you did on your mission. It's not easy to communicate so much truth to a society that is easily influenced by those with very evil intentions. But you have so much to offer and are a true leader. You just need a way to rid yourself of those shadows of days-gone-by, so that they don't keep following you around, haunting you with their wickedness every time you contemplate going back out into the public. Nicole, you must confront your true potential, or you will always be less than you really are. You must also learn who the enemy is. This Earth planet desperately needs artists like you."

"Earth planet. You almost talk as if you're an alien." Devon smiled.

"I get the feeling Athena really exists, but..." Nicole stopped short, stunned by the sparkle in Devon's bright turquoise eyes. She had been so wrapped up in her own problems that she had not noticed their unique color. Almost mesmerized by the orbs she was gazing at, Nicole flinched. They seemed to speak to her, without a word from Devon's mouth.

"This is too much. You're not going to tell me that you're from..."

Devon briefly closed her eyelids and nodded.

"My god! I've heard of people being visited by aliens, but usually it's some sort of abduction thing. This is so weird. You look so...so human. How did you know about me?"

Devon went on to explain about the Empress and her perception of Nicole, as Nicole's jaw dropped.

"Devon, this is unbelievable. What do you want to tell me?"

Devon's head whirled, and she nearly fainted.

"What's the matter? Are you okay?"

"I'm very weak. I must hurry."

Devon carefully pulled the chain with the coin from underneath her shirt. Nicole had a puzzled look on her face as she gazed at the coin. Devon was getting dizzier, and knew that she had to say as little as possible but still get through to Nicole. "That's nice, but what does it have to do with me, and Athena, or my goals?"

Devon coughed, as she grew sicker by the minute, and rested her head on the back of the couch, then sat up again. "It has a lot to do with them. I know this seems odd to you, but you must hold onto this coin," she said as she took it off of the chain and handed it to Nicole.

"What is it? Some sort of 'good luck' charm? I'm not particularly superstitious, you know. Will this help me fight the enemy? Who is the enemy anyway? Is there something you know that I don't?" she asked, bombarding Devon with swift questions, hoping to get them answered before Devon left her.

"It might be...." Devon said, then stopped, realizing she was on the brink of permanently losing her body if she didn't leave instantly. Being that she was running out of time, and didn't have total certainty of her evidence, she saved her final words for orders from the Empress.

"Who is it? Do you know?" Nicole asked desperately. Then she quickly took her attention off of her own problems afraid that Devon might die on her. "Is there anything I can do for you?"

"No, it's okay. There is something you have forgotten, which you must remember, and this is your ticket. There are instructions that I must get to you, but I must go now. I'll phone you and tell you what they are," Devon said, as she sat on the edge of the couch, about to pass out. She forced her body up. "Make sure you put that in a safe place," she said, looking at the coin.

Nicole opened a drawer next to her and put the coin inside. Then she stood up and walked Devon to the door. "Devon, what's the matter with you? Are you going to make it back all right? I don't want you to faint or anything."

"If I leave now, I'll be all right. It's just hard for me to exert much energy for long periods of time. Don't worry, though. I just need to go rest my body."

"Where are you going? Do you have a space ship to get to?"

"No," she said, thinking about getting to a place where she could take off her body.

"Can I give you a ride? I hate to see you leave in this shape."

"No, no, you don't need to bother." Devon looked at the clock on Nicole's wall.

"I must go," Devon said. "I'll call you soon."

After she had said good-bye to Nicole, Devon flew down the stairs away from her house with the same urgency that she had come there that night. She ran down the hilly street, using her strong willpower to keep her body from dropping. As she ran, Nicole watched her through a window and then, after she was out of sight, drew the curtain and went and sat on her couch thinking about the strange encounter she'd just had.

Devon ran until she came to a small park that was forested with bushes and trees. She walked into the thicket and just as she was about to faint, barely managed to de-molecularize. She instantly felt the relief and freedom that comes from not carrying around a toxic body. She knew that if she could rejuvenate for a couple of hours, she could then put her body on again for a brief time and phone Nicole.

Meanwhile, Nicole had gone to the drawer that held the mysterious coin. She took it out and contemplated its uniqueness. She hadn't remembered seeing many other pieces of jewelry that shined so brightly. She tried to make out the foreign writing on it but failed to decipher it. After about half an hour of being engrossed in the possible riddle of the coin, she then impatiently awaited a phone call that seemed like it was never going to happen.

Chapter 11

After a well needed rest, it was finally safe for Devon to put her body on again, though she was not looking forward to its discomforts. She materialized in her hotel room. She knew that her body would weaken quickly, so she had to work fast. Devon hurried out to a closed phone booth in the hotel lobby and put money into the coin slot. She shut the glass door and punched in Nicole's number. The ringing started and stopped and started and stopped and started and stopped about twenty times. She nervously stood in the phone booth for several moments, while getting no answer. A woman came up and knocked on the door.

"Are you done?" she asked.

"I, uh, I'm trying to reach someone and haven't been able to get through."

"Could I make a quick call?" the lady asked.

Devon didn't want to be discourteous, so she let the woman make the call.

There were two other phone booths, but both were being utilized. Devon waited in silent desperation trying not to stare at the humans making calls. The woman who said she was making a quick call was on for what seemed like forever. Then she noticed a man exiting a box. She sped over and went inside before anyone else had a chance to. Devon punched in Nicole's number quickly, not knowing what was going to happen. A wave of weakness splashed over her body.

"Hello," said Nicole as Devon felt relief.

"Nicole. This is Devon," She said while finding it hard to speak.

"Devon, hi, did you call before?"

"Yes, I let it ring and ring."

"I'm sorry. I was in the shower. I thought my phone was ringing, but wasn't sure. How are you feeling?"

Devon could hardly talk. At this point it was a true confront of mind over matter. "I'm okay, but still very weak. The rest helped but I will have to go to bed again soon. I need to tell you something. Please bear with me. I don't how long I can stay on the phone. You need to go someplace. Take the coin. Go to Griff..th park. Go tomorrow at eight PM."

"Devon, will you be okay?"

"Yes, yes I will. Please don't worry.. Just go there. You know where it's at?"

"You said Griffith Park. Yes, yes I do. What do I do there?"

"Go...near the ob....serva..tory. There is ...some sec..ret.. inf..or mation for you...go G...go to the.." She coughed and felt dizzier, not realizing she could ever feel so bad. "Go to.....les."

"Devon can I call you back later after you're feeling better? What's your number? Can't you tell me any more?" Devon hung up and headed back to her room practically knocking down a couple of people as she ran. She undressed from her body just as she felt like she was going to go into total unconsciousness. She couldn't even get her last words out. But Devon knew that if Nicole inquired at the observatory, she would probably find out where she was supposed to go.

Devon had pushed her body to the limit on this planet. She had no idea she could feel so bad. The next day she would have to put her body on one last time once she got to her space rider. Then she would rise above the LA smog where the toxins wouldn't hit her, and where she couldn't be seen. She'd hover over Griffith Park. Using a viewing device, much like very powerful binoculars, she'd make sure that Nicole got to her destination. This concerned Devon somewhat, but she knew that Earthlings were compelled to solve mysteries, and she had created such a big one for Nicole that it was likely she would follow through and resolve it. Once Nicole arrived at her destination, Devon would perform one more piece of magic. If Nicole didn't arrive, Devon would have to go back to Athena with a failed mission and face the Empress in shame. Devon put out a strong telepathic communication to Nicole, urging her to follow through with the message given to her on the phone.

* * * *

This was one of the weirdest encounters Nicole had ever had. There were so many questions she still had unanswered but couldn't ask, because Devon got off the phone so fast. She just hoped that Devon wasn't going to die! Nicole felt like a character in a mystery novel but wasn't sure what she was looking for.

It was now one A.M., and Nicole was exhausted. She thought of calling Tom and telling him what had happened, but she knew he would just laugh at her. She often wished she had someone with whom she had more in common, but she usually tried to lay those wishes aside. It was easier just to hang on to something even though it wasn't ideal.

Most of her attention kept going back to what was going to happen the next night. Questions like, "Why do I have to wait until eight A.M.? What is this 'less' thing I'm supposed to find? What if I can't find it?" kept going through her mind.

Nicole went to bed and tossed and turned most of the night until she was too tired to think anymore and then just fell asleep. The next day she woke up at noon, after finally getting six hours of sleep.

At six-thirty that night, Nicole's heart sped up as the hands of the clock moved into the future. She hurried into her room and opened a closet and looked for something to change into. She didn't want to wear the old sweat pants and T-shirt that she had on. Nicole was never told how to dress for this occasion, and just couldn't make up her mind what to wear. She pulled out a couple of dresses, and then put them back. Then she took out a pair of jeans and a T-shirt that she really liked, assuming that casual was going to be okay. She changed her clothes, then brushed her hair. While putting her brush down on a dresser, she was startled by the doorbell. She hastily hobbled toward her front door, hoping that perhaps Devon had returned again.

When she got to the door, she was let down as a tall blonde man wearing white overalls that were covered with splotches of paint greeted her.

"Nicole Jensen," he said, looking at the celebrity he was somewhat familiar with. He was surprised to see her holding a cane as she came to the door.

"Yes, how can I help you?"

"My name is Chris Sanders, the painter who was working on the Andrews' house. They said you liked the work I did and wanted me to come over and see you about doing your house," he said, starting to reach out a hand to shake hers, but then withdrawing it, realizing the blue paint on it hadn't dried yet. "Sorry, I guess I shouldn't be shaking your hand."

"Yes, I did want to get the outside of my house done, but right now, I'm in a big hurry and don't have time to talk to you. Can you leave a card or something? I'll get back to you later," she said abruptly.

"Sure, I'm sorry to bother you," he said, reaching into his pocket and pulling out a small white card that had a small picture of a wizard holding a paint brush. The card read "Sanders' Paint Magic."

Nicole's stomach growled as she took the card from Chris and quickly said good-bye to him, hoping she wouldn't have any more distractions. She almost forgot she'd hardly eaten anything that day, and rushed to the kitchen and grabbed some leftover chicken in the refrigerator. Not knowing exactly how long she was going to be gone, she thought it would be best to force herself to eat, even though she wasn't hungry. She managed to consume one small leg.

The two birds who had been silent most of the day were now singing more loudly than usual. "Mommy is going out for awhile. You have enough food there?" she asked while looking into the cage. "Looks like you have plenty, but I'll give you some of this chicken. "There that should make you guys happy," she said.

Nicole didn't like the idea of going out in public where there were lots of people, as she wasn't ready to face the celebrity gazers yet. She put on some tinted glasses and tucked her hair up into a brown beret, hoping she wouldn't be recognized. She grabbed her purse, and took the cane that made walking less painful. Then she walked out the front door. She remembered she hadn't checked her mail in two days, so quickly hobbled down to the bottom of the stairway in front of her house and took a handful of letters out of the mailbox. Just as she shut the box, she saw Mr. Milligan, her next-door neighbor, outside watering the lawn.

"Hello, Nicole," he said.

"Hi, Mr. Milligan."

"Looks like you're in a big hurry to get somewhere." he said.

"Yeah, you could say that."

"Well, honey, if you're not back too late, you're welcome to come over and have some of Martha's cookies, the chocolate chip ones you like so much."

"Thanks Mr. Milligan. I appreciate the offer," she said, not wanting to say anything about where she was going, as she had no idea what was going to happen or when she'd be back. "I'll see you later."

Nicole got into her car and sped out of her driveway, down the hilly road, ignoring the stop sign at the bottom of the street. She made a fast right turn and drove with anxiety toward Griffith Park. It was a place that she had been to several times before, mostly when she was a teenager.

After she was about half way to her destination she realized that she had forgotten something. "The coin!" she said aloud as she turned the car around, making an illegal U-turn.

Nicole sped back to her house, hardly aware of whether any policemen had noticed her wild driving. She got home and hobbled back up the stairs to her front door. Mr. Milligan gave her a curious look, while picking some dead leaves off of a bush in his yard. She opened the door to her house, went in and pulled out the drawer where the secret coin was kept. Nicole took the coin off the chain and looked at it for a second, then put it into a wallet in her purse. Taking a fast glance at the large golden clock in her living room, she saw it was almost seven o'clock.

As she walked out her front door, Mr. Milligan asked, "Forget something, Nicky?"

"Yeah. I forgot some money."

"That's not a good thing to be without. Can't get things for free in this world."

"That's for sure," she replied.

This time she had what she needed and was careful not to race down the road. She didn't want an encounter with a cop to delay her from wherever she was going. Although her mind was racing, her car maintained the correct speed limit. She kept thinking about where she was supposed to go.

She drove up a steep hill to the parking lot and arrived at seven-forty. She was glad to see that it wasn't very crowded. Getting out of her car, she took her cane and walked as rapidly as her physical condition would allow. There were a few people milling around by the observatory. Some were going inside the building and others were looking at the view outside. Devon's words played over and over in her mind. "Go to.....less."

Nicole walked up the wide stairway that led inside the dome shaped building, which looked like something that belonged on another planet. She went to the information desk. Nervously, she waited in line as she kept looking at her watch. Finally her turn came.

"May I help you miss?" asked the man behind the desk, in a rather bored tone.

"Yes, yes you may. I know this may sound like an odd question, but..."

He cut in. "It's okay. I've heard em all. You wouldn't believe what people want to know around this place."

She tried to smile. "That's good. Anyway, do you happen to know where the 'less' is, or something that sounds like that?"

"What is this, a game of Trivial Pursuit?" He snickered at his joke referring to a popular game.

The last thing I need is a wise guy, Nicole thought, but played along. "Yes, and if you guess the answer you win a thousand dollars."

"I'll have to give it more thought. Why don't you come back in ten minutes? Maybe I'll have the winning answer for you. Right now I can't think of anything off the top of my head. You can look at this here map and see if you can figure it out," he said as he handed her a map of the observatory and park. She looked at it but still couldn't figure it out. She walked away upset. Two people behind her in line gave her a curious look. She didn't know if they were trying to figure out who she was, or what she was talking about, but it wasn't important. Nicole walked around inside the observatory to see if she could find this "less" thing. She hobbled around looking at various objects, but no luck. Then she left and went down the wide stairway and panicked, not knowing if the thing was inside or out. Eight o'clock was getting closer and closer. She had over-exerted herself into a state of dizziness, so she went and sat on a bench and rested for a moment. She felt compelled to walk toward the edge of the hill that overlooked Los Angeles. Then something startled her. She heard a voice.

"Nicole. Nicky," a female voice said.

Her heart sped up as she turned around, thinking that perhaps Devon had come to find her, or maybe a long lost fan had noticed her, even though she was incognito. But all she saw was a lady waving to another lady.

"Over here," the lady said to another woman named Nicole, while trying to catch up with her friend.

As it got later, Nicole wondered what would happen if she didn't find this "less" thing by the eight o'clock deadline. She decided to stop being so frantic. What was the worst thing that could happen? She thought that her life would probably just keep going the way it was before all of this drama.

Her attention focused on the view from where she sat. In front of her she saw two kids trying to look through a telescope at the same time. This wasn't working out too well, and one kid said to the other, "Let me look first, Sammy."

Sammy stepped back, and the other kid looked through the small eyepiece. They were both really interested in what they saw.

"Okay Steven. Let me see now," said Sammy impatiently.

"Just a minute."

"Hurry up. Our time is running out."

As Nicole stood watching the two kids, something clicked in her mind. She said silently to herself, "Oh my god. less, les. Maybe Devon was trying to get the word telescope out. Is this what she was trying to say? Telescope. How could I have been so dumb? Of course. The coin. That must be it. She wanted me to go to the telescope and put the coin in! But what does looking at a bunch of stars have to do with anything? Is this some sort of a gag, like I'm on candid camera and don't know it?"

She walked closer to the telescope where the kids still gazed into space, and anxiously waited in the dark for her turn. Sammy was looking now, as Nicole watched him like a hawk. The view soon ended, and the kids turned around and saw her staring at them.

"How was the view?" she asked.

"Great!" said Steven. "I saw outer space. It was like Star Wars. There was a space ship flying around and everything."

Sammy looked at him. "You didn't see that. You're lying. He's just kidding, lady."

"Uh-huh. I did too see that."

She looked at them and smiled as they stepped away from the telescope. "Are you going to look at the space ship lady?" Steven asked.

"Yes," she replied, playing along with him. "I'd like to see it."

"'Bye," said Sammy.

"'Bye," said Steven.

Sammy turned to Steven. "You didn't see a space ship."

Nicole smiled to herself then looked at her watch and waited until the hands reached eight o'clock. She hastily dug in her purse, opened her wallet, took out the coin, and put it into the "les." Then she took her glasses off and peered into the eye piece. She saw sky and stars and more stars, and even a few shooting stars. Nicole looked and looked, but time ticked by, and the three-minute view was nearly up. Then something odd caught her eye. It appeared to be some kind of tiny UFO.

She wondered if this could have been what Steven was talking about and thought that maybe it could have been Devon's space ship.

The three minutes was up. She was frustrated and mad, and began to think that this was all a big joke. But why? Why would an alien come all the way from Athena to play a gag on her?

She cried a tear of frustration, and turned away from the telescope. Then she put her tinted glasses on and headed for her car. Her stomach growled so loudly that she couldn't ignore it. She thought it must have been complaining because of the minuscule amounts of food she had given it. Nicole couldn't stand it anymore and felt weak, as a wave of hunger came over her. She just had to get something quickly before driving herself and her humiliation home.

She noticed a man selling hot dogs out of a cart near the observatory and walked over to him.

"I'll have one hot dog."

"That will be a buck-fifty," the vendor said.

Nicole took a dollar out of her wallet and opened the change compartment and pulled out two quarters and gave them to him. He looked at the money to make sure it was the right amount. Then just as he was about to put it in a cash drawer, he did a double take.

"Hey, you gave me a dollar and one quarter, but this other thing looks like some sort of foreign coin or something." As he said this, Nicole's heart raced. She swiftly took the coin back from him as he held his hand out.

"I'm sorry. How silly of me. Here, let me get you another real quarter." She felt relieved as she put the golden coin back in her wallet.

It was so dark by the telescope that she realized she must have just grabbed any old quarter and put it in the slot. The man gave her a hot dog. She sat on a nearby bench, quickly gobbling it up. It was now ten minutes past eight and she didn't even know if it was worth it to go back to the telescope, but thought she'd give it one more try. This time she took the golden coin out and stuck it in a pocket in her pants. She hobbled over to the telescope, but before she got there a couple of teenagers beat her to it, and she had to wait again for her turn. It was now eight twenty!

Nicole took the golden coin out and looked at it for a few seconds. Finally her turn came, and she dashed to the telescope, almost managing to ignore the pain in her back, which gnawed incessantly. Without thinking any other thoughts, she took her glasses off, put the coin in the slot and glued her right eye to the eyepiece.

There, once again, were the same stars as last time. Nothing unusual. She got frustrated. Nicole wondered why she was putting herself through this, and lost hope about anything happening. The view just went on the same for two minutes. Then, just as she started to pull her eye away from the telescope in disappointment, she caught an odd sight out of the corner of her eye. Writing suddenly appeared on the lens in some sort of foreign language. She couldn't make it out at all but recognized that the letters were similar to those on the coin. Then the letters transformed into English, and it said, "Time and space alteration function." She couldn't figure out what this was supposed to mean, but it fascinated her, so she just kept looking. Nicole still saw stars and more stars. Then there was a small elliptical object floating around. She wondered if it was Devon's space ship again.

The UFO soon disappeared and there were still stars, and more stars. She was dying to know what the strange message meant. She was sure she had used up more than a quarter's worth of time. But the clock was still ticking. There were stars and stars and stars, even a few planets, but nothing unusual. Nothing weird except the writing on the lens. She started to get distracted by the wind that was blowing around her. When she first arrived there had merely been a gentle breeze, but now it was whipping harder and harder. Her hair was being slapped around, and she kept needing to push it out of her face in order to maintain her view. Nicole strained to see if there was anything else happening in outer space.

The wind howled at her, as the sky lit up with splashes of color that she hadn't noticed before. She wondered if they were various star clusters shining in different lights. It looked like a still picture of a fireworks display. Some of the colors started to fade. Then, all of a sudden, out of the blue, there was a very bright flash of light!

The wind died. Everything was very calm. Nicole backed off from the telescope, amazed at what had occurred.

All the things that were previously around her were gone! Poof! She no longer stood on a hill at Griffith Park! There were no people in sight! She was out of her body, and should have been terrified, but was amazingly relaxed. Just as she bathed in the calm stillness, some sort of motion stirred up. Lots of stars and strange shiny objects emerged, almost out of nowhere. Nicole was floating through space! Things moved very fast around her, as she rapidly sailed away from Earth.

The scenery changed while she weaved in and out of various solar systems. The speed was so fast that she barely had time to think about where she was. She felt like she was being magnetically pulled into another world. Sure enough, this was exactly what was happening! She slipped back in time hundreds of years. Swirls of color lit up the darkness. Then, all of a sudden she saw an object that stood out from all the rest. It was small and shiny and pink! She strained to see it as clearly as possible. It was unique.

The object, which she now figured to be a planet, started increasing in size. As she sailed closer to her destiny, the sky got lighter and lighter. The planet that had been mainly pink, now turned to shades of light blue, purple and magenta. She was awed by its magnificence and could barely make out the land formations, but they kind of looked like mountains. Tall purple mountains sprinkled with a glittery gold and silver coating. Crystal clear turquoise seas ebbed upon welcoming pale pink sands.

A feeling of elation and exhilaration came over her. She felt freer and more alive than she could ever remember. It seemed to her as though she were flying downward. More and more things became visible. She was able to see lots of trees. They were blue and green and yellow and red. Clusters of large, cheerful flowers decorated the ground beneath her. Then she spied giant castle-like buildings scattered throughout the land. They were the most incredible structures she had ever seen! Enormous gold and silver castles. In the distance were flowing streams, where velvety smooth water traversed the land.

The strange letters she had looked at on the coin and in the telescope flashed across the sky. Underneath the letters were the words, "Time and space alteration complete." These were the last English words she saw.

Nicole noticed a small village where the buildings seemed to be made of gold and marble. She floated towards them, feeling herself being lured to a particular home in the village. As she fell lower and lower, she felt like she was coming in for a landing on a runway. Closer and closer she sailed to the home, until nearly there. She spied a large triangular shaped window and looked inside. There, upon a large bed, was a pregnant woman wearing a very loose gown. A man was in the room with her. The woman looked like she was about to give birth. Nicole claimed the body and made it her own, as she saw the man hold out his arms, waiting to receive his new baby. The pregnant woman was quite relaxed. She simply caressed the top of her belly and then the head of the body came out, soon followed by the rest of the body. The man in the room gently took the baby into his arms. He snipped a small attachment that connected the baby's body to the woman. The man then put her in a silken blanket and wiped off a small amount of water that was on her body. He was smiling while looking at the new creation. Then he handed the child to the woman. She held and kissed the baby gently. The whole birth process was painless for her!

"Our little girl," said the man.

"She's beautiful," said the woman.

"Welcome," said the father to his new daughter as he tenderly stroked her head.

"We shall call you Rhianna - Spirit of hope and inspiration," said the mother.

Nicole had traveled back to another lifetime. While her body remained at the telescope in Earth time, the spirit of Nicole went back to relive a lifetime on Athena.

With a population of approximately one million, Athena was known as the "land of creation and home of the artists united!

Part II - Return to Athena

Chapter 1

Rhianna, now thirteen, was at home in the village of Alta where she lived with her parents, and a pet winged horse named Thaurus. Alone in the household meal room, she adjusted herself to a comfortable position on a chair. About to take a spoonful of red plant petals from a small bowl, she hesitated, looking at the picture painted on the black stone table in front of her. Although she had sat at this table for many of her weekly meals while growing up, she hadn't quite seen it in the same light as she saw it now. There in the center was a golden circle with a picture of the Empress Zeena holding a diamond-like necklace with a silver medal on it. She was placing it over the head of Rhianna's father, Andar, while, in the background, birds of various colors encircled them. Rhianna had been only three when her father had received this medal for a successful mission on a nearby planet.

Rhianna barely remembered the ceremony in Alta where Andar was presented with the table by one of their neighbors to acknowledge him for his first mission. Rhianna imagined being awarded by the Empress for going on a mission and helping another civilization, by creatively rehabilitating it after an invasion by the Black Knights.

Rhianna was usually content living in her pretty marble home in Alta with her parents. She enjoyed their company, as well as that of her pet Thaurus. Rhianna, however, was getting restless. Although a lifetime on Athena lasted up to six hundred years, she was eager to start expanding her own creative abilities. She wanted to contribute more to the aesthetic stronghold of her home planet, as well as to help other populations.

Picking a petal out of a small golden bowl, Rhianna put the sweet cherry-flavored flower into her mouth and savored it. As she ate another, a warm breeze came through an open widow, carrying a delicious smell. This was one of her favorite scents. It came from a large purple-and-yellow purla plant outside the window. As she experienced the warmth of the air, she felt glad that the climate on Athena was always a comfortable, warm temperature, unlike other planets she'd heard of with extremes of hot and cold. Rhianna thought about how she'd love to have some purla powder to embellish the red petals she was eating! Just then, some of the yellow powder complied, blowing off the plant and flying into her bowl. Happy to have her wish granted by simply intending it, she continued enjoying her feast. She traveled back to her imaginary world, dreaming of future adventures.

Rhianna was nearly full when her mother, Silka, came into the meal room. Silka sat across the rectangular table from her only child carrying one of the personally hand-crafted silken robes she had been nicknamed for. She sewed some golden thread onto the sleeves, putting the finishing touches on it as Rhianna spoke.

"Mama, you and father are back from your ride on Thaurus already?"

"Darling, we've been gone for a couple of hours already. You look as if you've been awfully preoccupied with something, Rhia." she said, calling her daughter by her nickname.

Rhia smiled and looked at the table; "Oh, well, maybe I was."

She confessed to her mother her impatience to go on a mission of her own.

Silka stroked her daughter's long shiny hair. "In time dear, in time. I know you're eager to help, but meanwhile you still have art lessons and other learning to do. The more skills you acquire, the more valuable you'll be."

Ignoring Silka's motherly advice, she said, "Mama, how is it that we are the only planet able to keep the Knights away so successfully?"

Silka smiled at her inquisitive daughter. "They are bitterly disturbed when they see the power of a united group of beings such as ourselves. Somehow, the more we flourish and the stronger our group intentions are to allow only goodness into our lands, the more it drives the Knights crazy. It's like a big, creative shield that keeps them from entering. Deep in their hearts they know that we are more powerful than they, as their supposed power comes from mere treachery."

Rhianna was nearly satisfied with this answer, yet she questioned her mother, "But Mama, in all these years, haven't they ever found a weak spot?"

Silka reflected back upon a story her mother had told her. "Long ago, before I was born, they nearly did."

Rhia grew wide eyed, "What do you mean Mama?"

"Hundreds of years ago one of the Empress' predecessors, Kovan, allowed himself to be corrupted by one of his staff."

"What did he do?"

"Kovan's staff member, a female named Liya, had been away on planet Ondog where she had procured the seeds of a magic plant called Hallucinatio. The leader of Ondog had convinced Liya that eating this plant could increase creativity by at least five times. Liya brought the plant back and persuaded Kovan to get the Athenians to try it. Thousands of people ended up addicted to the substance only to find that their imaginations went strangely wild when using it. After they went off of it, they became very frazzled and unable to create much at all." She paused.

"And then what?" asked her wide-eyed child.

"Fortunately, Kovan realized he'd made a huge mistake and had all Hallucinatio plants destroyed, forcing our people to painfully withdraw from this deadly addiction."

"So what do the Knights have to do with all this?"

"The Hallucinatio was originally brought to the leader of Ondog by Knights. It's just another case of these demons slyly planting a seed, which was allowed to blossom into a destructive entity. Fortunately, things have been pretty smooth since then, and a serious lesson has been learned. Of course, this doesn't stop the Knights from scheming of ways to do us in."

"But if they hate us so much, why don't they just get some weapons and destroy us?"

"That's not the way they operate. They use covert tactics. Weapons would be too obvious. Besides, we have so many allies in the galaxy that if they were to attempt such an attack, the Empress would summon an army here in no time."

Silka looked reassuringly at her serious daughter, and then joked with her, "I suppose if they ever did land and attempt to threaten us, we could get the wizards of Magic Isle to turn their weapons into flowers or some such thing."

Rhia laughed at the thought. At this point Rhia heard the footsteps of her father coming up the small winding staircase that led to the meal room. She slowly savored one last petal from her bowl.

"What's so funny?" asked Andar.

"The Knights. Do you think a Knight would look funnier with a Palon flower or a Pura for a gun?"

Andar was confused. "I think I've missed something."

Rhia quickly got out of her chair and affectionately threw her arms around Andar. "Oh Father, they go around causing all kinds of trouble on other planets, but if they dare to come here, poof! Their weapons would be turned into harmless flowers."

"I hadn't thought of that before. No need to, but sounds like a great idea."

"Why don't the members of the other planets get together and just blow up Trod?" she asked, referring to the home of the Knights.

Andar smiled at his daughter's rebellious, yet good, intentions.

"I wish I could say it was that easy. However, the main problem is that these demons have a number of populations tricked into thinking that they are true authorities. Besides, even if those who have become wise to their tricks decided to blow up the Knights, they wouldn't be able to."

"Why?"

"Trod has an indestructo shield around it, made of a substance that is impenetrable by any arms that exist anywhere in the galaxy."

"But, what about the...?"

Andar, cut his young daughter off by putting a strong, gentle finger up to her lips.

"Darling I know you have many questions, and I would love to give you a complete history lesson about the Knights, but we must depart soon. It's time for the three of us to go out to The Meadow and indulge in the creative festivities there."

"Okay, Father." She kissed him on the cheek and then ran down the meal room staircase through a large circular room and up another winding staircase, this one made of a ruby-like stone and leading to her bedroom chamber. From a large closet she chose a green silk dress that her mother had made for her. She tried it on and looked in a gold-framed mirror. Two years ago this dress had touched her mid-calves. Now it was almost up to her knees. She liked the fact that it wouldn't be long before she would be adult size. This was a height of six to seven feet for Athenian females and up to eight feet for males. As Rhia gazed in the mirror at her clear complexion, long golden hair and bright turquoise eyes, she rehearsed the words she would say to the Empress after returning from her first mission, "It is an honor to have completed the task to which I was assigned, and..."

"Rhianna, who are you talking to?" asked her mother who had walked into her room unnoticed.

"Mama, I didn't know you were there. You startled me. I was, oh, just dreaming about what I'd say to the Empress after a mission."

Silka smiled, "So anxious to grow up. You are very advanced for your age and I admire that. You have much natural talent, and with the training you'll get over the years, you'll be a great missionaire."

"Thank you Mama. I am looking forward to this, though with impatience."

Rhianna hugged her mother and the two of them went down the ruby staircase to the Music Room.

Andar was picking out a couple of instruments. "Hurry, my ladies, and choose your weapons."

Rhia went to a corner of the room and grabbed the small stringed T-harp. Silka made her selection and together they went outside to load the instruments into the back compartment of their beam glider.

Andar decided that he might also want to do some sky painting, so went back into the house for a collection of magic paint wands of various colors. While Silka waited in the glider, Rhia went over to the large covered stable where Thaurus was housed. She stroked the golden mane that flowed like honey over his white neck. He perceived the affinity she had for him and returned it by stroking her face with his snout. Then he grinned at her and wagged his tail.

"See you soon Thaur. Maybe I'll take you out later."

Thaurus shook his head up and down in approval. Although he couldn't speak in words, he was extremely perceptive, as were most animals on Athena.

"Rhia," called Andar.

"Coming, Father," she said, as she turned away from her loving horse and headed out to the beam glider.

Once Rhia was in the glider, Andar closed the bubble top and the three of them were off to enjoy a day of creation with their fellow Athenians. The glider rose above their home village, which rested on a plateau atop steep surrounding cliffs. As they sailed along, Rhianna observed a few large Tulu birds that flew near them. They were about six feet long and had splashes of blue and purple coloring their long slender bodies. Down below were several winged horses, some being ridden by Athenians, and others just out on their own enjoying the freedom of gliding through the air.

As Rhia and her parents flew between a couple of grand and glittery blue mountains, a stream of pink water suddenly came spilling over the peak to the left of them. The waterfall fell gracefully, then splashed into a large pool of blue water far below where the pool changed to purple. Then the water stopped flowing, suspended in midair. There, on the mountain, was someone changing the water to a shade of green before allowing the waterfall to drop into the purple pond below.

Approaching the huge area of blue velvety grass known as The Meadow were a number of beam gliders. More winged horses of varying shades from white to pink to green, colored the skies. Some of the horse riders sang or played small instruments and blended in harmony with one another.

Several tall turquoise trees with pink leaves, surrounding a parking area, stood and welcomed the guests as they landed their vehicles.

Rhia had been to The Meadow many times before, but she was especially excited about partaking in the group festivities today.

After a smooth landing, Andar lifted the glider's bubble top and the three of them disembarked, making their way to an attraction in the center of the large meadow.

In the middle of the meadow was a huge amphitheater where several musicians were happily improvising. Instruments were being put to use with great vigor, spilling out a cascade of harmonious song. In front of the amphitheater, sky painters colored their canvas with images evoked by the music. Rhia and her parents put their instruments down near the theater and joined the several hundred Athenians who now occupied The Meadow. The effects produced could be perceived near and far. Athenians came from all over to take part in the joy of creating simply for the sake of indulging in life's greatest pleasure.

Rhia bathed in the beauty of the aesthetics while her parents made plans.

Andar noticed a man named Karn doing a colorful sky painting of a planet and a rainbow. He chose to go over and add some embellishing touches to his work.

A friend of Silka's spotted her, and enthusiastically came over and thanked her for making her the lovely orange gown she was wearing.

Nothing delighted Silka more than adorning the people of Athena with aesthetic clothing. She smiled with pride as she did a cursory glance around the meadow noticing the many artists who were wearing garments that she'd designed.

Rhianna noticed some dancers stepping in sync to the music. She was fascinated by their routine and told her mother she was going to watch them. She grabbed her little T-harp and sat on the grass and played and watched with awe. The dancers held hands and rose up into the air while twirling around in a circle. Then they let go of one another's' hands and each contributed his own improvisational steps in midair. One girl, named Lesha, did several flips then frolicked gracefully upon the rainbow that Andar and Karn had created.

Joson, a resident sculptor, saw Lesha leaping toward the end of the rainbow. He waved to her then quickly molded a little lump of clay into a castle small enough to fit into the palm of his hand. Seeing her approach, he sprinkled some magic dust upon the clay, causing it to grow until one of its drawbridges reached up and touched the end of the rainbow. Lesha set foot on the drawbridge and danced onto one of the balconies of the miniature castle. She playfully hopped off again, landing on the grass three feet below, then continued her dance. Joson sprinkled more dust on the castle until it shrank into his palm. Lesha giggled and waved at him while blowing him a friendly kiss.

"Rhianna!" a voice called out. Rhianna pulled her attention away from Lesha's show and all the other marvelous sights. She put her harp down and turned to find a familiar face. It was a young female named Vaadra, whom she had met last year at an inter-planetary festival in the North Valley. These festivals were held every year for important guests from throughout the galaxy. Visitors from planets where space travel existed came to Athena to be entertained, as well as enlightened, by the messages in the Athenian works.

The year before, both Rhianna and Vaadra had been festival hostesses and had quickly become friends. Vaadra also had a small singing part of which she was extremely proud, considering the Empress personally chose the artists who would be part of the festival.

"Vaadra! Hi!" said Rhia, hugging her friend. "What have you been doing?"

"Working on my singing for the next inter-planetary festival. The Empress liked me so much that she wants me to do more next time."

"That's a great honor. Maybe someday I can be in one of the shows. I can sing, but I can't propel notes out for miles and miles the way you do."

Vaadra smiled as she put her arm around Rhia. "I can show you. It's easy."

"Yeah?"

"Sure. It's just one of many tricks. Someday I hope to get so good at so many things that I can find my own planet and be a leader just like the Empress. I want a castle and a whole bunch of people I rule over, but that's for later. As for now, come with me and I'll show you what I know."

Rhia found Vaadra's ambition rather odd, not under-standing how she could ever want to leave Athena. However, she didn't dwell on the remark too long, but instead, let Vaadra lead her to a barren area of the field.

"This spot needs to be filled with song. Too empty."

"You're right," agreed Rhia.

The ethereal music in The Meadow provided a nice background to Vaadra's vocal demonstration. She sang without words, however the message communicated by her pure aesthetic power was clear to those who heard her.

Rhia was fascinated by this new singing technique and couldn't wait to learn it.

"So, all you have to do is decide where you want to place the notes. You can start with that tree over there for example," Vaadra said, pointing to a pink tree that was about a thousand feet away.

Rhia was a little afraid to go for such a distant target but did as her friend instructed. She focused her attention on the music of The Meadow musicians and chose notes which blended with their melody. Then she let her thoughts guide her as she placed a firm intention for the notes to reach the tree. She stretched out and let herself go, blending harmoniously with the music. She was barely using her body to sing with! It was merely a device through which to propel physical sounds. She felt more like she was outside of her body and that she was the true source of the singing. Rhianna went on and on, not wanting to stop. Then Vaadra jumped in and joined her. The two of them sang so nicely that Silka, who was now on stage with the other musicians, took notice of the singing. She recognized the voice of her daughter and took pride in her new accomplishment.

Silka got off of the stage, saw a sculptor, and whispered something to him. Then she went and asked Rhia and Vaadra to come closer to the stage. The sculptor took a small, flat piece of clay and made a small platform. He sprinkled some magic dust on it, and it grew. He put it on the grass and asked Rhia and Vaadra to step on it. They weren't quite sure why, but they complied. Then the platform magically rose up in the air, growing longer and wider beneath their feet. Soon the two girls were about twenty feet above the stage. They looked at one another and smiled as Vaadra picked a target for them to sing to. Then they sang to another target, and another, until they were propelling notes almost three miles away. Rhia forgot all about the T-harp that she had brought to The Meadow, as she was more interested in her new form of singing. As they sang farther and farther, Rhianna began to hear notes bouncing back to them. She thought they were just an altered echo of their own voices, but Vaadra paused and told her that they had touched the ears of some other distance singers on another part of Athena. Those vocalists were contributing to their singing.

As more musicians added to the continuous song, Andar embellished the sky with several colorful floating bubbles. In a whimsical mood, Karn jumped in and drew wings on them. Then Andar drew a needle that burst one of the bubbles and out of it flew a large Tulu bird.

Andar was now in the mood to juggle some music along with his act. With the help of Karn, he learned how to make his zeechord, a small keyboard, emit various colors by striking the keys in a particular way. He watched with a playful spirit as colorful harmonies blended with the Meadow Song. Pink, yellow, blue, gold, magenta, turquoise and green streaks leaped out of the keyboard and twirled around like the dancers in the sky.

As Rhia and Vaadra continued to enchant the space around them with their golden voices, a dancer, who was also playing a small tri-flute, joined them on the suspended platform. Rhia was so impressed with the music he was making that she almost stopped singing. Then Vaadra nudged her in the arm and she continued. The three of them played on and on.

When at last they took a brief break, Vaadra introduced Rhia to her fifteen-year-old brother, Ladaar. They jumped back into the spontaneous performance, which would never be done again in exactly the same way. However, on Athena nobody cared about capturing performances for future enjoyment. There was such an abundance of fresh creating to be done that seizing it and throwing it into replay mode would only be a sign to the Athenians that creations were scarce and should be saved in case new ideas ran out.

After several hours three golden birds sailed by The Meadow, covering the entire grounds. Rhia looked at Vaadra as the birds passed overhead. She was filled with a feeling of pride, knowing the Empress was acknowledging her and the others.

Although the Empress was very pleased with the work of the artists, there were some others who were not at all happy with the festivities in The Meadow.

Driven to resentment by the sights and sounds beneath them, two Knights in a space ship hovered high above The Meadow, engaged in a surveillance of their foes. Their ship had an inviso-shield around it so they couldn't be spotted.

"Look at 'em. They're living in some sort of delusional fantasy world," said Libol, the driver, as a feeling of nausea hit him in the stomach. "Hey, Slandor, give me one of those pills." Libol practically grabbed the little white bottle labeled "Nerv-Calm" from his passenger's hand.

Slandor winced. "We'll never get them to face reality. They're a bunch of stubborn airheads who think they can just sing a song and make the world a better place.

Libol's lips twitched slightly, as he tried to suppress a smile. "Why the hell is it that we can so easily get through to the people on other planets but when it comes to these Athenians - - damn!"

"I don't know, Boss-man, but sometimes I think we should just deal with those we know we can influence. Besides, how can we ever get in when they're so united? I've never seen anything like it. The whole confounded population is one big team. It'll never work. That Zeena mentor of theirs has really got them in the palm of her hand. They're so loyal to their leaders. I don't see any way we could get around her command. Why don't we give it up?"

"Never, you oaf! We have to find a way to get through! We're already losing our position of authority on other planets because of their constant meddling in intergalactic affairs. They need to know they aren't gods, just ordinary beings just like the rest of 'em."

Slandor cowed a little at Libol's words. "All right, but what do you suggest we do?"

"Somehow, some way, we must weaken their "artistic" fortress. We've got to divide them. I'll figure it out. Just give me time. At least one of us has to do some of the thinking around here," said Libol. He cringed as glittery, brightly-colored swirls exploded in the sky, then anxiously sped back to their home base on Trod.

After a full seventy-hour day of play, the people in The Meadow sailed contentedly back to their homes.

When Rhia got home, she went to her room and sat on the edge of her bed looking out of a triangular window. She saw the daylight start to fade as the beams from the star known as Gastia got dimmer and dimmer. Rhia thought about the story her mother had told her, about an Athenian who placed a mechanism on Gastia that caused the beams to automatically turn off at a designated time every day. Rhia was impressed that someone could actually control such a large amount of light and energy production for an entire planet, keeping it all consistently light or dark.

Rhianna put on one of her sleeping gowns and sprawled on top of her red silken bed cover, resting her head on a small pillow. She reminisced about her day in The Meadow and how happy she was to be using her aesthetic powers; powers that made her feel the strength of being part of the Athenian team. She had further thoughts about going on a mission someday and replayed some words once spoken by the Empress via telecomm. "So, we must also rely on our keen ability to observe situations when we are on other planets. You see, once we spot what is going on, we can use our talent to get messages across where mere spoken words may fail. We pierce the heart of the being with aesthetics."

Rhianna was glad she was aware of the use of aesthetics to remind beings of their true abilities. She knew that this type of communication went straight to the heart of the being and everyone really longed to be a free creator.

Rhia was almost too excited to get her three hours of rejuvenation (the entire length of time without sunlight) when she would close her eyes and rise above her body, letting it sleep until it was re-energized. Obeying her body's demand, she fell fast asleep. A soft glow of light radiated from her young body. This was an indication that she was sleeping.

Chapter 2

Over the years, Rhianna spent many days expanding her artistic horizons beyond her main love, which was music. Although born with innate artistic potential, as all beings are, she became restless with her limited skills. Willing teachers helped her to learn to create new art forms such as sky dancing, painting, and sculpting.

As her talents blossomed and grew, she knew it was now her turn to help plant more creative seeds upon the lands of Athena. She ambitiously educated many young Athenians in the art forms that she had learned to produce. Rhianna indulged in a feeling of fulfillment, knowing that she was taking responsibility for others, which was just as important as her loyalty to her own goals.

Rhianna traveled, along with her ambition, to various regions of Athena giving lessons to thousands of eager people. She created such an impact that the Empress took notice of the rapid growth of creativity that was flourishing all over.

One day, the Empress called Rhianna to her palace. Rhianna sat in reverence, as she looked into the noble, warm eyes of the Empress, who was seated across from her in a golden chair. After acknowledging Rhia for her good work, Zeena continued on. "My dear Rhianna, there is another reason I have called you here. The time for planning of the Inter-Planetary Arts Festival is nearly upon us. The theme for the event this year will be "Making the Milky Way safe for Future Generations." I would like you to be in charge of designing the festival, utilizing the talent of the many young Athenians you have been instructing." She paused, noting Rhia's reaction.

Although Rhia was very honored, she got a knot of anxiety in her stomach, and tensed up inside. She didn't know if she was ready for such an assignment. Zeena perceived her reaction, and squeezed her shoulder with a comforting hand.

"I...I'm very honored that you have asked me to perform such an important task my Empress."

"Don't worry darling, you will have help. I normally choose those who have more experience with group productions, but I know that you can do it, that is, if you decide to take this offer."

"Of course, I'll do it!" she said, forgetting about her fears and jumping to the call of this new challenge.

As Rhia thought of seizing this opportunity, and not letting go, Jirmak, the Empress' assistant, walked into the room. She was carrying a platter, which held a pitcher with blue liquid and two empty goblets. Jirmak set the pitcher and glasses on a small table near Zeena.

"Thank you, Jirmak. Would you like some Seeva juice, Rhianna?" The Empress asked, referring to the blue plant liquid.

"Yes, please."

Jirmak picked up the pitcher very carefully, being over-cautious as she poured the juice into the glass. As Jirmak handed the goblet to Rhia, they made eye contact for a second. Then Jirmak's eyes quickly fleeted away from Rhia's gaze, as if pulled by a command to look elsewhere.

Jirmak then gave the Empress some juice. She picked up the platter, and just as she was about to leave the room, dropped it on the floor.

"I'm sorry for the disturbance," Jirmak apologized, while quickly picking it up. She exited, and closed the door to the room, giving the appearance that she'd left altogether. Unbeknownst to Zeena and Rhia, she was eavesdropping through a crack in the door.

Zeena could tell by Rhia's puzzled look, that she was wondering about the change in Jirmak.

"It was her trip to Sadan, Rhianna. She had a very rough time when I sent her there to help out. She was sleeping one night, when a couple of Knights knocked her out and drugged her. She was quite ill for some time. Fortunately, she is recovering from this incident, but still manifests some odd behavior. She'll be all right in due time."

Rhia left the palace of the Empress, with her sense of responsibility heightened several feet above and beyond where it had previously been.

After designing an outline for the event, her next step was to meet with her creative assistants at the Arena de Itrinia, where the festival would be held. The huge coliseum was named after the solar system where Athena was located.

Rhia thought about the artists who would be working with her. She looked forward to seeing Vaadra's brother, Ladaar, who was going to help with music for the event. He lived in the North Valley where the arena was.

Rhia chose to go to North Valley by horseback. She walked into Thaur's stable and stroked his snout. He slowly outstretched his grand white wings and then rested them back at his sides. "Yes Thaur. We're going for a nice ride," she said as he followed her out of his home. As they walked along, Thaurus suddenly stopped. He looked at a wooded area in the distance.

"Come on Thaur, let's go." She saw that he was gazing at a place known as "Taboo Forest," named because of the dangerous sand traps that were sprinkled throughout this area. It was the only place on the planet where Athenians feared to go. This was because of the spots that looked like they were covered with ordinary grass, but, in fact, had a thick, wet sandy substance beneath them, which magnetically pulled one in if they were stepped upon. There were certain animals that lived there because they fed off of a special kind of plant known as grana, which existed only in this forest.

Rhia remembered a recent time when Thaur had gone into the forest to see some of the animals that resided there. It was much easier for him to get around in the woods than it was for the people of Athena, because he had a better sense of where the traps were.

Thaurus made a snorting noise and then walked toward Rhia.

"You know that's not the best place for you to go. I know you like the animals in there, but I don't want you getting so playful with them that you accidentally stumble upon a trap."

He nodded with some reluctant agreement, and then she led him to the edge of a steep hill.

"Let's go, Boy," Rhia said affectionately, as Thaur took off over the precipice.

As they flew along, Rhia breathed deeply, delighting in the scent of ming flowers which sweetened the air. Thaurus was inspired by music he heard below and lifted his front legs and did a little dance, causing Rhia to slide down on his back a bit. "You silly horse, you're a real air dancer aren't you?" she joked. He replied by shaking his head up and down.

Soon they came to a mountain range known as the "Landis" that sparkled with gold and silver particles, and Rhia knew they were heading into the North Valley. She looked down and saw a red, grassy lowland that was sprinkled with black marble buildings with silver rooftops. Each was unique in structure. Splotches of bright white sand stood out like bald spots on the grassy area.

"There it is, Thaur," Rhia said with excitement, pointing to a golden, circular structure, which stood in its grandeur on the ground beneath them. They descended toward their destiny. When they arrived, Ladaar, the only other person there, greeted them. Rhia exchanged a hug with her friend's brother, whom she hadn't seen for ages. As a wave of affinity flowed back and forth between them, she was reminded of a time, many years ago, when she performed with him at The Meadow. Looking into his bright, emerald eyes, she noticed how he'd matured into an extremely attractive male.

"I'm so glad the Empress chose you as my musical assistant."

"Me too."

"It's too bad that Vaadra couldn't be here."

"Unfortunately, I don't even think she'll be back in time for the festival. Her mission on Sadan isn't going too well."

A wrinkle of worry crept upon Rhia's forehead. "I hope she's okay."

"She'll be fine. Vaadra's very strong," Ladaar said, as Rhia thought about Jirmak but said nothing.

"I know there have been others who have abandoned their duties on missions or even deserted Athena for good, but this hasn't happened too often," Ladaar said, as Rhia suddenly felt an intense concern for her friend.

"I don't..." Rhia stopped short in her sentence, as a couple of short men with curly, red hair and webbed feet walked towards her and Ladaar. Their names were Zak and Gar, a couple of the assistants. Although residing on Athena, they were quite different in appearance to the natives on the planet. These two were originally from the planet Chidon, now nearly a barren wasteland after Knights incited Chidon's leaders to get their army to exterminate most of the people there. The Empress took in a number of the survivors of Chidon, and they had become valuable assets on Athena.

Rhia and Ladaar watched as Zak and Gar did several jovial flips in the air, then landed next to them.

Gar bowed and took Rhia's hand and kissed it, "How do you do, my lady."

Rhia smiled warmly, "Hello Gar."

After they all exchanged greetings, the rest of the festival crew started showing up, including a couple hundred children. They all went to the enormous stage in the center of the arena, and engaged in their creative planning. They took Rhia's design and helped fill in the pieces.

Rhia wrote a script for a musical number called "The Enemy Within," and she and Ladaar whipped out some music for it while Zak did the choreography.

"Okay kids, so round and round you go. Step left, then right. Then, whee, up in the air. Ha ha, that's it," Zak said, as he delighted in seeing the kids follow along.

After this number, they rehearsed the other acts. Rhia had quite a sense of fulfillment, seeing the outline of her production being brought to life so nicely.

When the group was through with their meeting, they all parted ways, except for Rhia and Ladaar, who went back to Ladaar's home. It had been a long time since Rhia had been to the castle-like home where Vaadra and Laadar resided with their great grandfather, Bern. Ladaar's parents, grandparents, and great grandmother were all killed while on a mission long ago when caught in the midst of a devastating nuclear war. Rhia led Thaur to a large courtyard that separated Ladaar's home from another. She told him to wait for her there. He gave her a sad look but complied. Rhia and Ladaar talked for several hours and then worked on some music pieces that they would perform at the festival. As they filled the castle with song, Rhia forced herself to pull back from the magnetic attraction she was feeling for him. She still wasn't quite used to seeing the grown man who had played tri-flute in the meadow as a teenage boy.

As notes spilled into the air, so did several fleeting thoughts and feelings, which danced between them. When the music ended, their silent song of mutual affinity was only beginning.

Rhia's bashfulness caused her to turn away from Ladaar and go look out of a huge arched window. She gazed at the enormous mountain range in front of her.

Ladaar walked over and joined her, "Have you ever been up in the Landis before?"

"No, but I've heard there are some wonderful sights from up there."

"Some of the best," he paused. "Would you like to see what I'm talking about?"

Her heart sped up with anticipation, "I'd love to."
They decided to put Thaurus to work and use him as their transportation.

"You don't think your horse will mind an extra passenger do you?"

"No, he's strong enough to carry three people."
When Ladaar and Rhia went out to the courtyard to get Thaurus, much to their surprise, he was gone!

"Thaurus, where are you?" called Rhia as she looked around for him, not seeing anywhere he could have gone unless he flew away. But she knew this wasn't possible because he needed a bigger runway.

"He never goes far from where I leave him," she said as she noticed a picture on a canvas in front of her. It was a portrait of Thaurus.

"Must have been done by Klar, the painter that lives next door. She loves painting animals."

"Well she couldn't have done a better job. It looks exactly like him."

Just as they were gazing at the picture trying to figure out where the real Thaurus was, one of the wings on the canvas popped out. It looked like a miniature version of a real live wing. Then a leg poked out, and a snout. Then the rest of the head protruded along with another leg, until soon the whole body leaped out of the canvas. There in front of them was a real live midget Thaurus! Not a single hole was made in the canvas, and the picture of Thaur remained intact, just as they had first seen it.

"Okay Rhia, what were you saying about three people riding on his back?" asked Ladaar, as they both laughed.

Then the small horse started growing in size. He got bigger and bigger until he became life-sized.

"That's what I get for having a pet that comes from Magic Isle. He learned some funny tricks that fool me every time."

"Come on, you nut, we're going for a ride, so no more pranks," Rhia said to her mischievous pet. In front of the castle, they boarded Thaurus and took off. Rhia noticed a small model of a building that was growing larger and larger before her eyes. It was being produced by one of the planet architects by using a method similar to that used by the clay sculptors. "Ladaar, is that your grandfather who is making that building?"

"No, he's on Placid Isle, creating buildings at a resort village."

"Isn't that the place where guests from other planets stay when they're here?"

"Yes, primarily."

"Ooh, look at that one. It's huge," remarked Rhia, as a tall pink building with a dome shaped roof thrust up towards them."

"Yeah, those are fun to do. One of the things I like to create. They're pretty simple. Just paint all the trimmings and then sprinkle on some magic dust, and poof, watch it grow."

Thaurus ascended as Rhia and Ladaar continued their conversation. He soared closer and closer to the glorious mountains that twinkled brightly from the Athenian gold that was imbedded in them.

Ladaar led Thaur to some of his favorite scenic spots. They approached a section where shimmery purple water spilled over a steep cliff and landed in a sparkling silver pond.

As they flew higher, they saw several large yellow trees on a slope. Above the trees, emanating from a suspended pool of water, were large pink droplets of water that from time to time would fall upon the trees and nourish them. The sound of music could be heard, but Rhia didn't see its emanation point. Then Ladaar pointed to a couple of blue puffy clouds above, where sky dancers emerged as they danced and sang.

Ladaar led Thaurus to a plateau near the middle of the mountains, which was one of his favorite spots. "How about if we land here for a few minutes, and look at the view?"

"All right, " Rhia agreed, and instructed her horse to land. Thaurus rested near some large orange rocks while Ladaar led Rhia to one of the most breathtaking views she'd ever seen. To their right was the largest body of water on Athena, known as the Amagon Sea. The pure turquoise water was so clear that an array of colorful fish could be seen swimming around beneath the surface. From time to time, some of the fish would leap out of the water and twirl around, much like sky dancers, and then go back into the ocean.

In the distance was a small island suspended several feet above the water that glowed with pink and blue fluorescent colors. Images of various plants and animals popped into the sky and disappeared again. Rhia giggled as she noticed several trees on the island uprooting themselves, while flapping their branches around. "Magic Isle! What a great view from up here," Rhia said, as a holographic image of a wizard appeared in the sky. He waved a golden wand, and a shower of purple stars leaped out and changed into a multitude of different shapes. Then he rotated round in circles until his body was spinning so fast that it was a whirlpool of motion. Finally, after a couple of minutes, poof! He disappeared.

Below them, on another side, were many multi-colored waterfalls that formed half-circles around tall cliffs, all spilling into a pond that had several rainbows emanating from it. Rhia could see many large villages, which now appeared very tiny, down below them in the North Valley. Various artists looked like little dolls as they charmed the valley with their abundant creations. Even the Arena de Itrinia appeared to be a miniature theater from where they were.

Rhia looked out in front of her and spotted a familiar sight on a distant mountain range. She pointed at it as she touched Ladaar's right shoulder, "That looks like Etherea Palace," referring to where the Empress lived.

"That's precisely what it is," Ladaar acknowledged as they both stood with their attention riveted on one of the largest buildings on Athena, which housed Zeena and her staff.

Rhia took a deep breath, and bathed in a feeling of serenity, which emanated outward from her and stretched for miles and miles. "I can't imagine living anywhere else in the galaxy."

"I can't, either," replied Ladaar.

"I want to come back here lifetime after lifetime. I just couldn't think of ever breaking the bond I have with this incredible team, and..." Rhia's elation waned slightly, as her thoughts drifted.

"You know Ladaar, sometimes it saddens me to hear of the needless suffering that goes on around us on other planets. Look at all those who are less fortunate. I guess that sometimes it's hard for me to be totally happy when I think of some of our neighbors. After all, we're all part of the same galactic group, and it's hard to feel completely fulfilled when I know we are all connected to one another as spiritual beings. I just can't wait to go on mission and help out."

"Me, too, Rhia. It's great that the Empress has gained the trust of many of our neighbors by showing them we can assist during difficult times."

Just as they were deep into contemplation, Thaurus made a noise that drew Rhia's attention to him, "Thaurus is saying something, but I can't tell what it is from here. Do you mind if we go and see?"

"Not at all."

They turned around and walked back to the orange rock where Thaurus was now standing up swishing his tail.

"Thaurus, what is it?"

Thaurus turned his head and looked behind one of the rocks he'd been resting near. Rhia and Ladaar went to the spot he was pointing out. They saw what appeared to be a couple of small, brown balls of fur huddled up against one of the rocks. One of the fur balls moved and looked up at them with a pair of the brightest green eyes that Rhia had ever seen.

"It's a Bura," replied Ladaar, before Rhia could question him as to what they were. As he said this, the other Bura lifted his head, and both stood looking at Ladaar and Rhia, wondering for a moment whether any harm was going to be done to them. Then Ladaar bent down and put one open hand out in front of the fluffy brown creatures with the rounded ears and thin tails. One of the Buras made a soft chirp-like sound and timidly placed a paw on Ladaar's hand. Ladaar picked up the animal, which sensed Ladaar's good intentions and nuzzled lovingly against his hand. Rhia duplicated Ladaar's motions, and placed her hand down in front of the other Bura and picked him up.

Rhia and Ladaar sat down on a patch of grass holding the animals, and Thaurus resumed his sedentary position in front of one of the orange rocks. After gaining the trust of the creatures and stroking them for a moment, Ladaar and Rhia let them go.

"I've never seen any animals on this planet that are so afraid. This is unusual, Ladaar."

"That's because they're not from Athena."

"What?"

"They come from Thora, but few of them live there anymore. Many years ago, the Knights went to Thora and captured thousands of these animals and used them in experimentation projects. They would do things like inject certain chemicals into the Buras' bloodstream, and see how they reacted. Sometimes they'd even give electric shocks to their brains, to see if they became less active after the voltage was applied to them," Ladaar paused.

"But what for?"

"They thought that if they could manipulate the little animals physiologically, then the same could be done to people. The Knights believe that all beings are merely controlled by their brains and that there are no souls that occupy their bodies. So, of course they think that if you can control a body, then you are controlling a being."

Rhia's feeling of serenity turned to anger. "I don't understand how any soul could become so blackened as that of the Knights. Goodness is native, not evil!"

"You're right Rhianna, and deep in their hearts they know it but try to hide under a guise of pretending to help others. Unfortunately, many civilizations still fall for their schemes."

As they talked, another little Bura scampered over to where they were and looked up at them. Suddenly, bright light beams radiated from his glowing eyes and Rhia covered her own eyes with her arms for a moment to fend off the glare. The animal quickly turned off the bright beams as he saw that Rhia was uncomfortable. Then he scurried away.

"Those little creatures can be very helpful at night. Once you befriend them, if you're out in a dark area and can't see what is around, they will guide you," Ladaar explained.

"It's too bad that such sweet animals got so abused. How did they happen to make it here to the Landis?"

"The leaders on Thora found many of these animals trapped in cages, where Knights had left them and gave them to some Athenians who were there on a mission. After the Athenians returned home, they deposited the Buras in the Landis. I hear that some of them live in one of the deep forests of Alta, too. Thorians didn't want to take any more chances on having Knights come back to torture these animals," Ladaar explained.

Rhia barely heard the last few words he was saying, as she was wrapped up in the strong admiration she had for him that was getting harder to suppress. "I'm sorry Ladaar, what was the last thing you said after 'taking chances on having Knights come back?'" Rhia asked.

Ladaar almost forgot what he had said as he bathed in mutual affection for her. Both of them acted like the shy little Buras, hesitating to offer a timid paw to a loving hand.

"Oh, taking chances on Knights coming back and torturing the Buras," he said as he gazed into Rhia's turquoise eyes and noticed an extra sparkle in them that wasn't there before. Both perceived the intense feelings that were rapidly growing. Then Ladaar broke the silence by gently picking up one of Rhia's delicate hands and encircled it with his large fingers. He looked at the warm smile that lit up her pretty face, as they both spontaneously drew closer to each other until their lips met in a long-awaited, tender kiss. A sensation as sweet as ming flowers filled the space around them. Their lips parted, and Rhia put her hand up to Ladaar's' cheek and stroked it gently.

"Oh Ladaar, I know it's been a short time since we've been together, but I feel I know you well. You are such a pleasure to create with."

"My feelings exactly," he said as he ran his fingers through her long silken hair. "I didn't realize how much was missing before today. There is so much fulfillment that comes with being an artist on Athena that I almost forgot the extra power that comes with having a partner."

"I know, dear Ladaar, I know," she said, with tears of joy as Ladaar put his arms around her. They both fell into the soft grass beneath them. As he lay on top of her, they shared a passionate kiss while more strong sensations filled the air. Thaurus turned and looked at them out of the corner of his eye, and smiled to himself, then turned his attention to a couple of Buras that ran by.

After several romantic moments, they both sat up and leaned back against a couple of large rocks. Ladaar put his arm around Rhia's shoulder, as they silently bathed in admiration for one another. Then he hugged her as heartfelt words spilled from his lips, "I love you Rhianna, and I want to be with you for the rest of my life."

"I love you, too, Ladaar. I want the same, and I also want to find you again in lifetimes to come and share with you again."

After agreeing that they would be partners, they decided to have a marriage celebration after the Inter-planetary festival.

Chapter 3

Visitors from planets throughout the galaxy gathered at the Arena de Itrinia, creating a unique sight. One could look out and observe anything, from blue-haired Borians wearing refrigeration suits, to purple complexioned Varians with clawed hands and feet.

Rhianna and her team of artists, which consisted of a handful of adults and about two hundred children, bedazzled the audience with their performances.

Their first act, "The Enemy Within," enlightened the guests as to some of the covert tactics used by the Knights. As Rhia and Ladaar filled the arena with song, several children danced and sang playfully.

"Ooh, they're good. Good job," Gar whispered as he elbowed Zak who sat next to him in the audience.

The children made several motions in the sky, and colored it with beautiful images of various sorts. While the young Athenians indulged in creating, a man in a black pantsuit, pretending to be a Knight, slithered out from backstage. He joined in the singing but was slightly discordant. Then the Knight persuaded the children to come down and line up behind him. As he did this, the music got more discordant, and the spirit of play of the children lapsed into a mood of seriousness. Just as the Knight led the children around, controlling their moves, a couple of adult Athenians came out from backstage and started dancing around, encouraging some of the children to start creating again. A couple of the children timidly stepped out of line and shyly started dancing. Then more and more of them followed suit much to the Knight's dismay. Pretty soon they were all singing and dancing once again, and the Knight crouched away into a corner. As the music brought the children back into a playful spirit, many of the planetary leaders in the audience were coaxed into more hopeful spirits.

Lunok, a Varian, was one of them. When he first showed up, he had been wearing a dull complexion, but his bright purple skin was now glowing. He had been gravely concerned about many problems in his homeland. Now he was thinking of solutions.

Several other performances performed. At the end of the festival, the Empress addressed the audience.

"My dear friends, I am so pleased that you have come here for this special occasion. The primary purpose of these events is to encourage you to protect and advance your civilizations in spite of any opposition. Although our physical appearances vary markedly from one another, we are all part of the same galactic family.

"Here on Athena we have built a strong foundation. Our secret is simple yet powerful. We are united, and there isn't dissent amongst us. This is because everyone is encouraged to express the uniqueness of his own world of creation with others on the planet. There is room for one and all.

"It is very crucial at this time that we build more strength in the Milky Way. Some of you have fallen prey to the impure motives of the Knights. Although they can appear to come to you pretending to lend a helping hand, beware of the knife they carry behind their backs with their other hand. Unfortunately, they are not letting up on their devious quest and are often so surreptitious that they aren't spotted, even when they should look very obvious.

"The key thing you need to do is create harmony amongst yourselves. I do understand that friction can build up between your people at times, but you must set a good example and remind them they all are important players in your planetary games. Encourage your children at a young age to work toward positive goals that aid the advancement of your cultures. Build a strong base. Remember that the enemy is not within, but outside of your homelands. Although they put on an authoritative appearance of wisdom and strength, they are really afraid. Their only solution is to harm everyone else and keep people down so that others are less of a threat.

"I will be holding a United Council for Creative Freedom in the near future so that leaders of the various planets can meet to discuss and implement plans that will help our galaxy. You will be telecommed as to the first meeting and its location.

"The future is in our hands. I thank you for coming to our annual Inter-Planetary Arts Festival. I will end by performing the Athenian Anthem for you."

After the Empress finished her speech, several winged horses encircled the amphitheater. On their backs were musicians carrying various instruments. As the horses flew around the theater, they harmonized in celestial song. The Empress lifted her graceful limbs as the sleeves of her elegant gown draped down toward the ground. She started singing ethereally, while propelling breathtaking music for miles around her.

"Communication of the highest form that comes from the heart. That which is closest to a spiritual being, is the creation of art. Communication with a quality that produces a grand effect, Commanding notice and triggering ideas that spark great intellect. We are all responsible for the world that we build with one another There's no separation from our spiritual brothers..."

The golden voice of the Empress faded out and the musicians on horseback flew away from the arena. Several tall, luminous flowers surrounding the theater put on a dazzling light show. Each had their cue to color the sky at various intervals, adding to the spectacular grand finale. The audience roared with enthusiasm one last time, and then the Empress exited the stage.

A week after the Inter-Galactic festival, Rhia and Ladaar exchanged vows of commitment to be together and permanently work to forward the purpose of the Athenian civilization. The wedding was held in the foothills of the Landis Mountains and was attended by a small group of family and friends. Unfortunately, Vaadra was still on her mission and was not able to attend.

After the wedding, they flew to Placid Isle where Bern had designed a special building just for the two of them to spend their first night together. When they arrived, they met with Bern, who was busy decorating a model of a building.

Like a child with a toy, Bern playfully put the finishing touches on one of the rooms, "Yes, that's it. I got it. What you need is a nice little pool right in the middle. Hmm, and some dancing fish. Oh, lovely," he said aloud, amusing himself. He was so wrapped up in his world, that he didn't even notice Ladaar and Rhia standing near him smiling.

"I don't know, Grandfather, are you sure you don't want some dancing trees?"

Bern jumped, "Oh, kids, I didn't know you were there. Your old grandpa is getting a little imperceptive in his old age."

They exchanged hugs and then he told them where their wedding gift was. They went to inspect their gift, which was made of blue crystal with silver trim around the edges of the round roof. As they walked inside a large oval doorway, they were greeted by flowers and trees and animals carved into the walls.

Ladaar took Rhia's hand and led her up a spiral staircase that led to the bedroom.

Rhia looked around and noticed that the walls were made out of a rose-colored rock that was sprinkled with diamond glitter, "Bern's architecture is very lovely."

"Yes, my darling, he is quite good at what he does."

Rhia smiled as she looked at a picture that was painted on one of the bedroom walls. It was an image of the exact spot in the Landis Mountains where they had gotten married. There were lifelike drawings of Rhia, Ladaar, and the guests who attended the ceremony. A small waterfall spilled over one of the mountain cliffs, and next to a rock by the waterfall was a small Bura, poking his head out from behind the boulder. Rhia got closer to it and as she looked at the bottom right-hand corner. She noticed some familiar writing. It said, "Much love, Silka."

"Oh Ladaar, what a nice surprise from my mother."

"Yes it is," he said as he stood and looked at it while putting his arm around her shoulder.

While admiring the work of Silka, their attention was suddenly drawn to the sound of angelic music coming from outside of a large window. Ladaar took Rhia's hand and led her to a balcony that overlooked a colorful garden. Just as Rhia pointed to a couple of musicians below them, their attention was drawn to a picture being painted in the sky. It was an image of Ladaar and Rhia joining hands. One of the musicians then decorated the scenery with lyrics that were dedicated to them.

"A magic feeling was in the air one night.
Two people met and it was so right.
Talking, smiling and sharing what's inside.
At ease with each other, there's no need to hide.
A true love is a lifetime friend.
Growing stronger with no end.
Their journey is about to begin.
They'll work as a team and play to win...."

As the song was ending, words were written across the top of the images in the sky that said "Everlasting Spiritual Mates." Then there was a final embellishment to the performance. A couple of small bright blue birds flew to the balcony where Ladaar and Rhia were. They stood on part of the railing and sang. The birds, sent by the Empress in acknowledgment of their union, flew away after the music ended.

Ladaar and Rhia applauded. Then they walked back inside and sat on a large round bed in the middle of the room as passionate feelings flowed back and forth between them.

"Oh Ladaar, that was so nice. Do you know who it was from?"

"It was my father. He had it all planned for our arrival."

"It was so beautiful. We must thank him," Rhia said, looking into Ladaar's sparkling green eyes. Their feelings of passion intensified, and neither one could stand to hold back on the desire to get physically closer to each other.

Ladaar put his right hand up to Rhia's left cheek and stroked it, "How about if we thank my father tomorrow? I'm sure he won't mind. Right now, all I can think about is making love to you."

Rhia responded by throwing her arms around his broad shoulders and pulling him closer to her. After a night of romance, Ladaar and Rhia planned to spend the next day exploring the beauty of Placid Isle before going back to North Valley. Just as they were about to leave their wedding suite, a light on a telecomm that was in their room started flashing and beeping. Ladaar walked over to it and pushed a button that brought to view an image of a person on the screen. The male on the screen identified himself. "I am Ondor, mission assistant on the staff of Empress Zeena. I wish to make contact with Rhianna. I hear that she is there."

Rhia, who was looking out of a window, turned around as she heard her name mentioned. She saw the face of an unfamiliar man on the telecomm visio-monitor. "Yes, I am Rhianna."

"Rhianna, I am telecomming on behalf of the Empress. She needs you to report to Etherea palace. The mission that you were scheduled for has been moved up. She is sorry that your post-wedding respite may be interrupted prematurely, but there is an urgency for this mission to commence sooner than planned."

Rhia felt both a surge of excitement and disappointment all in the same breath. She turned and gave Ladaar a fleeting look. She could see he was trying not to let any feelings of objection come over him.

"How soon do I need to arrive?"

"Immediately Rhianna. From your location it will take you about one hour to get to Etherea. The Empress would like you here no later than one and a half hours."

Ladaar and Rhia hurried to thank Bern for their own private building, as well as for the special performance.

Rhia complied with the sudden request by the Empress, and had Ladaar fly her to the palace without delay.

Rhia's attention lingered on Ladaar for a few minutes as she walked away from the beam glider, and waved at him as he flew away.

At the front door of Etherea, a palace staff member greeted Rhia and led her to a mission briefing room. She entered a large white room with two rows of golden chairs and sat silently, along with a handful of others, until the Empress graced the room with her presence. Everyone stood up, as their leader took her place in front of the first row of chairs.

Zeena smiled at the small respectful group, "Please be seated," she said. They instantly complied.

The smile on Zeena's face turned into a look of concern. "My fellow Athenians, I have summoned you here today to inform you of a critical situation occurring on our neighboring planet,

Nera. After their lack of attendance at the Inter-Planetary festival for several years, I grew concerned about them. I telecommed one of their government officials, Zonat, and got an update on what was happening. Apparently, their new ruler, Bordak, has been having trouble with various members of his population who are in charge of transportation production. Many of the vehicle workers wanted to go into other areas of occupation. They refused to continue on with their duties, and as a result there has been a shortage of transport production and repair. Bordak and his staff then became troubled with an overburden of responsibility due to these non-compliant citizens. Worried and overwhelmed, Bordak took the advice of some over-ambitious Knights who seized this opportunity to instruct him and his staff on what to do to get compliance. The workers were put under the influence of some sort of mind manipulation to force them to produce.

"Although they are now working again and are no longer rebellious, they have become quite apathetic.

"Concerned that laborers in other areas might also become recalcitrant, Bordak has ordered more and more citizens to receive this manipulation therapy. I could not get all the details from Zonat. He was already stepping out on a dangerous limb just to give me this information. Bordak has become so swayed by these pseudo-authorities that anyone who dares to contest this scheme is considered a traitor. As we were talking, he had to quickly sever our connection. We did, however, rapidly make arrangements for a team of Athenians to go and meet him and some of the other disillusioned citizens to try and help get through to Bordak. You must get Bordak to see that he has been conned, and that unless he acts fast, he may witness the demise of his people altogether. Then you must use your artistic skills to help revitalize the life force and individual drive of their people. You see, at one time, Bordak had very high respect for us. But this was before evil influences threw him into a state of confusion."

Rhianna was both excited and apprehensive about such a challenge. She felt a little better, when she found out that the leader of their team, a male named Shero, had successfully completed several assignments, even tougher than this one, in the past.

The Empress went on to inform the group that they needed to stay until the Nerians started taking back the command of their lives and their planet.

The Athenians spent the rest of the day doing needed mission training that would assist them in their future tasks. They were further educated in the ways of the Nerians, and were informed of tactics that would aid them. Language assimilation boxes were used to quickly learn the dialect of the Nerians.

Although Rhia was excited about this new adventure, an unusual fear surfaced inside of her. She didn't know why. It was as if there was something she didn't want to face.

Chapter 4

The missionaires arrived on Nera and disembarked from their vehicle. They walked along a small landing strip in the direction of a spaceport terminal where Zonat waited for them.

Rhia looked to her right and took notice of a spaceship hanger where several workers were assembling various parts of a local transport vehicle. She caught a glimpse of one of the laborers, whose face was void of live expression, and had the appearance of an android that had been programmed to do the job. Then she noticed that many of the other mechanics looked the same way. It was a shock to her, being off of Athena for the first time, to observe beings that looked so unhappy.

A cold breeze, matching the feeling on Nera, whipped through the air as the Athenians arrived at the terminal. Zonat picked them up and shuttled them to a boxy looking gray building. The Athenians unpacked their gear, clothing that was suitable to the planet Nera, as well as a generous food supply of Athenian plants that would last them for several months. They got a short period of rejuvenation.

The next day, Zonat picked them up in a vanship, a long bus-like space vehicle. They headed for a meeting spot at the home of one of Zonat's associates, where a few other officials would also be.

Zonat was a tall, skinny, bald man of about sixty years in age. His complexion was pale green and he had long, bony fingers with yellow nails. It was hard for him to hide the anxiety that he felt, as his right hand compulsively shook while he clutched a steering device. He tried to cover up exactly how worried he was by turning to Shero for a few seconds and giving him a social smile. Shero smiled back, but could see through his veneer.

Zonat and the Athenians soon arrived at the home of Walusk, another disillusioned government worker, who was willing to do whatever it took to help the people of his homeland. Zonat introduced the missionaires to Walusk.

Walusk led them to a long, brown, oval table where the Athenians seated themselves. The missionaires waited patiently for other Nerians to arrive. Tama, a female missionaire who could hardly stand all the suspended seriousness in the air, made a comment to Walusk to break the silence. "That's a lovely painting you have on the wall over there. The pink flowers remind me of a type that we have on Athena."

Walusk's somber thoughts turned to the picture, and as he noticed its beauty for the first time in ages, he brightened up. "Thank you, Tama. It was a gift from a relative of mine."

Five minutes that seemed like hours went by before the other officials arrived. There were now ten people seated at the long oval table.

Zonat cleared his scratchy throat and opened the meeting, "First of all, I would like to thank Commissioner Walusk for allowing us to use his home for this conference." Walusk nodded in acknowledgment.

Zonat continued, "We are fortunate to have attained the devout assistance of the Athenians, who, as you know, happen to be from one of the most powerful planets in the galaxy. Empress Zeena has always been of service not only to us, but also to other populations, during dire times. It is now up to us to learn from them and take their lead in developing a way to rehabilitate our forlorn people." He turned to look at Shero. "We are open to your suggestions, and I would like to hear what you and the others have to say."

Shero went on to communicate that the first thing they needed was more knowledge as to exactly how the people were being successfully manipulated against their own will. He didn't understand how they suddenly turned from disgruntled workers into lifeless zombies.

Zonat reluctantly decided to show the Athenians, firsthand the method of torture being implemented on his people. They agreed to meet again after the missionaires had finished with their observation.

The next day, Zonat shuttled the five Athenians to the confines of one of several dismal buildings where the mind molding was being done. Zonat led the group to a secret entrance in the back of the building. Stepping into a small room, the six of them stood and looked through a one sided glass mirror and gazed into a large experimentation room.

The room was not as grim as Rhia had imagined it would be. She was surprised to see that it looked like some sort of theater, with several chairs facing a large white screen. It was empty when they arrived.

"They will be coming in at any moment," Zonat warned.

After a few minutes, the vertical door handle that led to the room came to life, as it moved to the right. In walked a procession of twenty people of all ages followed by Libol, a tall, gray complexioned Knight wearing a black jumpsuit. The people were instructed to take a seat. Libol slipped his hand into one of his pockets, and pulled out a handful of pills, known to the workers as Probot. Aloof from feeling for his victims, Libol started to go through the routine of handing each Nerian a pill.

Once a week, this group arrived for their ritual. After all of the Nerians had taken their drugs, Libol turned off the lights in the room and turned on a projector switch. Threatening images came to life upon the screen. There were various scenes of workers being tortured and electro-whipped into obedience, after having been defiant on the job. When the picture watching was over, the workers in Libol's theater were implanted with verbal suggestions. They chanted after him in sloppy unison, "I will work, or suffer pain. I will work or suffer pain. I will work or suffer pain."

The only break in his pattern was when a twelve- year-old in the last row started to scream in terror. Libol tried to ignore the plea of the child, but gave in to one of the few mildly warm spots in his cold heart. He left the other robots to continue their chant as he led the child out of the room into a small waiting area behind a partition. Libol then went back and conducted his choir.

"You, come on. You're whispering. Louder, louder!" he yelled as he approached an older man in the back row. The man was hunched over with feelings of nausea. His arms were folded across his stomach as he rocked back and forth. Then, before Libol could flinch, the man vomited on the floor, splattering Libol's boots.

Tempering cruel thoughts of having the man bend down and lick his feet, Libol simply walked away and wiped his shoes with a cloth. He unsympathetically left the older man in his misery. "I've seen enough, let's go," Shero whispered to Zonat.

The next day, they met again at Walusk's home. Shero communicated that the first thing they needed was a plan. He said that Bordak must quickly be made aware of the fact that his people were in very bad shape, and that the individuality of the beings on Nera was being usurped for the sake of creating a slave state. They were going to have to find a way to get through to him.

Then Rhia brought up a very important point to the whole scheme. She said they'd have to get through to as many Nerians as they could, and convince them of how bad the oppression was that they were being subjected to. Then they would need to be organized as a strong team, in order to rebel against the injustice.

The Athenians wrote several songs that addressed the situation on Nera. The songs were secretly played on an underground radio station, which could only be accessed by a secret code. Several Nerians tuned in to the impactful broadcast, and heeded the words of warning that hit their ears.

For the next several weeks, with the help of Zonat and the other officials, the missionaires secretly met with several of the people of Nera and surveyed them as to what their viewpoints were concerning their occupations and lives on Nera. Much unhappiness was found. The ones who were not yet subjected to Probot said they knew others who were on this drug who wanted to get off of it but couldn't because it was so addictive. Rhia talked to some Nerians on Probot. She worked hard to get them to rise above their drug laden fog and tap into the true goals they had once had, before they were suppressed.

While Rhia and the other missionaires were busy organizing a team of Nerians who would demand the end of the unfair obedience therapy, Shero and Zonat went to pay a visit to Bordak at the capital of Nera. Zonat was silent during their ride there. Thoughts of the worst possible outcome played over and over in his mind. He imagined what life in prison would be like, and even thought of being executed. Although he was tempted to cancel the appointment and go back to safer grounds, something told him not to back off. They arrived at the large oval building, known as White Dome on Headquarter Hill.

At the employee entrance, Zonat slipped a plastic card into a slot in a metal box. The silver doors obeyed the card's command and opened instantly. They walked down a long white corridor to Bordak's closed office.

After Zonat pushed a buzzer on the door, Bordak looked at a video camera through which he was able to spy on those who wanted to get in. Seeing that it was Zonat and Shero, he pushed a button that opened the protective doors.

As they walked into the large white office, Shero noticed that Bordak was nervously tapping a long skinny index finger on his large black desk. He sensed the uneasiness he was feeling, which seemed similar to the way Zonat appeared, when his hand shook as he clutched the steering device in the vanship.

"Please be seated," said Bordak, as he looked at his guests through pale yellow eyes, and then scratched one of his thick, gray eyebrows.

After the introduction, Shero sat in anticipation for Bordak to speak and cut through an initial moment of stiff silence. Shero would have spoken first, but he knew it wouldn't be proper etiquette.

Bordak cleared his throat and clenched the bony fingers of both his hands together, as he leaned forward and rested his elbows on the desk. He glanced at Zonat, then at Shero.

"I realize you have come here today to speak with me about your views regarding the obedience therapy," he said, and gave a threatening look to Zonat. "You must realize that if you choose to defy my orders regarding this program, you may be looked upon as a dissenter, and will have to pay the consequences.

Zonat leaned forward in his seat, knowing that he was leaning out on a fragile limb that was putting his job, and perhaps his life, in jeopardy, but at this point he didn't care. "My dear leader, there is something that you must realize," he swallowed and went on, "Too many people are decaying rapidly. They may still be productive at this point in time, but they are going downhill. The drug therapy might appear to be getting results, but it won't work forever. They will become too apathetic to do anything and then production will slow down tremendously."

Bordak stubbornly contemplated the words of Zonat, but then retaliated, "I was afraid of this! There is no other solution to get compliance. I need to keep the industry of this planet active, or it will fall apart and then we will be left at the mercy of other forces that try to come in and rule our lands. If you want to see the working machine of this planet die, and are working towards this end, then I will have to remove you from duty!"

Shero's purple eyes blazed with fire as he jumped in and addressed Bordak, "Leader Bordak, the working machine is closer to death than you think."

Bordak wrinkled his brow, giving a sign that he was somewhat willing to listen to the words of an Athenian. "What do you mean?"

"You have entrusted the care of your people to the Black Knights. Even though they may appear to be allies and want to help you, their intention is to destroy! You may not see this, because of the cunning way in which they operate, but Zonat is correct. I have been on other missions and have observed the same type of covert behavior. I know that you have only held the leadership position on the planet for two years, and don't have the tenure of your former commanders. This is one reason they are taking advantage of you. They often seek out young leaders who aren't yet alert to their schemes."

Bordak's eyes opened wide while Shero spoke. He was torn between whether he should believe this statement or not.

Meanwhile, as Bordak thought about his reply to Shero, something was occurring on the purple lawn in front of the White Dome. Rhia, Walusk and the other commissioners and missionaires were joined by about one hundred Nerians. They had organized a peaceful protest. The Nerians sat next to one another, forming several rows. A large canvas banner was being unrolled by a couple of ambitious Nerians. Meanwhile, Rhia carried a zeechord out to the lawn and set it down. She talked with a couple of the Nerians for a few moments, then went back to the vanship that she had come in. It was parked on a ramp several hundred feet away from the grass. She opened a cargo compartment door and pulled out a t-harp. As she shut the door, she felt someone's eyes blazing at her back. She promptly turned around and looked Libol right in the eye!

"Excuse me for alarming you, but are you part of the activities that are occurring down there on the lawn?" he asked.

Rhia felt an instant desire to yell at him, but decided to hold back. "Yes, I am. Why do you ask?"

"It appears that the good people of Nera are engaging in some sort of protest," he said suspiciously.

"Yes, you could say that. They are protesting the destruction of their individuality due to the use of obedience therapy!"

The social smile that embellished his face cracked, and was replaced by a look of resentment. "And why would they do such a thing?"

"Because it's not working. Those beings haven't been happy. Their power of choice has been subjugated against their own will."

"My dear, I doubt if you know the ramifications of turning the people against this therapy," Libol said, holding back his anger.

"And why is it that you seem to be in favor of such treatment?"

"I am an authority to these people and happened to have been given permission by Bordak to implement the therapy."

Rhia froze for a moment, but could no longer hold back her rage. "You won't get away with this, Libol!"

Libol went into shock, "How do you know who I am?"

"I have my ways."

"Who are you? You don't look like the other residents of Nera. How do you know about me?"

"My name is Rhianna. I'm from Athena," she said proudly. Libol restrained himself from the hostility he instantly felt for Rhia. He knew that if he expressed his emotions and killed her on the spot, he could too easily be identified as the obvious murderer. That was not the way he liked to do people in. He preferred slow torture. "So, I suppose you are here to try and abort my attempts to help Bordak."

Rhia took advantage of her confrontation with a real live Black Knight to tell him her point of view, "You are not here to help at all. Your purpose is to destroy in the name of help!"

"You have no idea what you're talking about. You're no expert on the behavior of people. You and your people are too busy doing useless activities such as painting the sky and singing songs, when there are planets in trouble in the galaxy."

"If it wasn't for you and your cohorts, there wouldn't be much trouble!" Rhia retaliated. "I must go and join the others now. I have nothing further to say to you."

Libol stood and steamed for awhile as Rhia walked away. "You'll get yours. You just wait," he said under his breath.

Her thoughts fixated on the run-in she had with Libol. Rhia walked over to Walusk, who was pulling up one side of the banner connected to a pole. He and another Nerian on the other side were adjusting it so it stood upright.

As the people on the lawn prepared to sing a protest song, Bordak was still in his office talking to Shero and Zonat. He was still not thoroughly persuaded to discontinue the obedience therapy.

Just as Bordak was about to comment on one of Zonat's remarks, his attention was drawn to the sound of the buzzer outside the door. He ignored it, thinking the person would give up and go away. However the buzzing continued. "Excuse me," Bordak said to Zonat. He looked at the video-cam attached to the top right corner of his desk. He saw the face of Libol and pushed a button connected to a speaker, "Libol, I am right in the middle of a meeting. Could you please put your request on electro-comm?"

"Sir, I need to speak with you immediately, before it is too late. Your people are becoming dissenters, and it is because of the Athenians that you allowed on your planet."

Bordak looked at Shero accusatively and then let Libol in. Shero turned and looked Libol right in the eye. "You have no idea what you are talking about. All you have done is created a group of unthinking zombies!"

"And I suppose you are ready to pay for the repercussions of a rebellion. Sir, I am here to prove my point. All you have to do is look out of your window and see there is a large group of protesters sitting on the grass."

Bordak was puzzled, "Very well, Libol. I will inspect this." Bordak immediately got up from his chair and walked over to the only window in his office. He looked down in surprise as he noticed how many of his people were there.

Rhia adjusted a few pegs on her t-harp, and Taus, a male missionaire, unfolded the legs on the zeechord. Then just as Bordak was looking at the banner, the musicians started playing. Shero and Zonat went over to the window to see what was happening. Then Libol reluctantly looked over Bordak's shoulder and strained to see.

Bordak and the others read the banner, which said, "We are Nerians, not Androids. No more obedience therapy!"

One of the Nerians spotted Bordak at the window and pointed a finger at him, glad to see that they had gotten his attention.

The confused thoughts in Bordak's mind were silent as he listened to the singing of his anguished people. Libol stewed in his resentment as he forced himself to watch the spectacle.

A chorus of Nerians sang these words while Rhia and Taus accompanied them.

"We are Nerians with our own goals.
We are not robots without souls.
We are individuals who are creators.
We are not destruction instigators.
All we ask is to be free
to be who we want to be."

These words were sung over and over and Bordak just gazed out the window, while beads of sweat emanated from his pale green forehead. He could see the suffering in the eyes of his people. Some even cried as they sang.

Feelings of guilt overcame him as he listened to the heartfelt lyrics. He tried to swallow any feelings of pride that he still had left, and realized that he'd never really wanted to implement the manipulation therapy, but just didn't know what else to do.

While listening to the Nerians, he turned around and instructed Libol, Zonat and Shero to take seats in front of his desk. With the music of his people in the background Bordak looked straight at Libol, "You and the others are to cease with the therapy at once. I will not subject my people to this means of control any longer!"

Libol was backed into a corner and was stumped for words for a second, "But,...uh Sir I don't know if you realize what the ramifications will be. I know their little song out there touches you, but you may be making a mistake. You see, many of those outside your window have not yet had the therapy and are acting rebelliously. Suppose everyone was off of Probot. Why they may try to overthrow you."

"At this point that would be better than continuing to turn them all into mindless Zombies! You and the others have ten hours to pack up and leave Nera!" Bordak said with more certainty than he'd had in a long time.

Libol and the other Knights resentfully complied with Bordak's enforced command. Bordak and his staff were grateful to the Athenians for coming to Nera and helping them out with a problem that could have led to the demise of their population. As it was, they were going to have to cope with the situation of getting many of their people off of a drug that they were now dependent on. This had been the first time their people had ever been on any chemical substance at all.

On their trip back to Athena, Rhia gazed out of a window. While the others cheerfully conversed, she was immersed in feelings of both relief and worry.

Shero approached her with a glass of festive purla juice. "Why so silent?"

"Oh, I was just thinking."

"That can be dangerous you know."

"Yes Shero, but perhaps my thoughts were mingled with some perceptions that gave me legitimate concern."

"What do you mean?"

"The Knights were so willing to leave. It just makes me suspicious. Whenever they pretend to accept defeat, they usually seek an even stronger revenge."

"That may be true, but I think Bordak will be wiser next time."

"It's not so much Bordak or Nera that I'm worried about!"

"Okay, Rhia, then what is it?"

"Who knows where they'll strike next. And who knows how hard. If they can't get vengeance on Nera, they'll just go somewhere else!"

Chapter 5

S everal months had passed since Rhianna's return from Nera. Her childhood dream had finally come true when she proudly received her own diamond necklace with a silver medal on it, for her successful mission.

One day, Rhia and Ladaar were at home in their palace in the North Valley watching planetary entertainment on the telecomm when a little green light started flashing on a panel beneath the screen. They both looked at one another, knowing there would soon be an interruption in the live performance they were viewing.

Outside the window, green lights which were the same color as those on the telecomm, flashed brightly in the sky. This was a signal for all Athenians to cease their activities and fly immediately to nearby telecomms so they could receive a message from the Empress.

Rhia, lying with her head in Ladaar's lap on a pink satin couch, sat up in anticipation of what the message might be. It had been a long time since there had been a planetary broadcast from Zeena. The fifteen-minute waiting period seemed to pass very slowly for Rhia and Ladaar.

Finally, the face of Zeena appeared. She was in a room in her palace, seated in a gold chair. Her direct assistant, Jirmak, sat next to her. Rhia noticed that Jirmak looked better than when she'd last seen her at Zeena's home, but the sparkle in her eyes wasn't quite as bright as it had been before her trip to Sadan.

The Empress addressed her people, "My dear friends and fellow Athenians, I have summoned you before me today in order to inform you of a temporary change on the planet.

"I have been called off of Athena to handle a crises. Although this is not a good time for me to be leaving the planet, because of the upcoming United Council For Creative Freedom, I am afraid that I have no choice. Two of our fellow planets, Gora and Atranus are in serious trouble. There has recently been such major conflict between these two Empires that the leaders are considering laser warfare against one another. If this sort of outbreak should occur, other planets may be pulled into the chaos and called upon to choose sides. This could cause the kind of major destruction in our galaxy that has never occurred before. The reason I must go and handle the dilemma directly is that I have been an opinion leader for the head of both Gora and Atranus. If I can reason with them logically, by spending time with each leader and their staffs, I may be able to prevent this debacle from occurring. Because of the nature of my mission, I will be gone for an indefinite period of time. I will be taking some of my palace staff with me as well.

"Jirmak will be taking my place during the time I am absent. She will be vested with supreme jurisdiction over Athena until I return to resume my position. She will have the authority to send qualified Athenians on missions, if need be. Jehra, who will fill his old position, will directly assist Jirmak, while Jirmak assumes mine.

"Two weeks from today the Creative Freedom Council will convene in a meeting hall on Placid Isle. Several officials from throughout the Milky Way will come to discuss ways in which to constructively forward the goals of their civilizations in alignment with the overall goals of the galaxy. There may be special proposals involving Athena after the conference, but before they are implemented, Jirmak will give final approval on them. I have worked with Jirmak for hundreds of years and am fully confident in entrusting my duties to her. Should there be any extreme emergencies I should know about, Jirmak will be able to telecomm me."

The day of the United Council For Creative Freedom soon arrived and guests flew in from throughout the galaxy and landed on a parking strip on Placid Isle. Bern was busy greeting the visitors and showing them to the rooms they'd be sleeping in during the three-day conference.

Rhia and Ladaar were part of the opening day entertainment for the council, and gave them a warm Athenian welcome that consisted of improvised music, created on the spot for the occasion.

Rhia badly wanted to attend the conference so that she could hear what they were discussing, but she wasn't allowed to attend. Ladaar, however, reminded her that she would get to hear the results soon after the meetings were over when Jirmak telecommed the people of Athena.

The day after the council, Rhia was at home anxiously waiting to see the blink of the flashing green lights on her telecomm. Ladaar was on Placid Isle with Bern, helping him paint a couple of buildings when he noticed green lights flashing in the sky. He thought of Rhia, and wished he were there in North Valley with her to receive Jirmak's message.

Jirmak sat in the same golden chair that the Empress had been seated in during the last planetary message. On her right was her assistant Jehra.

It took Rhia a few minutes to get used to the fact that the Empress Zeena wasn't the one addressing her people. However, if Zeena trusted Jirmak in her position, then Rhia did too. Athenians had always been recognized for having ultimate faith in their leaders, and not questioning their decisions.

Jirmak spoke in a confident manner, "Greetings my dear friends and fellow Athenians. I have signaled you before me to inform you of the results of the recent Creative Freedom Council.
"One of the things that was agreed upon is that there needs to be more interrelating and exchange amongst the people in the Galaxy. There are a number of citizens on Athena as well as on other planets who have never traveled beyond the bounds of their homelands. Taking more frequent trips to other lands would give us a better overview of other populations. This will also bring about a better interchange of products and ideas that could contribute to the overall expansion of many civilizations. It is important to broaden our horizons beyond our main education as artists. You see, something I have come to realize after the conference is that although we are one of the most powerful civilizations in the galaxy, we lack some of the practical skills that others have.

"It has been decided that a new shuttle station will be built here on Athena. This will accommodate the upcoming heavy traffic on and off of our planet.

"Also, several large new space riders will be built so that several people can travel together to other lands. In order to initiate this program, a number of Athenians will be called upon to take part in the creating of the station. Once the builders are chosen, they will be informed by telecomm as to who they are.

"The final thing that was brought to light at the conference affects every one of you on Athena. It was agreed upon by some of the officials from other planets that there may be room for improvement in the quality of our art. You see, my dear friends, it is true that we often create with wild abandon, not giving enough thought to how our works might be viewed by our neighbors. Since we are going to start having more involvement with them, it is important that we speculate on how we can do a better job. So from now on, when you are creating, take an even better look at your work and ask yourself how you can improve. Also, feel free to comment on the art of others and let them know what they could do that may be better.

"I will be having regular inspections conducted at various locations where there is continual group creating. Some of the main places will be The Meadow, Garden Valley, The Muse fields, and the Arena de Itrinia.

"Some of the visitors from the conference who have remained here on Athena will be going to the areas I've just mentioned, as well as others which will soon be announced. They will be residing at Etherea, and serving as temporary guest staff members. Our visitors will be assisting palace staff, and sharing their points of view regarding the impact of the work of our artists. I believe it will be helpful to all of us to be given the opinion of those other than fellow Athenians.

"This is all I have to report for now, and I look forward to working with all of you to upgrade the quality of life here on Athena so that you may better achieve your personal goals as well as those which contribute to the betterment of the planet and the galaxy."

Chapter 6

The creation of the shuttle was well underway. Because of Ladaar's experience with building projects, he was chosen to participate. Bern was also asked to go, and left the resort at Placid Isle in the charge of a man named Garun.

Since the shuttle station was being built about one thousand miles away from North Valley, Ladaar resided there during the time of the project. It saddened Rhia when he left, not knowing exactly how long he'd be gone.

After a couple of days of longing to be with him, she got busy with her own creations, and the urge to be with Ladaar was sublimated by the art that she worked on.

One day Rhia and Klar went to The Meadow to join the others who were creating there. When they arrived, Rhia noticed there weren't as many musicians on stage as she was used to seeing. The sky, which was normally filled with colorful paintings, was only sparsely decorated. Just as Rhia was gazing up into the sky, a man whom she'd never seen before approached her. Klar went off to talk to a friend of hers while the strange man spoke to Rhia, "Hello Rhianna," the man said.

"Hello. How do you know who I am?"

"My name is Beldar. I am from the planet Sadan, and was one of the attendees of the United Council For Creative Freedom. I saw your performance at the meeting hall on Placid Isle when I was there with the other guests. I met Bern after the conference, and he told me you were married to his son."

"Oh, I see. And you must be here at The Meadow to help Jirmak with your critique."

"Yes, precisely. Everybody knows that it is often hard for one to get a truly non-prejudicial view toward his own art, especially when you are trained to create so freely. So I am here along with another official to help with the upgrade project on Athena. It is quite an honor to be chosen by your leader Jirmak for such an assignment," Beldar said with a smile.

"So you heard me sing, huh?"

"Yes, I did. You have a lovely voice, but I can tell you are still training. Aren't you?"

Rhia suddenly felt her confidence in herself slipping slightly and thought she had to explain herself, "Well, no. Not at this time. Long ago I learned distance singing. In fact I was taught this by Bern's daughter, Vaadra, and..."

Beldar quickly looked away from Rhia, and then looked back into her eyes, cutting her off, "It's OK, my dear. You don't need to explain further. Sometimes one doesn't realize how lack of training can be detrimental. Just as a friendly word of advice, it wouldn't hurt for you to continue. One can't get too good, you know," Beldar said as Rhia questioned her own ability.

"Yes, I suppose that's true."

"Now, what is it that you came here to do today?"

"I, well, I was going to do some sky painting, and then perhaps some singing to enhance the instrumentalists."

"Oh my," Beldar said as he shook his head.

"What is it?" Rhia was concerned.

"You mustn't know."

"Know what?"

"About the new rule. You see, whoever is creating at a prime performance spot must pass an audition before they are allowed to participate in the activities at that location."

"But I haven't heard of this. All I knew about is that there were going to be inspections done. I've performed at The Meadow many times and all I ever had to do was just show up and start doing whatever I wanted."

"Yes, I know, Rhia. But this is something that has changed. The intention is to insure that the quality of talent here and at other locations is representative of Athena at her best. In order to bring this about, restrictions were put in. The artists you see here today were selected several days ago, and were told to come back today. They are a pre-selected example of what we are looking for. Some who auditioned days ago were rejected, unfortunately. Others that showed up today, not knowing the new rule, were told the same thing I am telling you. I apologize that you were not informed, but you may audition for a future performance. If you wish to do this, please wait over in Left Field with the group of artists who are in line. I can't guarantee that you will be chosen, as I have already informed you that your singing needs some work. But I haven't seen your sky painting yet, and perhaps it will pass inspection."

Rhia glanced over to a section of the Meadow where a group of artists anxiously waited their turns to audition for the new inspectors. She didn't like the idea of having to wait to create. "I think I'll just pass for today."

"That's fine my dear. Do feel free to go out and sit in the audience and watch the show if you wish."

"Perhaps I'll do this," she said as she looked and saw several artists observing those on stage. "By the way, how did the other performers respond to the news you are telling me?"

"Oh they took it quite well," Beldar said while placing a hand on Rhia's shoulder. "Please don't take this personally, Darling. I am simply following the new rules that have been approved by Jirmak. I know it may seem odd that officials from other planets are suddenly ordering your people around, but there's a reason for this."

"What's that?"

"We are able to act as non-biased observers."

"I understand," Rhia said, trying to get used to the new changes. Although she felt guilty for contesting the rules set by her leader, she sensed that something wasn't quite right. She tried to deny what she perceived, and wanted to convince herself to take on the attitude of other compliant Athenians. "I hope to see you singing in The Meadow at a time when you are truly ready."

Rhia walked away from Beldar, with less motivation than she brought with her that day. She saw her friend Klar, still talking to someone else, and walked over to the two of them. Klar and the other Athenian female stopped talking as Rhia approached. Klar then introduced Rhia to her friend Arna.

"Who were you talking to, Rhia?" Klar asked curiously.
"Oh, that was one of the inspectors that Jirmak sent out here to monitor the quality of artwork."

Arna spoke, "I was telling Klar about this new rule. I know that Jirmak is only trying to make improvements, and even though

I was hoping to perform today, I may just go and watch others for a while and see what it is they consider quality art."

"I don't know about this Arna. I came to entertain today, not to be entertained," Klar said, disappointed.

"But Klar, maybe you could learn something. Look at it this way. If the acts here today are the ones being selected by Jirmak and her staff, then we can see what they are looking for," said Arna.

"Yes, that may be so, but it's frustrating."

"I know my, dear friend, but personally I think there are some things you could change about your sky painting. You tend to use a lot of blues and greens, and maybe you could get more into reds and yellows as well, just like the painter who is doing a drawing as we speak," Arna said as she pointed to a picture of some large flowers and trees in the sky.

Klar got puzzled, "Yes, well maybe I could do that, but I don't know that I want to change."

Chapter 7

Early one morning Rhia tossed and turned in bed, wrinkling the satin covers that adorned the large round cushion she slept on. She was on the verge of awakening when the loud beeping of a telecomm in her room caused her to jump out of bed. She flipped on a switch that allowed her to get a picture of the caller. There in front of her was the face of her husband, whom she hadn't talked with for almost four months. He hadn't had immediate access to a telecomm while on his project, and when he beeped her, Rhia knew that he must have traveled a distance to get to one.

"Darling, it's so good to see you. I've missed you so much." Ladaar noticed Rhia's face was void of the cheerful expression he was used to seeing. "Rhianna, how are you doing?"

"I've been trying to adjust to all the new changes created by the upgrade project."

"What do you mean?"

"Well, things have gotten a lot stricter when it comes to performing at popular spots. You remember hearing about the inspections that were going to be done?"

"Yes."

"Well, one must go through auditions in front of Jirmak's staff, as well as inter-planetary leaders before they are allowed to do anything. I've had to do work on my distance singing and sky painting. As a result of all of this upgrade, I haven't been performing as much as I used to. There just aren't as many artists out in public places anymore."

"I see," Ladaar said with a questioning look of concern on his face.

"What are your thoughts, my darling? You look worried."

"If we don't produce enough artwork, we could become more vulnerable."

"I know what you are saying, but I don't think this has been a problem. Apparently there is still enough teamwork and intention to ward off the dark intruders," Rhia said as she held her right hand up to the telecomm screen and stroked Ladaar's cheek. As she did this, the color of his cheek glowed brightly. He closed his eyes briefly and felt a warm loving sensation come over him. "Oh Ladaar, there is something I must confess."

He waited.

"One of the other reasons I haven't been doing as much creating is that it's not the same without you. I miss the spiritual harmony that you and I share both in our artwork and our relationship. I've had a gnawing emptiness inside."

"I know what you mean. I've missed you very much too. I haven't minded working on the shuttle station because I know it's for a good cause, but it has worn me out. I'm not used to feeling this way. Somehow my inspiration for coming up with new creations has dwindled. I'm not used to following someone else's rigid rules for structural design. I'd rather be contributing my own ideas in conjunction with others, like when working with grandfather."

"So is there an end to this project you're on?" Rhia asked with a serious look.

"Yes, and this is the good news. In fact, this is one of the reasons I've contacted you."

Rhia's solemn look turned to a smile as she anticipated seeing Ladaar soon.

"We are done with the shuttle station. In fact, it is fully operational, and many people are already on their way to other planets."

"Then you will be coming home," she cut in before he could finish the rest of what he was going to say.

"I wish this was the case, but unfortunately I must go immediately to Placid Isle. Father and I found out that there was an inspection done at the village there, and some changes need to be made on many of the buildings."

"What kind of changes?" Rhia asked.

"The color scheme is wrong. There are too many varying colors, and we were told that the buildings need to be more uniform. In other words, instead of pink, blue, green and yellow, we need to choose only a couple of colors, such as blue and green, which are more coordinated. It shouldn't take long, perhaps only a week. What we need to do is get some blue and green magic paint that we can coat the pink and yellow buildings with. This will give them the apparency that they are made out of the same stones as those that are actually made of blue and green stone. This is the fastest way to go about the touch-ups."

Rhia sulked, so instead of further explaining the details to her, he interjected something else. "Rhia, I want to see you too, but it will not be long."

"I don't want to wait another week Ladaar. Can't you take a break and come home for at least a day?"

"I'd love to, but I can't."

Rhia got angry and could see the vibrations of her mood depicted by the wavy lines that altered Ladaar's picture on the telecomm monitor. Then she had an idea and calmed down, causing his face to go back to normal focus. "I'm coming to the village to see you."

"If you want to fly all the way over to Placid Isle, I would love that. Believe me, I don't like this delay any better than you do, but I have to follow orders. Maybe I can spend some time with you before we get to work," he said as he touched her cheek on the screen in the same loving manner that she had touched his, watching it sparkle and glow.

"Ladaar, I apologize for my selfishness, but it's just that this has been the longest period that we've been apart."

"Yes, Rhianna, I know. This will change though. Soon we'll be creating musical symphonies together. I just want to hurry and finish my work on Placid Isle so I can get back into other art forms."

"When will you and Bern arrive at the village?"

"Approximately ten hours. We will go to Grandfather's preparations room, and start working out our exact plan."

"Good. Then I will see you there in about ten hours. I know that I won't be able to be with you for very long, but it will be better than nothing."

"I love you Rhianna."

"I love you, too," Rhia said as she blew him a kiss.

They both turned off their telecomm picture switches.

Rhia decided to occupy her waiting time by going out to one of the fields of North Valley to practice her distance singing. She used to wander out to the red grassy area of the valley and see various musicians performing, while singers added nuances to the melodies with their golden vocals. Sky dancers often came around and did playful steps in the air, inspired by the liveliness and energy of the music. But today Rhia saw something different. She walked and walked and the only song she heard was the sound of silence. Then, as her bare feet approached a rocky area, she heard the faint echoing of a flute bouncing off of a cave wall. She stopped and listened for a while, and could tell the musician was doing a solo, with no one joining in.

Then she continued to walk around the large field. Stepping across a large white sandy spot, she heard the sound of another instrument, playing a completely different melody than the first player. She spied a man with a tri-flute near a tree, playing by himself. Off to the right of the man with the flute, several hundreds of feet away, she saw a lone sky dancer, taking steps that were out of sync with both of the musicians.

Rhia walked over to the man with the tri-flute, and faced him as he sat on a rock and played his instrument. He looked surprised to see her, and fumbled on a few notes as he continued to play. Rhia duplicated the melody he was playing, and started singing softly, then got louder and louder, throwing her voice out several hundred feet in front of her. Then the man on the flute stumbled again, and stopped playing his instrument. As soon as Rhia noticed this, she stopped singing.

"Why are you here?" he asked Rhia.

She was bewildered that he would question this, as it was usually so common for other artists to join one another in song. "I came out here to practice my distance singing, and I heard you playing flute, and thought I'd accent your playing with some vocals," she said, feeling like she had to justify her actions.

"I understand that your intentions are good, but if you don't mind, I'd rather just work on my craft by myself," he said as he started to pick up the flute.

As the man nearly had the instrument to his lips Rhia spoke, "What has happened here in the valley? Last time I was out in the fields, people were creating together. Now I see you over here and another tri-flute player in a cave. I know there's more stress on perfecting our work, but why not join together. Aren't we a team anymore?"

The man wrinkled his brow as he put his flute down. "Yes, of course we are. Uh, you are?" wanting to say her name, he realized he didn't know what it was.

"My name is Rhia, and who are you?"

"Rhia, I am Vanaar."

Vanaar went on. "I just need my own space at this time to keep perfecting my playing. You see, I am determined to keep being accepted in The Muse Fields. I have played there a few times, and don't wish to be replaced by others, such as that other flute player. He is trying very hard to take my place, and assures me that next time there are auditions, he will be the one who gets to play. He and I have been together at some of the auditions, and I have been the one chosen at these tryouts. He hasn't been accepted yet."

Rhia was confused, "You mean they are only allowing one tri-flute player at the main performances?"

"Yes, Rhia. With the abundance of instruments on this planet, they want to see a larger variety of players. So instead of having several flute players, they'd rather give the open spaces on stage to other instrumentalists. When I perform at the Muse Fields, I feel very much a part of the group there. I think this pre-selection of artists is a good thing because it allows the best creators on the planet to work together, while others are improving and trying to get up to our standards. But meanwhile, I don't want to be copied by other jealous tri-flute players, trying to replace me. That man over there, may very well try and do just that."

Several thoughts tumbled around in Rhia's mind while thinking of a reply. She didn't think that Vanaar was any better than the other tri-flute player, but for some reason, probably just having to do with personal taste, some auditioner merely decided to chose him over the other player. She withheld from telling him her viewpoint.

"So you have an objection to me singing along with you?"

"It's not so much that I object to the company. You do have a lovely voice. It's just that right now, I need to be alone to work out certain techniques. The singing is a bit of a distraction."

"I see," Rhia said, not totally convinced that she did see.

Rhia ended her conversation with Vanaar and then slowly meandered around the valley until she came to a secluded area by a small purple pond. With some of her motivation lost, she did her best to sing an improvised melody. It spilled from her like a viscous liquid, instead of the free flowing cascade of song that usually poured out. After a while, the fluid thinned and she started propelling her music several thousand feet in front of her, but it was with more effort than she was used to.

After several hours in the field, Rhia went back home to get ready to meet with Ladaar. When she arrived at her mansion, she rushed down a long corridor toward her bedchambers, and pulled out a blue gown that her mother had made for her several years ago. She changed into the dress and then headed out to the courtyard behind her house. Lying down on a patch of velvet grass was Thaurus, who had been residing with Ladaar and Rhia ever since they got married. Rhia's parents knew how much she loved him and said she could take him to live at her new home. Rhia had decided to go on horseback to meet Ladaar, as there were still three hours before he would arrive, and this is how long it would take her to fly to Placid Isle on Thaurus. Besides, Thaurus hadn't been out for some time, and she knew he needed to stretch his wings as much as she needed to stretch hers.

As Rhia approached Thaurus, her attention was drawn to the sound of two people arguing. She pet Thaur's neck and then asked him, "Where are those people that I hear?"

Thaurus made a pointing motion with his snout, directing Rhia's attention to Klar's home next door, which shared the same courtyard. She quit petting Thaur and then slowly started walking toward Klar's home. She didn't see anyone, so she started walking around toward the front of the building. There, by an open entranceway, she saw Klar talking to another female neighbor named Lara. She ducked her head behind a wall so as not to be seen eavesdropping.

Klar was speaking, "I don't find it necessary to put paintings up in the sky that aren't permanent and are only going to be there for a few moments. This type of painting is on its way out, and so are other forms of spontaneous creating. What is becoming more important are those things that last and can be carried forward to future generations. That is why I have decided to stick to doing strictly canvas paintings."

"But Klar, creating is spontaneous, and I believe that one should be able to have an abundance of ideas that they can portray at any instant they wish. If we limit our artwork to merely those things that must be carried forward, and have to 'save' our art then we are stunting our growth and holding on to the past. If we can discard our creations, then there isn't a feeling of scarcity of ideas. We can continue to create whatever we want, at will, whenever we want. Our imaginations remain freer to bloom."

"Yes Lara, but now we are concentrating on those things we can more tangibly exchange with our neighbors on other planets. I just don't see how you can give them a sky painting when it is only going to be around for a few minutes," Klar retaliated.

"But Klar, some of my greatest moments have been pleasing people with my work at a special instant in time, knowing I have given them something pleasureful that will live on in memory. There's no limit to the amount of creations I can do. I don't have to clutch onto something as if it's so valuable I can't part with it. After all, we are supposed to be setting examples of creative freedom, not bondage."

Their debate went on for a few moments longer, but Rhia had heard enough and decided to get Thaurus and take him for his long overdue ride.

Rhia told her animal friend that she was ready to go. Thaurus proceeded to lift himself up from his comfortably lazy position on the grass that he'd been in for hours. He stood upright with his head towering way above Rhia and then walked behind her.

"Okay Thaur, we finally get to go see Ladaar in Placid Isle."

Just as Rhia was about to board Thaur's back, he started shaking his head and making a funny sound.

"What is it Thaurus?" she couldn't make out exactly what he was trying to say, and she had so much attention on getting to her husband that she didn't grant his noises much importance. Although it was not like her to ignore him, at this time she just didn't care about his nagging.

Rhia anxiously climbed on his back. He walked out towards the red fields of North Valley. Then he started trotting faster and faster until his trotting turned into a gallop. Soon he was up and flying, and much to Rhia's amazement he started deliberately heading in the wrong direction, "Thaurus, we're going to Placid Isle. What are you doing?"

He replied by making a similar noise to the one he made before.

"Oh Thaur, are you trying to lead me to Alta for some reason? My parents might be trying to reach me, huh?"

Thaur shook his head, as Rhia perceived that her parents in fact, may be trying to get in touch with her. She didn't have time to be taking any detours now, and informed Thaurus of this. After she straightened Thaur out, he started heading toward the correct destination.

As they flew along, passing large red and blue trees, Rhia started to feel better, being above all the problems below. She knew that some artists on Athena had gotten too serious recently, and this didn't seem right to her.

In short order they came to the Amagon Sea, where Rhia looked down and saw colorful fish swimming below the surface. Some of them leaped out of the water and danced in the air then dove back in. She was glad to see that at least the fish were creating together harmoniously.

When they finally approached Placid Isle, Rhia looked out in front of her and saw the beautiful buildings that Bern had designed. She liked the array of colors, and wasn't happy about the more uniform change he was requested to make.

Thaur came in for a landing on a patch of blue grass with a small pond connected to it. They were right near the building where Bern's preparation room was. Rhia quickly jumped off of Thaur's back and instructed him to wait on the grass for her. He shook his head in compliance, and then loudly slurped water from the pond. Then he found a comfortable spot on the grass and lay down, resting his tired body.

Rhia ran to Bern's building, and was greeted by Garun at the entranceway. "Hello, Rhia."

"Hello, Garun. Are Bern and Ladaar inside the preparation room yet?" she quickly asked.

"Yes, they are. You seem as though you're in a hurry."

She smiled, "You could say that. I didn't see my husband during the whole time he was working on the shuttle."

He smiled back at her. "I see. Well, then, you better hurry." Rhia hugged Garun, and then ran to the end of the long hallway. She was out of breath when she arrived at the doorway and stopped short before going in. She noticed Ladaar and Bern seated at a shiny black table peering over a square, glass planning board. The board had a picture layout of every building on Placid Isle. Bern was coloring over one of the pink buildings with a blue drawing implement to see how it would look in its new, darker shade. Rhia gazed at Ladaar with such affinity that he felt it from across the room and looked up at her. When their eyes met, she rushed inside the room and into his arms. They hugged and kissed one another affectionately.

"I hope you saved one of those hugs for me," Bern said, waiting patiently for them to end their moment of passion.

"Oh, I certainly did," Rhia said as she walked over and hugged him.

After their embrace Rhia went and sat in Ladaar's lap. She looked at the miniature map of the village on the planning board, noticing the color changes.

"We were just discussing some details regarding the plans to change the building colors here at the village," Bern said.

"I see. I'm sorry for interrupting you two, but..."

"I know you two missed each other very much. You needn't be sorry. I heard about you day and night. You were all he could talk about."

As Rhia sat in Ladaar's lap with her right arm wrapped around his shoulder, she looked at him and noticed that his face was more pale than usual. He'd also lost some of the sparkle in his bright emerald eyes.

"What's the matter Rhia?"

"Your face looks different. There's a glow I used to see that is missing."

"What do you expect? After what I've been through, I don't feel as bright," he said with a tone of resentment.

Bern busied himself with some details on a couple of the buildings, as Rhia and Ladaar continued their conversation.

"I know you've been working hard, darling. I don't know, but something just doesn't seem right. Forgive me for saying anything. Maybe I should just be quiet," she said as she gently stoked Ladaar's head.

"It's okay. I'm sure you are right about the way I look. I have been feeling worse than I usually do. The shuttle project really drained me. Now we're forced to make these building changes."

"Well, if you don't agree, why don't you telecomm Jirmak and let her know how you feel, and perhaps you won't have to do it," Rhia said as she looked at Bern who was coloring the last of one of the buildings on the board. "That is, if Bern feels the same way."

Bern looked up, giving full attention to Rhia and Ladaar, whom he'd only half been listening to. "My dear, I don't want to go against the wishes of the palace staff. I know they have their reasons for all of this, and just because Ladaar and I disagree doesn't mean it's going to do any good. We are only a couple of voices in the crowd, and Jirmak is acting for the Empress now."

"Yes, but each voice in the crowd makes up a group of voices, and if everyone spoke out for what he believes in, then a change could be made, but...." she said as Bern and Ladaar looked at her blankly.

"Okay, well if you don't, then it's up to you, but...." Rhia sighed and started to regret saying anything at all. She knew that if she didn't start keeping her mouth shut, she'd get a bad reputation and look like an enemy.

At that point, a telecomm on a table in a corner of the room started beeping. Bern excused himself and got up to see who the caller was. Rhia and Ladaar went back to talking with each other.

"Well, regardless of what you do, at least I can spend some time with you, and this is what I came here for anyway," Rhia said as she smiled at Ladaar.

Ladaar didn't return the smile, but instead looked at the pink stone floor beneath his feet for a few seconds. He took Rhia's right hand and held it between both of his hands then looked at her. "Rhia, there is something I must tell you."

"Now what is wrong?"

"We have to get started right away. I found this out when father and I arrived. I thought we would have some time to delay, but Garun said he was informed by palace staff that they want the buildings done in six days instead of seven. There will be some visitors coming to Placid Isle in seven days, and we need to be ready for them. With such a tight deadline, we need to get to work after this meeting. I would have telecommed you, but I knew you were already on your way. Of course you are welcome to stay here while father and I work, and you can even assist if you want, but I know it's not the way you want to be spending time with me."

Rhia got up off of his lap, disappointed. "It's all right. That's what I get for being so impatient. I won't stay," she said, as she suddenly had thought about her parents, and wondered how they were doing. "I think you'd get more done if I left you and Bern alone so you can continue your planning and then get on with what you have to do. Besides, I need to go see my parents. They're not far from here, so my trip wasn't totally wasted," she said with a little resentment.

Ladaar stood up and walked her down the long corridor that led to the front entranceway of the building. "Cheer up, Rhia. The sooner I get done here, the sooner we will have lots of time together again, just like we used to."

Rhia looked out the doorway and noticed Thaurus gazing up at a purple winged horse flying through the sky. Then Thaurus perceived Rhia's eyes on him and turned and looked at her from a distance and started swishing his tail while making a few noises.

"So you rode here on Thaur."

"Yes, he needed to get out as much as I did."

Rhia and Ladaar stood silently looking at each other for a moment, which they made stretch as long as possible. Then Rhia threw her arms around Ladaar's neck. They hugged one another tightly.

"I wish you could stay longer."

"I know, but like you said, the sooner you get through, the sooner we can be together. Anyway, I'm starting to worry about my parents. Thaurus tried to lead me to them before I came to Placid Isle, and I don't know why he was so insistent, but I want to find out. I will see you back at the castle when you are done, my love."

They kissed each other good-bye. Thaur watched them for a second and then bashfully turned his head away.

Chapter 8

Rhia walked over to Thaurus, who had been faithfully waiting for her. He instantly got up and started walking in circles around her, while making funny noises.

"Thaurus, what kind of strange greeting is this?"

He stopped.

"I know. You want to take me to Alta. That's exactly where we're going next."

Thaur nodded in approval as Rhia climbed aboard his back. He quickly ran along, until they were up and flying. Thaur was in such a hurry that he traveled at a speed which was much faster than Rhia was used to.

Rhia saw the village of Alta in the distance and got nervous as they approached it. Then Thaur slowed himself down as he came in for a landing on a flat plateau. Rhia disembarked from her pet and ran towards her old home. As she walked through the large arched entranceway, she didn't see anyone, and noticed that everything was very silent. "Hello, Mama, Father. Where are you?" she asked as she sensed that they might be upstairs. She climbed the spiral staircase that led to her parents' bedchambers. When she got to the room, there in front of her on the bed was Rhia's mother dressed in a light purple gown, with her eyes closed. Rhia was stunned to see her looking sick and pale.

Her father Andar was seated right beside her on a silver chair. Rhia was so focused on them that she didn't even notice that Thaur had followed her into the house, up the stairs and was standing right behind her.

"Rhianna, you have come. I tried to telecomm you, but you were not at home. I see that you and Thaurus got my message anyway. It's so good to see both of you," said Andar.

Rhia turned and saw Thaur looking over her shoulder, "Oh, Thaur. I do have to thank you for getting me here, but you know you're not supposed to come in the house. Why don't you go outside and wait for me near your old stable," she said petting him on the snout. He complied and walked back down the staircase, then out the front doorway. He was proud of his good deed.

Rhia walked over to her father and hugged him, then went to her mother's bedside and sat next to her on the round bed, and kissed her gently on the forehead.

Silka's heavy, closed, eyelids opened slightly, "Rhia, is that you?" she asked, reaching a hand out.

Rhia took her mother's frail hand in her own, "Yes, Mama. It's me. What has happened to you?" she said as tears of grief watered her eyes.

When Silka didn't reply, Andar gently put his right hand on Rhia's shoulder and pulled her away from her mother. "Darling, she's having a hard time speaking. I don't want her to strain herself, so I will tell you what is going on."

"Your mother is very ill."

"But why?" Rhia, asked loudly.

"Shhh, please talk more quietly so you don't disturb her." Andar looked at his wife, then turned to Rhia. "Let's go next door to your old room, so we can let her rest while we talk. I'll meet you over there in a minute. I just want to put some petals on her forehead," Andar said, as he took some pink flower petals from a bowl that rested on a silver bed stand. They were used for healing various physical ills, and were most effectively used by putting them on the forehead.

As Rhia walked into her old bedroom, which she hadn't been in for years, she noticed the gold framed mirror that she used to look at herself in. She flashed back to a time when she was wearing a green silk gown that her mother made for her, and was standing in front of the mirror, rehearsing what she'd say to the Empress after a successful mission. Then she sat on her old round bed that she used to dream on and realized how many of those dreams had come true since her childhood. Although she knew she'd achieved a lot of things since the time she resided at her home in Alta and generally felt good about her accomplishments, at this time she only felt the suffering of her mother.

Soon Andar walked in and sat next to Rhia on her bed. He solemnly looked at her. "Mother is suffering from Dream Demise, which has caused her body to collapse with weakness. She has trouble talking for any length of time, as this makes her dizzy."

Rhia jumped in, "But how did this happen? I've never ever seen Mama in this state."

"As you know, Mother has been making beautiful silken gowns for years."

Rhia nodded.

"Well, recently some of mother's gowns were put on display in front of some palace staff who are in charge of garment design inspection. Mother was told that her gowns needed to be improved upon, and that they were not as satisfactory as the gowns by other designers. She was instructed to change some of her pattern making and to use other designers' works as examples of the standards she needed to meet. She had to telecomm all the women for whom she'd been designing clothing for over the years, and tell them that she couldn't create items for them until she bettered her skills. Some of these women were upset but then decided to switch over to 'approved' designers. Meanwhile, mother tried to do as instructed and change her styles, but she got very frustrated, and didn't like what she was coming up with.

"When she left home she'd observe some of her old patrons wearing garments made for them by other designers. This caused her to become very jealous. She couldn't stand to be left out so she finally came up with a couple of designs that were closer to accepted standards. She telecommed some one of the women she used to design for, and had them come over and see her new garments.

"Unfortunately, when the women arrived, and saw the clothes, they weren't impressed and decided to stick with other designers. This upset mother so much that she stopped creating. After getting over her anger, she felt sorry for herself, and then became ill over the whole matter."

Rhia became outraged, surprising Andar with the scorn in her voice, "This is so unfair! Mama was doing so well for so many years! I am really starting to doubt Jirmak's motives!"

"Shhh, not so loud," Andar said, "Honey, Jirmak is royal staff. I'm sure her intentions are good. It's just that we have to get used to some of these new changes. Mother just needs time to recover. I'm sure that when she gets better she'll try her hand at designing again."

Rhia held back from shouting and spoke in a normal tone, "How do you know this, Father? She now has to follow a set of rules that are modifying her creativity. I've never seen her look so bad."

Andar tried to comfort Rhia by moving closer to her and holding her in his arms. She hugged him back but didn't feel as much affection as usual. Their realities had grown further apart.

"Father, I don't like this," Rhia said, standing up, and walking out of her room, back toward her parents' bedroom. Andar followed after her, as she stood at the edge of their doorway, and sadly looked inside at her mother. Then she walked up to the bed where Silka lay with her eyes shut. She put her hand on Silka's right arm and talked tenderly to her, "Mama," she said, as Silka gradually opened her eyes. "Mama, I can't stand seeing you like this. You need to stop doing this to yourself. You're much too talented to be lying here. Oh, Mama." She broke into tears, leaned down on the bed next to Silka and wept for a while. Water from her eyes left marks on Silka's gown. Then Rhia lifted her head up. "Mama I love you. You are such an incredible artist, with so much to offer. I know that designing is your favorite art form, but you're also very talented in other areas. You taught me so much when I was younger."

Silka brightened up a little bit after hearing her daughter's words, and then spoke to her in a soft voice. "Rhianna, my spirit of hope and inspiration, I've had a pretty fulfilling life, and even if I don't make it, I am still thankful for the things I've experienced here on Athena. Silk making was my main contribution, and if I can't do that, I feel pretty worthless."

"Is there anything at all that I can do for you?" Rhia asked in desperation.

"Just continue creating the works of beauty that you always have. This will make me happy."

Andar walked over to them and pulled Rhia away from her ill mother. "Rhia, she needs her rest. Come on, Darling," Andar said as he walked her out of the bedroom and down to the meal room.

They both sat at the table with the golden circle in the middle of it that contained the picture of Andar receiving a medal from the Empress. Rhia looked at it, realizing she'd lost some of the pride she used to feel for her homeland, and all it stood for.

"Father, things on Athena haven't felt right for a while. There are so many new restrictions. I'm sick of it! I know all these new changes are supposed to be for the good of the people, but I've seen sights that aren't native to Athena.

"And now I come to see mother and she has never looked worse! There's something awfully wrong! She's suffering from one of the most deadly afflictions there is!"

"Rhianna, the Empress and her staff have never done us wrong before. Why would they start now?"

"I don't know, but this all seems to have occurred when the Empress left and Jirmak brought in a bunch of officials from other planets."

"Yes, I know that, Rhia, but these neighbors are our allies and have the good of all in mind. I don't think they would intentionally do anything to try and hurt us. Besides, Jirmak would be wise to this."

Rhia couldn't stand listening to any more of her father's reasonableness, and stood up, "I'm going to be leaving now!"

"Rhianna, stop it! You've got to get hold of your senses!"

Rhia headed for the front entranceway to the house. Andar followed. "Rhia, wait! I don't want you to leave so soon! I hardly ever see you anymore!"

She stopped and turned and saw the longing look on Andar's face and numbed her feelings for him, "I have to go father. There's too much sorrow around here!" She turned her back on him and continued walking in the direction of Thaur's stable.

"Thaurus! Thaur! Where are you?" she said, walking into the stable. He wasn't there. "Thaurus! Thaurus! I told you to wait around here for me. Where have you gone? Come here now!" she yelled, knowing that she shouldn't be raising her voice so angrily, but didn't care.

It was not like Thaurus to just wander away from where she instructed him to wait. She couldn't figure out what he was up to. Rhia walked out toward the precipice that he normally took off over when he flew away from Alta. He wasn't there, either.

"Thaurus! Thaurus!" she called again. She went over to a big crystal rock near a large blue tree, and sat down on it. She started feeling exasperated, and tried to calm herself down. She sat and thought about some of the old places she and Thaur used to go to when they lived on Alta.

Rhia went over to a bright rainbow colored stream that trickled over transparent rocks. She remembered how Thaurus used to go to that spot and make himself blend in with the colors of the rainbow by doing a trick that he learned on Magic Isle. Some of her tension abated momentarily when she got a picture of her multi-colored horse and how funny he looked. He wasn't there, however, so she continued her search.

She walked to the house of one of her old neighbors who had a horse that Thaur used to like to visit, and checked to see if he was there. The Athenians who lived there said they hadn't seen him.

Rhia continued strolling along, until she came to the outskirts of Alta. She was getting more and more discouraged. With the homes of the village far behind, she looked in front of her and saw Taboo Forest, the distant wooded area that was not trespassed by anyone because of the sand traps there.

Rhia remembered a couple of times when Thaur, who had a mind of his own, had decided he was going to disappear from her and go hide in the forest and visit his animals friends. After having exhausted her resources as to where else he might be, she suddenly had the funny feeling he might have traveled into this dangerous area for some reason. Rhia looked for signs of Thaur's presence. Staring at the ground like a detective, she spotted some hoof prints. "Thaurus, where are you?" she asked aloud, looking between a row of tall red trees.

Hating to step beyond safe bounds into a place she'd never been Rhia felt she had no other choice. She hesitated for a while, knowing that she'd have to be extra careful not to allow herself to slip into the dangerous traps. She walked toward the trees, and was dwarfed by their giant size as she cautiously wandered inward toward the heart of the forest. She was glad it was still light so she could watch the ground below and test it before stepping on the wrong spot.

She continued on, passing shiny green rocks that sparkled with diamond chips. She gingerly stepped on the narrow margins of red dirt that surrounded patches of blue grass. Rhia started to regret coming into the forest when she got to a spot where she was surrounded by nothing but grass. She stopped for a moment as her heart raced on. "Should I stay or turn back?" she thought aloud. Compelled by her concern for Thaurus, she moved on, taking chances on whether she'd be eaten up by a sand trap or not. Pointing one dainty foot, she tiptoed out on the grass. Then she put her foot down, and felt solid ground beneath her. She was relieved, as she told her other foot it was safe to follow. As she stood on a safe island in the middle of the grassy spot, she leaped to a trail of red dirt, knowing that there wouldn't be a trap there.

Approaching a patch of tall purple flowers, she heard a rustling in the trees and was startled, "Thaurus. Is that you?" she asked. Then she saw a small, striped animal, known as a zeela, come out from behind some bushes. He walked over to her and she pet his back. "Hey, what are you doing in here?" He just gave her a blank look.

"By the way, have you seen a white winged horse with a gold mane?"

He shook his head, as if to say "no," and then went on his way.

Rhia suddenly sensed that Thaurus was nearby, and that he had some reason for leading her into the woods. She just couldn't understand why he didn't wait for her.

She kept walking until she came to a break in the dense growth. She stepped out into an area of bald, blue dirt, and as she moved along, she noticed a funny looking imprint in the sand. There were three round indentations that formed a large triangle. She had never seen anything like it before. She was sure it was too large to be any kind of animal paw.

With puzzled thoughts, she kept going until she came to another patch of trees. Spotting a narrow dirt path, she started treading on it. Her attention was still on the odd imprint in the sand as she walked. She failed to notice that she'd put her foot right on a red patch of grass, which started pulling her leg into it. She quickly took both hands and grabbed her leg out as fast as she could, before it had a chance to suck her in. This scared Rhia, and made her aware of the fact that she needed to continue to be very watchful of her moves.

Rhia heard some tree branches moving, and just as she was about to call out for Thaurus, she heard the sound of a voice. Then she heard another voice. It sounded to her like two people talking. She looked around to see where they were coming from, but saw nothing. Then she moved in the direction of the voices. As they grew louder, an eerie feeling came over her. Instead of rushing out to where the people were, she chose to remain hidden from their sight. She looked through a small crack between a couple of trees, and could barely make out two figures in front of her. Then she noticed there was some sort of vehicle to the left of the two unclear figures. It didn't appear to be a space rider or a beam glider. Moving closer to the vehicle, she noticed that it rested on three legs that formed the shape of a triangle, and realized that it was the same kind of ship that was responsible for making the indentations that she had previously seen in the blue dirt.

Desperate to get a better view, Rhia wove her way around the trees that were blocking her vision, still careful not to be seen. She didn't quite understand the reason for her fear. She just sensed that she didn't dare make herself known. Then, quietly wading through tall purple grass that was nearly as tall as she was, Rhia finally came to a spot behind a tree, where she was able to peer out and get a better look at the people in the woods. Her jaw practically fell off of its hinges as she saw and heard something that shocked her like never before. There in front of her was her old friend Vaadra, talking to a Black Knight!

"Their defenses are weakening. It won't be much longer before others can come in unnoticed," said Vaadra to the Knight.

"That may be true, but I'm getting impatient. There are still Knights that don't want to come near this place. Still makes them sick. I guess they'll just have to wait till things get worse here."

As the two of them stood there talking, Rhia could hardly believe that one of her best friends had disaffected and taken on the dark color of the enemy. Rhia knew there was something suspicious about Vaadra's mission on Sadan taking so long, but she had no idea why. She wondered if they'd given her some kind of hypnotic command.

Her thoughts were interrupted by a beam glider, which was landing on a small bald spot of sand near Vaadra and the Knight. A familiar figure of a man approached them. "Libol, what took you so long? We can't remain in these woods after dark, you know. Could get swallowed up in a sand trap."

"Hey, I'm aware of that, Slandor. That's why we have our meetings here in the first place, though. No one else dares enter these parts."

"You'll be happy to know that Jirmak has been robotically following my suggestions. Good thing we hypnotized her back on Sadan. You never know when these officials can be used as handy traitors."

Rhia had known something was odd about Jirmak, but she never dreamed this was what it was! She was puzzled as she looked at the man being called Libol who carried a small laser gun and had a body that was identical to that of Beldar, the official from Sadan, who had been helping out with inspections at The Meadow!

Slandor looked Libol up and down, "Gee, I kind of like you in that dead guy Beldar's body better than that other one you usually wear," he said while laughing snidely.

Libol gave him a dirty look. Rhia was still trying to make sense of all this. The more she listened the more she realized how right she was about the recent crisis she had perceived on Athena.

"Yeah, well, I might have to wear this disguise for a while, so I'm glad you like it," he said blowing Slandor a kiss. "Thanks to Vaadra, after I knocked off the real Beldar she was able to do her hocus pocus stuff on me that she learned at some Magic Isle place.

She made me look just like him. That way, I had it easy coming here for that Creative Council thing. I do admit that it's been a bit tough tolerating all this art stuff. But thanks to Vaadra, I learned how to fake like I had good intentions. That was the hardest thing I had to do, but so far, so good." Libol looked around him, "Bring any more disaffected Athenians with you, Slandor, or just Vaadra?"

"No, she's it for now. The others have gone back to Trod to learn more about our covert tactics. We may use them for missions on some of the other planets. They're quite valuable to have around, with their ability to create illusions and things. Some have agreed to use their little songs and artwork to promote our cause in a nice logical way to leaders of other planets. And speaking of leaders, how are the rest of the pseudo officials doing? I have to report back to Kilbor."

"They're doing just fine, old boy. All of them are playing their roles quite nicely, almost as good as me. We're weakening this place. Those artists are starting to fight amongst themselves," he said with a wicked laugh. "They don't even know anything is wrong," Libol said. He walked over to Vaadra and ran one of his index fingers across her chin as a sign of feigned affection. "All these years, all we needed was someone like Vaadra to come along and help us out."

Vaadra had a cold, wicked look on her face, which made her countenance appear much different than the bright, cheerful Athenian that Rhia once knew. As she spoke, she answered the question in Rhia's mind as to why she turned into a traitor. "Yeah, well, I just expect to get my reward for what I've done. You know I want my own planet, with a whole bunch of people under my command. I don't want to wait forever, either."

"Yes, yes, my pretty one. We promised that for helping us get into Athena, we would reward you in that way. Of course, if you are in a big hurry, I could always knock off one of the planetary leaders, and you could just disguise yourself in their body and," Libol stopped as Vaadra cut him off.

"You know I don't want to do that! I want my own place, with disaffected members from other planets that want to have a place of their own. You said you'd help me to round them up."

Rhia's eyes opened wider as she recalled a time many years ago when Vaadra had first mentioned she wanted to rule her own planet. At the time, Rhia only thought this was slightly odd, as she couldn't understand how Vaadra would want to leave Athena. Rhia never imagined the true motives behind Vaadra's communication.

"Of course. We will do this," Slandor assured her. "I know that you want your own planet, just like Zeena has. Meanwhile, why don't you get out of hiding, and go back home to your brother and father."

Vaadra looked down at the ground, experiencing some suppressed guilt, "I don't know about that. I'm not ready to face them."

"Well, that's up to you. But it may be a little while before we can assist you."

"Hey, and besides, maybe you'd like to go and meet your brother's new wife," Libol said with a sickeningly sweet smile on his face.

"What?"

"That's right. Ladaar married that old Rhia friend of yours."

Vaadra was shocked and numb, all at the same time. "How do you know?"

"The two love-birds entertained us on Placid Isle before the Council thing. They were introduced as husband and wife. Isn't that cute?"

"Oh, I see," said Vaadra, looking through her drug fog at a pleasureful memory of a time when she and Ladaar and Rhia were creating together at The Meadow. She tried not to let any sadness penetrate her numbness. "I'll think about going back," she said with reluctance.

"Speaking of Zeena, that was a very clever trick you pulled off, getting her to leave Athena. What did you do exactly?" asked Libol, addressing Slandor.

He laughed in a wicked, arrogant way, overly proud of his tactics. "You like that, huh? I just used an old scheme I'd learned from Kilbor. Just got the leader of Atranus convinced that he and his people were going to be invaded by the people of Gora. It's simple. Then I told the Atranium leader not to believe the leader of Gora if he denied such a planned invasion. I told him to tell the leader of Gora that the Atraniuns would come invade them before they got a chance to get to Atranus. Anyway, there's quite a bit more detail, but you get the picture. In any case, it's what had to be done to get the Empress to leave Athena at a time when she should have been here for that Creative Council deal."

"That's great, we got ol Zeena to disappear, and with that new shuttle station trick, more Athenians will be shipped to distant planets," Libol said with joy.

Rhia had heard enough to get the idea of what was going on. All she could think about was informing the Empress of her findings as soon as possible! As Rhia stood eavesdropping she felt something rubbing her on the back of her right leg. She jumped and made a slight rustling noise in the grass. A little bura brushed against her.

"What was that?" Slandor fearfully asked. Rhia slid behind a large rock and sat down, hoping she wouldn't be noticed at all.

"Probably just some little animal. Don't be so fearful," Libol replied.

The little animal came back and sat next to Rhia. She nervously picked it up and held it in her hands. She saw that it just wanted some affection and was happy to be held by her. She let it go, and started to get concerned about finding Thaurus and sneaking out of the forest unnoticed. She thought he mustn't be far away, since this was the spot he had intended to lead her to. She slowly got up and hid behind a tree as she looked around trying to spot Thaur. Then, just as she was trying to walk carefully, she tripped on a tree branch that was lying on the ground. It snapped and caught the attention of Vaadra and the Knights. She saw them start to walk in her direction! Rhia quickly got up and ran and hid behind another large rock.

"There's no one here," Vaadra assured them. "I told you that nobody enters this forest. The only reason we're even here is because I used that sensor device on your spaceship to locate this hideout. Athenian ships don't have those mechanisms, so don't worry about it. It was probably just an animal that you heard."

Rhia froze in her hiding place.

The bura went up to Vaadra and rubbed against her leg. She picked him up. "See this. This is all you heard."

"Yeah, well that little ball of fuzz had me pretty scared," Slandor said, as he took the bura from Vaadra. He held it by the scruff of its neck and it got frightened. Then he threw it down on the ground and stepped on it with one of his heavy black boots. The animal squealed in pain under all the impact.

"Stop it!" yelled Libol, "Leave the animal alone."

Libol's anger was so strong that Slandor removed his foot, and the bura just lay there dying.

"Damn it, Libol, there you go being a whimp. What is it with you and animals? It's no wonder they didn't send you to Thora to do the testing on these critters. You probably would have taken them all back to Trod to keep as pets."

"Shut up, Slandor! Enough of your sarcasm."

Rhia, who was sitting in fear, had heard what was going on and got infuriated. She couldn't stand to see an innocent animal tortured like that.

Vaadra and the Knights turned and went back to their meeting spot, and Rhia pulled herself up and continued moving back in the direction in which she originally came. She realized that the little bura losing his life might have saved hers. She thought that if the Knights hadn't seen him and assumed he was the source of the noise, they might have further investigated the area and could have found her.

Rhia moved as quickly and silently as possible. She came to a blue, grassy area and ran across it, not even thinking about the traps. Before she knew it, she was going down, and fast! She restrained from screaming, lunged her arms forward and grabbed hold of a tree trunk. She played tug of war with the magnetic sand. Finally, she won. Her pink gown, which had taken a sand bath, was now dull gray. She made sure she was more careful as she made her way back into a thickly wooded area. Rhia fled in fear as she heard some footsteps coming toward her faster than she could get away from them. She came to a large rock and ducked behind it, frozen and still, wondering if perhaps some other Knights in the forest had spotted her. Remaining as still as the boulder she hid behind, she was terrified as she felt the presence of someone near her. She knew that she had been discovered, and didn't know what to do. Then, knowing it was too late to try and run, she mustered up some bravery. Feeling trapped, she knew that all she could now do was to confront her pursuer, and blast he or she with the words that had previously been tied up in a knot inside of her. Rhia slowly lifted herself up. Just as the top of her head came up over the top of the rock, she heard a step on her right. She looked down at the ground, and there in front of her was the hoof of her pet Thaurus! He had been very careful not to startle her too much, for she may have screamed, causing the Knights to become hot on the trail to find her.

When Rhia saw Thaur she jumped up, experiencing great relief, hugged him, and climbed on his back. He quickly led her out of the maze that he'd gotten her into. When they got outside of the woods, and were on safe ground in Alta, Thaurus walked over to a small pond, and put his head down to take a drink. Then he lifted his head up and Rhia talked to him, "Oh, Thaurus, if it hadn't been for you, it would have taken me quite a while to find out what was really going on here in our homeland," she said as she hugged his neck. "But one thing I want to know is why didn't you wait for me outside of Mother and Father's house? Did you think I wouldn't follow you here? You had to pretend you were missing in order for me to come into the woods, didn't you?"

He nodded as if to agree with her. He knew her all too well.

"Okay, Thaurus. I'm sorry I was angry at you. You did the right thing, leading me in there. Right now, time is of the essence. I've got to do something about this right away."

Thaur started walking in the direction of Rhia's parents' home, thinking that she may want to tell them what occurred in the woods.

"No, Thaur! I don't want to go there. Mother is in very bad shape. That's all she needs is to know that a couple of Knights are hiding out in the woods of Alta, and that my old best friend is a traitor! And Father, well I don't know if he'd believe me. We must go back to the North Valley right away!"

Thaur understood and obeying Rhia's command, took her back. All Rhia could think about was how she had to help undo the injustice that had been done to her mother and the others on Athena.

Chapter 9

Riding anxiously home to the North Valley, Rhia calculated a plan for getting through to the Empress on Atranus. She needed to get a special telecomm code number in order to reach Zeena, which only certain palace staff had access to. She knew that she wouldn't be given the number, or even allowed to come to the palace, without a very good reason. If she let her newly found secrets slip out to the staff at Etherea, she could be considered some kind of liar or traitor.

Rhia insisted that Thaurus travel at breakneck speed. He complied, breaking his old flying record of their trip to Alta. When they arrived at the palace in North Valley, Thaur went to the courtyard to rest, and Rhia ran to Klar's home to get her assistance.

"Klar, Klar. Are you there?" Rhia called as she walked down a corridor that led into the heart of the large home, where Klar lived by herself. Rhia hurried past a picture on a wall of a handsome man with white hair and purple eyes. It was Klar's six hundred-year-old husband, who had recently passed away. Next to his picture was a painting of Klar, who was now about four hundred. She passed a room with a triangular doorway and called again, "Klar, Klar."

As she stepped anxiously upon the marbled floor, Rhia heard the footsteps of someone walking through the front entranceway.

"Rhia, I am here," the voice of Klar said. Rhia stopped in her tracks and turned around. Rhia took Klar by the hand and led her to a large red silken couch in the hallway.

"Klar, is anyone else in your home right now?"

"No. Why? I have never seen you like this. What on Athena is going on?"

"I will tell you in a minute," Rhia said, scuttling to shut the entranceway door and return to face Klar who sat speechless, just gaping at Rhia.

There were a few seconds of silence as Rhia carefully chose her words, "Klar, there is something I must tell you that you cannot reveal to anyone else on this entire planet. This is highly confidential and I need your Athenian oath that you will not disclose what I tell you," Rhia insisted, referring to a vow that missionaires took when given secret data regarding planets where they were doing missions. They were often only allowed to expose data to select individuals.

"But Rhia, we are not on a mission, and..."

Rhia cut in. "Klar, I know, but you've got to trust me on this. I need your vow because of the nature of what I have discovered."

Feeling the impact of Rhia's words, Klar went along with her desires, "All right Rhia," she said, holding her right hand up to her forehead, symbolizing that the spirit residing in her body would hold true to her promise. She then recited these words, "Under the trust vested in me as an Athenian missionary I pledge that I will not impart to anyone the words given to me in confidence by Rhianna of the North Valley."

Klar removed her hand from her forehead and impatiently awaited the message from Rhia.

"Klar, the Knights have started to covertly invade Athena," she paused.

Klar was shocked, and thought of asking a million questions, but just let Rhia continue.

"You're probably wondering how I know this, and I'll tell you," Rhia said as she went on to tell her about the conversation in Taboo Forest.

"I never thought we could be so tricked! These Knights want to make a scarcity of opportunities for us to create publicly, and to put us into competition. In other words, they want to destroy our strong united team and make us fight one another! And if that isn't enough, the whole reason for the shuttle station was really for getting many of us to leave our planet, making it even easier for them to come in and slyly wreak havoc!"

Rhia paused. Klar, whose temperature had been rising while Rhia talked, took a deep breath.

"At first I was reluctant to believe you, but then when you spoke of the effects that have been produced since the new rules have been out, I saw it! I've recently had the type of disagreements with fellow Athenians that I'm not used to having. In all the hundreds of years that I've lived here, I've never felt so out of sync with others. And here I was, just thinking it must be me, and I'm growing older and all, and trying to figure out all kinds of reasons for this. But it's not me at all. This is the very tactic they've often used to destroy other civilizations! How could we fall for it?" she asked. The wind, which had been whipping outside the window before, started to scream louder.

"It's that old weakness. We trust our leaders too much. But they aren't perfect."

"Oh Rhia, this leads to the worst kind of destruction imaginable. I don't have any qualms about improving my skills, but I want to be able to choose my style and what I decide to communicate in my artwork!"

Rhia was glad that she got Klar to so quickly understand what was going on. She knew she had to make haste and get on with the next step of her plan. "So, my good friend, now that you get the gruesome picture, I need your help."

"How? Why have you come to me? What can I do?"

"I need to contact the Empress immediately and tell her of my observations."

"But Rhianna, there must be other Athenians who can see that something is awfully wrong here! Don't you think we should try and get a group together and..."

Rhia cut in, "I don't know about that. My own mother, who is very ill, won't really even take a look at what is going on! And my father won't look at the fact that Jirmak may be doing the wrong thing. Then there are all those others I've seen that are so wrapped up with trying to impress the royal staff, or arguing with each other, that I just don't know how many people are aware of the situation at all. The only solution is to get Zeena's telecomm code number on Atranus and communicate to her directly!"

"And you need me to help with this?"

"Yes, I do. I need a connection at Etherea."

Klar thought about her daughter who worked at the palace, "So, you want to go through Alandra?"

"Yes, I need her help. I must let the Empress know what is going on behind her back!"

"But, I don't know that Alandra has access to the codes or permission to reveal them even if she does have access. How are we going to get her to help us without putting her in danger? Besides, I don't know what her present views are regarding the current scene on Athena. Being palace staff, she may not readily accept your words about the Knights, and..."

Rhia cut in, "Klar, there's no time to waste. You must telecomm Alandra right away. If we cannot safely utilize her to get the code, or if we can't confide in her without risk, then we will have to find another way to get the number. The main thing I need right now is to use her as a palace connection. Then you can let her know that we have a message to get to the Empress. We don't have to tell her what the message is, but just that we must communicate to the Empress in private."

Unfortunately, as Klar suspected, Alandra wasn't the one who had direct authority to give out the code. She told her mother that the only way to get the number was to get final approval to communicate with the Empress from a staff member who was the code keeper and relay officer for the Empress. To do this, Klar would have to come to the palace. The only thing Alandra could offer was to do the initial screening of Rhia and Klar, and then if their request was approved, turn them over to the code keeper for final approval. They were determined to do whatever it took to get the number.

Rhia and Klar had no choice but to go straight to Etherea. Alandra told them that she could meet with them the next day before her work shift, as it was already quite late, and nearing rejuvenation time. She could then arrange for them to see the code keeper. Klar told her that they wanted to fly to Etherea that night, as the message was very urgent. Even though Alandra warned them that the code keeper may be retiring by the time they got there, Klar insisted upon coming anyway and not waiting until the following day. Alandra agreed, as this would also give her a little more time to spend with her mother, who she hadn't seen for a while.

Rhia and Klar headed immediately for Klar's beam glider and took off in the direction of the palace. When they arrived, they were greeted at the doorway by a guard who questioned them as to why they were there at such a late hour. Klar informed him of their meeting with her daughter. The man looked at them out of the corner of his eye, while punching Alandra's office number into a small box.

Rhia did her best to calm the nervousness that nearly caused her body to shake. Alandra's voice came through the speaker on the box and the guard informed her that her guests had arrived. The guard led them into the palace, and took them to a reception area, where he instructed them to be seated until Alandra came to receive them. As they sat still and quiet, having walked into the teeth of the trap on Athena, Rhia noticed a couple of people walking by them that were definitely not Athenians. She couldn't help but wonder if the bodies they wore were those of actual inter-planetary officials, or those of dead ones that had been knocked off by the Knights. While her thoughts lingered on this question, a tall Athenian woman with long red hair approached them. She looked somewhat tired and pale, but seemed to brighten up when she saw Klar.

"Mother," she said, as Klar stood up and embraced her.

"Alandra, darling. It is so good to see you. You have no idea how good," Klar replied, "I want you to meet Rhianna, my friend and next door neighbor."

Rhia stood up and embraced Alandra warmly. After exchanging greetings, Alandra led them up a long golden staircase to an office. She then shut and locked a solid silver door behind her, giving the three of them privacy. Alandra took a seat behind one of three large silver desks in the room, and Klar and Rhia seated themselves in chairs in front of the desk.

"Now, tell me Mother, what is all this urgency about? You were in such a hurry to get over here, that I hardly got a chance to question you further."

Klar quickly glanced over at Rhia, thinking of what to say.

"Before I tell you darling, I'd like to ask you something," Klar said, knowing that it was best to avoid answering her question at that point and to find out if she and Rhia could confide their secrets to Alandra safely.

"What is it?"

"Tell me dear, how effective are the new programs that Jirmak is implementing?"

"Why do you ask, Mother? Don't you see the results in your daily life?"

"Oh, yes. Well I can see to some degree what is happening, but since you are staff here, I thought maybe you could tell me more about the overall effect on the planet."

"I suppose I can give you a brief summary of the results from my understanding. First off, I can tell you that the shuttling of Athenians to other planets is working quite well. Many people have been transported out to other locations in the galaxy and are gathering new information to bring back here to put into use in the expansion of our overall base of knowledge.

"As far as the plan to improve our artistic presentations, I hear from other staff that this is going quite well but have not been out to observe this directly. Being here in the palace most of the time, I don't get much of a chance to see what is really happening with the people. I know that there are not as many people taking part in the creations being done at some of the main spots on the planet. I suppose this is because they are at home improving their skills before going out and attempting to audition for public events."

"Are you no longer helping the Empress with mission briefings? You didn't used to work so many hours when you were doing that job. What is it you do now that keeps you occupied for so many hours Alandra?"

"Right now, I'm primarily doing research on the language and customs of other populations. This is so that when our people arrive to acquire knowledge, they can communicate with the natives.

Klar contemplated her next move. It was now clear to her that Alandra didn't have any awareness of the harmful effects being created. To try and convince her of what Rhia had seen in the woods could be a terrible mistake.

Alandra broke the silence, "Well mother, have I sufficiently answered your question?"

"Yes, yes darling. Thank you."

Alandra then asked the question that Klar and Rhia were hoping not to have to answer. "And what is it that is so important to tell the Empress that you came all the way to the palace for?" she asked. She then looked at Rhia who was sitting at the edge of her seat. Klar answered, "Darling, I cannot tell you. All I know is that the Empress needs this information right away."

Rhia jumped in. "In the past the Empress has insured me that it would be all right to communicate with her in private if there was an absolute need to do so."

"I wish I could help both of you out, but, unfortunately, I am not the one that can authorize this. Any communication to the Empress would have to be approved by Maron, who is her personal communication relay officer. I'm not saying that you cannot get in touch with her, but you must understand that because of the nature of the project she is on, she cannot be disturbed by unnecessary interruptions. The only way to determine whether a message is vital or not is to inform Maron as to its contents so that he can decide if it's important enough to give approval to talk with her. If only you could tell me what this information is that you are keeping to yourself, perhaps I could direct you to the correct personnel to help you out. It would be easier to get through to Jirmak than the Empress. Is there some reason you cannot inform her of the data you have?"

"Yes, Alandra, there is. This is something specifically for the Empress," Rhia said, trying to hide her frustration, "Alandra, you have worked with missionaires."

Alandra nodded.

"You know that sometimes things come up which can only be revealed to certain people because of their confidentiality and that there is a risk in disclosing these things to anyone other than specifically designated personnel, right?"

"Yes. I am aware of this fact, but you are not now on a mission, and without getting any data, it is hard for me to see the relevance of informing the Empress specifically. The staff here are all very competent and trustworthy."

Rhia thought, "If you only knew."

Klar then addressed her daughter, "Believe me, Alandra, we are not trying to hold this secret from you because we want to. It is just that Rhia and I know that there is a certain risk in what we have to say and..."

Rhia tuned out as her eyes were drawn to a small black box set on a table to the left of Alandra's desk. She could barely make out the engraved heading on the box, but focused her eyes more acutely and read the words "code number index." She jumped into the conversation during a pause by Klar. "Alandra, do you personally have the number of the Empress?"

Alandra didn't answer for a few seconds, "Rhia, you are a very determined woman. I can appreciate this. I'm sure that your motives are good, but even if I did have the code, I could not give it to you. I will, however, inform Maron that you have passed my initial screening and that I would like him to see you both for final, direct approval. Of course, you will most likely have to give him more information than you have given me. This still does not guarantee that he will let you speak with the Empress in private, or at all for that matter, but at least you will have a good shot at it."

Klar gave a fleeting look to Rhia, who was trying to decide what to do next. Rhia then spoke, "So where is Maron now?"

"He is off duty at this time. I warned you that it might be too late to see him today. Since it is nearly rejuvenation hour, why don't we go and get some sleep. When we wake in the morning I will speak with Maron before he begins his daily duties and tell him you need to see him right away."

Rhia tensed up inside, knowing that the longer they put this off, the worse things would get. Then she started to wonder if she could really convince the Empress of her findings in the woods, and if Zeena would have doubts about what she was being told. She knew she shouldn't be having thoughts like that, as she had the truth in her hands, but for some reason she was losing some self-confidence.

"All right Alandra. If this is what we have to do, then we will wait until morning," said Rhia

"Very well," said Alandra. "Now, since it is so late, I will not be able to get you your own rooms. You will have to stay with me in my quarters. Fortunately, I do have an extra sleeping cushion which will be big enough to accommodate both of you."

The three of them got up, and walked toward the heavy silver door, and Alandra let them out. Then, as she shut the door, Rhia saw her take a small red key out of a pocket in her gown and lock it, then put it back in her pocket. They walked a short distance down a hallway. The palace was very quiet, and Rhia didn't notice anyone in the area where they walked.

Alandra whispered, "We must be quiet. It is past the sleeping time of most of the staff."

Klar and Rhia nodded at her.

When they got to Alandra's room, Rhia saw Alandra take the red key out of her gown pocket and place it on a crystal stand next to her bed. Rhia was exhausted from such a long, wearing day but formulated an idea of something she wanted to do which would keep her from going to sleep right away.

Alandra opened a red crystal closet door in her room and pulled out a tiny white cushion. She placed it on the floor on the side of the room opposite from where her single bed was.

Klar smiled, breaking some of the seriousness in the air as she looked at Alandra who stood next to the little bed. "Darling, I know that Rhia and I are not the tallest of Athenians, but I don't even know if either of us could fit our big toes on that cushion."

Alandra smiled back at her mother who stood beside her. "Well, in that case let me see what I can do for you," she said as she waved her hand over the mattress several times until it grew into a bed that was at least as big as the one that Rhia shared with Ladaar at their home.

"Much better," said Klar.

Rhia yawned as she looked at the comforting bed. Alandra glanced at her, and noticed the heaviness of Rhia's eyelids, "You must be very sleepy,"

"Yes, I sure am. It's been a very long day. Gone by slower than usual too."

"Well then you should fall fast asleep and get considerably reinvigorated here. The palace is a very calming place to be, and guests that come here say that they sleep quite well, often better than usual."

"That sounds great. I could use a nice rest," Rhia said.

Alandra then took two gowns out of a drawer and handed one to Rhia and one to Klar. "Here is some sleepwear for you."
After they were all in their gowns, Klar hugged and kissed her daughter, who then went to her bed. Alandra lay down and instantly shut her eyes.

Klar and Rhia crawled on top of the cushion and lay down. Rhia was glad that Alandra's bed was so far away, which made her feel safe enough to whisper something to Klar without being overheard. "Klar. Don't fall asleep yet. I need to tell you something in a few minutes, once Alandra has left her body for rejuvenation."

Klar nodded, and waited with Rhia for Alandra's body to emit a soft light around it, indicating that she had left for her sleep revitalization period. After this signal appeared, Rhia inched closer to Klar and spoke quietly. "Klar, I am going to get the key to Alandra's office that she keeps on her bed stand. Then I'm going to go to her office and get the code number of the Empress. There's a little black box on a table in her office that reads "code number index."

Klar didn't say anything for a moment.

"Rhia, you are taking a big risk. We don't even know that she has the number."

"I have a strong feeling that she does. If she didn't have it, why wouldn't she just have said so when I questioned her?"

"I don't know, Rhia. That's a good point," Klar said. She heard Alandra stirring in her bed and touched Rhia on the arm and put her right index finger up to her lips. Both of them waited until Alandra stopped moving and then Klar spoke, "If you are going to do this, just wait a little while. Her glow has faded a bit. Give her enough time to cause her body to radiate again, and then make sure the glow remains steadily bright for about five minutes. You are already playing very dangerously, but if you insist on getting the key, then do as I say."

Rhia agreed, and then worked to fight off her own exhaustion, forcing herself to stay awake long enough to make her next move. She knew that this could mean the fatal difference between getting to the Empress and not doing so. After all, there was no guarantee that Maron was going to buy some story that she and Klar made up about why they needed to communicate to the Empress. Even though Rhia had anxiety about this risky strategy of hers, she wasn't about to back off.

Klar had been keeping a watchful eye on Alandra, and when the right time came, she nudged Rhia and informed her that Alandra was sound asleep. Rhia then quietly got off the cushion and walked over to the table where the little red key was. She carefully picked it up and slipped it into her gown pocket. She then tiptoed over to the door that led to Alandra's room and gently opened it, insuring that no sound was made. She gazed at Klar who had her eyes open, and fixed on Rhia's every move. Then she shut the door and proceeded down the dark hallway toward her destiny.

When she got to the silver office door she looked around and didn't see anyone. She took the shiny red key out of her pocket and unlocked the door. She didn't realize how heavy the door actually was until she felt herself straining just to get it open. She went inside the dimly lit room and rapidly pulled the door shut behind her and locked it. Because of her haste, she accidentally allowed the door to close too fast, making a clicking noise as it shut. She hoped that no one heard it. She walked over to the small black box that rested peacefully on a table. Rhia reached out and attempted to pry open the box, only to find that it was locked tightly. As disappointment mounted inside of her, she refused to just turn around and go back to Alandra's room, defeated. Instead, she picked up the box and looked it over. There was a small keyhole in the back of the container. Perhaps there was a key somewhere in Alandra's office that would open it.

Doing a cursory glance around the room, she tried to spot any places where keys might be kept. She noticed a lone shelf that was mounted into one of the walls and towered about three feet above her head. It appeared that there was some sort of purple container atop the shelf. Rhia's instincts told her to get closer to it and examine its contents. It was well above her reach. She then got a chair to help her out. Stepping up on the chair, she reached an arm up and just barely clutched onto the receptacle, pulling it from the shelf and into both of her hands. Stepping down, she took the container and then placed it on the table where the black box was. She opened the lid that was securely placed on top of it. There inside was a colorful array of keys of various sizes and shapes. Rhia quietly took out one key at a time, examining each until she came to any that looked small enough to fit in the hole in the black box. There were five that looked like they might fit. She tried one key at a time, and after four of them failed the test, assumed that the last one was going to work the magic she'd been looking for. Placing the fifth key in the lock she twisted it to the left, then to the right, and much to her surprise, it didn't work! She panicked, as the odds were now starting to stack up against her. Still, she was not about to give up on her quest. Leaving the keys scattered on the table, she carefully walked around the room inspecting every nook she could find, to see if there was any other place where keys might be hiding.

Seeing nothing, she went back to the table with all the scattered keys, and dug through once more, hoping to find a small one that perhaps she had missed. Meticulously, she inspected the keys, pushing them around on the table while looking them over. While she was checking one of the keys, she managed to fumble and drop it on the floor. As she reached down to pick it up, Rhia noticed a small black slot on the side of one of the legs of the table. She saw a small, metal, shiny object poking its head up from inside the slot. Going along with her intuitions she put her index finger up against the metal head and pulled it up slowly, until she could grasp what turned out to be a little key. She took this potential new treasure and stuck it in the hole in the black box, turning it left, then right until, sure enough, the container opened!

There in the box were a bunch of neatly placed metal cards, all in planetary alphabetical order. Rhia's fingers scrambled through the cards until she came to "Atranus." Lifting out this card, she saw the code numbers of a couple of the officials from this planet. There was nothing on it that referred to a number where the Empress might be. Rhia further searched the box, hoping that perhaps she'd get a better reference point than the one she had. In the back of the box, Rhia saw a section that read "temporary codes." She looked at some of the cards and noticed names of various Athenians and numbers of where they could be reached while currently on mission. These, too, were in alphabetical order, this time by name of missionaire. Rhia looked in the "E" section, hoping to find a number for the Empress, but nothing was there. Then her fingers scurried to the back of the temporary code section and looked under "Z." There, in the back, on the second-to-last card was the name "Zeena," inscribed in the metal. It read "Empress Zeena, currently on Atranus. Code number v98*9**-89/^^~'~o^8."

Rhia took a blank metal card from the back of the box, and then pulled out an inscribing utensil that was inside the black box, and quickly copied the numbers and symbols down on the file card. Then she closed the box, and put the key back in its slot beneath the table. She cleaned up the mess she had made with the other keys, placing them all back in the purple container and placed it back on the shelf where she found it. Then she returned the chair, which she'd used as a stepping stool, to its proper position. She slipped the metal card, with the Empress' number, into her gown pocket. Then she exited Alandra's office, locked the door, and started walking back toward the bedroom. As she walked, she barely heard the sound of faint footsteps in the distance. Not daring to look behind her, she continued on. Then she got to Alandra's room and opened the door and quietly stepped inside. She started to shut the door from inside of the room and as she did, noticed a faint shadow that moved across the hallway. She couldn't make out who the figure was, but she worried for a moment that someone might have noticed her. She hoped that if someone did see her they just thought it was Alandra.

Rhia quickly shut the door and put the key back on Alandra's table and then lay down next to Klar.

"Did you get it?" Klar whispered to her.

"Yes," Rhia said proudly.

Klar squeezed Rhia's arm as a sign of approval, "Well, that was easy, wasn't it?"

"Of course," Rhia said, refraining from telling Klar exactly how "easy" it was. She'd save that story for later, after they left the palace.

The next day Alandra arranged for Rhia and Klar to meet with Maron early in the morning. Klar told Maron that they really needed to get in touch with the Empress but couldn't tell him what it was about. Maron kept insisting on knowing what the message was, because he couldn't give his consent to communicate without knowing the nature of the data himself, just as Alandra had warned.

Since Klar was no longer worried about being turned down, she made up a story. Klar told Maron that both she and Rhia had heard a rumor about possible trouble stirring up on planet Nera, the planet where Rhia had been on a mission in the past. Klar said that she thought the Empress might want to check into this matter herself, as she was the one who originally sent the missions out to Nera.

Maron asked Klar who the source of this rumor was, and Klar replied by telling him it was someone she had met in the Muse Fields recently. She couldn't remember the woman's name.

Just as Rhia and Klar suspected, their request got turned down, and they were told that there was no need to inform the Empress of such a matter. Jirmak was carefully monitoring any disturbances on other planets, and if there was anything serious enough to worry about, it would be looked into and handled.

Alandra was relieved to hear that the situation they were worried about was not as important as Rhia and Klar made it sound. She figured that their franticness was an over reaction to someone's gossip.

Chapter 11

ecause of Rhia, not only had Thaurus broken his all time speed record, but so did Klar as she raced back to the North Valley. She didn't know if her small vehicle could hold up under the two thousand mile an hour limit that she pushed it to. The speedometer was off its dial, and a shake could be felt in the vehicle.

When they arrived back at the North Valley, she and Rhia ran straight for the nearest telecomm in Rhia's house. Rhia took the metal card with the Empress' code and looked at it, then entered the code into the telecomm number keypad.

They anticipated seeing the face of Zeena appear on the screen, but as they waited, nothing occurred. Then, red letters flashed across the screen saying "Transmission failure. Please wait five minutes before re-entering code."

Rhia glanced at Klar with severe impatience in her eyes. The five minutes was the slowest she could ever remember spending in her life, even slower than when she was waiting for several hours to see Ladaar at Placid Isle after his return from the shuttle station project.

At the exact second that the time calculator on the telecomm signaled five minutes had passed, Rhia re-entered the code again. This time several green lines appeared across the monitor, and words flashed stating, "Connection in progress, please wait." Rhia had never tried to reach anyone on another planet before, and saw that it was taking a lot longer to get through than if she were simply trying to contact somebody locally on Athena.

After a few minutes, a green light started flashing on the screen and another message flashed before her, which read, "Connection made." The green light disappeared, along with some of Rhia's extreme anxiety.

"You did it!" Klar said with a sigh of relief.

"Now, let's just hope she's there."

A picture started to form on the screen, and Rhia, expecting to see Zeena's face, was let down when a picture of a man with bright orange hair and dark pink skin appeared. His yellow eyes nearly pierced through the screen as he gazed at Rhia.

"Greetings. How may I assist you?" asked the man, whose Atraniun language was instantly translated into Athenian through a device on the telecomm that allowed beings to communicate with each other, even though they spoke in different tongues.

"Greetings, I am Rhianna from the planet Athena. I wish to speak with the Empress Zeena, from my planet. This is the contact number I have for her. Is she there?"

"The Empress Zeena is in a consultation at this time and cannot be interrupted. My name is Ranu and I was assigned to receive any incoming messages that may be transmitted to her from outside of Atranus. What is it that you request of her?"

"I need to speak with her immediately about an emergency situation here on Athena."

"And what is the nature of this emergency?"

"I prefer not to say anything at this time," Rhia said, not wanting this type of message to be made from a relay point. "Please sir, there is a major crisis here in her homeland and I would not be telecomming over such a great distance if there was any other way this could be handled!"

Ranu felt a strong beam of sincere intention coming through from Rhia, and this prompted him to comply with her wishes, "Very well, I will see if she is willing to receive you. Please wait." Ranu understood that very few Athenians had access to Zeena while on Atranus, and if Rhia telecommed with such urgency then perhaps he had better get the Empress.

As they waited, a flashing light appeared on one of the incoming lines on the telecomm and carried with it a beeping sound. Someone was trying to get through, and normally Rhia would have put the current call on hold and taken the second incoming caller, but at this point she didn't want to take any chance of losing her only line to the Empress. She ignored the other signal. Several moments went by. The picture of Ranu came back on the screen, "Rhianna, the Empress wants to know why you have not gone to Jirmak if there is a crisis on Athena, and for what reason Maron gave approval for you to contact her directly on Atranus."

Rhia looked over at Klar and shut her eyes tightly for a couple seconds and then opened them. Ranu could see her frustration mounting.

"Please sir, tell her I cannot go to Jirmak, because of the nature of this message. I can only reveal this to her! This information is highly confidential!"

"My dear Rhianna, the Empress is in a very important conference which could determine the future of our planet, and she does not wish to be interrupted. If you can give me more specific information regarding the nature of your communication then perhaps I can be of more assistance. However, without further data, I'm afraid I will have to end this conversation, and go back to my other duties," Ranu said, tired of getting nowhere with Rhia.

Rhia was now desperate and felt she had no choice but to tell Ranu what was happening and just hope that the Empress would believe her. "Sir, I understand that the future of your planet is being determined at this time, but you must know that the future of Athena is at stake at this very moment also!"

Ranu's eyes grew wide, "Yes, and how is that?"

"We are being insidiously infiltrated by Black Knights. I cannot tell this to Jirmak or any of her staff, because they are being badly tricked by disguised Knights and wouldn't believe me! In fact the reason that the Empress left to come to Atranus was because of a conspiracy set up by Black Knights to plot your people against the Gorians. I uncovered this data by accidentally discovering a couple of Knights hiding out in a forest on Athena. They got onto our planet with the help of an Athenian named Vaadra, turned traitor while on a mission! She helped Knights to disguise themselves as planetary officials. One of them that I personally observed is named Beldar, whose real identity is Libol!"

Ranu was rapidly typing the information into a small communications device, which made it possible for him to relay the urgent message to the Empress. Ranu said that he would go back to Zeena and inform her of the information immediately. Klar and Rhia waited in dire anticipation.

Rhia had ignored the flashing light and beeping on the telecomm which persisted during her conversation with Ranu. Now that she was on hold, she got curious as to who was so anxious to get through. "Klar, could you do me a favor and go to the telecomm in my bed chambers and see if you can do a code decipher and get me the number of whoever is calling. In spite of the importance of talking with the Empress, I still don't want to miss any vital messages," Rhia said, thinking about her sick mother in Alta, and wondered if her father was trying to give her any news.

Klar complied.

Several minutes went by, and Rhia's attention was averted from the telecomm by the sound of footsteps coming in through the front entranceway of her home. Ladaar or Bern were probably coming back early for some reason. She ignored the steps and turned back to the telecomm. She jumped as she heard a familiar female voice.

"Hello, anybody home? Ladaar, father?"

Rhia's eyes remained glued to the telecomm as confused thoughts raced through her mind. "Should I tell Vaadra what I know of her right now, or should I feign ignorance? And what if she comes in and sees me talking with the Empress? How will she react?" Rhia wasn't sure what to do, but she did know that the most important thing at this point was to convince the Empress to come back to Athena. Rhia did and said nothing, except to wait diligently and unmoving in the position she was in.

The footsteps of Vaadra got closer and closer. Rhia felt an unwanted confrontation about to happen.

"Rhia, what are you doing here?" Vaadra asked, pretending to be surprised.

Rhia turned around and looked at her with tempered rage, "What am I doing here? Perhaps I should ask, what are you doing here?"

Vaadra was shocked, "What, what do you mean? I am back from my mission on Sadan and am home," she said as she looked around nervously. "I don't see Ladaar or Bern. Where are they?"

"They're not here," Rhia said as she heard a clicking noise on the telecomm and turned back to it. Then it ceased and she looked at Vaadra.

"Rhia, why aren't you happy to see me, old friend?"

"You've got that right. 'old friend.' That's exactly what I am. I don't remain befriended to traitors!"

Vaadra stood at the doorway trembling, and looking more ragged than Rhia had ever seen her. She couldn't imagine how Rhia could have ever found out, "What ever are you talking about?"

"Come on Vaadra, don't try and play games with me! You know exactly what I am saying. I'm not going to cater to your pretended ignorance, not when I know more truth about you than I care to admit!"

At that moment, Vaadra couldn't take any more, "Damn it, Rhia! So what do you know?"

"I know that you have willfully put your foot into the biggest sand trap there is. Even though your body is standing here in front of me, the spirit of Vaadra is sinking deep!"

Vaadra's wide bloodshot eyes just stared at Rhia blankly, as she tried to justify her actions.

"I only want more than I have. Is there anything wrong with that?"

"What's wrong is how you have been trying to get it. Those Knights aren't going to reward you. They are probably just using you in order to get what THEY want. Helping disguise those creatures as planetary officials so they can covertly sneak in here and having secret meetings in Alta with them is one of the highest acts of treason you could possibly commit!"

Vaadra couldn't stand any more of Rhia's verbal assaults so started wildly attacking her. "You think you're such a great Athenian. Well, Athena has its flaws and I don't see why I need to stick around on this planet when I could be where I want. I don't know how you ever found out about what happened in the woods at Alta, but my business has nothing to do with you. I don't care if I never see you again because you are no longer my friend either. In fact, when Slandor and Libol get here, I probably won't see you again."

"What are you talking about?" Rhia asked, She glancing quickly at the telecomm, which just remained silent.

"You're not going to get away with this, Rhia," she said with a wicked look. "They know you are here. You thought your little trick was so clever about slipping into the palace and getting the telecomm number of the Empress, but you can't sneak past the masterminds of the Knights. They are the cleverest organization in the galaxy, even smarter than the Athenians! Libol, or should I say Beldar, saw someone go into the office where the codes are and when he found out from Alandra and Maron who their little guests were, he instantly notified me, and got me to inform him as to where 'our' home was. He suspected you were onto him. You should just be glad that he was kind enough not to say anything about you breaking into Alandra's office! He spared you that humiliation. He simply was concerned about your request to telecomm the Empress. Of course he didn't for one minute buy the story that you and Klar told to Maron. Not when he knew perfectly well that Nera has been void of Knights, ever since you got his crew deported from that planet! And then.."

As Vaadra continued talking, Rhia tuned her out and heard the sound of Thaurus. It was the "urgent warning" noise that Rhia was familiar with, the same noise that told her she needed to go to Alta. Only this time his distress signal was for another reason. She sensed that the Knights were approaching and had no choice but to flee before they came in and attempted to kidnap her. She only hoped that Ranu did a good enough job of getting through to Zeena and convincing her of the tragedy on Athena. Rhia nervously picked up the code card with Zeena's number on it and put it in her pocket. She knew that if she got away from the Knights, she could try the Empress again later.

Rhia got up and started walking toward the back of the house, while Vaadra shouted after her, "Where are you going?"

Rhia said nothing, and Vaadra just stood silently, looking at the telecomm screen, trying to figure out if any contact with the Empress had been made yet. She saw that it was blank, and assumed that Rhia hadn't gotten through, but was probably about to dial her code number when she was interrupted.

Rhia quickly got to the room where Klar was and startled her as she tapped her on the back.

"Rhia, I just deciphered the code. It was Ladaar, trying to reach you. Did you get the Empress?"

"No, almost," she whispered, "but you must get out of here. Vaadra is here and the Knights are on their way. Libol discovered me sneaking into Alandra's office, and Vaadra led them here. They may be desperate enough to be carrying laser guns, and could come after you. You must flee. Exit the door of this room, and get your space rider and fly out of the North Valley.

Klar was scared, "But, the Empress?"

"Don't worry, I'll stay a little longer and see if she comes on the telecomm."

Klar obeyed Rhia's command and slipped out the door and ran to where her space rider was parked, and left.

Rhia's thoughts were flying at lightning speed, thinking of what to say to Zeena, and thinking about how she could escape from the Knights. She knew her time was running out. She heard the sound of footsteps coming down the long hallway, accompanied by a male voice. She now knew she had no other choice but to flee. Before she left, she flipped a switch on the telecomm that Klar had been sitting in front of. It was a 'body detection' device that would allow the Empress to view whoever was in the house, wherever they were, at the time that she came to the monitor.

Just as Rhia was about to exit out the same door that Klar left from, she heard the sound of Zeena's voice, "Rhianna, this is the Empress Zeena. I have received your information..."

Rhia swiftly ran back to the telecomm, "My dear Empress, there are two Knights in the house right now. You can see them for yourself. Please come back immediately. I must run away fast!" Rhia said as she heard Vaadra and Libol about to enter her room. She fled out the back door and was going to try and get to Thaur, but saw Slandor near him by the courtyard, carrying a laser gun.

Rhia ran as fast as she could, heading out toward a wooded area in the valley, hoping she would get away. Then she heard the sound of a beam glider coming in her direction. She had been spotted. The glider landed a few feet ahead of her, and then she changed directions, trying desperately to get away. The two Knights got out of the vehicle and were chasing her. Then she heard the sound of Thaurus' voice, as he ran. "Thaurus! Help!"

Thaurus was gaining speed, and Rhia turned and could see him on Libol's tail, about to attack him. But instead, Slandor turned to Thaurus and aimed his weapon at him, shooting him in the leg. Thaurus fell to the ground in pain! Then Slandor took another shot at Thaur, this time hitting him in a muscular thigh.

"No! No!" Rhia yelled, as she kept running until she came to an area with a steep cliff and realized she had nowhere else to run without going over the edge. She stopped and fell to the ground, out of breath. Crying loudly, she buried her face in her hands.

Then she lifted her head, and out of her blurry eyes saw Libol's two black boots. He was standing right beside her, and there behind him was Slandor!

"Nice try, my dear. Not bad for an amateur. But do you really think you can outsmart the most brilliant group of all?" Libol laughed wickedly.

"Be a gentleman Libol and help the lady up." Slandor said as Libol grabbed her by the arm and pulled her up. Rhia tried to resist him but he was too strong and she ended up standing against her own will while he held her limp arm.

"Oh look, you dirtied your gown. What a shame," Libol said as Rhia glanced at the front of one of her favorite blue dresses, made by her mother, and saw how stained it was. "So you thought you and your friend could just enter the palace and get away with your little plan. You almost did, too. Not bad for a couple of novice spies. In fact, you have lots of potential. Very good cover up. Trouble on Nera. Very good. But that is certainly a big joke isn't it? I've been waiting patiently for my chance to get revenge for what you did to me and the other Knights! And now here we are, face to face again."

A swell of rage emerged in Rhia. "You won't get away with any of this!"

"If you shut up, perhaps we may be able to work out a deal with you to make your future less miserable," Slandor said.

There was a moment of silence and then Slandor continued, "You know we could use someone like you on our team. You already have some of the basic spy tactics down, but of course we'd have to train you in more advanced techniques. And of course you'd have to learn some of our control procedures. I realize that this may be foreign to you, being an Athenian, and thinking that all you need to do is create art, and that this somehow gives you power," Slandor said in a resentful tone.

"Who are you trying to fool?" Libol added, as Rhia struggled to get her arm loose from his strong grip. "Now, now, you shouldn't try to escape, when you know that there is no way out for you."

"The Empress already knows about you and when she comes back to Athena it will be all over for you and the rest of your decoys!" Rhia yelled.

"I don't care about your damned Empress. By the time she gets all the way back from her little mission on Atranus, this planet will be known as Trod Two!"

Rhia spit in Libol's face. He wiped the annoying saliva from his cheek and went on, "There's no need to even discuss this now. You are the one who we are interested in at the moment. You have your choice. Either come and be part of our Empire, or suffer the consequences of a slow, painful death!"

As Libol gave her this choice, Slandor went to the space rider, and got a got a small electro-shock device. Rhia saw him return, carrying the mechanism that she had learned was used by the Knights to destroy the brain tissue of their victims, giving them chronic amnesia.

"I would rather die than become part of your group! Because as far as I'm concerned that would be a pain worse than death! You're asking me to commit the most treasonous act in the galaxy when you ask me to become a Knight. What you stand for is the opposite of everything I believe in! You may think that you are having some sort of victory by sneaking onto Athena, and holding me captive here. The fact is that you have been digging your spiritual graves for a long, long time! If I die now, I know that I'll still have my honor and that at least I will be reborn next lifetime with a clean conscience!"

Rhia stopped talking as she was drawn to the sight of Thaurus, struggling in pain, trying to get up to rescue her. Tears ran down her cheeks as she saw the agony he was in. She knew she couldn't just let him lie there suffering. "Please, I have one request, please. It has nothing to do with me," she cried.

Both Knights gazed at Rhia with a blank, questioning, look. Then she forced some of the most difficult words she'd ever spoken out of her mouth, "Shoot my horse!"

Slandor and Libol looked at each other as if to consult one another as to whether they should honor her request. Then Slandor smiled slyly as an idea occurred to him. "No. We couldn't kill such a nice animal. How could you do this to your pet? Shame, shame. If you won't come with us, then I think we'll take Thaurus instead. He'd be perfect for our experimentation projects. Of course he won't be able to walk or run again, now that I've disabled two of his legs, but we could certainly use him for drug testing, and other things. After all, he is only a soulless animal."

Rhia had so much wild fury for what Slandor was saying that she fought twice as hard as before to get away from his grip. "My horse is not going to be a traitor any more than I am!" she said while Libol loosened his hold on her slightly. He was tired of having to fight with her while she squirmed.

Libol felt a bit of sympathy for Rhia, but more so for Thaurus, and did something that angered Slandor. He granted Rhia's one last wish, and turned to Thaurus and fired the shot that ended his life. He hated to admit that his soft spot for animals caused him to spare Thaurus the misery of experimentation.

Rhia squirmed some more, and with intention stronger than Libol's grip, finally broke loose. She fell to the ground with exhaustion.

"Now dear Rhia. One last chance to save your own life, before we have to torture you slowly, the way we did to your pet,"

Libol said as he dug the heel of his boot into her lower back. He yanked her up and held her over the edge of the cliff. "You can't escape. You have nowhere to run." She looked down at what appeared to be over a two hundred foot drop. Libol again offered her the option that would save her life.

She struggled with Libol and screamed, "I would rather die with my integrity than live in treason!" She pushed against Libol and his hold on her slipped. Rhia fell over the precipice and took the step that saved her from what would have been a living death if she had chosen to keep her body alive.

Rhia felt herself falling rapidly, with a speed that exceeded that of the pink waterfall that was making its way over a cliff to her left. Falling, falling, falling. Downward she went and just as she was about to hit the ground below her, something happened. Everything around her disappeared and all she could see was sky and stars and planets. There, behind her, was the pink and turquoise planet that had been her home. She was now out of her body, sailing away from Athena.

She then encountered a very strange force field, one that she found herself fighting to get out of. Feeling like she was trapped in an electronic maze, she wondered if she'd ever make her way back into the physical universe. There in front of her was the image of a Knight. He was shooting her with some sort of energy beams from a weapon that caused her to surrender some of her spiritual powers, which had previously been intact on Athena. Fighting with all the might and intention she could muster up, she tried to make her way out of the deadly trap. She had the feeling she was losing control of her destiny.

She saw stars and planets as well as comets. All of these things increased in number as she traveled at a very rapid rate, forward in time, on and on and on and on into the future. She was lost and confused, not knowing where she would end up next. Then she saw planet Earth in the distance, and started moving closer and closer and closer to it. A light flashed, like lightning in the sky, and before she had time to think about anything, she came in for a landing on Earth, and found herself in her current body, that of thirty-seven-year old Nicole Jensen. She was standing on the hill at the Griffith Park Observatory, looking through the same telescope where she had inserted the magic coin that had taken her on the most incredible journey of her life. Glued to the eyepiece, she saw the words, "Time and space alteration completed. Normal operation of device resumed."

Part III - The Final Battle

Chapter 1

Nicole unglued her eye from the telescope. She slowly backed away from it, feeling very disoriented as she looked at the view in front of her. She gazed out at the lights of the city and stared at them for a couple of minutes, while adjusting to this old, familiar sight. As she stood staring into space, she didn't even notice that someone was standing behind her. She jumped at the tap of a finger on her shoulder.

"Sorry to startle you, Miss, but are you through with the telescope?" a man asked.

She looked at the chubby, older man with a bald head, and was speechless for a few seconds. She was barely able to get any words out of her mouth, "Yes..I um, I think so."

"What did you see in that thing, life on Mars or something?" the man asked as he snickered at his own comment.

"No, not there, no life there, but somewhere else, much farther away."

Nicole stepped away from the telescope and let the man take his turn. As she walked away, he turned and watched her for a moment as she clutched her cane and wandered aimlessly.

Nicole walked in circles, touching her body, checking it from time to time to make sure that it wasn't just going to up and disappear on her. Confused thoughts and feelings danced around in her mind as she tried to digest everything that had just occurred. She felt as if she'd just woken up from an incredible dream that had turned into a nightmare near the end, only she knew it wasn't a dream because she wasn't in her bed. She was on top of a hill several miles away from her home, much further than she could have ever walked in her sleep.

Nicole looked at her watch and saw it was eight-thirty. Only ten minutes had passed since she had put the magical coin in the slot! She looked to her left and saw the large dome-shaped building where only about twenty minutes ago she had asked the man at the information desk how to get to the "les." Her sense of time was so twisted that she now had to adjust to the fact that time was no longer stopped, but in fact was now continuing to march on into the future. It had almost seemed to her as if time itself didn't really exist, but was something that depended strictly on what people decided to do with it.

Nicole's attention was drawn to various people milling around. She had a hard time getting used to seeing them dressed in the wide array of attire that was much different from that which Athenians wore. She continued to walk around, forgetting that she had put her sunglasses in her purse. She was reminded of the fact that she had wanted to be incognito when she noticed a couple of people pointing at her from a distance. She quickly fumbled around in her purse for the glasses and put them on as she made her way to a bench in a secluded area and sat down.

She looked out over a hill at the lights that dotted the city below. The view didn't compare with the majestic beauty on Athena. Nicole began to take in the whole experience she had just gone through. She started to understand what the vision had to do with her goals. She realized the amount of power she had had as Rhianna and knew that she still had the same incredible potential. Although she had resided in different bodies since her lifetime on Athena, she knew that she was still the same spirit. Any slight doubts others had instilled in her mind about the credibility of past lives were completely erased.

Nicole was dying to know what had happened to Athena. Had the Empress returned in time to salvage the planet? She wished that somehow she could have gotten the answer before she came back to Earth.

Nicole's thoughts turned to the viciousness of the Knights and the time she was being pursued by them in North Valley. She grew angry as she thought about all the havoc they'd wreaked on Athena and the other planets in the galaxy. Nicole remembered her head-on confrontation with Libol and Slandor and the words she said to Libol rang through her mind over and over, "I'd rather die than be part of your group." Then she felt the pain of his heel digging into her back as she lay collapsed on the ground. She put her hand on her back as it throbbed while she allowed herself to feel the pain of this ancient wound that was very similar to the injury she had incurred after her attack at the concert the year before. She removed her hand from her back and felt a surge of strength that she hadn't experienced in a long, long time. "My God! I was willing to die for my group. My honor was more important to me than my life!" she thought so loudly that her words were almost audible. Then her thoughts briefly fleeted to the time she was attacked after her last concert and how quickly she'd just given up on her career. "I've been a weakling for all these months, letting myself and so many others down, just because of one assault. I've been a coward! I must go back and follow the road I chose for myself. Even if I do eventually get killed, at least I'll know that I've done something to make things better on this planet. I'd just come back next lifetime and pursue similar goals. It's much more important to die fighting for a good cause than to give up on a course while still living. That's the most insidious form of death there is."

Her thoughts drifted back to the time she left Athena. She recalled how she had deserted her group there. She sensed that she never went back after the Knight attack, but instead had been living out lives on various planets, and had developed the bad habit of "leaving when the going gets tough." She knew that she had to quit doing this, and could no longer let down her fellow human beings on planet Earth. Whether she liked it or not, this small, backwards planet was now her home. It was just as much her responsibility as the others that lived here to take care of it. She grew angry at the fact that the people on Athena had allowed the specious perpetration of the Knights, much as the people on Earth had allowed evil influences to determine the course of this planet.

Nicole was ready to leave the park and go home. She got off the bench and started walking towards her car. All of a sudden she stopped short in her tracks and realized that she had forgotten something. "My cane," she said to herself, as she suddenly noticed that she had been standing upright and felt no pain whatsoever when she walked! "My God. It's gone," she whispered loudly, and then touched her lower back with her hands. "The pain, it seems to have disappeared when I recalled the scene with Libol, and what happened in the North Valley! I feel so much better. She looked over at the bench she'd been sitting on and saw her light brown cane lying inanimate on the seat. She walked towards it, still testing her renewed ability to take strides without it. When she got to the bench, she reached down, wondering if she'd feel any remnants of pain as she bent over. She felt none. Nicole looked at the cane and said "confronting," that's the secret. One has to be willing to face things, no matter how painful. That's where true strength comes from!" She ran her left hand over the shiny crutch she'd been carrying around for what seemed like ages. Then she carried it under her arm as she headed back in the direction of her car. Nicole stopped and examined the cane one more time. She hesitated, with some slight reluctance, before making her next move. "No more crutches. I've got to learn to walk free now," she said to herself as she took the cane and bravely deposited it in a trash receptacle next to her.

Nicole arrived at her car and nervously dug in her purse for a few seconds, searching for her keys. She glanced over at the trash can where she tossed her cane, and paused for a moment, reassuring herself that she'd done the right thing. Then she unlocked the car door and got in. She refamiliarized herself with the inside of the red BMW that she'd had for five years. Although considered to be state-of-the-art technology on planet Earth, it seemed archaic to Nicole, after having ridden in the high-tech space vehicles on Athena.

When she arrived at the driveway of her home, she opened the glove compartment of her car and realized she'd forgotten to take the automatic garage door opener with her. She got out of her car and walked toward the heavy garage door. Then she bent down and started pulling on the handle. She was about to lift it up, when she felt someone's attention fixated on her, and turned to her right to face Mr. Milligan. He was taking out the garbage.

"Nicole, I don't believe it. Seems like I just saw you, not long ago hobbling out of your house. Here you are only about an hour later, walking like a normal person!" he yelled to her from several feet away, "You go away to some sort of magic healing place?"

She smiled as she stood up straight, "Yeah, as a matter of fact, I did," she said and winked at him.

"But it happened so quickly. You were hardly away at all, and...I just don't believe it."

"Well, I'm finding that some things in life are very hard to believe myself."

"I'm so happy to see you walking normal again dear. What's your secret?"

"Not really a secret. It's just..." she paused, stopping herself from saying too much, "It's just that if you want something badly enough, you can get it."

Mr. Milligan scratched his head, still harboring some disbelief in what he was seeing, "Well, whatever happened, I'm happy for you, dear."

"Thanks," said Nicole, as she knelt back down, grabbed the handle, and lifted the bulky door.

After parking her car in the garage, Nicole went inside of her home and was greeted warmly by the singing of her birds.

She then went over to a couch and sat down. She was still flashing back to various scenes from her life on Athena, much like she'd done after just having watched a movie, where the pictures and words of the characters were still fresh in mind. A feeling of loneliness crept through her as she thought of Ladaar, and how much she missed the relationship that she'd had with him. Longing for his love, tears started swelling in her eyes, as she wondered what had happened to him after she left Athena. And where was he now?

With one foot shakily planted back on planet Earth, she tried to remove the other one, which was still resting firmly on Athena. Although she was having a hard time doing this, she knew that she could no longer live in the past, neither on Athena, nor on Earth. Although not totally certain of what her next move was going to be, she liked the fact that she definitely felt freed from some of the mental and physical shackles that had bound her to the trauma of her recent assault.

The birds were now quiet as they sensed Nicole's serious contemplation as if they respected her need for silence.

As she sat in a comfortable, slouched position on the couch, she started noticing things in her living room. There in front of her, she saw the large TV screen, which rested by itself on a stand on the floor. She knew that if she turned it on she'd be bombarded with a lot of the plagues that are found on Earth. "Drugs, violence, crime. How did things get so degraded?" She asked herself, as if determined to get an answer somehow.

Then Nicole put her head in her hands, as an unharnessed realization started to emerge in her mind, "The team! On Athena we were so strong because we were united. I was trying to do it all on my own here on Earth, as many others have. No wonder I was having such a hard time. I had no group!"

She pulled her head up and took a deep breath, as she started forming an idea for a song. Then she stood up and walked over to a small closet and quickly opened it. She felt like a child who had just been handed a gift and couldn't wait to tear the paper off the package to see what was inside. Though, in this case, she knew very well what was there. It was her guitar, which she hadn't picked up since her assault. She stepped into the closet and hesitated for a few seconds, then pulled it out. Carrying it by its neck over to the couch, she sat down and put the instrument in her lap. She used the sleeve of her blouse to wipe off some of the dust that had accumulated on its shiny rosewood face. Then she lifted it up and gazed at it, admiring the beauty of the custom-made instrument. She remembered some of the concerts she'd done with it.

Reacquainting herself with her old friend, Nicole put it back in her lap and timidly strummed it. The fingertips of her left hand stung a bit as she pressed them onto the steel strings, forming various chords. The calluses on her fingers had faded away during her long hiatus.

Forcing herself to overcome the biting sensation in her fingertips, she plucked a melody from her mind and placed it onto the guitar. Then she started painting words over the melody, and before she knew it, a song about Athena was flowing from her heart. Remembering that she was on Earth, and that it was now important to capture songs for future use, Nicole put the guitar down and got a pen and paper. Then she went back over to where her instrument anxiously awaited her return. She picked up the guitar and recaptured the melody and lyrics that she'd been creating. Still bathing in the intense emotions involved with her recent experience on Athena, her heart sped up and chills ran down her spine, as she wrote down the chords and lyrics to the first song she'd composed in over a year.

Chapter 2

The next day, Nicole was in bed restlessly tossing and turning at ten in the morning. Thoughts churned around in her mind, about re-awakening her old career. Just as she pictured herself up on stage, facing an audience, the telephone rang and startled her. She sat up and fumbled for the receiver.

"Hello."

"Nicky. It's Dale. What happened with that Devon lady?"

"Would you believe that she turned out to be an alien who abducted me and took me to another planet?"

Dale smiled, "Hey, anything is possible if you're on the right drugs. If I didn't know you better, I might assume she came over and gave you some good hallucinogenics. So, okay, what really happened?"

Nicole hesitated for a moment, "Dale, I know we've been friends for a long time and have shared a lot of common experiences, but I'm afraid that if I told you the truth about this one, you would still be asking me 'Okay, but what really happened?' I'll just say that by taking a look at the past, I was helped to see that I have a lot more potential than I've been using. I was allowing myself to stop short on the way to my goals, because of my attack last year. I became aware of some of the key things I need to do in order to succeed."

Dale was silent, and Nicole had the urge to go on and further explain what happened, but decided that the less she said, the better.

"Nicky, I still don't quite get what happened exactly. But whatever it was, you sound different, more confident or something, and that's great, except..." he paused.

"What Dale?"

"Well, I just really care about you, and I don't want any slime-bags threatening your life again. I just think that you should maybe try and find out who your attacker was before you go out and become a sitting duck again. These aren't the safest times for celebrities, you know?"

Had she been having this conversation a couple of days ago, Nicole might have let Dale's words sway her, but now she knew better. "Don't worry Dale. I appreciate your concern, and, in time, I'll find out what that attack was all about. But for now, I need to make up for lost time. I let too many people down when my performances stopped."

"So what are you going to do?"

"Play. That's the first step. I've got to get out again and communicate and make it known that I'm back. I'll do one of the main things that I failed to do before."

"What's that?"

"Put together a team of artists who have similar goals to mine, those who want to create a better world, and will do whatever it takes to be seen by the broad public. After all, it's the messages of the artists that set the precedents for the civilization. And besides, with all the crazy things that can happen to celebrities, it's much safer to have a supportive team, just like on Ath... like other successful movements throughout history," she said with a re-kindled, fiery determination in her voice.

Dale almost didn't know what to say, "Nicky, it's good to hear you talking like that, kind of scary, but good. You haven't sounded this self-assured since the time, several years ago, when you swore to me that you were going to do whatever it took to get a record deal. I still don't know what Devon did to you, but she sounds like some sort of emissary from God."

"You could say that," Nicole said, as she instantly thought of the Empress.

"Well, if my old friend is going to make a comeback, then I want to be the first to support her. I want you to know that I'm behind you all the way and am willing to help you out with any new demo CD's that you might need, or any bass parts you want played live."

"Thanks, Dale."

"Why don't you and your actor boyfriend come over to my house and join Lori and me for dinner tonight. We can celebrate your new comeback."

"That sounds great Dale, but I'm afraid Tom probably has another dinner date in Germany. He just left to go direct a movie there."

"Well if your physical ailments aren't bothering you too much, why don't you come over by yourself."

"Oh, I'm up to it. In fact I feel great, healthier than ever."

"Yeah, well, with all this hocus-pocus going on, I wouldn't be surprised if the next thing you tell me is that your all your aches and pains are now gone."

"They are."

"You're pulling my leg on this one. I mean it's hard enough to understand the revitalization bit, but you're not telling me that this Devon lady was also some sort of spiritual healer are you?"

"That one you'll just have to see to believe."

"Hey, do you know how to get hold of her? There are some problems in my own life I'd like her to handle for me."

"It's not quite like that, Dale. She didn't just wave a magic wand and heal me, not really."

"Well then what's the big secret to her powers?"

"It's not really a secret. It's something that anyone can do for themselves. They just have to be willing to."

Dale eagerly awaited her words, expecting some complexly worded formula, "Well?"

"Are you ready?"

"Sure, I've even got a pen and paper to write it down."

"Okay, then here goes,"

Dale poised the pen in his hand, not wanting to miss a word.

"Confront it."

"Confront what?"

"Whatever it is that you're backing away from, whatever your weaknesses are. If you can't face the music, then you'll never be able to sing the songs you want to sing."

"Okay, Miss Philosopher, so you're saying that if I don't confront things, nothing else is going to get done."

"Simple, but true. That's really all I can tell you for now."

After her talk with Dale, Nicole dug her old repertoire of songs off of a shelf in her room where they'd silently remained, slowly yellowing on sheets of music paper. She spent the rest of the week practicing some of her favorite tunes until she had fully re-memorized most of them. Doing vocal exercises, she worked out the instrument she used to sing with, unleashing the natural beauty of her voice, that was now amplified by the amount of newly born passion she sang with.

At the end of her musical workout Nicole knew that the next step was to call her old agent, Carl James, and get his assistance in getting booked and promoted. She thought that with his help, it would be easier to get gigs and to eventually get a record deal. Nicole knew that he would be surprised to hear from her and rehearsed the words that she'd say to him. Then she dialed his number.

"Carl James here," the deep voice of the fifty-something-year-old man said.

"Carl, this is a ghost out of your past."

Carl was puzzled, "Okay, so who is it that is calling to haunt me? I can't tell by your voice."

"It's Nicole, Carl, remember me, that rebellious artist."

"Nicole, how could I forget? What did you do, wake from the living dead?"

"Yes, I did," she said as she sensed a touch of irritation in his voice.

"I'm right in the middle of six things, so you'll have to make it quick. What can I do for you?"

"Book a concert for me."

He was silent, then gave her a quick, snide laugh and replied, "I tried to do that last year, and all I got from you was adamant rejection. I couldn't have budged you, even if your house was on fire, and here you are out of the blue, mustering up enough nerve to call me with this request. Dear, you had your chance back then. I did everything in my power to salvage the record deal, and you let me down. Not to mention that it took me several months to pay back your disgruntled fans who paid for tickets to a concert but didn't get a performance from you."

Nicole tried not to be affected by his condemning words, "Carl, I'm sorry about that, but I've recovered, and as soon as I start making more money, I will reimburse you for the damage I did, I promise. I'm not living in the shadows of my past anymore, and all I ask is for some help so that I can get the show on the road again."

Carl was speechless for a moment, and felt somewhat better having expressed his upset about the past. "Nicole, dear, I am glad that you have had this recent re-awakening, but it's just too risky at this time for me to take you on. I guess I'm just not convinced that history won't repeat itself," he said. "I have to go now. I've got an important client on hold for me."

"Okay, Carl, I understand,"

He abruptly said good-bye to her. As Nicole got off the phone, she was somewhat shaken up by their conversation. She felt one of her past misdeeds slapping her in the face, and knew that she never should have agreed to do a concert after her attack. Making promises that she couldn't keep was not the way she liked to operate.

Nicole felt like she was truly on her own. She decided that, since she was starting over again, she would have to do it the way she did years ago, before she reached stardom. She knew that her return to the music world would not be as glamorous as it would have been if she had the backup of producers or promotion people with lots of money. But, somehow, this was no longer important. She knew that the most important ingredient to her success right now was her own die-hard determination.

* * * *

Nicole could hardly believe that three months had gone by as she stood in front of a full-length mirror. Dressed in a calf-length black skirt, boots, and a white blouse, she inspected herself, making sure that she looked acceptable for her "coming out" concert at the Rose Club in Los Angeles. She picked up an old brush and ran it quickly through her silky dark hair. She was drawn closer to the mirror by something she'd noticed about her face. Some of the wrinkles that had previously revealed signs of aging seemed to be gone. She was astounded at this. Maybe it was due to her recent vision of Athena. Perhaps being true to her goals had something to do with this phenomenon. She remembered the long lifetimes that Athenians led and how much freer and alive they were than the people on Earth. She thought that perhaps this had something to do with staying young. "It's no wonder so many people on Earth age so quickly. There's so much loss of hope, so much apathy. I was starting to fall into this rut myself, giving up too easily. What a sure sign of suicide," she said to herself. She heard the gong of the grandfather clock in the living room telling her it was time to leave for her performance.

As Nicole drove along, some anxiety lodged itself in her stomach as she wondered how many people would actually show up for her concert. She remembered the performances she used to do at the Rose Club many years ago when she was just starting her career. The owners had welcomed her with open arms as her following got larger and larger, packing their club with people.

Nicole looked back at the obstacles she had to overcome a few months ago, not only in being rejected by her old agent, but in trying to convince the owners of the club to book her. She thought of parts of the conversation she had with the owner, Mr. Lang, as she drove along.

"Yes, I think I can still fill the club."

"Is your old agent friend, Carl, going to help you?"

"No, he's not, but it doesn't matter," she said with some resentment, "I started out on my own years ago, and I can do it again. I know it's been a long time, but I'm willing to do whatever it takes."

"I understand, Nicole, but what makes you think that your old fans will just eagerly await your arrival here. They may not be as interested in you as they were before. After all, you just up and deserted them."

"I know, Mr. Lang, but I need another chance to show them I'm back for good this time. Besides, I won't entirely depend on your assistance in promoting me. I'll do a large promotion to my own mailing list and make lots of calls letting people know that things have changed. Believe me, I'm going to make it this time."

As Nicole waited at a stoplight of a busy intersection the conversation with Mr. Lang faded and the words to one of her songs danced through her mind. She looked forward to performing it with Dale, who would play bass, as well as one other musician named John, who would accompany her on keyboards. John was one of the musicians who often used to play with her in some of her concerts years ago.

Approaching the Rose Club, she noticed a sign above the marquee, bordered with flashing little lights that read,

"The return of Nicole Jensen! Wednesday evening at 8 PM."

She drove by the front entrance on her way to a parking lot in the back of the building. Then she saw a small line of people waiting for the box office to open. After parking her car, she got out, grabbed her newly dusted guitar from the trunk, and went inside the performers' entrance. There in the backstage area, she greeted Dale and John, who had just arrived moments before her.

A club employee wearing blue jeans and a black T-shirt approached the three of them. "You'd better hurry and do the sound check. We're opening the doors soon."

"Yeah, you're right. Let's get this done now," Nicole said.

The three of them walked out to the stage and proceeded to adjust their instruments to sound levels set by Dale, who used his engineering skills to assist in this pre-concert routine.

As Nicole sang into the microphone, testing its volume, her vision of the seats in front of her was impeded by bright lights. She could barely make out the figure of a man approaching the stage. She put her right hand up to her forehead, blocking the annoying lights and was able to see who it was. She finished up the microphone check and walked off the front of the stage, "Mr. Lang," she said as she shook his hand.

He looked at her, semi-smiling. "Nicole, good to see you."

"You don't look so sure about that," she said, noticing that he seemed to be holding back from giving her the kind of warm greeting she'd been used to in the past.

"I'm just kind of worried. There's not a whole lot of people out there, and it's only twenty minutes until show time, dear."

Nicole's spirits sank a bit while listening to his solemn words, "Oh, I see. Well maybe they're just running late," she said, trying to hide any discouragement. She didn't want to further discuss anything negative, and changed the subject by introducing Mr. Lang to John and Dale. After the greetings, Mr. Lang went off to open the club doors, and Nicole and her band went to wait backstage.

Ten minutes before show time Nicole anxiously peered out to the main part of the club from an opening in a set of curtains that separated her from the audience. She saw small groups of people spread out sporadically throughout the club, and recognized some familiar faces, including her sister Cheryl and her husband Dan, who brought with them several of their friends. As the time slowly passed she noticed a few more people filing in from the club entrance, but she was disappointed that only half of the two hundred seats were filled.

"Anybody out there?" asked John, who approached Nicole.

"Oh, a few. Take a look," she said, trading places with him.

"I know it's a far cry from the crowds you were used to during your prime, but it's a start."

"We're on in thirty seconds," Dale said as the club emcee took the stage.

"Ladies and gentlemen, it gives me great pleasure to bring back a very special lady, who started her career here at the Rose Club over six years ago. In spite of an attempt on her life last year, she has made the decision to bring her inspiring music back out to the public. I bring to you Nicole Jensen and her band."

Nicole's heart raced to keep up with both her excitement and her stage fright.

"Let's go," she whispered to John and Dale.

The three of them emerged from an opening in a wall behind the stage and took their places as the sound of applause welcomed them. Nicole approached the mike and was barely able to see the people in front of her. She motioned for the lighting man in the back of the room to dim the bright lights, "There, that's better. I can see you now," she said looking around at the smiling audience. "Thank you so much for your welcome. It feels great to be here," she said, blowing a kiss to her fans.

She heard whistles coming from some old fans, and then heard someone loudly say, "You don't have a cane anymore."

"That's right. I've thrown away that poor excuse of a crutch, and have decided to stop running away from life. A year of hiding is just too long. I don't even think bears go into hibernation that long," she said as she heard some laughter coming from the audience.

"I have learned the hard way that the surest way to a quick death is to give up on ones dreams. And this is where I was headed until I had the privilege of meeting someone who helped give me back my life again. You could say I had an advanced case of what is called 'Dream Demise,' not a pleasant thing to experience, as anyone who has ever given up on their goals would know." Nicole said and then walked over to where her guitar rested against a metal stand. She carefully picked it up and placed its strap around her shoulders, then went back and stood by the mike. She paused for a few seconds and looked at the audience. She was almost glad that the house wasn't too packed, as a small crowd was easier to get used to. Shaking a bit, she introduced her first tune, "I'd now like to play for you a song called "Dream Star."

Nicole strummed a few chords and then Dale and John joined in. Nicole sang to her captive audience,

"There is a star that shines in the sky.
It's where your dreams are; it shines way up high.
You spend your life chasing after that star
And when you reach it you'll know you've gone far.
So, reach up, reach high and grab hold of your dreams,
no matter how far away they may seem.
Sometimes the clouds come and block your view
It starts to rain and you think it's all through,
But after the storm the sun will shine.
You'll say once again, 'that star is mine'...."

She ended the song after holding a high note, stretching it longer than ever before, using one of the distance singing techniques from Athena. The audience roared with applause and some even gave a standing ovation.

Cheryl got choked up seeing her sister's performance. She was happy to see her fighting again. Over the past year, Cheryl had taken on much of the blame for Nicole's attack. Cheryl remembered how she'd talked to her about all the drug abuse in her daughter's school. This got Nicole so enraged that she started on an anti-drug crusade.

Cheryl and Jenny had been at Nicole's last concert a year ago and recalled some of the words that Nicole spoke at the end of her performance, just before going backstage where her predator lurked. "I dedicate a part of my crusade to all those children on drugs who died before they ever really had a chance to live. I urge all parents to do what they can to alert their children to the life threatening dangers of substance abuse. Those who are responsible for infesting children with one of the worst plagues in history should be brought to justice for their crimes." The memory faded away as tears came to her eyes when she thought about Jenny. She wondered if Jenny would have ever taken her own life, if Nicole hadn't been attacked and quit being such a big influence in her life.

Dale's wife Lori, who was sitting in the front row, had come to the club after working her day job as a legal secretary. She had been feeling over-burdened by all the daily pressures of her business and was becoming more and more disheartened by many of the legal documents she had to type. These were nothing more than complexly worded justifications as to why criminals should be allowed to get away with their crimes. As she listened to Nicole's uplifting lyrics, her own dreams were being revitalized, and she was aroused to anger by the fact that she had been so far off her own true path in life. She envisioned herself taking the tops off of her old set of oil paints, squeezing the different colors onto a palette, then dipping into them with a clean brush and stroking a canvass. She remembered her true love in life, and how many months had flown by with only fleeting thoughts about it. Lori thought about an idea for a painting that she was dying to go home and create.

Nicole went on to treat the crowd to a feast of songs. Nothing made her happier than looking out to the group and gazing upon many smiling faces, feeling the positive energy, initially generated by herself and her band, but then intensified by the audiences' contribution to it.

She finished her performance that night with a feeling of satisfaction that she hadn't felt in a very long time. She knew, however, that this was merely the first small step on her quest.

Chapter 3

Discouraged by the small turnout at his club, Mr. Lang wasn't willing to have Nicole back until she had a bigger following. He decided to stick with more popular names. Although this discouraged Nicole, she wasn't about to stop on her path. She'd just find other places to play, even though they might not be as well known as the Rose Club.

She had no idea how hard she'd have to work to convince others to book her. Old rumors were still floating around amongst club owners, and some feared that if she scheduled a show, she might not show up. Some even thought their reputations might be at stake.

After several months of playing promoter and performer, and putting out old fires, Nicole managed to start making a good name for herself again. She was ready to take her next step forward.

Nicole impatiently sat on a sterile white couch in one of the reception rooms of Horizon records. She was there to discuss a possible record deal. She picked up a Music News magazine from a small table, and flipped through it. She was about to put it down when her eyes were drawn to a bold caption on one of the pages, "Pop singer Neal Sherman mysteriously disappears after revealing source of a large drug scandal." Nicole quickly read the article about the singer with whom she had been friendly during the height of her career. Nicole didn't see any mention of who the "source" was. The article stated the possibility that the singer may have been murdered, with his body not yet found. Nicole threw the magazine down on the table and cursed to herself about the injustice of this. The receptionist, who was the only other person in the room, turned away from her computer briefly to glance at Nicole.

Crossing her arms and tapping a foot on the floor, she waited for her lawyer to show up. She was upset that he was late even though she didn't necessarily like the idea that one never made appointments with record company executives without lawyers. But she knew that was the only way to keep from getting ripped off.

"Excuse me," Nicole said to the receptionist.

She stopped in the middle of a sentence she was typing and looked at Nicole. "Yes, Miss Jensen."

"I've been waiting for over an hour to speak with Mr. Jacobs. Is he still in conference?" she asked,

"Yes, he is, but let me call him for you, and see if there's any prediction on when he'll be through."

The receptionist picked up the phone on her desk, "Mr. Jacobs, it's Hilary. Miss Jensen would like to know how much longer you will be."

"I'm not sure, I'm still in the middle of some important decisions regarding Nicole, as well as a couple of other artists. It could be anywhere from ten minutes to half an hour. Please give Nicole my apologies."

Hilary reported the news back to Nicole. She was annoyed about the delay, but what bothered her more was the fact that she had been waiting for several months, trying to build back up a following, before she could even justify contacting a record company. She had to go through the routine all over again of proving that people would come to her concerts. Time ticked by, and she knew that it was vital for her to get signed to a label so that the momentum of her career could be moved forward even faster. She was pushing forty years old, and still had a tremendous amount of work to do. She wished she were able to live to even one-third the life expectancy of an Athenian.

Imbedded in her thoughts, Nicole had taken her attention off of the lengthy wait.

"Nicole, Mr. Jacobs is ready for you," Hilary said as she got up from behind her desk and walked towards Nicole.

Nicole followed Hilary towards a door at the end of a hallway. She was looking forward to finally getting the support she needed in her career. Hilary picked up a few small Dictaphone tapes from a basket in the room, and then left the two of them alone. Nicole sunk into a large, leather chair in front of Mr. Jacobs' desk. She looked out of a window that nearly covered an entire wall, and could see what looked like toy cars, moving along on the streets way beneath the twenty-seventh floor suite.

Stan Jacobs got off the phone, then shook hands with Nicole and smiled, "Miss Jensen, I see that you are here representing yourself today."

"I guess if I have to, I will. My lawyer was supposed to be here an hour ago."

"Well, we can wait a few more minutes, but I'm afraid if we don't get started soon, we'll have to re-schedule our meeting."

Nicole panicked, "Can't you discuss the deal with me? Then I could go over the contracts with Sam later."

"I don't really like to do business that way, but if that's your decision, then I'll go along with it."

"I'd like to get started."

"All right, then first of all I want to say that I am pleased to see that you are currently engaged with the renewal of your career. I'm not one to hold grudges against past wrongdoings for great lengths of time. However, if you are going to sign with Horizon, we will have to make agreements that are mutually beneficial. I don't want to lose money like your last record company did."

Nicole listened in mild interest to his words, feeling over-confident about her recent ambitious nature, and not worrying about causing any betrayals that were similar to that of the past. "I understand your concern Mr. Jacobs. I can assure you that won't happen. I've learned my lesson, and wouldn't dream of breaking my commitments."

Stan pulled a manila file from a basket on his desk and took out a recording contract. He placed it on the left side of his desk and put his hand on it as he continued talking. He enjoyed hearing the sound of his own voice. "You can take this and read it in a moment, but before you do I want to make sure that you are willing to work in alignment with Horizon's rules."

Having been down this road before, Nicole knew what she had to do. "Of course, Mr. Jacobs, as I've said, I'll keep my agreements. I will perform at all engagements that are set for me, and will not let Horizon, nor my fans down," she said as if under oath.

"Very good, then starting out on the right foot, for the second time, there are some lessons I'm sure you've learned which you know are not worth repeating."

"Of course," she said, thinking that Stan was starting to sound overly cautious. She sat forward and eyed the contract under his large palm, eagerly waiting to take it with her and carry on with her plans.

"Good, then I need your agreement not to bombard the public with controversial songs that may set you up for attacks by angered listeners."

Nicole's eagerness waned, and she suddenly found herself battling between the desire to do whatever it took to become more well known, and the undying commitment to her own integrity. She was tired of the long trek back up an old familiar hill, and like a hiker who gets weary near the top of the slope, she felt like taking a rest.

"If I do as you say, then what do you have in mind for me?"

"The old image has to go. You need to sing more contemporary material. Your lyrics should deal more with sex and relationships. This is the material that sells. I want to see you trade in the baggy skirts and blouses for some short, tight dresses, and high heels. Don't be afraid to show some cleavage. You've got the figure for this type of look. I don't know why you insist on hiding it. Your sensuality is what I want to knock 'em out with." He paused for a moment and lit a pipe.

"Take a look at some of the female pop singers like Mara Lary, and Dawn Winters. Just a couple of examples who aren't afraid to show what they've got. I'd like to promote the return of the new Nicole. What you did in the past nearly cost you your life, anyway."

Out of breath, trying to climb back up the mountain to stardom, Nicole let Stan's words sink in deeper than she should have. She sat in silence as he pushed the contract towards her. Then she started getting pictures of herself on stage slinking around in some tight red mini dress singing about making love. She knew this might get her popular faster and liked this part of it. But she quickly snapped herself out of the trance she was in. She couldn't stand that this music industry glamour sometimes had nothing to do with the art itself, but was used to lure the public into buying a pretty toy. She'd be nothing more than a new doll.

Then she remembered how many other artists had weakened under this temptation and had lost themselves before they ever even tried to stand up for who they really were. She cleared her throat. "I cannot do that, Mr. Jacobs. I need the independence to communicate what I want. If I can't do this freely, then I will face my own Dream Demise."

"Dream Demise. That's an interesting concept, and I can understand your concern and fear of giving up your ideals. But I'm afraid that, because of your past, you must be put under the close scrutiny of our company if we are to sign you. We cannot take risks with you. It's too dangerous to just let you run the show." He leaned forward and put his elbows on the desk, clasped his large hands together, and rotated his thick thumbs.

Nicole leaned back in the cushioned chair and sulked for a moment. Mr. Jacobs stopped his thumb twiddling as he looked into her fiery eyes, waiting for her to say something.

"I understand your worries, but I just can't..."

Stan opened his desk drawer and fumbled around for something. He pulled out a copy of Music News and turned it to the page with the article about Neal Sherman. "You see this?"

"Yes, I read it out in the reception area while I was waiting for you. It incensed me that something so horrible could happen to a guy like Neal."

"Don't think it didn't shake things up here at Horizon either. He was scheduled to record a new CD two weeks after his disappearance occurred. Now we don't know if we'll ever hear from him again. Money was already paid out to promoters and distribution companies, and, again, Horizon took a loss. I'm telling you Nicole, in spite of how talented you are and how much passion you have to change the world, sometimes you just have to step back and play it safe. You're at a point right now where your name is starting to emerge on the local music scene again, but you have a chance to protect yourself this time, under the guise of noncontroversial, commercial success. This company deals mainly with pop stars. You have this chance to become another one."

Nicole was sickened by his condescending words, "A guise! That's what it would be, a guise. There are too many people on this planet who are hiding behind false identities. I refuse to be one of them. If I can't stand up for what I believe in, then what good am I? I'm sorry Mr. Jacobs, but if this is what my relationship with Horizon would be, then I'm afraid I can't do business with your company. And trust me, I will be a big success, with or without this record deal. I may have gotten attacked unjustly, but at least I did manage to get a lot of people off of drugs, and prevent others from starting to take them. Besides, if artists don't communicate the truth about what's really going on in the world and inspire positive change, then what's the use of us? I don't need my lawyer here to tell me this is not a deal for me."

Stan Jacobs separated his hands, and picked up the contract and placed it back in the manila folder. He barely even heard the words of her last sentence as he was too busy being appalled at her sudden outburst at what he considered to be an equitable deal. "All right, Miss Jensen," he said as he stood up and adjusted his blue tie. "I see that we won't be doing business. But I warn you, be careful."

Nicole stood up and pushed back the black chair, while tossing the strap of her red purse over her shoulder. "Thanks for your concern and your time," she said resentfully as she walked out of his office.

As she hurried past the reception area, Hilary called to her. "Nicole, your lawyer called and said he was stuck in a major traffic jam, but will be here in ten minutes."

"Thanks Hilary, I'll call him on his cell phone and tell him he doesn't need to show up," she said and stormed out.

Hilary gave her a puzzled look then went back to typing.

Chapter 4

Seriousness hung in the air of Nicole's home. She sat on a couch with her arms folded, talking with Tom, who was just back from Germany.

"So I will probably have to move by the end of the month," Tom said. He had taken a new directing position with a German film company.

"I know it's what you want, Tom, and I'm glad for you. But I didn't expect you to just walk out of my life so suddenly. I..." she stopped.

He moved closer to her on the couch and put his arm around her. A feeling of panic and fear came over Nicole. She never did well with break-ups, even with relationships that weren't quite right.

"Sorry, but I gotta do it. Why don't you come with me Nicky?"

"What about my career and my crusade? I'm just getting back on my feet again and..."

"You can be a rebellious artist in Europe. It may even be a better place for you to be one. Fewer lunatics trying to kill you over there."

Nicole thought about his words and went into deep contemplation. She almost didn't respond to the knock she heard on her front door.

"Aren't you going to get that?"

"Oh, yeah," she said. She got up and opened the door. She was greeted with a friendly smile from Chris Andrews, the painter she'd met a while back, who was there to start on her house. She went outside with Chris and quickly gave him instructions on what to do. She was in such a hurry to get back to Tom that she almost forgot to tell Chris something, but caught herself. "So as far as the trim, I'd like it dark brown instead of gold. Let me know if you need anything."

Chris wondered why all the abruptness as she hurried away. He thought that maybe he had bad breath from the onions in the sandwich he just ate. Or was she just another cold celebrity? This didn't seem like the Nicole he'd seen on TV and in concert in the past.

She sat back down next to Tom and put her arms around him, "I don't know, Tommy. I don't like the idea of being alone, and I know you don't either, but I just..."

"Just what, hon?"

"I've been working so hard to get re-established here."

"Yeah, and you told me it's not going as well as you'd like. I hear of American artists going to Germany and getting known even faster than they ever would here in the States. Besides, you won't have as many bad rumors from the past haunting you."

She withdrew from Tom, "Why do I have to be the one to make this decision? Why can't you just get a directing job here in Los Angeles? What if it meant the difference between staying together or not?"

"I don't want to. I've already made my decision, and it's a firm one. Besides, why don't you look at the fact that you're not the big deal you used to be. Not many people would miss you anymore."

"How can you insult me like that!"

Tom was silent. "It's the truth. Why don't you just get off of your cloud and look at it."

Nicole slammed her fist into the seat of the couch and turned her back to him, "Damn you! Why do I put up with this?"

"Why do I?" Tom yelled, then stormed out, slamming the door behind him.

After Tom left, Nicole looked out her kitchen window and stared blankly at Chris painting a wall. Her attention was fixed on Tom. She thought about whether to go to Europe or not. Back and forth she went, remembering the words of an old rock song, "Should I stay or should I go?" Why was it so difficult for her to just say "no?" This had always been a problem with her and men. She remembered a time when she even stayed with a guy who physically abused her. She knew this was her weakness. Chris turned and looked at her and smiled. She didn't even notice. After a moment, she walked away from the window and sat at her desk in the living room, trying to decide what to do. Here she was back from Athena, revitalized and ready to fight any barriers that stood in her way, but this was one thing she hadn't expected. With Tom's selfish attitude, it should have been easier for her to dump him, but for some reason she hadn't done it. She'd have to become braver.

A couple of days had gone by, and Nicole was still dizzy with indecision about whether to run away to Europe with Tom or to stay in America. Although her name was coming back to life to some degree in the Los Angeles area, she grew frustrated at not being on the record charts yet. After turning down Horizon the next plan of action was to promote herself to other record companies, inviting them to come to her self-booked concerts. She had already sent out a couple of mailings to several companies and was ready to do some more promoting.

It was a warm spring day as Nicole busily sat in front of her computer. She pulled up a file with a list of record companies. Then she printed out a sheet of address labels. As she started placing a label onto an envelope, the smell of paint fumes came slipping into her house from an open widow in the kitchen. She walked over to the window with the intention of shutting it. When she got there, she looked out and saw Chris putting a brown trim around the kitchen window.

"I don't mean to be rude, but the toxic smell is starting to get to me, so I thought I'd close this," Nicole said, looking at Chris' paint smudged face.

"Hey, it happens all the time, women shutting me out of their lives just like that."

Nicole smiled at his humor. "I understand."

"Hey, I better not say anything else. Here I am ruining my reputation with you. I better get back to work. I know you want your place done as soon as possible."

"You can take your time. Just have it all wrapped up by tomorrow."

Chris gritted his teeth and shook his head, "Tomorrow, huh. Well I guess in that case you leave me only one choice."

"What's that?"

"I'll just have to shrink your whole house down into a little miniature model. Then I'll paint it with all the trimmings. After I'm done I'll sprinkle some magic dust upon it and make it grow back into a life-sized house. What do you think of that idea?"

She instantly recalled the technique that Ladaar and others had used on Athena when they were designing and coloring buildings, "That's a great idea. In fact, I can really picture you doing this, better than you think."

"Well, unfortunately I don't think I can really pull this off," he said with a bit of sadness, "but it sure would be fun and quite economical. I don't know exactly where I got this idea, but think it has something to do with another lifetime. I know this sounds weird. I've been told I have a pretty wild imagination."

"Hey, don't deny what you perceive."

Chris paused as he let her words sink in. "Thanks for making me feel better. No one has said that to me before," he said, forcing himself to pull back from any attraction he was starting to feel for Nicole.

"I bet you're much more of an artist than you let on to be."

"Well, it's a sensitive area. I suppose I tend to hide behind this house painter disguise. Right now, it pays the bills better than my oil paintings at home."

"What do you paint?"

He hesitated, "Oh, mostly scenes from other magical planets. I get these incredible pictures and just let my imagination control my paint brush."

"Hey, you can't knock imagination. After all, it's creative ideas that are responsible for instigating many of the great realities that exist."

Chris smiled at Nicole as he put the final stroke on her window ledge. "There's a wisdom about you that's real cool. You aren't afraid to share your visions. If I ever get famous, I'd like to share some of mine."

"Thanks," she said looking into his sparkling blue eyes, "I, uh, I'll let you get back to work."

"Okay," he said nonchalantly, still puzzled by what she meant about "picturing you doing this better than you think."

Nicole shut the window and went back to work on her mailing. Her attention was still riveted on Chris' words about shrinking and painting the house. She didn't even notice that she was placing the labels upside down on envelopes until she'd stuck about ten of them on and happened to glance down at her careless work. As she threw away the useless envelopes, the words of the brief conversation with Chris played over and over again in her mind.

Nicole felt guilty about the wave of Spring fever that came slipping in through the window, just as swiftly as the paint fumes had touched her nose. She fought with her feelings as she thought about Tom.

Losing concentration and interest in the simple tasks she was doing, she decided to take a break. Nicole sat in a large rocking chair in the living room. She rocked back and forth, as her heart raced to keep up with the speed of the thoughts flitting about in her mind. She kept trying to convince herself that the words Chris had spoken were just coincidentally similar to those of Ladaar. Besides, they really didn't have much of a conversation and there wasn't enough evidence for her to verify anything. But for some reason, she couldn't stop her wishful longing.

Feeling like a teenager, who had fallen prey to the bashfulness that comes from a sudden crush on someone, she kept trying to reassure herself that she was acting ridiculously. After all, she was well past the crush stage, and even old enough to have teenage kids of her own. But the thoughts she was having would not let her go. Could her wish from lifetimes ago finally be coming true? Or was she just hoping for a fairy tale ending? For all she knew, Chris was happily married, anyway.

Nicole couldn't stand the suspense she was wading in, so out of desperation, decided to overcome her shyness and do something about her dilemma. She sprang out of the chair, leaving it to rock back and forth on its own, then walked back over to the kitchen window and looked out. Chris was not within sight. She hoped that he hadn't already left for the day. She went to the sliding glass door in her kitchen, and walked outside. Looking around, she didn't see him anywhere, so she walked around to the back of her house. There he stood near the top of a large ladder, painting a section of her house right beneath the roof. She looked up at him and was hit with another wave of Spring fever as she watched his muscular arm gracefully stroke a brush across one of the wooden beams. He didn't notice her, so she moved closer. Then, compelled by her steady gaze, he looked down and spotted her. He stopped painting for a moment. "Hi. Did you come to check up on me?"

"Well, sort of. Actually, there's something I wanted to ask you, but I don't want to yell all the way up there. Do you think you could come down for a moment?"

"Sure. You're the boss," he said as he put his brush in a tray on the top of the ladder. He climbed down to the ground.

"I wanted to know if you'd like to be a guest at my concert tomorrow night."

"Guest? I must be doing something right to get an invitation like that. I, well, I don't think I have anything planned. Sure, I'd love to," Chris said, noting how much nicer Nicole had been to him lately. He smiled to himself as he realized he hadn't had any onions in his sandwiches recently.

Nicole forced herself to ask the question that was the hardest for her to confront, "Is there anyone you'd like to bring, like your wife or a girlfriend?"

"How about if I bring one of each?" he joked.

"Sure, the more the merrier."

"Well, I'd like to say that my wife wouldn't mind if I also brought my girlfriend," he said as Nicole's heart sank, "but since I don't have a wife or a girlfriend, I guess it will just be me. Unfortunately, I broke up with my girlfriend a couple of months ago," he said with downcast eyes. Nicole's heart bounced right back up.

"Oh, well I'm sorry to hear that," she said, trying to feel some sincerity. "Why don't you see me before you leave tonight, and I'll give you a guest pass."

"Sure. Thanks," he said as he started to climb back up his ladder while looking down at Nicole.

The following night, Nicole and Dale were backstage at the Rose Club. Mr. Lang had decided to give her another chance to try and fill up his club. They nervously waited for John, the keyboard player, to arrive. John, who was notorious for being the first performer to arrive for a show, was mysteriously missing, with only ten minutes to go before their concert. Nicole had tried calling his house, but got no answer, and was periodically checking the parking lot, hoping that somehow this would lessen her worries. The sound of overlapping conversations kept intensifying as more and more groups of people entered the club. Mr. Lang, who had been busy making sure that there were extra tables set up for the overflow of people coming, walked backstage wearing a smile of contentment. Then, as he noticed the wrinkled brow and look on Nicole's face, his smile faded.

"Nicole, what's the matter?"

"John's not here."

"What? Doesn't he know he's on in five minutes?"

"Sure he does. This is very odd. He's usually the first one to a gig. I called his house and got no answer, and thought he may be running late for some odd reason, but this is so unlike him. I just hope he's okay."

"So do I," he said, partly with concern about John, and partially with selfish thoughts about what might happen to his club's reputation if there was no concert. He started to have regrets about booking Nicole again. "We can delay your fans for a little while, but you know how upset people get when they have to wait for a show."

"Believe me, I know, Mr. Lang. I don't want to let them down," Nicole said. Not only was it bad enough that this was happening, but it was occurring on a night when she expected both Chris and possible record company personnel to show up.

Dale, who had just come back from the bathroom, was walking towards Nicole and Mr. Lang. He caught Nicole's attention and pointed to his watch, indicating that it was time to go on. Nicole felt like she was sandwiched between the intense thoughts of both Mr. Lang and Dale. All she knew is that she had to make a decision quickly.

"Okay, Nicole, so what are you going to do? I need to know now. If you don't think you can perform without John, then I'll have to make an announcement to the audience. You can wait about ten more minutes for him. But I can't just keep those people out there forever."

Nicole thought about how much better her songs sounded with keyboards and really regretted going on without John. She tensed up as she looked at Dale, who was now standing beside her, and then replied to Mr. Lang, "We have to go on. You're right. I can't keep them hanging. As far as I'm concerned, ten minutes is just too long. I'm sure if John isn't here by now, he won't be coming at all."

"Okay, then, do your best. I wish you luck," Mr. Lang said as he squeezed Nicole's shoulder.

Nicole and Dale stepped out onto the black wooden stage and were instantly greeted by warm, welcoming applause, embellished with various whistles and cat calls. Many of Nicole's old fans were filled with joy at the fact that they once again had the pleasure of being treated to her inspiring music. After greeting the audience Nicole informed them that she regretted that her keyboard player would not be with them. There were some thoughts of discouragement amongst the crowd, but for the most part the people were not as remorseful as Nicole was.

Entirely disregarding the words of Stan Jacobs of Horizon records, Nicole proceeded to open her set with a rebellious old song of hers entitled "Time for Making Changes."

After she fired up the audience with this tune, she played several more songs. She now hardly noticed the absence of her keyboard player. She overcompensated for his vacancy by pouring more passion into her own performance. Dale helped as well, adding unique improvisational effects on the bass. After about an hour of back to back songs, there was a brief ten-minute intermission.

Nicole and Dale walked backstage and slapped one another's right palms in acknowledgment of the success of their performance. Both of them knew that because of John's absence, they had both expanded their creativity beyond previous bounds

After the quick break, Dale and Nicole went back on stage, and imbued the audience with another array of songs.

As she finished the second to the last song of the set, Nicole addressed the audience. She experienced a slight feeling of self-consciousness, trying to think of how to introduce the next song. "I'd like to end tonight with the newest addition to my repertoire, and in fact the first song I've written in a whole year," she paused as some loud whistles came from the audience. "Thanks. It was a nice accomplishment, but not just because I haven't written in so long. You see, this particular song was inspired by a vision that I had, a concept of a land far more ideal than Earth, where creation, not destruction, is nurtured. It is with great pleasure that I share with you tonight the song entitled Athena." Instantly she thought about Chris, wondering if he was listening. As she sang about the good old days, her voice quivered.

"If I could travel back in time, there's a place I'd like to be.
Enchanted land so far away, a place of ancient beauty
Golden castles and bright clear sky,
winged horses that fly up high.
Artists who were free to do
Whatever they wanted to.
Oh Athena, how I long to be there.
Land of ancient beauty. A place I used to roam,
a place I could call home........."

The spirit of the audience crescendoed along with Nicole's angelic voice as she finished her grand finale. After a standing ovation, and then a performance of one last song as requested by the crowd, Nicole and Dale exited backstage. Nicole hugged Dale and thanked him for pulling off such an incredible feat on his bass, and he returned the praise by telling her how well she played and sang that night.

Nicole started to walk towards an opening in the backstage curtains. She intended to look out and see if she could spot Chris. However, before she got there, a tall man wearing a black leather jacket approached her.

"Miss Jensen," the man said with an air of importance.

"Yes, what can I do for you?"

He smiled warmly at her, "How about discussing a contract with my company, New Civilization Records?"

Her eyes grew wide with delight, "I'm happy that you are interested, but I never heard of this company."

"We are fairly new, but because of some wise investments that our board of directors has made, we have access to a fair amount of funds."

Nicole was hesitant. This was her first offer, and she knew that in this business she had to be careful not to make the wrong moves. "I can't make a quick decision. I'll need to consult my lawyer."

"I understand. You have to be wary of shady deals in the music biz. I just want you to know that my partner and I have chosen the name of our company for a specific reason," he said.

"Oh, what's that?"

"We only want to sign artists who are serious about bettering conditions in the lives of others on the planet."

This all sounded good to Nicole, but she had some skepticism.

"Miss Jensen, I just want you to know that the reason I rushed back here to meet you tonight is that I was extremely inspired by your material. I found myself so moved by the end of your concert that I felt like going on a campaign against the injustices in society. You got me encouraged to donate some of my time to helping stop the rampant decay I see. After your grand finale with that song about Athena, I really saw the contrast between the way things are in this world and the way they could be in a more ideal one."

"I'm glad to hear that. Then I'm doing my job," Nicole said, melting down some of her earlier suspicions of this stranger. "I'm glad to hear that you are interested in my type of material, especially when there are so many people in the business who are wrapped up with motives that merely aid their own selfish ends."

"I know exactly what you're talking about."

"It's too bad it has to be this way."

"Yeah, well, it can be a real insidious trap."

"What do you mean?"

"I once worked for a record company where "selfishness" became a way of life. Fortunately, my conscience kept reminding me that I was in the wrong place."

"Really? Who did you work for?"

"Twisted Records. Name's Ralph Carson," he said, then shook her hand. He pulled out a business card and handed it to her. "Sorry, I got carried away talking to you and forgot to formally introduce myself."

Nicole was a little hesitant to fully trust Ralph, although he seemed like a nice guy. "Nice to meet you."

Ralph sensed some timidness on her part. "You know I'd really like to have a meeting with you."

"I, uh, well, I've got your card, and I'll think about it. Thank you."

Chapter 5

This could be the deal that would boost her back up to the
level where she used to be in the music business. When she
first started promoting to record companies, she had no idea
that it would take three months of such hard work before they
would even come to her shows. Although she had originally hoped
to be signed by a larger, more well-known label, she now found
this of less importance. She felt that her freedom as an artist would
be better protected with a company such as New Civilization
records.

Walking into her dark bedroom, Nicole looked at the
blinking, red light on her answering machine. She turned on the
bedroom light and pushed the playback button on the machine.
Words of anguish filled the room as she listened to the voice of
John's wife, "Nicole, it's Claire. There's been an emergency with
John. Call me at Oakwood Hospital in Sherman Oaks. I don't have
the number with me, but you can get it from information. Ask for
the trauma ward," Claire said, barely able to keep from crying as
she spoke.

Nicole pressed the "stop" button on the machine, not even
bothering to listen to the other two messages. She was so shaken
up by Clarie's message that she tripped on the phone chord,
knocking the telephone off of her dresser. She quickly picked the
phone up off the floor, got the hospital number from the
information operator, and made her call.

"Trauma ward, please," she said to a hospital operator, then
waited for a couple of agonizingly slow minutes before being put
through. "Hello, is Claire Stevens there? She's the wife of John
Stevens, one of your patients?"

"One moment, please," a woman said with a monotone
voice.

Again, she was put on hold, and waited and waited, until
finally the woman came back on the line, "Have you been helped?"
"I was waiting for Claire Stevens, wife of John Stevens. Is she
there?"

"One moment, please," the woman once again said, putting Nicole on hold, before she had a chance to plead her urgency.

"Hello," a female voice said.

"Claire?"

"Yes, it's Claire. Who is this?"

"Claire, this is Nicole, what on Earth happened? Is John going to be okay?"

"Nicky, I don't know right now. He's in critical condition. He was assaulted."

"What?"

"It's hard for me to talk about it, but I'll try. I would have left a message at the club, but you had to perform. I didn't want to upset you. I got the story from the liquor store owner who saw the whole thing.

"On his way to the club, John stopped to get a pack of cigarettes. When he left, he was attacked by a couple of teenage kids, who tried to take his wallet. John fought back. One of the kids snatched the wallet out of his pocket and John held him by his neck, so he dropped the wallet. The other kid took out a knife and stabbed John in the chest and neck," Claire paused and cried.

"Oh my God, Claire!" Nicole cried.

Claire continued, "One of the kids picked up the wallet, took out the money, and then threw it back on the ground, along with John who was..." Claire got choked up, "who was lying in a pool of his own blood."

"My God, how could they be so cruel?"

Claire's voice softly quivered, "I don't know, but the owner said this isn't the first time this sort of thing happened outside of his store. These kids are part of some gang that attacks people and robs them to get money for their vicious drug habits."

"So what is being done with John now?"

"They are trying to keep enough blood pumped into him to keep him alive. There was a lot of internal hemorrhaging, and they already did one operation, to patch up a couple of main arteries, but they're not sure that they stopped it all."

"Is there anything I can do for you Claire?"

"No, nothing at all right now. I'm still hoping for a miracle, and at this point I don't know if one will happen," she said as her tears started covering the telephone receiver.

"Mrs. Stevens," said a nurse, approaching Claire. "Excuse me, but John's doctor needs to see you right away."

"Nicole, I've got to go."

"I understand," Nicole said, as she got off of the phone and sat still on her bed, while suspended in the mystery of what was going to happen with her friend John. All she could think about was John's smiling face after their last concert at the Rose Club and how he'd mentioned that he was proud to be performing with her again. He told her that he'd be her keyboard player as long as she wanted him.

Then she flashed back to the time she was attacked after her concert a year ago and remembered John's voice yelling, "it's Nicole!" after she had let out a scream.

Nicole cried as she recalled that if it hadn't been for John coming to her rescue she might have been in the same condition he was now in. She got angry, as the injustice of this matter just gave her a higher level of necessity to get back on her old path of putting a stop to one of society's greatest ills. "Drugs! Damn it!" she said aloud, as she lay down on her bed, unable to put aside thoughts of John. She yawned, and grew more and more tired. She had only gotten a few hours of sleep the night before, since she was up rehearsing for her performance.

Nicole forced herself to put on a pair of pajamas and crawl into bed. She fell asleep with her attention still glued to John, wondering if she'd ever see him again. After a couple hours of sleep, Nicole started fidgeting in bed while having a nightmare, the likes of which she hadn't had since her attack last year. There on the screen in her mind, playing like a motion picture film, was a vivid picture of her niece Jenny. She was with a few teenage boys with shaved heads and baggy pants. The boys used their pants pockets as scabbards to carry knives, and were walking down a busy city sidewalk. A couple of the boys had guns, also positioned silently in their pockets. One of the boys put his arm around Jenny, and looked into her drugged eyes as she put her arm around his waist.

Like scavengers, waiting to swoop down on their prey, the boys silently walked along eyeing possible victims. Then, as a well-dressed man and woman approached them on the sidewalk, one of the boys with a gun nodded his head, indicating to the others that they should attack. Jenny coldly stood with her arms folded and watched the action. Without hesitation, one of the boys grabbed the woman, and another seized the man, while other group members held threatening knives over them as the woman screamed, and the man struggled to get away. They picked the man's pocket and snatched the woman's purse. Then the woman looked at the boy who was holding her with big, frightened eyes and said, "please don't hurt me." The boy just gazed into her eyes with a wicked, empty stare and then slammed her head against a cement wall, knocking her unconscious. The man, seeing the condition of his wife, managed to turn and punch his wife's attacker in the face. Nicole heard several gunshots, which sounded like loud pounding. Then Nicole suddenly jumped, opened her eyes, and sat up in bed with the sound of pounding still coming through loud and clear. She was confused and terrified for a moment until she realized that the pounding was now coming from her front door, and that was what had woken her up. She turned and looked at the clock on her bed stand and saw that it was already nine in the morning, an hour later than she had intended to sleep.

Nicole got out of bed and put on her robe, went to the door and looked through a small peephole to see who was outside. There in a set of beige overalls was Chris. She opened the door. "Chris, hi."

"Boy, you must have really been sound asleep. You look kind of shaken up."

"Bad dream. I'm glad you woke me. I'm sorry that the doorbell doesn't work, and you had to stand out there and knock. How long have you been here?" she asked.

"Oh, I don't know, a few minutes I guess. Not too long." Chris put his hands in the pockets of his overalls and looked at the ground, and then straight into Nicole's waking eyes. "I don't want to disturb you for long. I know you've got things to do, and I have to get back to work on your house, but I just wanted to thank you for inviting me to your concert last night."

"You're welcome," Nicole said, brightening up from some of the gloom she was sitting in.

Chris tried to fight back the feelings he had developed for Nicole since the concert last night, thinking that a celebrity like her probably wouldn't be interested in someone like him. "All your songs are pretty powerful, but the one that touched me the most was the last one that you played, about that Athena place."

Nicole's hopes opened wide, along with her eyes, as she listened to the words Chris spoke, looking beyond the surface of his communication and once again sensing the familiarity of this being. "Thank you, Lad..., uh Chris. I feel sort of rude having you just stand here at the door. Would you like to come in and join me for breakfast?"

"Sure. But you don't need to feed me much. I just ate."

"Okay." She led him to her dining room table.

Anxiety welled up in her as she started worrying about John again. She put her head in her hands.

"What's the matter? Did I do something wrong?"

"No, no, not at all. I might as well tell you. A friend of mine is in critical condition in the hospital. I've got to call and see how he is. Please excuse me for a minute."

Nicole went to call Claire, and got a report on John. There was no change; nothing new to report.

"How is you friend?"

"No change. I'm sorry, you just got me at a bad time," she said and went on to give Chris a brief summary of what had occurred with John.

"Should I just get to work, and skip the breakfast offer?"

"No, no, that's all right. I invited you in, and besides I could use the company. I need to get my mind off of him for now. There's nothing I can do anyway."

Nicole put her attention on Chris. "What would you like? I've got toast, eggs, coffee, orange juice?"

He smiled and laughed a little, "Wow, this is an honor, being served breakfast by a celebrity like you."

"Hey, before I got into the music business, I was serving a lot of meals for a living," Nicole said, sensing some of Chris' nervousness.

"Really? Anyway, to answer your question, how about a couple pieces of toast and coffee?"

"Coming right up."

Chris gazed at her as she turned her back and went to the refrigerator and took out a loaf of bread. She felt his eyes fixed upon her and turned and looked at him. He then looked away.

"By the way Chris," Nicole said warmly, "I just want you to know that I've never had the idea that just because I was a celebrity, I was some sort of god-like human that deserved special treatment and couldn't do things that others did."

"I admire that."

Nicole toasted some bread, made the coffee, poured herself some orange juice, and then when everything was ready, brought it all to the table.

There was silence for a few minutes, as Nicole drank her juice, and Chris ate a piece of toast.

Chris watched Nicole, who was engrossed in spreading just the right amount of jelly on her toast. He waited until she was done, carefully chose his words and spoke, "I know this may sound kind of odd, but there was a haunting familiarity to that song about Athena. You painted such a real picture, that I felt like such a place may actually have existed. I, it actually brought tears to my eyes and then broke through some of the numbness I didn't know I had been so entrenched in. There's something unexplainable which I can't quite put my finger on, but..."

Nicole found herself holding back from expressing all the things that were racing through her mind. She felt that she couldn't reveal too much too soon about her vision, as it may be too much of a shock. She just played it cool, and let Chris' curiosity reach for further answers, "I'm glad my song touched you that way."

"Nicole, I was just wondering, do you believe in past lives?"

"Yes, I do."

"Yeah, me too. In fact, I sometimes think that the ideas I get for my paintings come from perceptions I have of other lifetimes. I sure know that they aren't related to modern day Earth realities. When you sang that song about Athena, a very vivid picture leapt to mind. You may think this is weird, but I got some vague notion that I may have actually been to a place like that. Do you think I'm nuts?"

"No, just deluded."

"Ooh, that's pretty bad," he laughed, "Call the guys in the white coats to come and take me away."

Nicole joined him in laughter. The feelings that danced between them got warmer and warmer. By now they had both finished their meal and were busy feasting on their conversation for desert.

Sensing that it was now safe for her to take the next step in sharing her vision, Nicole spoke, "Chris, I want you to know a little secret."

He nodded, encouraging her to go on.

"That song I wrote about Athena is about a past life, one that was so special I wanted to capture it in a song. Some people will only view it as a fantasy, and that's all right, but there's a lot more depth to it than that."

"You seem to have a lot of certainty about this place. How come?"

Nicole almost spilled out the story about Devon and the telescope, but then hesitated, again holding back, "Let's just say I had a vision. You know how sometimes you read a story and it seems like a place where you have actually been?"

Chris contemplated her words. "Yeah, I know what you mean. My paintings take me to worlds that seem familiar to me."

"I'd love to see your paintings sometime," said Nicole.

"I'd love to show them to you, in fact I was just thinking about that," he smiled.

"That's what sometimes happens with people I've shared a lot of common reality with. Our thoughts seem to often fall right into sync."

Chris never had this kind of experience with anyone, and knew whatever he was feeling for Nicole, it was something not of this world, "How about tonight? If you're not doing a show, maybe you could come over after I'm off work. I've got a job to do for this lovely lady, but when my shift is over then maybe you could come and see my paintings."

"Well, unfortunately that isn't going to work because I have a meeting with my lawyer tonight regarding a possible record deal, but I have another idea," Nicole said, not wanting to delay her pursuit of the possible Ladaar.

"What's that?"

"How about if you get permission from that lady you are working for to let you start work a couple of hours late, and if she approves, we can look at your paintings now?"

Chris was both flattered, and a bit surprised at her aggressiveness. "Oh, well sure, let me ask her right away then," he said, changing from a playful attitude to one that was serious and businesslike. "Pardon me, Miss Jensen, but I would like to know if you'd allow me to leave work, even though I haven't started yet, and come back in a couple of hours."

"I don't know. Do you have a good reason?"

"Why, yes, I've been requested to give a tour of the Andrews Art Gallery by an important person who is only available this morning. I'd really like to show her where the true heart of Chris Andrews resides. Not that I dislike painting houses, but it just doesn't compare to creating a whole visual universe on a canvas."

"If you put it that way, then I guess you don't leave me much choice. Go ahead and give your tour, but don't get so wrapped up with this guest that you forget to come back and paint my house."

"Yes ma'am," he complied as they both laughed softly, enjoying the spirit of playfulness in the air. Nicole was so involved with Chris that she didn't even notice the knocking on the door.

"Did you want to get that?" Chris asked.

"What?" she asked, as the knocking got louder. "Oh, yeah."

She wasn't expecting anyone, and was curious who had arrived unannounced. Looking through the peephole, her heart sank as she looked at Tom. She hesitated, then reluctantly opened the door. "Tom."

"Hello, Nicky. Sorry I haven't called for a while. I've just been real busy trying to get everything arranged for my move. I was in your area today, and thought I'd take a chance and see if you were home. You gonna let me in, or just stand there?" He asked, then kissed her on the cheek.

"Sorry. Come in."

This time Chris' heart sank along with his hopes, as he saw Tom walking toward the table with his arm around Nicole. Nicole introduced them to each other.

"My girl's been treating you real good I see?"

"Can't complain."

"Nicole, I want to talk to you alone, but I see you're in the middle of entertaining."

"Hey, it's okay. I can go outside and get back to work," Chris said, quickly gulping down the last bit of coffee in his cup and abruptly exiting.

Nicole's head was spinning as Chris left the table and politely walked outside. Tom sat on one end of a couch, and Nicole, wanting to keep her distance, sat on the other end.

Tom broke the silence, as he moved closer to Nicole. "Nicky, you've had a real 'attitude' towards me ever since I told you about my offer in Germany. Why don't you just give in and come with me? I'm going to be making big money, probably more than you'll make. I can help you pay for your promotion and recording expenses."

"Tom, I can't! I've thought about it, but I need to stay."

"Why? You starting something with that painter guy out there?" he asked, raising his voice intentionally. Chris strained to hear their conversation while casually pretending to work.

Nicole got defensive, but wanted to avoid his question. Instead she told him the main reason she wasn't joining him. "Tom, my friend John is in critical condition. Druggies attacked and robbed him. He might not live. I need to help put an end to this injustice! I started to take responsibility for this sort of thing before, and then dropped it. I have a mission here that I need to complete."

Tom moved back to the far end of the couch, "Oh, so you think that by staying here and singing your songs, this society's troubles are just going to go away."

Nicole thought about the promise to herself she needed to keep, of not giving up when the going gets tough. "I've made my decision, Tom."

He got off the couch and walked out of her life. Nicole grabbed and squeezed one of the throw pillows next to her while the argument with Tom replayed in her mind. She thought about how it took all this drama for her to get up the courage to say no. She regretted the fact that she hadn't turned his offer down the day he made it.

After Tom left, Nicole told Chris he could come out of hiding. He came back in her house and she explained what had happened with Tom. Chris didn't quite know what was going to happen between him and Nicole, but somehow felt that things might work out in his favor.

"So, where were we before this interruption?" Nicole asked.

"I had just gotten permission by my boss to give Nicole a tour of my art gallery."

"Great, then why don't we take a break from all this seriousness and go do that."

Chris chauffeured Nicole in his paint truck to his house, about forty minutes away. They soon arrived at the small home in Sherman Oaks. As Nicole walked in, one of the first things she noticed was an upright piano standing proudly against a wall in the living room. Chris shut and locked the front door and stood beside Nicole as she gazed at the instrument, "You play piano too?"

"Yeah, not as much as I'd like, but once in a while. I used to play a lot more years ago and was even in a band for a while, but then I decided to quit." Chris said, leading Nicole over to a couch where they both had a seat.

"Why is that?"

"Drugs. Three of the five members were getting into a really bad state because of their habits. A few times they messed up so badly in concert that this one club didn't want anything to do with us any more. I just couldn't deal with their weird head trips. But that was a long time ago. Lately I've been mostly into my paintings when I have spare time. I love music, but I've had it on hold ever since the band broke up about six years ago."

"I see."

"Yeah, drugs. Aren't they lovely? I think some artists have this false idea about how they're supposed to enhance your creativity, but I think they just make people more crazy. I had some good highs back in "high" school, but after a while just felt worse after taking them."

"I know what you mean. I'm definitely going to go back on my anti-drug campaign again, as soon as I get another record deal. In fact, you just gave me an idea."

"Oh, well I guess I owe you one after you inspired me the other night. What's your idea?"

"I thought of getting a group of artists together and doing something called "Get High on Art," encouraging people to use their creativity as a "high", instead of those nasty chemical substances that warp their bodies and minds."

"Sounds good to me. I'll support you on that one."

"Thanks," she said as she smiled at him, then turned to her left, noticing a large, brightly colored painting on a wall, "Well, now that we've discussed the lovely subject of drugs, how about showing me your world of art that adorns the walls of your gallery."

"Sure, right this way ma'am," he said as he took Nicole's hand and led her toward the painting she was glancing at, "Leaving the guest reception area, we come to our first display over here on the west wall."

Nicole's attention was instantly awed by one of the paintings. It had a bright blue sky sprinkled with glowing stars, and in the center of it was a transparent wizard. The wizard stood on top of a bright red planet and whirled his wand around as a swirl of bright yellow lights formed and various animals emerged as if out of nowhere.

Nicole was silent as she closely inspected all the pictures on the wall. Then Chris led her to a room that had been a den, which he had transformed into an art room. Covering each of the walls in the room were several framed paintings. Nicole was in awe as she took her time looking at each one, confirming her certainty that they were definitely images that looked very similar to scenes from Athena. She went into pleasant shock as she focused on a painting that was in the middle of the right wall. Up in the left hand corner of the painting was a young woman and man riding on the back of a gold colored winged horse. The man was blowing into a flute-like instrument and the girl was singing as golden notes flowed out of her mouth. She got sad for a moment, as she looked at the horse, and thought about the fate of her pet, Thaurus. Down below them was a field with a large glittery castle on it. Surrounding the castle were a group of dancers and musicians. Nicole's jaw would have dropped if she hadn't commanded it to stay in place, as she looked at Chris.

"You look as if you've seen a ghost."

"I think I have."

"Oh, who is it?"

"I think it's you," she said, as Chris' own, already strong feelings for her intensified, and his heart raced with passion that he was holding back from expressing.

He stepped closer to her as they both bashfully stood and looked at each other, much like the time when they were first getting to know one another on Athena. "Nicole, why is it that when you say this, I get the feeling that what I'm experiencing is the haunting memory of something from the past?"

"Well, I don't know how to tell you this, other than to say that that is probably exactly what is happening between us."

"It's almost too good to be true. I feel like I'm living inside one of my dreams, and that at any moment I'm going to be woken up by my alarm clock, and 'poof' you'll be gone, and there I'll be, jumping out of bed getting ready for work."

Nicole smiled, "No, no, that already happened hours ago."

"Then, are you saying that this is real?"

"Very."

"I'm standing next to the kind of woman I've dreamed about for years."

They stood silently for a moment, while this time, not only did Nicole's eyes look through the present and into the past, but so did Chris', recognizing the fact that she was someone very familiar to him. "Athena," Chris said, pointing to a painting of a bright pink and turquoise planet that took up almost the full size of one of the canvasses in his gallery. "So, that's what it was called. My God, I've been there too."

She smiled warmly in acknowledgment.

"God, it's so good to see you again, my darling," he said as he softly touched her cheek. Then she could hold back no longer, and threw her arms around his broad shoulders, which led to a very, very long awaited embrace.

Nicole lifted her head from Chris' warm chest and as their eyes met, their moment of affection led them into a sweet passionate kiss.

"Now that I've found you again, I don't want to let you slip away for another eternity," said Nicole.

"Neither do I," Chris replied. "We must have had a very special relationship back on Athena. It seems like there was more to it than just the love that we had for one another."

"There was more, much more. We not only had each other, but we worked together with the strongest team of artists ever."

"Yeah? Just like the lyrics in your song, that's what it was. What was that one line you had, something about a big family?"

"We were taught to help each other, one big family with one another," Nicole sang.

"That's it. That's what is so needed here on Earth today. More unity with artists helping each other as part of one big team. There's too much damn jealousy and competition."

"That's for sure."

Chris took Nicole's hand and led her back to the couch in the living room, "Boy, do I feel revitalized talking to you. It's like these old ideas I had are just bouncing back up from some deep well from the past."

"What kind of ideas?" Nicole asked curiously.

"I wanted to inject more beauty into the world with my art and the art of others by putting on shows with messages that inspire people.

"There are just too many others out there like me, who end up getting engulfed in a daily routine that is detrimental to their dreams. Sometimes I feel like I'm on one of those little hamster wheels going round and round, forgetting that it's me who can stop the wheel and get off and do something else. The times I've gotten off, I've just ended right back on again, because of the security."

"I know exactly what you mean, but Chris, your paintings are so extraordinary. Why not make a living selling them?"

"I wish it was that easy. I have sold some of them, but it just hasn't been a stable enough gig, not enough money to live on consistently. To sell them for what they're really worth, I have to put a high price tag on them, and with people cutting down on expenditures these days, they're hard to sell. Unfortunately, it takes so much of my time to complete them that it's just not viable to do this full time."

"That's too bad. I'd sure like to see more of your works adorning the walls of homes and offices instead of some of the garbage that I've seen out there."

"Thanks for the encouragement."

Nicole smiled, then changed subjects, "So you say that you want to put on shows with other artists?"

"Yes, this is another dream of mine, which is resting somewhere on a back burner with the heat kept on low."

Nicole's feelings for Chris heightened even more as she imagined producing a show with Chris. She started feeling a bond with Chris that was similar to that she'd had with Ladaar during the inter-planetary festival. "We just need to round up other artists that have visions like ours. This is something I plan to do after I get my record deal. It may be a big challenge, but I'm determined to overcome whatever obstacles present themselves. This may be a difficult task on this planet, because I know artists often think they can't be part of a group."

"Yeah, but strength comes in numbers, and you want to know something interesting?"

"What's that?"

"Years ago I looked up the word 'art' in the dictionary, and I found something fascinating. Do you know what the derivation of that word is?"

"No I don't."

"Let me show you," Chris said, as he got up and went over to a bookshelf and pulled out a dictionary. He flipped to the word "art" and sat down and showed Nicole the derivation.

She read aloud from the book, "Art, from Ars, Artis, which means To Join Together." Nicole shut the dictionary in amazement and handed it back to Chris, "We sure have pulled up our roots on this planet, haven't we?"

"Yeah, that's one tree that badly needs re-planting."

"Sure does, and it's up to those of us who want to take the responsibility to do it."

They looked at each other with a confirmed agreement, and then hugged one another.

In the middle of their embrace they were interrupted by the sound of a key turning in Chris' front door. Nicole jumped, and let go of Chris.

A boy carrying some books walked in and looked at Chris and Nicole.

"Jeremy, why are you home so early?" Chris asked.

Jeremy gave him a puzzled look. "What do you mean, dad? This is the time I always come home."

Chris and Nicole look at each other and laugh. They hadn't realized how much time had gone by.

"Jeremy, go put your books down, then come back."

"Okay Dad," he said as he dropped his heavy books on the kitchen table, then walked towards them.

"Jeremy, I want you to meet uh..a friend of mine. This is Nicole Jensen."

"Hello, Jeremy," Nicole said as she shook the hand of the twelve-year-old blonde boy.

"Hi. I've heard of you. You're famous, aren't you?"

"Well, I was a while back. I'm working on it again."

"Cool. How do you know my dad?" he asked as Nicole looked at Chris, her thoughts winking at him.

Then she gave Jeremy an acceptable answer, "He's been painting my house. I found out he had his own art gallery here and I wanted to come see it."

"Cool. Can I have your autograph?" Jeremy asked as he grabbed a pen and paper and handed it to Nicole.

Nicole smiled, then wrote a note, "To Jeremy, may your dreams come true. Love, Nicole Jensen."

"Thanks. I don't get to meet stars too much. This is great because I know you're not just a plain old celebrity. You helped a lot of people, huh?"

"Well, I did some anti-drug campaigns last year, if that's what you mean."

"Yeah, I remember. Well, nice to meet you. I gotta go do my homework now."

"Nice to meet you too," said Nicole, as Jeremy walked over to the kitchen table and put the paper with Nicole's autograph into a slot in his notebook. Then he picked up all his books and went to his room.

Nicole looked at Chris and smiled, "Cute kid. He kind of looks like you, but where does he get those big brown eyes?"

"From my ex-wife Sarah."

"And he lives with you instead of her?"

"Yeah, it was a fight getting him, but it's much better this way."

"Why's that?"

Chris hesitated, feeling some embarrassment, "Sara is a lesbian."

"Oh, really?"

"Yeah, when she split she decided that she would be better off with another woman, someone who understood her emotional needs better."

255

"Seems to be more and more of that kind of thing these days, huh?"

"Yeah, thanks to some psychotherapists out there promoting it."

"Lovely planet we live on."

"Yeah, isn't it," Chris said as he looked at his watch. "Hey, I just realized I'm about a half hour late getting back to work. If I don't leave now, my employer might fire me."

"She just might. In fact, I bet she's waiting for you right now, wondering why you haven't shown up."

"Well, then I better get going," he said as he pulled Nicole up by the hand, "Why don't you come with me?"

"Sure, I'm heading in your direction anyway," she smiled.

Chris knocked on Jeremy's door and told him he was going back to work.

On the way to Nicole's, Chris kept prying for more information about Athena and how she knew so much about it. Nicole finally decided to break down and tell him what had occurred with Devon and how she was led to the telescope. She figured the worst that could happen is that he'd just think she was slightly nuts. However, because of Chris' own hidden memories, he believed her. The fact that an actual Athenian came to Earth and gave her a magic coin seemed somewhat far fetched, but then again, he knew that aliens landed on Earth and abducted people, so why not?

When they arrived at Nicole's, Chris unloaded some paint cans from his truck and carried them to the side of the house. Nicole went inside and admired the mess on the table left over from breakfast, while recalling their conversation earlier that day. She started picking up a plate. The mundane chore of doing the dishes was so much more enjoyable with Chris around. Just as she was putting the last couple of dishes in the sink, the phone rang.

"Hello," Nicole said cheerfully.

"Nicky," a female voice said in a sullen tone.

"Yes, hello. Who is this?"

"Nicky, it's Claire."

Nicole's cheerful mood suddenly dropped to one of instant worry, "Claire, how is John?"

"Nicky," Claire said, her voice quivering, hardly able to speak. "He didn't make it," she cried.

Nicole's heart dropped to her stomach. For a moment she was stunned and numb, then her own tears of grief emerged, "Oh Claire, my God. I'm so sorry. So, sorry," Nicole said, as both she and Claire sat in silent mournfulness.

"I am calling to let you know that there will be a small service Wednesday afternoon at three p.m. at the Park Lawn cemetery. Then there will be a reception at my house."

Nicole thought about an appointment at two p.m. Wednesday that she'd scheduled with Ralph Carson. Then she thought about the funeral of her friend. She knew she had no choice but to re-schedule the meeting. "I'll be there Claire. Is there anything I can do for you now?"

"There is something I'd very much like."

"What's that?"

"Find out why there is so much senseless violence. Why did my Johnny and so many others have to pay the price of some juvenile criminal's drug habit? Why, Nicole, why? You were on the right path last year. You did so much good, and I'm glad you're making a comeback. But do be careful Nicole. I don't want you to get hurt again. I'll assist you in any way I can. I can't..stand.. it, " Claire said, unable to control herself as she sobbed loudly into the receiver.

Nicole's grief turned into a fiery anger, "Claire, I want you to know that I am more intent than ever to see that justice is done, and that innocent lives don't continue to get taken!"

"Thank you, Nicole,"

"I will see you Wednesday," said Nicole. She got off the phone, and flopped down on her couch in disgust. It still hadn't fully hit her that John was really gone, and she just kept thinking about him, and what a good friend he was. She buried her face in her hands and started crying. Her two birds watched in silence as she wept.

After a couple of minutes, Nicole lifted her head and remained deep in thought as she sat on the very couch that had been the recipient of so many of her ups and downs. She heard a knocking on her back door, and jumped, as she heard Chris turn the handle and let himself in, something that he wouldn't have done so overtly a couple of days ago. She wiped her eyes, trying to hide some of the grief that had blurred her vision. Then Chris knocked on a wall in the kitchen, hesitating before entering the rest of Nicole's domain.

"Come in, Chris, I'm in the living room." she said.

He was surprised to see her sulking and sat a comfortable distance away from her. "What's the matter?"

"My friend John died."

"Oh, no. I'm sorry to hear that."

"I am too, very sorry," she said.

He moved next to her, comforting her by putting his arm around her slender shoulder.

She rested her head on his muscular chest, not caring that her cheek was leaning on a spot of wet brown paint. "Chris, it's so unfair, so unfair sometimes."

"I know."

She hugged him tightly for a few minutes. "Chris, will you stay with me tonight?"

"Of course, " he said, stroking her soft hair. "Let me call Jeremy and make arrangements for him to spend the night with a friend."

Chapter 6

It was several months since the death of John. Nicole had signed a contract with New Civilization records in October. Her following was growing at a decent rate.

Nicole offered Chris the opportunity to perform with her as her regular keyboard player. He gladly took the position, stepping off of the hamster wheel of the work-a-day world. He now spent most of his time doing the things he loved most, which were playing piano, painting and being with Nicole. Nicole was also busy starting to unite other artists on her "Get High on Art" campaign. She had recently recorded a brand new CD with some of her old songs on it, as well as new ones.

Carl James, Nicole's old agent was both surprised and delighted to receive a check for five thousand dollars, more than making up the damage for the concert she didn't show up for last year.

* * * *

Rodney, of Rodney and the Gutter Rats, who had been getting more and more discouraged with his life and was ready for a major change, was at home one day, lying on the couch recovering from a hangover and a fight with a band member the night before. He had barely noticed the music coming from the radio in the background, until some lyrics hit his ears, which caused him to spring up from his reclining position. He walked over to the stereo, turned up the volume and went back and sat on the couch, continuing to listen to the song.

"Dreams you've had throughout the years,
at times may slip away.
But go my creative one and find them today.
There is room for everyone to share their own art,
for each and every one of us play an important part
But if we want our dreams to waken, it's up to you and me,
for we're the only ones who make them into a reality.

Fellow artist who fell to drugs, or such insanity,
you can throw away your crutches and learn to walk free.
Oh, darkened ages of the century, it's your time to
shine......."

After the song ended, a disc jockey came on and said, "You have just been listening to a song entitled 'The Renaissance,' a new tune by Nicole Jensen. Nicole is a bold and controversial artist who has recently made a successful return to the music scene and has recorded a new CD. She has also started a campaign encouraging people to get addicted to creativity instead of drugs. She plans to work with other artists to put on shows locally and nationally, using their messages to help heal the ills of society. For more information on her program, you can write to her at Get High on Art, or GHOA for short."

As the DJ spoke, Rodney got a pen and paper to write down the address. "We here at KNEW wish her all the best and hope she gets the support she needs in her endeavors."

Rodney lay back down on the couch, noticing that the pounding of his head, which had absorbed most of his energy, had diminished considerably after listening to the Renaissance song.

He stared up at the white plaster, cottage cheese ceiling with his eyes opened wider than they'd been in a long time. "Shit, man, I need to improve this poor excuse of a life. This trap I'm in is a bitch," he said to himself as one of the lines in Nicole's song played over and over again in his mind, "Fellow artist who fell to drugs or such insanity, you can throw away your crutches and learn to walk free." This was the line he remembered most, and put his hand over his eyes and rubbed them as he sickened at the thought of how he'd turned to drugs as a solution to his problems when all they really did was create an excuse not to confront life. Although he'd recently cut back on most of the drugs he'd been taking, he hadn't made the decision to completely get rid of the habit. After listening to the Renaissance song, however, Rodney was reminded of the fact that he was either going to go "up or down," and he was certainly fed up with the latter.

"I have no choice, I've got to throw away my crutches," he said to himself as he remembered a time, years ago, before he ever became a druggy. He recalled how he used to play his original songs, which were far better than the ones he'd been doing with The Rats. Even though he now had a record deal, his agent told him that he shouldn't start playing his old songs, as it may ruin his popularity. "Damn him!" he thought, "Look at me, man! I'm a wreck," he said to himself as he sat up and picked up a newspaper resting on a coffee table and threw it down hard. Just as he did this, the front door opened and he turned his head to face his wife.

"Marla, you're home from work early."

"Good observation," she said resentfully, trying to say as little as possible as she walked into the bedroom and proceeded to pull a suitcase out of the closet.

Rodney walked to the doorway of the room and noticed a familiar scene that he'd previously regarded with anger. This time he just blankly stood and watched as Marla opened a dresser drawer and pulled her clothes out of it, tossing them in piles on the bed. Then she opened another drawer and did the same thing. Rodney walked over to where she busily worked and put his hand on her shoulder, "Mar, I want to talk to you."

She ignored his presence, as if he were invisible and walked away from him and went to get her suitcase, throwing it on the bed with the clothes. She then started stuffing the clothes into it. When it was full, she got another large suitcase, put it on the bed, and stuffed more clothes into the bag.

Rodney observed that she was taking more than the usual amount of clothing with her this time, and grew desperate, thinking this time she was really going for good. "Mar, I'm changing. I'm not the same, I swear I'm not. Please, before you leave me, I need to speak with you," he said with such strong intention that she actually paused from her activities for a moment and looked at him.

"How many times have I heard that line? Why should I suddenly take your word for this, or for anything? I don't think you've changed a bit!"

"I've cut way down on the drugs, honest! And I've made the decision to quit altogether."

"Great, I hope your little hussy friends like you just as well when you do."

Marla continued to pack clothing into the suitcase as Rodney walked closer to her, about to talk, when she cut in, "You can go now, I let you speak. Now leave me alone, so I can finish."

He got down on his hands and knees like a beggar. "Marla, there's more. Please, please stop what you're doing for just a few minutes and come talk to me. Just this one last time, then I'll let you go. I'll leave you alone, honest," he said. He looked at her with such pathetic eyes that she gave in to him, partly because of a molecular sized place in her heart she still reserved for him, but mostly because he wouldn't leave her alone.

"Okay, damn it, hurry up. I don't want to be here all night," she said as she followed him out to the living room. She stood and folded her arms, reluctantly waiting for him to talk.

Rodney sat forward on a chair. "Marla, babe, I've made so many mistakes that I don't know if I can ever make things up to you. I just keep thinking about how rotten I've been. This whole music scene is a nightmare. I may be getting more famous, but I hate what I've become." He put his head in his hands and continued, "I feel like some sort of male prostitute, selling myself out to some jerks in the record biz so they can make a big buck. I've become a lying, cheating son of a bitch, and you don't deserve any of this."

"So what else is new?" she said, although noticing that Rodney was speaking to her in a tone that was a little more sincere than usual.

"Marla, please, don't disregard my words, please babe. I just want to express something I haven't admitted before. I used to say I didn't need you, and you didn't really do anything for me. Well, this is a total lie. I know you backed me up and believed in me during some of my roughest times, and me, I've just been a real asshole. Mar, I don't want to live my life without you."

"Rodney, it's been a living hell and you know it! You may tell me all these things about wanting to change, and how good you're going to be, but I can't trust you so easily, not with your history! I'm not going to sit around this apartment night after night, wondering if you're going to come home or if you're out getting smashed with some little whore! I just won't play that game anymore," she said as she stood up and started to go back to what she was doing.

Rodney shouted, this time with tears streaming from his eyes, "Marla, please! Please listen to me. I'm not done. I'm quitting my band! I'm getting out of the Rat trap!" he said as she stopped and turned around and looked at him.

"I'll believe that one when I see it."

"I swear it, Mar! I'm going to throw away my drug crutches and learn to walk free!"

"I'll believe that one when I see it too, no matter how poetically noble it sounds."

"Those are lyrics in a song that inspired me, helped push me over the edge. That's how powerful an artist's message can be. And that's the kind of message I'd like to be communicating, instead of all this other crap!"

Marla still wasn't convinced, and just as she turned, about to walk back to the bedroom, Rodney yelled, "Marla, no, just one more thing! I'm going to call Jim Scott right now and tell him I'm through! I want you to witness this, so you don't think I'm lying. Please come here."

She just stood with her arms crossed as Rodney dialed Jim's number. Marla stared at him, wondering if he was really calling Jim or just pretending. She didn't believe he would just up and quit the Gutter Rats with a simple phone call.

"Hello Jim, it's Rod,"

"Hey, it's the lead Rat? Whatcha need pal? You run out of pills or something?"

"No, thanks I've got plenty. In fact I'm gonna give you back the ones I've got."

Marla walked closer to Rodney, wondering whether there was really anyone on the other line. She went over to a desk drawer near where Rodney stood, and started emptying some of her things out of it. She pretended not to show much interest as she listened to see if she could hear Jim's voice.

"Yeah, I've flipped, Scott. No more drugs. This is the flip side of Rodney's CD. The first song is entitled "I'm Going Straight" and the second song is called "I'm Telling my Manager to Shove it!"

Scott laughed loudly into the phone, "Very funny Rod."

"You don't believe me, do you? Well maybe you'll see what I mean when I don't show up for my next gig. I'm quitting the band, man! I'm tired of being a Gutter Rat, cause that's what I've been feeling like. No more band. No more drugs! You and your shrink don't have me as a customer anymore. Go find some other sucker!"

There was yelling coming through the receiver and Rodney held the phone away from his ear. Marla could hear all kinds of profanities, and she turned from what she was doing and looked at Rodney with some amazement. Then Rodney slammed the phone down.

Seconds later the phone rang and Marla grabbed it, intercepting Rodney, "Let me get it," she said as she looked Rodney in the eye, "Hello."

Jim, about to yell some more, realized it was Marla, and quickly put the brakes on his temper, "Marla, it's Jim, I need to speak with Rodney."

"Oh Jim, I'm sorry, Rodney's not here," she said as she hung up the phone, not giving Jim a chance to say more.

Rodney pulled the phone cord out of the wall so it wouldn't ring and disturb them again. Then he walked over to Marla, and just looked at her, holding back on any desire to pull her close and hug her. "There! Do you believe me now, Mar? I'm finished. I couldn't have done it without you."

She looked puzzled, as he went on, "Don't you remember, long ago you told me I was mixed up with the wrong people and was too good for this type of lifestyle. I was a stubborn ass and wouldn't listen. It took a pretty hard crash before your words of wisdom sank in," he said. He walked over to a nearby chair and sat down. "Oh Mar, you have no idea how hard it's been."

Marla stood, unmoving, still reluctant to fully believe that all of a sudden everything was changed and that Rodney would just go back to leading a normal life.

Rodney saw her staring at the wall in front of her, her eyes flitting around, as thoughts he was unable to read ran through her mind.

"What do you want from me, Marla? I will do whatever you ask."

She walked over and sat in a chair opposite Rodney. "I want to see actions. I want to know that it's permanent this time! I can't go through any more of this torment, and at this point I think I'd be a fool if I forgave you so easily like every time I did in the past. Calling Scott was a good start, and I'm glad that you did, but..."

"So, you're not going to still move out are you?" Rodney asked desperately.

"Yes, Rodney, I am. I think it's best. I don't want to live here, not until you can really prove to me that you've changed for good and that the Rodney I used to know is back. I know it's not easy to get off of those drugs, and every time I've seen you try in the past, you've failed."

"Oh, Marla, babe, if that's the way you want it, then I have no other choice. I'll do whatever it takes. I don't care what kind of withdrawals I have to go through, or even if I have to go back to construction work for a while to make extra money. I'll make up the damage to you. I promise. No more drugs or promiscuity. Just please don't go running off with some other dude, unless I fail to do what I said I would," he pleaded. For the first time in ages he noticed how pretty Marla was as he gazed at her long blonde, curly hair and brown eyes, then did a cursory glance at her whole body. It was as if he'd been blinded by the stage lights and his sinful behavior all this time, just blocking her out of his life.

"You have a lot of nerve telling me not to run off with anyone. I didn't cheat on you once, not ever. But if you must know, being with another man isn't even on my mind right now. I just need to be on my own for a while," she said as she stood up and started walking back toward the bedroom.

"Marla, wait!"

"What is it Rodney?"

"Give me sixty days. If I haven't stuck to my word and changed my ways completely, then I'll give you a divorce."

Marla contemplated this for a minute, "Okay Rodney, I can agree to that. And if you have changed?"

"Then, then please come back to me."

"I can't make any promises, but I'll think about it," she said and then went to the bedroom to finish packing her bags and gathering the things she needed.

Rodney felt lonely and desperate.

Chapter 7

Two weeks after Rodney vowed to his wife he'd quit his band, Nicole was at the post office picking up mail that regularly came in from her "Get High on Art" project. She was greeted by a nice handful of letters and postcards. She always looked forward to her trips to the post office, knowing she'd come home and be rewarded with an array of mostly positive communication from various people.

When she got home she placed the mail on her desk in the living room and picked a letter off the top of the pile and read it. It was from a boy at one of the colleges where she and others had recently done a show. A feeling of satisfaction came over Nicole as she read the words in the letter: "Thank you much, everyone in GHOA. You got me to look at some very bad things I was doing. For years I was taking drugs just cause my friends were doing them. Sometimes my friend Billy, he'd make me come with him and his gang. They went shoplifting to get things to sell so they could buy more drugs. I stealed a couple of things but didn't feel good about it.

"At your show I cried. I remembered I used to play drums and had fun. Then I did drugs. This was supposed to be a good thing and it seemed like I was happy on drugs. But it was badder than I thought. I stopped learning things and gave up on music. All I cared was to do drugs. But at your show, your messages broke through my numb brain. You made me see I was on the wrong track. I decided to quit drugs and even not to hang around Billy and those guys anymore. I want to be a professional drummer, and a good one. I can't do that if I do drugs. I will practice very hard now. My mom even said she'd buy me a new drum set. Love, Danny Jordan."

Nicole put Danny's letter back in the envelope, then laid it to the side of the desk, intending to read it to the artists who came to monthly meetings for GHOA. She was very happy to read such a nice success story but felt badly about the poor level of literacy that came across in Danny's communication. She had seen this sort of thing with other letters from teenagers, and couldn't help but be disturbed by how poorly educated kids were these days. Nicole knew that her own schooling was poor, but nothing compared to what she'd seen lately.

She picked up the next letter in the pile and pulled out the note inside. She could barely read the scribbly handwriting but did make out the key parts of it. This person had heard a song of hers on the radio and wanted to help out in her campaign. She read the signature on the bottom, and was shocked to see a familiar name. It was signed "Rodney Nelson, formerly of Rodney and the Gutter Rats." Below the signature was a P.S. that read, "Thanks for carrying the torch out there and helping me to see the light at the end of the dark tunnel I was in. I have now joined the ranks of ex-druggies, and won't be turning back to the dark side again."

Nicole read the letter a second time, trying to decipher more of it. This time, she got more of the story from Rodney and how he wanted to get his wife and his life back together. She noticed an address and phone number stamped underneath Rodney's signature and decided that before going on to the other letters, she'd give him a call.

Just as she was about to dial his number, the phone rang, startling her, "Hello," she said.

"Nicole Jensen?"

"Yes."

A man on the other end cleared his throat, "Nicole, it's Mr. Jacobs from Horizon Records."

Nicole wrinkled her brow, puzzled as to why he would be calling, "Yes?"

"Nicole, I know our last meeting didn't go too well and I would like to personally apologize for being so hard on you."

"Oh, okay, well thanks for your apology," she said, wanting to get off the phone as soon as possible so she could call Rodney.

"Nicole," he cleared his throat again, "the executives here at Horizon recently had a board meeting and were looking at all possible prospects that could be signed to the label. The staff here has noted that your popularity has been rapidly growing, and I want to compliment you on that. Had I known that you would be such a big success with your material, I wouldn't have been so insistent upon your switch to more commercial types of songs. It's just that I was concerned about you at the time and wanted to be more cautious in my decision. I know that you are currently signed to some rinky-dink label that couldn't possibly do what we could for you, so I am calling to get your consent to come back to Horizon, with the promise that we will help triple your current CD distribution in the next few months. We can meet with your lawyer and work out a contract that is favorable to you."

The words of Mr. Jacobs echoed in Nicole's mind as she sat in silence for a few seconds.

"Nicole, hello, are you there?"

"Yes, I'm here."

"Look, I know this deal sounds too good to be true."

"Mr. Jacobs, I appreciate the offer, and even though it does tempt me, I can't accept it."

This time Mr. Jacobs was silent, and sat in surprise. He thought for sure she'd just up and rush into the arms of Horizon.

"Mr. Jacobs, are you there?"

"Yes, yes, Nicole, I just can't believe you're giving me a flat rejection on the offer."

"You have to understand, I have an allegiance to my rinky-dink record label, and even though this deal sounds great, I just can't walk away from them. They might not have the big bucks that Horizon has, but they've stood by me and helped me through some slow times when I was getting back on my feet. It would be against my sense of business ethics just to leave. I'm sorry I can't help you."

"All right, Nicole, then all I can do is wish you well," he said with a tone of both sincerity and resentment.

Nicole nonchalantly got off the phone with Stan Jacobs, only giving fleeting thoughts to the conversation. She phoned Rodney. He was quite flattered Nicole would call personally. They set up a meeting time and place to get together and talk.

Two days later, at a small uncrowded cafe on a hill in Topanga Canyon, Nicole met with Rodney in the middle of a weekday afternoon. Sitting at a round metal table with an umbrella in the center, Rodney took intermittent sips from a cup of steamy hot cappuccino, as he told Nicole the full story of how he came to his decision to quit the Gutter Rats.

"I admire your strength in pulling yourself out like that," Nicole said.

"Thanks. It was the hardest thing I've ever done in my life."

"I bet. People get very inspired when they see celebrities turn their lives around, and I don't see why you couldn't make a huge impact, especially on all the kids and teens that were big fans of yours."

"Yeah, I owe it to them. After all, I was probably partly responsible for getting them screwed up in the first place. You know how it is. Some kid says, 'There's Rodney, and he does drugs and messes around, so why shouldn't I?' I gotta make a bigger positive impact than the negative one I just left behind."

"Well, it sure sounds like you've taken the right first step, quitting the habit."

"Yeah, and I'm sure my shrink and his cohorts are gonna love the fact that I'm not giving them any more business."

"What do you mean? I thought you had to get those kind of drugs from a pusher.

"Yeah, well, maybe some druggies do, but hey, I was a high class addict. I got my stuff from the guys at the top. You know, the ones who are responsible for giving the pushers jobs in the first place."

"What?"

"You don't know what I'm talking about do you? You must have had a pretty straight life huh?"

"Well, not totally, I did my share of drugs and alcohol when I was a teenager, but you're right, I don't exactly know what you're talking about."

Rodney leaned toward Nicole, and gave her a smile of one who was old and wise, then put his hand on her shoulder and started talking in a feigned German accent, "My dear, you must listen to the advice of Dr. Delusion. I vant you to know that I gan geev you vat you need to escape from your problems. Ve have Barbiturates, Amphetamines, Heroin, LSD, you name it. Just take your pick and ve vill see to it that all your vorries are handled. You just need to stay on zee drugs and everyzing vill be fine." Rodney stopped and took his hand off of Nicole's shoulder, leaving her with an expression of surprise and enlightenment.

"You are telling me that all those street drugs originated with psychiatrists?"

"Vould I lie? Ve just send them out with street names, and nobody knows ve did it."

"No, I don't see why you would lie, but if what you're saying is true, then you've just put a piece of a puzzle together which I didn't even realize was missing. You mean many of those harmful street drugs were once, or still are, prescription drugs? Holy cow! Why would they do such a thing to people?"

"For control, Nicole. For profit and control. Pretty sneaky, huh?"

"Yeah, I'll say. What a ploy, boy. Go in with the pretense of wanting to help someone, and then give them something that destroys their mind."

"That's the deal, all right. Ain't no different with those other prescribed drugs they're giving out today, like Prozac and Ritalin. They don't have as bad a reputation as the older drugs, but just wait till they hit the streets."

"People need to know about this, Rodney. Look at all the school kids that are put on them. I had no idea they were as damaging as street drugs."

"After those nasty chemicals ripped me apart, I started researching this whole area, and have been reading about lots of actual cases of people who have been duped after taking the advice of the friendly 'men in white coats'. What the public doesn't realize is how insidiously these guys have been operating for years and years, with their aims to dope up the entire nation."

As Rodney said the word "years," Nicole had an eye-opening flashback, of going to the planet Nera after the Black Knights had introduced the drug "Probot" for use in controlling people. The similarity between the Knights and the psychiatrists was almost too inconceivable.

"Hey, Nicole, where did you go? Looks like you took off somewhere. Was it something I said?"

"Well, yeah, but it's okay. You've just got me looking at a very interesting perspective in regards to this whole scene. Sorry to just space out like that," Nicole said, after taking the last bite out of a chicken croissant sandwich. She then took some vitamins out of her purse. While holding them in her hand and leaning forward to grab a glass of water, the click of a stealthy camera went off, capturing a picture of her and Rodney, unbeknownst to either one of them.

"Don't be sorry."

"Rodney, I'd really like to use you in our next show. I think the first step would be to let the public know why you quit your band and that you have really turned around. Do you have any special songs you could perform, that would relay this message to them?"

Rodney gave this some thought and came up with an idea, "There is one that I started writing, a very special one that I've dedicated to my wife. I think it would get the point across."

"Great. I want to feature you. And in this performance I want to do something I haven't yet done."

"What's that?"

"I want to find some celebrities who have suffered from the abuses of psychiatric drugs and get them to be part of the show, sharing their stories as well," Nicole said with a newfound zealousness.

Nicole and Rodney finished their rendezvous and walked out to the street where their cars were parked. They hugged each other then both of them left.

Chapter 8

The day of the event arrived, with Rodney as the featured artist. Many of his old fans came to see the metamorphosis that had taken place in his life.

There was a lot of curiosity as to why the Gutter Rats broke up and what had happened to Rodney. Many of the people who attended wanted to get the story straight from the "horse's mouth" rather than rely on the rumors that were floating around in various publications.

Three thousand people filled the seats of a pavilion at a large college in the San Fernando Valley. Nicole's sister Cheryl and John's wife Claire had done a lot of promotion to local high schools, and their work contributed to the arrival of many of the attendees at the show.

"Good evening, everybody. I'm happy to see so many people here attending my fifth concert featuring members of "Get High on Art." Nicole said, opening the show for the evening. "It's so easy in this day and age to get wrapped up in a world where individual goals and dreams get suffocated underneath elements such as drugs and peer pressure. I'd like to dedicate my opening song tonight to one brave teenager who managed to break out from underneath these two elements to find his way back to what he loves to do best, which is to play drums. In fact you will have the opportunity to see him here on stage tonight, doing a special performance with my band. His name is Danny Jordan, and I'd like him to come out and say a few words."

The audience applauded and whistled as Danny, a tall black boy, came out from backstage and bashfully walked up to the mike as Nicole stood to his left. "Thanks. I never thought I'd be doing this, and if it wasn't for Nicole and her crusade, I might have been out with my old friends tonight getting high on drugs. Instead I'm here getting high on art! I've also been working on my illiteracy problem and have actually started to write songs, too," Danny said as the audience roared with applause. Then Danny went to take his place at a drum set on the stage. Chris came out from backstage and stood by the keyboards, and Dale came out and strapped his bass around his shoulders and stood in a position near Nicole, who was now holding her guitar and standing in front of a mike. The introduction to the song started out on piano and bass. Then Nicole started playing her guitar, and soon Danny hit the drums. Nicole sang.

"If you've got something to say, then say it.
If you've got a game to play, then play it.
If you've got something to do, don't wait around.
If you've got a song to sing, then sing it.
If you've got a message to bring, then bring it.
You can do anything you want right now, because
you're the spirit, the inspiration. You're the
life of vast creation. You're the maker of
anything that you dream........"

The song ended and the audience once more howled in approval. Then after Nicole acknowledged Danny, Dale and Chris, they exited the stage and Nicole remained.

"It is now my pleasure and privilege to bring to you one of the main people you have come here to see. I won't be introducing him the way that he was used to being presented in the past, because he no longer has his old image. He is a very strong individual who, much like Danny, has recently pulled himself up out of a deep hole in his life. I'd like to bring out Rodney Nelson!" Nicole said as Rodney walked towards the front of the stage waving at the adoring audience. He hugged Nicole and then traded places with her. She walked off backstage.

"Thanks for coming out here tonight. It's good to see so many of you guys here. I don't have a formal speech prepared, so bear with me. I want you to know that these past few months have been some of the most difficult yet rewarding times of my life." He cleared his throat and went on to spill his heart out to the crowd, who had their ears glued to his words. "Let me just say that the Rodney you knew, who was part of the Gutter Rats was an impostor, an actor who had on professional looking stage makeup that was all composed of garbage and lies.

"Many years ago when I was in my early twenties, I had written some really neat songs, ones that got people to take a look at things in the world that weren't right, much like Nicole's songs. I used to play them in an old band of mine, one that was very supportive of me and liked my lyrics a lot. But unfortunately, I let the band down. We'd been playing for low pay for so long, and even though I made a promise to stick it out until we got a record deal, I went against my word and quit. Yep, I was a traitor.

"It all happened one night when a man by the name of Jim Scott came to one of our gigs. Jim fell in love with my voice and encouraged me to quit my band and come and be the lead singer for a group known as the Gutter Rats. He told me not to worry about my band, because the important thing was to "look out for number one," as his shrink had told him. So I arrogantly left my old band behind and headed out to 'Hollyweird' and signed a contract to be a Rat," he said as he snickered at his put-down of himself. "Here I thought that all I'd have to do was sing a bunch of sleazy songs and then eventually, when I got a big name for myself, I'd get to do some of the originals I'd done with my old band. But that never happened. I just got caught up in all the "Sex and drugs and Rock N Roll" and ended up losing my sanity and developing a 'Twisted Mind', as 'pun' ishment.

"Before becoming a Rat, drugs were a small part of my life, but then I became convinced that I needed them. You name it I did it. Even tried some Prozac and Xanax, which are no better than street drugs.

"So, meanwhile, while I was on this sleigh ride going down the tubes at a rapid rate, my old lady and I were fighting all the time. She couldn't stand to see me getting worse and worse. Marla, she was one hell of a supporter and before I joined the Rats she'd just kept backing me up all the way, but then I let her down. I just lost control, and to make matters worse I took the advice of Jim Scott, who used to say, "when your love life ain't heatin, there's nothin wrong with a little cheatin." So there I went, down, down, down, until finally I really crashed. It was a good thing I did, because when I hit my head hard enough, it finally knocked some sense into me.

"I told Marla I was quitting my band and getting off drugs for good. Unfortunately, the hard part was getting her to believe in me again, because of all the times I'd lied to her in the past. She decided to move out in spite of my pleas, and I don't know that she'll ever want to come back, but at least if I really make it this time, I've got another slim chance with her," he said as he forced himself to hold back his grief. "Anyway, I'm "going straight," and that's the title of a new song I've written which I'd like to dedicate to my wife Marla. I hope she'll let me play it for her someday," he said as he went over and picked up his guitar and sang.

"I've been sitting in a drug delusion.
My life has been a total confusion.
I've betrayed myself for so long,
betrayed you. I've done wrong.
I didn't want it to turn out this way,
living lies from day to day.
I've been away from myself for so long,
got lost in a rock n roll song.
I'm not what I was pretending to be.
I've got good intentions inside of me.
So I'm going straight.
I'm going straight.
I'm going straight.
I'm going straight.
I'll make up the damage I've done to you,
because I know what I've put you through.
I want to give you what you want from me.
I just want to make you happy.
Just want to be like we were before,
working together and reaching for more.
I just want a normal life,
without drugs and with you as my wife........."

Rodney finished, and was saluted with a standing ovation. He dried the inescapable tears that meandered from his eyes while some members of the audience also dried theirs. Then he brought out a drummer and keyboard player and went on to play several more songs, all earlier ones that he'd written before he became a Rat.

When he finished the last song of his set, the other musicians exited and Rodney addressed the audience. "You have no idea how good it feels to be up here. This is the first time I've played these tunes in many, many years, and I hope I was able to touch your lives in a positive way," he said, as there was some howling and whistling in the crowd.

Rodney smiled contentedly and went on, "Thanks. Let me tell you, it's been absolute hell not going back to my old habit, but no matter what suffering I've had to endure, I know that I've climbed back out of a deep, dark ditch and am seeing a light I haven't seen for years. I don't know how many of you out there are currently doing drugs, and I won't ask you to raise your hands so I can target you as bad guys or anything. But I just want you to know that I really care about you, and feel that I need to make up the damage I did when I may have influenced some of you in the wrong way. Many of you are still pretty young and have the potential to live long and happy lives. All I hope is that you don't blow it by becoming a living dead man like I was. In the early stages of addiction I didn't ever think I'd turn out to be such a deluded basket case, but over the years I saw just how low I could go. One time I was going through a real dry spell as a songwriter and was told that I just needed the right type of hallucinogenics to expand my creativity. Well, let me tell you that after going down this road, I almost hit the most disastrous dead end of all. I nearly committed suicide. I don't care what temporary, magical pictures I had in my mind, they did nothing for my songwriting. This is another blatant lie, about drugs enhancing creativity, which the psychiatrists have used for ages, and too many artists have fallen prey to it. Now I want you all to leave tonight remembering that 'Rodney says NO.'

"One last thing. I'd just like to say that the worst part of what occurred with me wasn't my addiction, believe it or not. That was a horrible symptom of an underlying disease, one that Nicole Jensen refers to as "Dream Demise," and it comes from self-betrayal. I became my own worst enemy, and when you can't be a friend to yourself how can you truly care about anyone else? And I didn't. So I've learned that you've got to be true to your own goals and stand up for what you believe in no matter what evil influences try to lead you astray.

"Thanks for being here. I hope to see you again soon. My profound appreciation goes out to Nicole and her group, of which I have recently become a member. Good-night." The audience once again gave a standing ovation. Then Rodney waved to them and went backstage.

Nicole came out and announced the next celebrity guest, an actress by the name of Shawna Dunn, who had recently quit using Prozac, after nearly killing herself and another passenger in a car accident. As Shawna addressed the audience, Rodney talked with some of the other artists and show personnel backstage. Just as Rodney was speaking to a couple of people, he stopped short, as his attention was drawn to someone approaching him, "Excuse me guys, I don't mean to be rude, but I've got to go. I'll get back to you." Both of the people he was talking with turned and looked at each other and then continued on with their conversation.

"Marla, you're here," Rodney said with the surprise of a kid who has just seen Santa Clause. He stood in front of her, once again suppressing the desire to throw his arms around her, but didn't know if it would be appropriate yet.

"Hello Rodney," she said, still somewhat walling herself behind the earlier grudge she'd had for him.

They stood silently, staring into one another's eyes until Rodney spoke, "So, you saw my show?"

"Mmm hmm,"

Rodney nervously ran his fingers through his hair, feeling some tenseness between them, "And you, uh, how did you get backstage?"

"I said I was your wife. I had to show ID to prove it too."

"Oh," Rodney liked hearing her still referring to herself as his wife, "Well, it's good to see you Mar."

Marla moved closer to him, as she made the decision to allow some of the wall to crumble around her, "Rodney, I just want you to know that I was very proud of you tonight. It seems to me that you're really doing it this time. Something's different."

"It is Marla, very different. I'm not alone Mar. I have a group, a group of other people who want to see a drug free world as badly as I do. With all this encouragement and support, it makes things a lot easier."

Marla's solemn lips curved upward into a smile, the first one that Rodney had seen on her face for ages. Then he closed his eyes tightly for a second and took a deep breath. When he opened them they were watery. "Marla, God, Mar. Do you know how good it makes me feel inside, to see that look on your face again? It's one that I destroyed over the years, when I turned your life into a nightmare. Seeing you here, looking at me like that is such a nice reward."

Marla reached inside of her purse and pulled out a Kleenex and held it up to his cheek and started to dry his tear, "How would you like an even nicer reward?"

"What's that?"

"Your reward for having successfully gotten through your probation period?" she asked as she put the Kleenex back in her purse.

Rodney couldn't hold back any longer and gave her a long awaited embrace, "Oh Marla, I'd love to have you back. I've missed you so much, babe."

Chapter 9

After Rodney's successful college performance, many kids started turning their lives around. Some made decisions to quit taking drugs and join the GHOA project.

Performances by the GHOA artists were more and more in demand. As a result, several events were done simultaneously in various locations. There were also newspaper and magazine interviews featuring Nicole, Rodney, Chris, and other artists and celebrities. Much of the press was favorable, although there were some critical articles, as can be expected from the journalistic field. More and more people were taking themselves off the detrimental psychiatric drugs that they'd previously befriended as aids to their survival. Parents who became enraged about the truth behind the drug scene ensured that Ritalin, Prozac, or other such mental toxins would not poison their kids.

While many people throughout the country were joyously ridding themselves of the torments of substance addiction, the ones who weren't celebrating at all were the big drug dealers (psychiatrists and other pushers), and IB Dilly, the largest drug manufacturer in the U.S. So much money was lost by IB Dilly, that they nearly went out of business, which would have made their remaining supportive customers very upset.

Chris and Nicole managed to take a break in their hectic touring schedule and had a small wedding celebration with intimate family and friends. Chris and Jeremy moved out of the house they were renting in Sherman Oaks, and moved into the Brentwood townhouse that Nicole owned.

Two weeks after the wedding, Chris was out of town doing a big art show at a national exhibition. He was there along with other drug-free visual artists, who were successfully displaying and selling their paintings and inspiring the spectators that came to the show.

Nicole was home one day, typing a letter to Chris on her computer. Although he had only been gone for a week, she felt lonely without him there. As she wrote, the melody to the wedding song she'd written for them danced through her mind. The song held a very special place in her heart because she'd taken it from the song which was played for her and Ladaar on their honeymoon on Placid Isle

After finishing the letter, Nicole flipped through a photo album that contained pictures of her and Chris at their wedding and reception. She stopped and looked at a particular picture. It was one where a friend of theirs was playing her wedding song, entitled "A Magic Feeling," while she and Chris, and their guests, listened. As she gazed at this pleasurable moment in the near past, Nicole sang some of the words to the song aloud.

"A true love is a lifetime friend.
Growing stronger with no end.
On and on and on and on.
Their journey is about to begin.
They'll work as a team and play to win....

"Nicole finished singing and closed the album. Then she went to her mailbox to send off the letter to Chris at his temporary residence in Arizona, where he'd be staying for another two weeks. After Nicole put the letter in the brass box, she took a deep breath and her nostrils were treated to the sweet scent of honeysuckle. She looked above her at the clear blue sky which was adorned with white, puffy clouds and felt a sense of fulfillment she couldn't remember ever feeling before. She quickly thought about the large number of artists and other supporters she'd been working with over the past several months and still found herself amazed at how many others shared her views on changing society for the better. Then, just as she bathed in her gratification and was about to walk back in the house, she heard her name being called. She turned to her right, and there was Mr. Milligan, frantically running over to her while carrying a newspaper in his hands.

"Nicole, honey, I hate to be a harbinger of bad tidings, but when I saw this article in the paper, I thought you'd want to know about it if you hadn't seen it already," Mr. Milligan said, as he stood next to her, slightly out of breath. He opened the large,

"National News" paper, which he'd had folded in half, and showed Nicole one of the headlines and pictures on the front page.

Nicole came down off of the cloud she was in as she took the paper from him. There was a picture of Rodney and her sitting at the table at the Topanga cafe where they first met, several months ago. Nicole held some "pills" in her right hand, and was reaching for a glass of water. The caption read, "Nicole Jensen, 'pusher' for a drug-free America, is a hypocrite."

She went on to read the first paragraph of the short, libelous article which read, "Nicole, who claims that one of societies biggest ills is drugs, seems to be a user herself. Although she has been promoting to others that they should stay off of all sorts of drugs, even those that are prescribed by psychiatrists for medicinal purposes, she seems to have a need for them. Nicole, who has been making a comeback, over the past year, is now slandering the use of beneficial substances that are needed in the treatment of many mentally ill patients. It appears that Nicole doesn't fully believe in the cause she is fighting for. Rather she is using this controversial public issue merely to gain popularity by convincing those who really need these substances to function properly that they don't. Her followers have been buying into her anti-drug preaching."

Nicole stopped reading and looked up at Mr. Milligan who stood on her porch with a sympathetic look on his face, "No, I haven't seen this one yet," Nicole said, trying to numb some of the anger that she'd felt.

"Sorry to ruin your day, dear, but I thought you might have wanted to see it," he said and then put a fatherly hand on her right shoulder. "Dear, I feel bad for you. It seemed like you were doing such a good thing, but I had no idea that you also had a habit yourself. Must be a lot of pressure in your business and I can understand where you might have to fall back on some pills once in awhile. But why, why Nicole, would you try to tell all those other people not to take their medications?"

Some of Nicole's anger surfaced, "Mr. Milligan, first of all, I want you to know something. Those pills you see me taking in that photo are vitamins!"

"But, I..." Mr. Milligan practically fell over from Nicole's blast.

"Yeah, I have a real bad habit. I pop those little pills every day. Let me tell you what hypocrisy is. Many of those same doctors who claim that their medicine is so good, would love to see my type of pills, the ones that cure people without bad effects, taken off the market!

"The next thing I want you to know is that the pills prescribed by the psychiatrists are the very drugs that end up on the streets and damage innocent lives!" she said as she folded the paper and slapped it against the side of her house. She wasn't quite sure why she was so over-reactive to this particular article. Nicole had been used to getting bad press from time to time, but there was something about this one which enraged her more than usual. She didn't know if it was because she'd suddenly made national headlines in this way, or if there was some other unknown reason for her upset that she couldn't put her finger on.

"Calm down, dear. I hate to see you get so shaken up. Martha and I still respect you, getting all those kids off of street drugs. But, just watch out when you start encroaching on the territory of the doctors that have gone to school for years to study up on how to treat people with medications."

Nicole could see that Mr. Milligan did not take her words about the psychiatrists to heart, as he wasn't willing to accept this shocking new reality. Rather than pursue the matter further, Nicole decided not to try and convince him. She had enough other supporters, and had to accept the fact that not everyone was going to be ready for the truth yet.

"I should really get back to work. Do you mind if I keep this article?"

"No, by all means go ahead. In fact, take the whole newspaper. Martha and I are done with it."

"Thanks."

"Just be careful, sweetheart," Mr. Milligan said and then went back to his home.

Nicole walked into her house and threw the paper down on her kitchen table, then sat down in a chair and sighed. She read the rest of the nasty editorial and wondered whether she should take action in the form of a lawsuit. Then she thought about all the time and money involved with such a pursuit and didn't know if she should bother. Nicole knew that one of the dangers of being a celebrity on planet Earth was being subjected to injustice in the media, a deadly force that was often hard to fight back against. As she sat and sulked, while looking at the picture in the paper, she wondered who had taken the photo without Rodney or herself noticing.

Chapter 10

Lester Sherman Dopum, an executive of the American Psychiatric Association, was at home in his Beverly Hills mansion, talking on the phone. He sat behind a desk in his office on the third floor of the large, Southern style home when he heard the front door open and shut. Taking his feet off of a large, mahogany desk, he got up and looked out of the office door. He saw his eleven-year-old son looking out of a window, waving good-bye to his mother. The wrinkles on Lester's face pulled together, aging him more than his forty something years, as he cringed at the sight below him. After satisfying his curiosity, he went back and sat in his chair. He fiddled with a personally monogrammed pen, staring at the letters LSD, as he spoke, "Sorry, I didn't hear what you said, Jim. Peter just got out of school and Pam brought him over. She had to go to her lawyer to get more legal documents for us to go over before we finalize this divorce thing," he said. He was about to continue, but was interrupted by a teenage boy walking into the room.

"Dad," said his other son, who Lester considered his only real friend.

"What is it, Troy?" Troy was the only family member who shared the large home with him since his wife Pam had moved out, taking Peter with her.

"I don't feel right. I'm depressed."

"I'm sorry, but I can't counsel you now, I'm busy. When was the last time you took your Prozac?"

Troy tensely twisting his hands together, "I, um..."

Before he could answer, Lester cut in, "Look, why don't you go and take a pill now. I can see that you need something to calm you down. I gotta get back to this conversation. I'll spend some time with you later. I promise," he said with some sincerity.

"Okay, Dad." Troy nervously ran out of the room, down a long hallway to his bedroom, where he rushed to the medicine cabinet and pulled out a pill. He turned on the faucet with a shaky left hand while cupping his right hand under the spout, catching some water in it.

He then threw the water in his mouth followed by the drug, which his father had him taking regularly now for the past two years. Then Troy turned on the TV in his room and pounced on his double bed, wrinkling the bedspread.

Lester opened a drawer in the center of his desk and pulled out a newspaper, smiling in a wickedly pleased manner, at the picture on the front of it. "Scott, I gotta hand it to you, using those spy tactics of yours to get someone to track Rodney and Nicole like that a couple of months ago was ingenious. It gave us a real good caption. I knew that I could finally come up with a big enough payoff to that paper, so they'd do an article. Too bad it took this long, but we did it, man."

They both indulged in a few seconds of evil laughter, then Jim spoke, "Hey, I don't know whose enjoying this more, me or you."

"I don't know, but wait till I show Bud. He'll get a kick out of it too," Lester said, referring to one of his good friends on the Board, who was also Jim's psychiatrist.

"Yup, Nicole deserves all the bad publicity we can get on her. If it wasn't for her little Get High on Art scheme, Rodney might never have tried to become something other than a Rat. What a waste, man, just as he was getting real famous, bam, some chick comes along and ruins me. Women, what are they good for?"

"Women are sick creatures, often very neurotic. In the case of Nicole, she suffers from Hyper-Utopia syndrome, wanting to make the world a perfect place, at the expense of anyone who should stand in her path."

"Hey, maybe you should try and get her committed. Then you could get your hands on her and give her the kind of therapy she really needs, like you've done with so many other women."

Lester pounded his fist on his solid desk, "Damn it, man! I wouldn't give her that kind of treatment. Demonstrative sexual confidence therapy is only for those depressed females who come to me after they've had failures in their relationships with a man. In order to boost their self-esteem and make them feel they can fulfill their role as a woman, I appeal to their sensuality by seducing them.

"As far as Nicole, I just want to strangle her little neck. Do you know that my huge shares in IB Dilly are only worth pennies now! That monster is responsible for cutting my drug money to shreds, with her damn crusade, not to mention the drop in business that has occurred in my respectable profession!"

"That's too bad. I was thinking of joining you in your field, after my career took a recent dip into the dumps; just so I could fondle some more females, but now I don't know if it would be worth it. I may not get much business."

Lester's nostrils flared, and he started yelling as Jim held the phone receiver away from his ear. "Hey, watch it, man! How dare you insinuate that I'm in the business of fondling females! I'm a highly regarded expert, and my treatment of women is only for therapeutic means! Got it?"

"Okay, okay. Sorry, I didn't mean to pull the bull by the horns."

As they continued their heated conversation, Peter carried a couple of schoolbooks and sauntered up the long stairway leading to the third floor. He was on his way to his old bedroom, the one he'd slept in nearly every night for nine years until he moved out with his mother after she decided to divorce Lester. Peter hated his father and resented having to come to his old house at all. As he got near the top of the stairway, he heard Lester, whom he'd referred to as "the ogre," talking loudly and obnoxiously on the phone. He stood still for a moment, listening to his dad's husky voice, while recalling a time about two years ago when he and his mother verbally tore each other apart in that very office. Peter remembered crying in the hallway by the office door while listening to Pam being tormented as she insisted that Peter be permanently taken off the Ritalin that Lester had him on. Lester refused to comply with Pam's wishes and told Pam that she was out of line to ever counter his authority on what was best for the children.

Then he recalled Pam throwing several of Lester's textbooks off of a large bookshelf where they'd been neatly arranged. She spoke with fury, "Listen to me, would you. You've wrecked me and now you are destroying our children! I'm leaving you for good Lester! This is the last straw. Peter doesn't want to stay on Ritalin! It's making him violent and messing up his mind."

"Quit ruining my office, you bitch! He's hyperactive. He needs it!"

"No, he doesn't! It's made him worse! He made a decision to go off of it after going to the anti-drug concert last week!"

"Damn it! You go to some stupid performance by this Nicole lunatic, who thinks that no one should do street drugs, and then you come home ranting and raving! Ritalin isn't even a street drug, and he's on it for a very good reason!"

Peter caught Lester, about to slap Pam, and cried "stop!" Lester complied. He didn't really have the heart to hit her in front of him. "You're a psychotic woman, Pam, a real psycho-delusive."

"That's right, make something up, just whip up a name for me out of your handy-dandy imaginary dictionary!"

"You're just plain nuts! I should give you a taste of your own medicine and drop some Ritalin in your coffee."

"I'm afraid you're the one who's nuts! You know that your damn prescription drugs are just as nasty as many of those hard core street drugs! I hear Ritalin is even being sold on the streets now, under a different name!"

"Enough woman! Get out of my life, both of you! Go ahead. Take our child. But you're not taking Troy. He's mine."

"Don't worry. Troy won't come with me. He refuses to quit your drugs. He thinks he needs you, and that I'm the enemy! Hopefully he'll wake up before it's too late!"

The memory faded from Peter's mind as his attention was drawn to the discussion between Lester and Jim. Peter quietly slipped around to a side wall of the office, pressing his ear against a wooden panel, unnoticed.

"I seriously am considering hiring another hit man to go to Nicole's next show and just take her out once and for all. She's apparently recovered from her injuries that my man inflicted on her last time. The dope had to go and manage to get himself caught, but this time it'll be different."

"You don't think that's overreacting a bit, do you?"

"Not after she wrecked my income recently, as well as my marriage a couple of years ago! She's a vicious one, and I think my personal vendetta for her is pretty well justified. Between the bad press and the prior attack, I didn't have to worry about her for a while, but now she's wreaking havoc on my life again."

Jim Scott said nothing, and for a few seconds grew worried about Nicole.

"Well partner, what's the silent treatment about?"

"I, well...uh, I don't know if I'd go that far."

Lester grinned wickedly, "Since when did you become a wuss?"

"Hey, watch who you're calling a wuss. I got you that prize photo."

"Yeah, and I paid you a pretty penny for it. Why don't you help me out with this one, and I'll really make it worth your while." Again, there was silence on Jim's end. He felt a sudden headache coming on as his thoughts jumped back and forth. He was torn between the death of Nicole and more material wealth, or settling for his current financial condition and keeping Nicole alive.

"I can't do it buddy. You'll need to find another sniper. As much as I resent her, I just can't go out and have her shot, other than from a camera."

"Damn it, Scott! If you won't do it, then I'll have to find someone else I can rely on," Lester said, feeling a well of hatred for Nicole that ran deeper than seemed logical. There was something unusual about his disgust for her that he couldn't analyze.

As Lester got off the phone with Jim, Peter scurried to his old bedroom and put his schoolbooks down on his desk. He sat down on a chair, threw open a book, and pretended to study as he heard the footsteps of his father coming down the hallway. Peter snarled to himself as Lester stopped in front of the doorway and looked in, "Hello, son."

"Hi."

"Good to see you sitting there in your old room. Too bad your mother had to steal you away from me. I kind of miss seeing you here."

Peter cringed as Lester walked over to where he sat pretending to ponder over a page in a book. Lester glanced at the page and then ruffled Peter's short brown hair in a playful manner, "So, how's school?"

"Fine."

"Just fine? You don't seem too happy. Aren't they employing the program that my board recommended, the one where they are supposed to be getting you kids in touch with your inner feelings instead of doing so much intellectual studying about history and English and other academic subjects?

"Yeah, we do that."

"Good, I'm glad to hear that, because we have enough scientists and engineers out there. People need to know more about the emotional side of life," he said, as Peter clumsily dropped the book on the floor, and said nothing in response to Lester's comment.

"Well you're awfully silent. What have you got to say?"

"I don't think the program is so good,"

"What are you talking about Peter?"

"Every year, I've been learning less and less. We talk about our feelings too much."

"Well, that's wonderful. Do you see something wrong with that?"

He turned resentfully and looked into the dull brown eyes of his father, "Yeah, how can I grow up and go do something useful in the world if all I know is what kind of mood I'm in that day."

"Don't be ridiculous, son. I can tell you've been listening to your mother about this again. She's the one who always feeds these ludicrous ideas into your brain." He heard the sound of the front door being closed shut, "Well, speak of the devil, I think Pam is back. I better go see what that lawyer of hers said."

Peter sat with tightly pursed lips and sneered at his father's back as Lester started walking towards the doorway and then headed down the long staircase to confront Pam.

Meanwhile, as Lester was wrapped up with Pam, Troy was in his room attempting to paint a picture. He had placed a canvas on an easel, but instead of being creatively inspired, he just stared at the canvas with a look as blank as "it" was. Dreaming up pictures in his mind and making them come to life, which used to be very easy for him a few years ago, now seemed to be a laborious task. Nevertheless, he tried to overcome his frustrations. However, the more he sat, the angrier he became. Outraged by the fact that he felt he could no longer paint the kind of pictures that once won him prizes in contests, he took a tube of red paint, squeezed it and smashed it against the canvas. Then he took a tube of blue paint and repeated this action. He watched the oozing colors overlap one another and drip upon a white carpet. As the Prozac caused more fury to well up inside of him, he took a paintbrush and violently jabbed its handle into the canvas, poking several holes into it.

"Peter," Pam yelled, twenty minutes later, signaling her son to come downstairs. She was now ready to leave.

As Pam drove off with Peter, Troy was driving himself crazy with his uncontrolled frenzy. He had taken the canvas down and smashed it over a sharp, pointed bedpost, leaving it there as a decoration. Then he squeezed swirls of red paint onto his carpet, as if he was garnishing a hamburger with ketchup.

Lester's attention was yanked away from his own activities when he heard the sound of glass being shattered. He ran up the stairs to Troy's room in time to observe him smashing an expensive mirror with a baseball bat.

"Troy! Put that down!" Lester yelled with enough force to cause Troy to drop the bat.

Lester ran over to his son and grabbed and held him. Troy tried to get free from his strong grip. Then he gave in and broke down and cried. "Dad, I'm so confused."

Lester pulled his son over to the bed and sat and comforted him, "I understand. You're just having a crisis. It will be okay. Just keep taking the Prozac and everything will be fine," he said sympathetically, not knowing what else to do for his son's depression. He tried hard to hide his own anxiety over his concern for Troy.

"Come on, let's get out of the house for a while and go for a walk on the beach. You always feel better when we do this."

"Okay" Troy agreed, following Lester out to his car.

They arrived at a secluded beach area in Palos Verdes and spent time walking and talking.

"Dad, you know, sometimes I get real scared and think I'm going to die."

"Oh Troy, don't torment yourself. You're just going through the normal pains of adolescence. You'll be fine. I'll help you get through it," Lester said, affectionately putting his arm around his son as the sound of a wave crashed upon the shore.

"Come on Troy, let's go over there. I'll race you," Lester playfully said as he ran to a wall of rocks that jutted out into the sea.

Troy snapped out of his gloom for the moment and attempted to keep pace with his father. Lester stepped foot on a giant boulder and over-zealously ran along. Troy was close behind. Just as Lester was maintaining his lead, he lost his foothold and twisted his ankle, taking a near fatal step that almost plunged him into the crashing water below.

"Dad!" Troy yelled as he raced to grab Lester's arm. Playing tug of war with the force of gravity, Troy managed to win as he helped his father stand up.

Chapter 11

It was 12:30 p.m. when the bell rang at Hillside elementary school in Beverly Hills, ending lunch period. Peter Dopum, late for class, carried his books and ran at full speed down a long corridor. Peter slipped into the back door of the course room. Mrs. Smeech, a short chubby teacher, had just finished doing roll call. She had her back turned to the students, about to write something on a blackboard, when she was distracted by the sound of footsteps. She turned around and saw Peter trying to sneak into his seat without being noticed by her.

"Mr. Dopum, how nice of you to join us today," she said as Peter turned red with embarrassment. "No, don't sit up here, dear. These front seats are for my punctual pupils. You've been late four days in a row. If this happens one more time, I'm sending you to the principal's office for a counseling session to determine the true cause of your continued tardiness. I want you to sit in the back of the room in that empty seat next to Mr. Andrews, in the far right corner, until you can prove to me that you can make it here on time," she said. The Mr. Andrews she was referring to was Jeremy, Chris' son, who had just transferred to Hillside school a couple of weeks ago when the new semester started.

Peter said nothing and just walked to his newly assigned seat. The eyes of every student gazed at him as if they were watching a game of darts with Peter as the target.

Mrs. Smeech went back to the blackboard, picked up some chalk and wrote the words, "Morals = principles or standards in regard to right or wrong conduct."

"Now children, can you tell me why this word is no longer applicable to our lives?"

A girl with long red hair and freckles raised her hand.

"Yes, Amy."

"We follow our own emotions and if something feels good then we use that as a judgment, not what is supposed to be right or wrong,"

"Very good," Mrs. Smeech said and continued on with this topic a while longer. Then she went on to what had become a favorite subject in her classroom, "All right, now we will spend some time on sex education. We have recently been watching a number of films on sexual behavior. These films may very well tempt many of you to go out and try it for yourself at some point. However, boys and girls, it is very, very important that you protect yourselves from unwanted pregnancies," she said as she proceeded to pull two cucumbers out of a drawer along with two condoms.

"Now I would like to have two boys volunteer for our live condom fitting demonstration."

The students looked around at each other and Mrs. Smeech smirked, "All right, don't you all raise your hands at once. Am I going to have to do the picking?" she asked, as one boy put his hand up, and then another bashfully raised his.

"Very good. Now, you two brave students come up here."
As Mrs. Smeech proudly continued, Jeremy opened his notebook. He didn't even notice that the front cover nearly hit Peter on the arm. Then he started to open a plastic utensil pouch. As he unzipped it and pulled out a pencil, Peter's eyes were drawn to a piece of paper that stuck out of a slot on the inside of Jeremy's notebook. Peter quickly read the words, "To Jeremy, may your dreams come true. Love, Nicole Jensen."

Peter was surprised at what he saw and turned to Jeremy and lightly tapped him on the arm, getting his classmate's attention. Jeremy started to close the notebook as he looked at Peter, but Peter shook his head and whispered, "No, don't close it."

Jeremy complied and re-opened it. Peter pointed to the note by Nicole and continued to whisper, "Do you know her?"

"Yeah, why? You want her autograph or something?"

"No, it's not that. I have another..."

"Okay, you two. That's enough. Mr. Dopum, I want you to go to the principal's office immediately. Not only have you been coming to class late, but when you're here, you just end up talking to other students. You haven't been doing well in your studies, and when I speak with you, you seem to be miles away. I'm worried about you Peter, and I want you to be checked out for possible Attention Deficit Disorder."

Peter resentfully stood up as Jeremy looked at him wondering what he was going to say about Nicole. Again, the eyes of the students all turned to Peter as he pushed back his chair and started to comply with Mrs. Smeech's orders. Before Peter left, he quickly whispered to Jeremy, "I need to see you after school."

"Peter, you just can't control yourself can you? It's too bad you ever moved away from your father. I'm sure he could have helped you with your inadequacies," she said as she got a piece of paper and a pen and wrote a note to the principal about Peter. "Now, pick up your books and take them with you. I don't know if you'll make it back to class today. Come here and get this note and give it to Mr. Sneglwhurt."

Peter got the note, and reluctantly left the classroom and made his way to the building where the principal's office was. When he got there, he gave the receptionist the note from Mrs. Smeech, and then was told to take a seat at one of the small desk/chairs in the office. About ten desk/chair sets lined the walls of the sterile office. Six of them were filled with other students who resentfully sat in the stuffy room as if they were waiting to be summoned before a judge to plead guilty or not guilty for their crimes.

"Students, if you are not studying, please do so. The wait may be long, and I'm sure you could make better use of your time if you were being studious," the receptionist said, noticing that there were only a few who were bothering to study. Peter reluctantly opened a book and pretended to read. His bluffing was partially because he didn't want to study and partially because his understanding of the English language was so poor that he couldn't read very well. He thought for a moment about the fact that even when he'd wanted to learn something, he had an incredibly hard time and blamed this on the teachers who were more concerned with his feelings than his education.

Three hours ticked slowly by and Peter couldn't understand what was taking so long. He was glad to be away from Mrs.

Smeech and only really wanted to get back to class so he could catch Jeremy after school.

"Peter Dopum," the receptionist called, as Peter jumped out of his thoughts and looked up at a tall, skinny woman with a hooknose. "Peter, Mr. Sneglwhurt is ready for you."

Peter followed the woman to the office of the principal. He went into the large, boxy room, which smelled just as much like a classroom as any other room in the school. Peter sat in front of the principal's desk and watched the plump, bald man in the gray suit read the note from his teacher. After talking with Peter for several minutes, Mr. Sneglwhurt decided to send him to the school psychologist, to determine what to do about Peter's possible case of Attention Deficit Disorder.

The tall skinny receptionist came back to the principal's office and led Peter down the hallway of what felt to him like a juvenile prison. He arrived at the room of the psychologist and sat in the back of her office along with three other kids. Again, the time painfully ticked away as Peter waited his turn to be sentenced for his crimes. This time, only one hour went by before his turn came.

The three other kids had finished their consultations and it was now Peter's turn. He sat in front of the desk of Miss Noos, the psychologist, who questioned him about various habits that he had at school and at home. She carefully took notes, then compared Peter's answers to a reference chart which listed out the symptoms of ADD. Then she sympathetically leaned forward and told Peter that he very definitely had ADD, and that his mother would be consulted about putting him in a special education class for the learning disabled. As Peter sat silently, Miss Noos looked in a book that gave a listing of teachers in the area that taught sixth grade children with ADD.

Peter hated school so much, that it didn't matter a whole lot to him what kind of classroom he was in. He just wanted the years to go by so he could get free of the educational system. He despised coming to school every day not knowing which of his friends or classmates was going to be pronounced dead from a drug overdose or shot by the psychotic frenzy of another student who carried a gun. He remembered a time when he himself went berserk on Ritalin, and started beating up a friend of his. It was as if he were being controlled by a demon living inside of him over which he'd had no control.

Peter almost didn't hear Miss Noos as she started to speak, until he heard the word of the dreaded drug he used to be on, "and so Ritalin would be the next choice, should the special education fail."

Peter sat erect in his chair and squinted his eyes and gave Miss Noos a look which nearly strangled the words that she was about to say, "Peter, my god, you look as if you've seen the devil."
"I have!"

"Why, what do you mean?"

"Ritalin is the devil, and I'm never being burned by it again!"

"Again?"

"Yeah, again. I was on it once and I hated it! It ruined me!"

She forced a smile on her perturbed face, knowing that she had to handle Peter's delusion about such a miracle drug. "Now, Peter, it couldn't have been the Ritalin that did anything to you. It may have been the fact that you already had a psychological disorder, and that the chemical imbalance in your brain was disturbed, but I assure you that Ritalin didn't harm you one little bit."

Peter knew that it was useless arguing with these psych types, because they always think they know best, besides, he knew that his mother would protect him against anyone who tried to get him back on the evil substance.

As Peter sat there with Miss Noos around his neck, the sound of crying could be heard as the receptionist led a girl into the room.

"Excuse me, Peter," said Miss Noos, who frantically got up and went over to greet the young girl, whom she'd just recently treated. She thought the girl was doing better, but by the looks of the outbreak, she was having a relapse. As Miss Noos comforted her, the receptionist left and walked back down the sterile hallway.

Peter heard the loud clicking of the minute hand on the clock on the wall. There were only two more minutes before class let out for the day. He got up and walked over to where Miss Noos was standing with the girl, "I gotta go to the bathroom."

"Okay, dear, but hurry back. We're not quite...," she said, unable to finish her sentence, as she was distracted by compulsive kicking and clawing being delivered to her by the girl

"Ouch!"

Peter took advantage of this commotion, and walked out of her office. He surreptitiously made his way past the front desk where the receptionist was. Just as he thought he was going to make a cool exit, he heard his name being called, "Mr. Dopum."

Peter turned around and looked at the receptionist.

"I need to see your dismissal notice showing that you have clearance to leave the building. Normally Miss Noos has one of the receptionists come and pick the notices up from her office, but I see she is just letting you loose on your own," she said. Peter felt like a convict who was breaking out of jail. He suddenly perceived the weight of the ball and chain around his leg.

"I uh, I'm not done yet. I'm just going out to the bathroom. I'll be back."

"We do have a bathroom in this building you know, just down that hallway to the right," she said pointing, as Peter quickly thought of another excuse to leave.

"I, thanks, but I have to go get something from my class that I forgot. I'll be back real soon."

She gave him a suspicious look, as he turned and walked out the door, not giving her a chance to question him further or to try and stop him. He walked fast, and then when he heard the bell ring, ran down a corridor toward his old classroom. All the classrooms started to empty, and his movement was now hindered by students spilling out into the hallways.

"Hey, watch it!" said a girl who Peter practically knocked over.

"Sorry," he said as he turned back and apologized.

Peter arrived at Mrs. Smeech's room and noticed that many of the students had already left. Not wanting to be spotted by his teacher, he attempted to look in the doorway without being noticed. Much to his dismay, it appeared that Jeremy had already left. Out of breath, Peter turned away from the classroom, discouraged that he wouldn't even get to do the good deed he'd set out to accomplish that day. Then, just as he slowly walked back in the direction of the building of the principal, he felt a tap on his shoulder and turned around.

"Jeremy," he said, suddenly feeling a renewed sense of purpose. "Were you waiting for me?"

"Well, not really. I didn't know if you'd be coming back. I was already down the hallway when I realized I forgot one of my books, so turned around and came back. Then I saw you."

Peter looked to his right and noticed Mrs. Smeech walking out of the classroom, "Come over here," he said to Jeremy, pulling on his shirtsleeve and leading him around a corner.

"What?"

"I don't want Mrs. Smeech to see me."

"Why? Are you in more trouble?"

"Kind of, but Nicole Jensen is in bigger trouble."

"What do you mean?"

"Before I tell you, I gotta know if you know how to get in touch with her."

"Well, yeah, if I want to," Jeremy said, not wanting to divulge his connection yet.

"Jeremy, someone wants to kill Nicole, and I need to warn her."

Jeremy noticed the worried look painted all over Peter's face, "No, not again. She was nearly knocked off a couple years ago. Is it the same attacker?"

"Yeah. I can't say too much now, cause I've gotta get back to the psychs' office. I just snuck out so I could catch you. So, how can I reach Nicole? Do you know?"

Jeremy hesitated, "Yeah, she's my stepmother."

"Really? That's great! Then you can help. Quick, give me your number."

Jeremy complied. He opened his notebook and took a pencil out of a plastic pouch and started to write his number down on a piece of paper. As he was halfway through, Peter heard his name being called, "Mr. Dopum, what are you doing?" asked Mrs. Smeech, who approached them as Jeremy swiftly finished writing. "I, uh, just getting uh talking to Jeremy," he said, off guard.

"Are you done at Mr. Sneglwhurt's office?"

"I, no, I was talking to Miss Noos, but then another girl came in. I had to go to the bathroom, and I, that's what I did. Then I ran into Jeremy."

"Okay, well, I don't know if I trust your shenanigans, so why don't I walk you back to Miss Noos's myself."

"I can go on my own. I promise," Peter nervously said.

"No, young man. I will take you myself," she said, starting to take his arm and walk him along.

Jeremy quickly ripped the notebook paper from the three metal rings, nearly tearing the phone number in half. He managed to sneak it into Peter's back pocket, as Mrs. Smeech continued to hold onto his arm and lead him back to jail. Peter felt something, and reached for his butt pocket and felt the piece of paper there. He shoved it down deeper so it wouldn't fall out.

After Peter was escorted back to Miss Noos' office, he sat back in front of her desk while she called his mother. Pam was told that she needed to come in for a consultation about the future of Peter's education.

When Pam arrived at the office, and found out her son was diagnosed as having ADD, she became outraged and refused to commit him to a special education class or to have him put back onto Ritalin. Miss Noos was frightened by Pam's anger, and didn't want any more parent complaints written up on her, so told Pam she'd allow Peter to go back to his regular classroom on a trial basis, to see if he could keep up with the normal kids. Pam then took Peter's hand and told Miss Noos that as soon as she got final custody over Peter, after her divorce settlement, she'd be putting Peter in a private school. Then she took her son and stormed out of the office.

Peter sat in the front seat of Pam's red Mercedes as she drove him away from the beautiful facade of lovely architecture and lush, green grounds, which merely hid some of the ugliness that ensued at the elementary school.

As they drove along, Peter spoke, "Mom, I'm worried about something."

"What is it darling? Are you afraid of the new school program they want to put you on?"

"No, not that. Something else. It's something I didn't have time to tell you last night because we got back so late from Dad's house, and you were all upset, so I thought I'd just tell you today," Peter said. He went on to explain to Pam that Lester had been responsible for having Nicole attacked a couple of years ago, and was planning to do it again. He told his mother that he'd met Nicole's stepson, and got his phone number from him so that he could call and reveal this information to Nicole.

As Pam pulled her car into the long, stone driveway of her small Beverly Hills home, she quickly put on the brakes, making a screeching halt. Then she and Peter rushed out of the car and went into the nice three-bedroom home, located in the "poor" section of the wealthiest city in Southern California.

"That slime bag, he just doesn't know when to quit!" said Pam, as she threw her purse down on a kitchen counter. "Where's that number, darling? Why don't you let me make the initial call. Then you can let Nicole know what you heard. There are some other things I want her to be aware of, too. If Lester thinks he's going to get away with murder, he's got a nice surprise coming!" she said as Peter followed her. Peter put his books down on the counter and took the crumpled piece of notebook paper out of the back pocket of his baggy blue jeans and handed it to his mother.

Pam could barely make out the lightly penciled phone number. "Can you tell if this is a three or an eight?"

"Mmm, looks like an eight mom."

Pam punched the number into a phone as Peter sat at the kitchen table. His eyes were glued in suspense at his mother, thinking about how fortunate he was to have been rescued from the clutches of his father a couple of years ago. He only hoped that Nicole could be saved from his devious plans.

The phone rang and rang and Pam grew frustrated as she heard the voice of a man come on the line. "Hello, you have reached the home of Nicole Jensen and Chris and Jeremy Andrews. We are unable to come to the phone right now, but would like to know who called and any message you have. Please leave a message after the beep. Thank you."

Pam left an urgent message.

Chapter 12

Although Nicole had been doing quite well in her career, she was recently feeling more perturbed than she had for some time. There had been some dissension amongst some of the artists in her group. Jealousy and competition were creeping into the domain of the team, causing unnecessary fighting. Some of the artists who had been helping out with promotion and organization decided that they didn't want to contribute to the cause anymore, and just wanted to leave the group, and work on their own careers. A couple of musicians, also executives in the group, who were both married to other people, decided to have an affair with each other. Both of them were unwilling to take responsibility for their actions, and when violent repercussions occurred in their home lives, Nicole was targeted as the reason for their affair. They both stated that if they hadn't joined her team, they never would have met one another, and this wouldn't have happened.

On top of all this, she got some more negative press, and some of her supporters began to doubt her true intentions. One school that had wanted her group to come and perform canceled their invitation after being effected by some of the rumors about Nicole.

Nicole came home at eight o'clock after having been out all day, busy with rehearsals and meetings for upcoming performances. She knew that, in spite of the recent upheavals with her team, she wouldn't quit her crusade, but she was feeling weaker than usual. Her mood of anxiety was intensified as she was greeted by Jeremy, who told her that she was in trouble. He didn't know exactly why, just that one of his new classmates warned him she was in danger. Then she played back the messages on her answering machine and heard the seriousness in Pam's communication as she listened to her voice. She rewound the tape, feeling like she was living through a replay of her past. She played Pam's message again, this time writing down the telephone number that she left.

Nicole was tired and had a headache from all the recent stress. Before calling Pam and getting bombarded with more bad news, she called Chris' pager in Arizona, "Please get my call. I need you," she said to herself, as she hung up the phone waiting for him to call back.

Within ten minutes the phone rang, "Hi honey," she said as she answered the phone, knowing it was him. Jeremy, who was doing his homework in his room, looked out his door and noticed Nicole sitting hunched over her desk as she held her head in her hands.

"Nicky, I wasn't expecting you."

"I wasn't expecting me, either. But, I needed to talk to you," she said as her voice quivered while she attempted to hold back her tears.

"What's the matter? You don't sound like your usual bubbly self."

"I'm not, Chris. I've been a wreck lately. Things were going so well and then this negative force came along like a tidal wave and hit me in the head. I wish you were back here, honey," she said as she went on to tell him some of the nasty things that had been happening during the last month, and also informed him that she had this illogical feeling about taking a break for a while.

"Nicky, you've got to keep focused on the positive. Don't back off. I know that when you're sitting in a pile of garbage, it's hard to look out and see all the good things happening around you, but I think you're just starting to let some of the evil out there run you down. That's not a healthy thing to do, especially when the world so badly needs you."

Tears of frustration came to Nicole's eyes as Chris continued to give her a pep talk, "Come on, babe. Look how far you've come. You can't put that torch down and take a rest now, not at this crucial time. You know that the show must go on. Just remember Athena."

"I love you," she sobbed, feeling more energized by his encouraging words.

"I love you too. I can't wait to get back and see you next week," he said.

They talked a while longer then got off the phone.

Nicole took a deep breath, dried her eyes, and replayed Chris' final words to her, "Just remember Athena," rang through her mind over and over, as she recalled her old home and felt some renewed strength. The intent to carry on with her mission moved to the forefront of her thoughts as she dialed Pam's number, now willing to hear whatever urgent message she had to deliver.

After talking to Chris, she once again felt strong enough to confront the evils of the world without falling apart at the seams. She appreciated the special relationship she shared with him. It made such a difference having a partner who shared similar viewpoints to her own.

"Hello," said Pam.

"Pam, its Nicole Jensen."

"Oh Nicole, I'm so glad you returned my call. I know you're a busy celebrity and all, and I didn't know when I'd hear from you. I was hoping that my call didn't disturb you too much, or that you didn't think it was just some sort of useless annoyance."

"No, I didn't think any of that. Jeremy warned me that something was wrong which I should find out about."

Pam turned off the kitchen faucet, getting rid of the sound of running water splattering on the dirty dishes she'd just been washing. She wiped her hands on her apron, while holding the phone between her head and shoulder, and carefully chose her words, "Nicole, I have some news for you, and I don't know how to break this to you in an easy way, I, uh..is there any way we can meet?"

"If you think it's necessary, I guess we can arrange it. Do you want me to come to your home?"

"No, I don't think that would be a good idea. I'll explain why when I see you," she said, picturing Lester barging in.

"Why don't you come to my home then. You mustn't live very far away, if our children go to the same school," Nicole said. Pam agreed to come over that evening with Peter.

A half-hour later, Pam drove up in front of Nicole's home, screeched on her breaks, and parked her red Mercedes. Then she and Peter got out of the car and went to meet the celebrity they both admired.

Nicole opened the door, and let the two new guests into her home, leading them to the couches in the living room. Pam, a tall blonde woman of forty years, sat down and adjusted her long skirt. Peter quietly sat next to her, and Nicole sat in a chair next to them. Then Jeremy, distracted by the mystery of what was going to be said, came out of his room and joined them.

"Nicole, the first thing I want you to know is that Peter and I are eternally grateful for what you did for us last year. After one of your concerts, I made two very important decisions," she paused, "I decided to take Peter off of Ritalin for good, and I chose to leave my husband for good."

Nicole was pleased and puzzled, not liking the idea of causing anyone's marriage to break up, "Oh, well, I'm happy to hear about the Ritalin, but,..."

Pam smiled, "Believe me, leaving my husband was a good thing. He was the one responsible for keeping Peter on Ritalin, as well as many other poor kids,"

"What do you mean?"

"He's one of the executives of the American Psychiatric Association, and also still has an active practice of his own. Nicole, I can beat around the bush for a while, but I might as well get right to the point," she said, as Nicole and Jeremy's eyes grew wider. Pam tensely closed her own eyes for a second, then opened them, "My husband was responsible for some of the bad press you unjustly received, as well as hiring someone to attack you last year. He couldn't tolerate what I did to him after being inspired by you, and sought to get revenge."

"My God, all this time I figured that someday I'd get the answer to who did that to me, and here, right in my own house the truth is finally being revealed."

"Nicole, one of the reasons I rushed over here to tell you this is because," she hesitated, and looked at Peter who was tensely twisting his baggy yellow T-shirt, "Peter overheard something that he needs to tell you," she said. Then Peter shyly told her of the conversation that he'd heard between Lester and Jim Scott.

"He really hates me, doesn't he? Maybe this is one of the reasons I've been feeling so awful lately. It's all the bad vibes in the air."

"Nicole, I just want you to know that Peter and I are on your side and are willing to help you in any way we can, no matter what consequences we may face by 'the ogre.' You're one of the most valuable artists I know, and I'd hate to see you hurt in any way. You stand for the opposite of everything my ex-husband and his profession represent," she said with profound resentment.

"I knew these guys were bad, but not totally to what extent."

Pam leaned forward, "My dear, the main type of therapy that those guys in white coats give is help which turns out to be betrayal. That whole profession slithered into the open arms of society under the pretense of wanting to help people with their afflictions. I'm afraid to say that, in most areas they've touched, they've only made lives worse! I feel that what I have to say can aid you in your crusade to create a better world."

Nicole heeded her words while flashing back to a time when the Empress was briefing a group of missionaires on the devious ways of the Black Knights. "I'm interested in your information. Sounds like you have a lot of firsthand knowledge."

"Pardon my language, but I was sleeping with the enemy, and believe me it was the worst rape I've ever experienced. I know by your campaign that you're now well aware of the source of the infiltration of drugs into society, so I won't go into that, but do you know that the rising crime and violence in the nation are primarily a result of drug abuse?"

"I had some idea of this and have recently lost a good friend because of an assault by some druggies, but I don't know the extent of this dilemma."

"I'm sorry to hear about your friend. Let me tell you that the onset of senseless crime occurred right after massive drug use was introduced into our mental hospitals in the mid-fifties. This then led to an outburst of drug use in the streets. Ever since this time, the statistics on crime rose markedly. Fortunately, you and your group are helping to lower these statistics by getting more and more people off of drugs and keeping people away from the clutches of money grubbing psychs, but the extent of damage goes beyond just the drug and crime arena."

"Yeah, like in my school," Peter cut in, with all eyes now focused on him as he explained to Nicole some of the things that occurred in the classroom. Jeremy, who had just assumed that he was getting a usual education, was now seeing things in a new light.

"It gets even more atrocious than that Nicole. Peter is only telling you some of the things that have been occurring to keep kids from getting a decent schooling."

"You mean there's more corruption that goes on?"

"Yes, thanks to my husband and all his wonderful cohorts, who have spread their influence into this delicate sphere. You want to know why there's so much immoral sexual behavior in society?"

"I've often wondered about that."

"It starts in our elementary schools, believe it or not. Did you know that graphic sexual films are shown to these kids on a regular basis?"

"No, I..." Nicole looked at Jeremy whose face was slightly reddening. "Well, that certainly explains the high rates of teenage pregnancy I've been hearing about."

"Exactly."

"Nicole, I'm afraid that the main purpose behind all of this is to rip the very fabric of society to shreds, and create the downfall of the human population."

The wheels in Nicole's mind started turning as she quickly thought about all the corruption she'd seen with artists and other people in society. She was putting the missing pieces of the puzzle together, which now created a picture of the very reason why she'd run up against so many obstacles in her crusade. There in her mind was the roadmap taken by the enemy, laid out for her more clearly than she'd ever seen it before. The only thing she had to compare it with was the similar strategy used by the Knights!

After listening to the words of Pam, Nicole had experienced some old, familiar fear in regards to having her life threatened. But then a surge of bravery welled up inside of her, as she realized that things were much different now than they were a couple of years ago. She was stronger, and no longer alone. She still had a team, in spite of recent troubles with some members. She also had her fans, who supported her, and in this case she had Peter as a key witness to the phone conversation between Lester and Jim Scott. The only problem is that his words were not recorded, and these days it was very easy for criminals to dodge the justice system. Nicole knew that there was no use worrying about this possible conflict, and that perhaps with her newly found confidence, under the right circumstances, she would even confront her enemy face to face and let him know that she was aware of his scheme!

Chapter 13

When Chris returned from Arizona, Nicole gave him more information about the recent battle that was occurring on the home front, and how the conversation with Pam enlightened her as to who the true enemy was. They decided that Chris would oversee the continued expansion of GHOA, while Nicole worked on putting out some of the forest fires that were blazing within the group.

Nicole drove down Hollywood Boulevard on her way to a group meeting with key GHOA members and executives. Her palms sweat, as she was engrossed with figuring out how to put the thoughts in her mind into words that would communicate the things she wanted to say.

Nicole's heart sped up as her car came to a stop in a parking lot behind a large building. Today she was more nervous than usual, not knowing what to expect when she addressed the group. She had stressed the urgency of today's meeting and only hoped that the people who most needed to hear what she was going to say showed up.

Nicole sat tensely in her car for a moment, then pulled down the rearview mirror and looked at her face. She noticed that she looked more pale than normal. To remedy this she pulled a makeup container out of her purse and rubbed some blush onto her dull cheeks.

Nicole walked into the building, tightly clenching her purse in one hand and a thin blue notebook in the other hand. Then she went to the front door of a large, three hundred-seat room, ten minutes before meeting time. She looked ahead of her and saw that over half of the seats in the room were already filled, which was a good sign. Doing a cursory glance around the room, she noticed that some of the people who had recently caused dissension and troubles had actually shown up. There were still others who were not there yet, who she hoped would attend.

While waiting to start the meeting, Nicole talked with Shawna Dunn, who was very active in the group. While talking with Shawna, Nicole's eyes were constantly shifting to see who was walking in through the back door. Some of the other people who she'd hoped would attend walked in. She was glad to see that although there were problems with some of these people, they still found it important enough to show up. She thought that perhaps this was due to the urgency and mystery used to promote the meeting that day.

Nicole looked at her watch and noticed that it was nearly three o'clock. With two minutes to the designated meeting time, she said good-bye to Shawna and hugged her, then took fast steps towards the stage.

On her way to center stage, she tripped on a microphone chord. The mike and its stand went crashing to the floor, along with Nicole's stomach. The thud got the attention of the attendees, many of which stopped talking with one another and focused on Nicole. Nicole picked up the mike stand and put her notebook on a small table.

Normally there was a spirit of playfulness and enthusiasm amongst the crowd, but today the air was infiltrated with a feeling of seriousness and resentment that clouded the usual excitement. Nicole wished she didn't have to say some of the things that were necessary to reveal, as she much preferred to just carry on with the news of the successes of the group, and plans for the future. The crowd got silent as the knots in Nicole's stomach twisted tighter. Then she began the meeting, trying to ward off as much of her own stress as possible.

"Hello, hello everyone."

"Hello," the audience echoed back.

"I'm pleased to see so many of you here today. Although there have been some mounting problems, I'd first just like to acknowledge all of you for the support you've given to this cause over the past year. I want you to know that I could never ever have made such an impact alone, without a group. One artist may be a powerful influence in society, as those of you who have played that role may know. But it also can be a dangerous position. Before I get to the crux of the matter of today's meeting, I'd like to spend a few moments informing you of some of the recent statistics in regards to our progress in creating a drug free, creative society. Would you like that?" Nicole said. There was some mild applause in the audience, not the usual roar of strong interest.

She picked up the notebook and opened it quickly, wanting to break the thick silence as soon as possible. She looked up from her notes and spoke, "Okay, first of all, two of the areas we've had big victories in nationwide are high schools and colleges. The percentage of students on drugs has dropped by fifty percent on the campuses where we've performed. Many of these students have taken part in art workshops set up by Chris Andrews, who is helping teens and young adults channel their energies into the art form of their choice. Students are learning the skills they need in order to forward artistic hobbies and careers. As I stand here right now, Chris is painting a large mural on a freeway wall in Washington State. About sixty teenagers from local high schools are assisting him. The theme of the mural is "The highway to happiness." He tells me that part of the mural contains pictures of cars driving down a road that comes to a fork. One side is called Drug Road. The other side is labeled Happiness Highway. The cars driving down drug road end up crashing into all sorts of obstacles. The ones that choose happiness highway, a rainbow colored road, make their way towards their dreams. As soon as the mural is done, Chris will have a picture taken of it, so that you can all see.

"Another recent development has been the attraction of a few new top celebrities to our crusade. One of them is the popular actor, Gerald Johnson. Gerald has taken it upon himself to unite a troupe of actors that have been going from town to town doing shows. He is currently in Chicago, where his show has been a regular sellout, attracting thousands of people. When he is not performing, he is working with local actors, who have decided to become drug free and is producing a show with them." Nicole paused as the group applauded.

"As our anti-drug statistics continue to go up, there is a group whose statistics continue to soar downward as many of you are aware. Yes, I'm afraid to say that the shares of IB Dilly are plummeting downward thanks to our efforts. Since we've made the public aware of the damaging effects of psychiatric drugs, there has been a nice decline in this area. However, I'm afraid to say that the monsters actively behind the drugging of society refuse to let our wins overcome their losses completely. Unfortunately, I have taken the brunt of an attack by one of the main stockholders of the Dilly Company. However, thanks to the support of Pam Dopum, I was recently made aware of exactly who this mysterious enemy was. He has been libeling me in the media and in fact was the one responsible for hiring someone to assault me two years ago after a concert," she said. Nicole began to go on but was interrupted by a man in the audience.

"What about the photo of you taking drugs in the National News? What was that all about?" asked the man in a somewhat skeptical tone.

"I was framed," she paused. "Those were vitamins. This is the very type of behavior that some of these stockholders and their cohorts have been pursuing. In the near future there will be some ads coming out in that very newspaper, promoting our group and exposing the lies that have been printed. Unfortunately, because of some of this untruthful press, we've lost some members of the group, who chose to believe the "authority" of the media and took it to heart to turn against me."

"So you want us to defend you?" a woman in the audience asked.

"I'm not necessarily telling you these things about the press to persuade you to defend me, but what I would like to convince you to do is to talk up all the successes of the group. Show the good press to people. Inform them of what has occurred at our events. Invite them to upcoming performances. Please, don't get detoured into having to explain away all the bad things that have occurred. You'll only get backed into a corner and end up fixating your attention on destruction rather than creation," Nicole said with such strong conviction that she received some cheers from the audience.

"Thank you. Now I have to bring up another sore issue that has been plaguing us for a while. Over the last several months there has been some fighting amongst our members, with concentration being put onto what others have done wrong as artists or administrators. There are others who are tired of being part of the team and who have left the group altogether or who are currently contemplating leaving. I'm certainly not going to force anyone to remain on our team, but I would definitely like to handle any unnecessary abandonment due to petty causes.

"This is a dangerous condition and needs to be handled so that things don't get worse. The first thing I ask you to do is to look and see if you are doing anything that has been detrimental to the group. This could be as apparently insignificant as just being nasty to another member or failing to carry out a duty you agreed to do, or whatever else it might be. I know that groups can often fall apart when people start transgressing against agreements they promised to keep or doing things to injure others. So please understand that you are all very valuable and your work has been greatly appreciated. I just hate to see anyone leave because of their conflicts with others, when deep inside, the real reason they're leaving is because they feel their acts may be damaging the rest of us.

"Although it's the responsibility of each one of us to realize any harm that we've done to one another, there is another underlying demon in the world who may be contributing to some of the troubles we've had. This monster is responsible for supporting destructive behavior and often makes it difficult to see the true source of injurious ideas that lie harbored in unsuspecting minds. I have recently become more aware of the extent of the damage that this beast has inflicted upon society. The way in which he operates is so tricky that he has managed to tread upon many areas of life, without being noticed as the cause of small and large disasters. The very nickname which he goes by is an adequate description of what he seeks to cause to happen to others he comes in contact with."

"Shrink," someone in the group said.

"Yes, exactly. Most of you know by now that these men in white coats originally waged the drug war we've been fighting. But they have other weapons that are being used to destroy society as well. We are a prime target for assault by them. Our group stands for growth and creation, and they stand for decay and destruction. When I hear that people don't need a group, and..."

"But sometimes you have to look out for yourself, take care of number one. Being in a group can be a distraction," a female voice in the audience said loudly, interrupting Nicole.

"Who said that?"

A young woman named Gina raised her hand.

"Gina, could you come up here please," Nicole boldly requested.

Gina gladly confronted Nicole on the stage.

"Gina, I know that you've recently been thinking about leaving our team and..."

"Yeah, and I was hoping I'd have this moment up here to make a point."

Nicole quickly hit the ball back in Gina's court, "Where did you hear that you have to look out for number one?"

Gina looked down at the wooden platform and tried to honestly answer Nicole, "I don't know, from a friend of mine I think."

"Yeah, and what did your friend say to you about this?"

"That she was tired of dealing with others, and that they didn't have anything to do with her anyway, so she was going to go out and do her own thing in life and forget about people who were a pain to her."

"I see. Do you know where your friend got this idea from?"

"I don't know. I think she read some sort of motivational book that...", Gina paused and then reluctantly smiled.

"That what?"

"Oh, just some book by some mental health expert. Now I remember. She said that this book stressed the fact that a person had to do what felt right to them at the time, and not worry about the consequences...and,"

"And what?"

"Nothing. I don't want to stand here and get interrogated anymore."

"Gina, I'm not going to make you stay up here if you don't want to, but I was just trying to get you to take a look at one of the lines that our rivals use to cause the disintegration of groups."

"Fine, well I'm just not ready to accept all this yet," she said, and walked offstage and then out the back entrance of the room.

Nicole got a little nervous as she watched Gina exit, and then went back to her talk, not knowing the overall reaction of the group after her interview with Gina.

"Nicole, can I say something?" a man named Dean asked.

"Sure Dean, would you like to come up here?" Nicole asked, as he walked up to the stage.

"Thank you. There have been times when I've just wanted to shelve responsibility to this group and even to my wife and kids when things got too tough, but I can now see that this was based on some false information I'd gotten. I thought that all I needed was myself, in order to survive, but this is ridiculous. After Nicole pointed out the source of where such an absurd idea comes from, I started to look at how bad it would be if everyone just went out and fended for themselves. Nicole, I just want to say that I'm on your side," Dean said and then walked off the stage as the people applauded.

"Thank you, Dean," Nicole said, and then went on to inform everyone of many of the other ways in which society has been destroyed by this stealthy enemy.

"So it's vitally important that we remain connected to our roots, and by that I mean the very place where the word 'art' itself comes from. Yes, the derivation of this word is, 'to join together.'

Although we're making good strides in the improvement of society, it's vital that we rekindle our purposes and retain a stronghold so that we can advance our position more successfully. It's up to us to continue to carry the brightest torches, the ones that shine the light that the majority of people are going to follow. We need to lead them in the right way so that our positive dreams waken as realities."

Chapter 14

I t was a week after the meeting, and several musicians who were part of GHOA were frantically worrying about whether anyone would show up for a performance they were scheduled to give at a local amphitheater that evening. Gina, who was an expert at promotion, was supposed to have been doing major advertising for the upcoming event. Instead, she had hardly done anything at all. This was unlike her earlier actions, when she'd genuinely done a lot of work that greatly enhanced the attendance at various shows. While pretending to be on the phone contacting media, and doing ticket sales, she had actually been talking to various agents and managers about helping her to get her own career off the ground.

After she left, some of the other more dedicated members of the group did as much last minute promotion as they could, to help ensure there would be an audience.

* * * *

Over several previous months Gina not only dropped her commitments in GHOA, but had also started dumping the responsibility of the care for her two kids. Normally she shared the task with her ex-husband Bill. She cared for the children during the week, and Bill got them on weekends. Gina started getting so wrapped up in her own singing career that she told Bill she was too busy to tend to the kids during the week, and refused to care for them until her career was off the ground. Bill wasn't happy with the extra burden that was being put upon on him, but Gina was so convincing about her certainty of becoming a success that Bill resentfully went along with her demands.

Gina quit her day job as a secretary in order to have time for rehearsals, and spent many nights performing in local clubs with a band she'd put together. The band did a variety of original rock songs, mainly written by Gina to show off her voice. She had been performing for low or no pay, with the hopes that she'd attract the attention of someone who believed in her enough to want to help her record a CD and get paying gigs. In the heat of her frustration, with lack of money and overdue rent, she managed to find an agent who said he saw enough potential in her to help her out. Gina was relieved after getting this offer. She knew that she'd proven herself right by putting all her energies into doing what counted most which was "looking out for number one."

Mark Snow, Gina's new agent, managed to get Gina and her band a few low paying gigs. Then he told Gina that the next step was to have a CD made in order to more broadly promote the beauty of her voice. He told Gina that she needed to come up with fifteen thousand dollars in order to get the CD produced properly. He said that he customarily had his clients pay for their own recordings, as it wasn't his job to front them the money. Although Gina's hopes dropped when Mark told her the amount of the CD, he convinced her that he'd make the expenditure well worth the price she had to pay.

It was at this point, Gina felt confident enough to quit GHOA. Gina got on the phone and called everyone she knew, trying to convince people to lend her all or part of the money she needed to help her get the break she knew she deserved. After begging several people to give her the money but getting turned down, she finally convinced her mother and sister to help her out. She then took the handout and swiftly handed it to Mark Snow, who said he would take care of all the arrangements of making her first CD. Snow told Gina that he'd call her in a couple of days after he set up the studio time and hired the correct engineer.

However, after a week went by with no call from Snow, Gina got tired of waiting, and took the initiative of phoning him. Much to Gina's shock, the voice that came on the telephone wasn't Mark, but the recording of a woman's voice saying "We're sorry. The number you have dialed has been disconnected and is no longer in service. If you feel you have reached this number in error, please check the number and try your call again."

Gina dropped her jaw and just let the phone receiver dangle by its long, twisted chord as she regretfully thought about all the money she'd just paid to this so-called agent she'd trusted to help her out. She picked the receiver back up and clicked the button on the phone that eliminated the dial tone she'd been listening to. She dialed Mark's number again, hoping that perhaps she'd dialed it incorrectly and that had been the reason for the recording. Unfortunately, to her further dismay, the same woman came back on the line saying, "We're sorry. The number you have dialed has been disconnected..."

Her last desperate attempt was to call the operator and get verification that the number was, in fact, disconnected. The operator confirmed Gina's conclusion. Then she called the information operator and tried to see if there was any other listing for Mark. There was none. Gina slammed down the receiver so hard that she nearly broke it. "I never should have trusted anyone with a last name like Snow!"

Thoughts raced through Gina's mind as to how she was going to explain this misfortune to her mother and sister. She just hoped that they'd have enough sympathy to forgive the debt. After all, this whole circumstance was not her fault. They'd have to understand. For several days, Gina just stayed in her small apartment, sulking. She was now two months behind on the rent and starting to receive eviction notices.

Gina's mother called and asked how it was going with the making of her CD. She stumbled around, trying to find the right words to say that would emphasize the fact that she was the victim of an unfair scheme. She told her mother what had happened, and although her mother had some sympathy, she still wanted Gina to pay her back.

After she was done talking with her mother, Gina heeded the sounds of her stomach, which was growling at her, telling her that she'd better feed it. She went to her cupboards and saw that they were nearly bare, and if she wanted to be rid of the faint feeling in her head, she'd better go to the store and buy some food. Gina went to her bedroom and opened up a dresser drawer and took out several rolls of nickels and pennies that she'd been saving for emergency occasions such as this one. She rushed out of her apartment, slammed the door, and drove to a nearby grocery store.

Carrying a red, plastic grocery basket down an isle, Gina stopped at the section that housed a variety of sizes and types of beans. She quickly looked at the packages, searching for the cheapest ones she could find. She came across a bag that was ninety-five cents, and threw it into her cart. She walked along until she came to the area where the rice was, again looking for the cheapest bag, and threw it into her basket. As she hurried down the isle, she barely noticed someone coming towards her pushing a cart, and smacked into his arm as she walked. "I'm sorry," Gina said, now looking right at the guy with the familiar face.

"Gina, hi."

"Oh, hi, Danny. Funny who you run into at the grocery store sometimes," she said, reluctant to carry on a conversation with Danny Jordan, who was an active member of GHOA. She glanced in his metal grocery cart and noticed there was a variety of expensive meats. Her mouth silently watered at the sight.

"Yeah, I know. How have things been going?" he said, looking in her basket.

"Uh, fine, okay. They've been all right," she replied as her eyes fleeted about nervously.

"How's the singing career?"

"It's, well, I don't want to talk about that right now. I have to go and finish my shopping."

"Okay, I was just wondering if you had achieved any of the goals you'd set out for yourself."

"Some, how about you?" she asked, attempting to avert the attention off of herself.

"Things have been going better than ever for me. The band I'm with for got signed to New Civilization Records."

Gina's ears perked up with both jealousy and curiosity, "Band, which band are you in now?"

"One with Rodney Nelson called Integrity."

"Oh, well, that's nice," she said managing to eke out a small smile, now interested in prying Danny for hints as to how she could get such a deal. "How did your group happen to pull off a record deal?"

"Well, you may not believe this, but I think it has a lot to do with the fact that all the band members have been very active with the Get High on Art crusade. It seems like the more I help on this cause, the more good things happen in my life. Just kind of works that way. I never would have believed this myself last year when I was playing in bands with guys that insisted on taking drugs before every gig. I didn't care about anything but getting wasted and pounding on my drums. There was no one very important to me, not even my own friends and family. They were just people to use to get money from when I needed something, mainly drugs," he said as Gina cringed, not wanting to face the fact that she knew she was using her family for selfish reasons.

"Anyway, I won't go into all that. All I can say is that I'm getting far more done than I ever thought possible. Seems like the time spent helping this valuable group always enhances my own career as well. This may sound corny to you, but I realized recently that all people are directly or indirectly connected to each other on some level. This planet belongs to all of us, and if we don't do what it takes to make things better for ourselves and others then things will just continue to go downhill."

Gina painfully digested his words, and although she understood what he was saying, she was not yet ready to humiliate herself by fully admitting to her own errors. "Well, that's nice Danny. I'm glad that you got your record deal."

"Thanks," he said, wondering if what he'd said had sunk in. "I've gotta go now."

They said good-bye to one another and then Gina went and finished her shopping. Her attention was riveted on Danny's words.

As she stood in the checkout line, a wave of grief welled up inside of her as she thought about the foolishness of her past actions and forced herself to look at how she'd harmed the group by not doing what she'd promised them in regards to her promotional duties. She wondered if there was any way to make up for the damage she'd done.

Chapter 15

Lester Dopum hobbled swiftly as he bounced a basketball around a court in his backyard, while his son Troy tried to intercept him and take it away.

"Oh, no, you don't," he said to Troy who nearly got the ball. Then Lester dunked the ball into a hoop above his head, "scored," he said, looking at his son who had a look of defeat on his face, "Okay, here you go. Don't let me take it from you, son."

Troy got back into the swing of the game as he proceeded to take awkward steps around the large court, trying to imitate the strategy of his father. Lester nearly grabbed the ball from him, but Troy was fast enough to prevent the interference. Troy got away from his father and ran over to the orange hoop and aimed the ball at it, missing his target. The ball bounced off of the rim as Troy's hopes bounced back down as well. "I'm just not as good as you, Dad, even with your bad leg," Troy said, referring to the injury Lester incurred after slipping on some rocks at the beach. Troy let the ball roll away into a large patch of nearby lawn.

"Oh, come on, of course you are. Just be as quick as you were at the beach when you grabbed my hand and pulled me up. I know you can get it in the basket," Lester said, going after the ball that lay at rest next to a neatly trimmed rosebush. After he fetched the ball, he brought it back over to the front of the hoop and instructed Troy as to how he could get a better shot. Then he handed it to his son, and watched as Troy imitated him, this time getting it directly into the hoop. Troy smiled, and held the ball in his left hand, "Give me five," the fifteen-year-old boy said to his father. They both slapped one another's right palms.

Just as Troy was about to take the ball to attempt another shot, his vision suddenly blurred, and he could barely make out the scenery in front of him. He dropped the ball and covered his eyes with his hands.

Lester became worried about his behavior, "Troy, what's the matter?"

"Don't know. Everything just got all fuzzy. I couldn't see you very well."

"All right, you're just going through a temporary stress relapse," he said, as he noticed the butler approaching.

"Why don't you sit down over there on a lawn chair by the pool, and just relax for a little while."

"I'm afraid to walk."

"Okay," he said, lifting up his son. "Do you want something Pierre?"

"Yes, sir. Ms. Pam has arrived here to see you."

Lester cringed, "All right, tell her I'll be right there," he said, dismissing the butler and carrying Troy over to a lounge chair. He lay him down on the chair by the large pool, facing him in a direction where he had a view of the sights below the hill on which the house rested. "You rest here. Take a nap if you need to. I'll go see what bad news your mother has for me now."

Lester turned away from Troy and walked towards the back door of his mansion. The sun beat down on his slightly balding head as he picked up the basketball and dunked it into the hoop. "That woman isn't going to beat me in the game of life. Damn neurotic females," he thought to himself.

Lester opened the glass door that led to a recreation room. Before he entered the house, he turned and looked at Troy in the distance, more worried about him than usual. Then he stomped through the house, until he came to the main reception area where he saw Pam sitting on a chair, "What is it now? More good news from your lawyer?"

"Not yet. But real soon I'm sure there will be," she said with a tone of suppressed resentment that rang through the room.

Lester didn't want to discuss personal matters in that part of the house, so he led Pam to a small den on the first floor. He sat down on a couch, while she just stood and slowly paced in front of him like a tiger that was about to pounce on its prey.

"So you found a way to outsmart me? That was very clever, Lester, but I'm afraid that this battle is not over."

"And whatever are you talking about my dear?" he asked, feigning ignorance.

"Oh, come on. Don't pull that one on me. You don't have to hide the fact that you've been talking to Miss Noos."

"Pamela, darling. The school wants to put Peter back on Ritalin. I don't know why you ever agreed to have him come off of it in the first place. He's only gotten worse since he's stopped."

"He's had to go through withdrawals. That only appeared to make him look like he was getting worse. That's the whole trap that you and your damn profession set up with this thing. Make it look like someone was doing better when they were drugged. Devious Lester, very devious."

Lester tried to maintain his calm demeanor, knowing that in this case he had the edge over Pam.

"You don't know what you're talking about. I'm only thinking of Peter's welfare. Don't be so illogical. Miss Noos called me, knowing that I would give my consent for him to go back on this useful substance that would allow him to be able to carry on with his studies. She knew that you disapproved, and since she only needs the consent of one legal parent, she called me. It was quite the reasonable thing to do."

"Just because the divorce isn't final, and I don't have sole custody, you think you can just weasel your way into the life of the son you hurt and try and wreck his life further."

"Now, now Pam, I was trying to help. I didn't wreck..."

"Oh, knock it off! Who are you trying to fool? Do you want your son to turn out like Johnny Bryan?"

There was silence as Lester contemplated a memory of a very bright child he'd treated who ended up on the streets selling drugs.

"Maintain yourself, Pam. You appear to be suffering from an unnecessary hyper-adrenal-dysfunction, which is exciting your anger."

"My rage is not physically induced. It's mental, and you are the source of it!"

"What do you know? You always thought you could tell me more about the area that I have been studying for twenty years, and you still haven't learned that you know nothing."

"I know more than you! And another thing I know is that if you don't immediately withdraw your consent of the drugging of Peter, I'm going to retaliate in a way you've never seen before. You and your cronies are already swiftly fading as authorities in the mental health field, but there's one last blow which you haven't suffered yet."

Lester's armpits started to perspire as he continued to attempt to cover up any fear that Pam tried to induce in him, "Let me guess, you're going to have someone burn down my house."

"Worse than that. I'm going to burn your reputation."

He flinched, realizing that his name had remained hidden from public scorn, although the good reputation of his field was losing ground.

"That's right, you heard me. I'm going to go to the press, and inform them, not only of what you've done to Peter, but the fact that you nearly killed a major celebrity two years ago and plan to do it again."

This time Pam was successful at injecting a shot of fear that was painful enough to run through the cold, blue veins of Lester's personality. His beady brown eyes looked at Pam in an angry, nervous manner, as he gripped the arm of the small couch with his right hand. "What are you talking about?"

"You know perfectly well what I mean," she said, pulling a copy of a parental consent form out of her purse, and putting it on Lester's desk. "Show me your signature on the disapproval line of this, and then perhaps I'll spare you some public misery. I'll give you two days to bring me this. If I don't hear from you by then, I'm proceeding with my plans," she said and then walked towards the front door of the house.

"You're a menace to my life, Pam!" Lester shouted at her right before she walked out. He wondered how in the world she could have found out about his plans for Nicole. His feelings of paranoia led him to a medicine chest where he swallowed a couple of self-prescribed barbiturates to calm himself down. Thoughts of hatred raced through his mind as he schemed of ways he would be able to still follow through with his plan for Nicole without being targeted as a suspect. He contemplated having Pam killed first, so she couldn't talk. However he didn't know if he'd be as lucky as the popular black football player who was awarded the not-guilty verdict in the murder trial of his ex-wife by a sympathetic jury.

Lester went and lay down on his bed, wrinkling the bedspread decorated with naked women, as he twisted his desperate ideas around.

Chapter 16

P am went home and was greeted by the ringing of her phone. It was Nicole, calling to thank her for all the information she'd recently imparted to her about the true nature of psychiatry. She said her group was becoming a supportive team again. They became so enraged about who the enemy really was that they were more interested in attacking this beast than in fighting amongst themselves.

Pam told Nicole about the conversation she'd just had with Lester, and the threat that she'd just made to him regarding exposing his name publicly.

"That's great, Pam. I'm glad you've been holding your ground, but, meanwhile, "the ogre" has continued to pay off some journalist to put out more bad press on me. He's also sent me a couple of anonymous letters."

"Well, that's because you've thrown a nice big rock at the hornet's nest, dear."

"Yeah, and I'm getting tired of having this obstacle in my path. Pam, I know this may sound pretty risky, but I'd actually like to meet this opponent of mine. I have some things I'd like to say to him in person."

"Nicole, I...that's very brave but I'm worried about you doing that."

"What do you mean? Just because he wants me dead?"

"Well, yeah, the man is crazy. There's no telling what he'd do to you. You can't reason with Lester."

"Pam, I'm willing to take that chance. I think he's got a lot more to be scared of than I do."

"Well, I know that but..."

"If he's going to have me attacked, then what does it matter if I face him first or he faces me? Or should I say, has someone else face me for him."

"Nicole, why don't you let me try to get Lester's name in the press, revealing him as the source of your attack a couple of years ago. I just don't think it's a good idea to see him," she said, picturing the worst of what might happen to her.

"Pam, even if we did expose him, he could do a cover up and deny the whole thing. I've tossed this about in my mind over and over. Unfortunately, I still don't have enough concrete evidence to show that he was the source behind the attack. Besides, he might still try to have me knocked off, even if you did get those articles printed."

"But Nicole, you're not looking at something."

"What?"

"You've been making good strides at getting people to see that psychiatric drugs are destructive. Don't you think that if Lester was exposed as the source of your attack, he could appear to be an obvious enemy?"

Nicole paused and looked at this. She saw Pam's point, but there was something driving her to stick to her original plan. "I see what you're saying, but I still want to meet him. I know if you can truly confront things, they aren't as dangerous to you as when you run away in fear. I'm tired of this monster at my back, and I'm willing to take the risk of any consequences I might face."

"But why is it that you have this urgency to talk to him about it in person?"

"Pam, I want one chance, just one opportunity to really nail him verbally for all the damage he's done," she said, feeling a zealousness beyond reason regarding her pursuit.

After arguing with Pam on this issue, Nicole finally persuaded Pam to give her Lester's address and tell her of a time when he was likely to be at home. Nicole's compulsion to meet him grew stronger and more desperate.

Chris, who had walked in the house at the tail end of Nicole's conversation with Pam, overheard part of what they were talking about. After Nicole hung up the phone he asked, "Honey, what was that I heard about confronting things that are dangerous to you?"

"I'm going to meet Lester."

"What?"

"I have to do it Chris."

"But why? I won't allow it. He's vicious!"

"Maybe so, but it's just something I need to do. You aren't going to get in my way! I've thought about this for weeks. I haven't been able to sleep at night. My attention has been glued to this threat. The nightmare I face is one that haunts me daily. The only difference between now and before my vision of Athena is that I'm now willing to stand up to things like this. I wasn't able to do that before, Chris! You have to understand," she said and then stood up and walked towards the kitchen table where her purse was.

Chris panicked, "Are you going right now?"

"Yes. Pam said he's probably home."

"Nicole, I don't like this idea! At least let me come with you if you're going to be so damn stubborn!"

Nicole walked to the door and opened it slightly. "No, Chris. This is something I have to do on my own!" she said as she stormed out of the door, taking steps as fast as her heart was racing. She got in her car, which was parked out on the street. She turned and saw Chris staring at her. He had thrown open the front door of the house, and was starting to run towards her. She ignored him and just turned the ignition on and drove off.

Chris cursed at her and then angrily walked back through the front door and slammed it. He stood by the living room window and looked out. All sorts of frightening thoughts entered his mind as to what might happen to his wife. He even feared that he might not see her again, "Damn her! She thinks she's some kind of superwoman!"

With Nicole's attention focused on her target whom she'd never seen before, she didn't notice that the light in front of her had turned red. She became aware of this fact after she drove right through the intersection, and heard some nasty honks coming from a couple of cars. Then she forced herself to concentrate on her driving. Riding up the long and winding Beverly 'Hills,' Nicole got closer and closer to the address she was looking for. She went past several mansions that were hidden behind towering trees and bushes. Slowing down, she tensed as she carefully looked at the addresses on the curbs, trying to figure out exactly where Lester's home was. She finally reached her destiny, and parked on the street in front of the ominous looking mansion. She sat in her car for a couple of minutes and took deep breaths.

Nicole got out of the car and slowly walked down a long U-shaped, brick driveway, until she got to the large door of the foreboding estate. A couple of crows flew overhead and landed on the top of an apricot tree. Nicole held her finger up to the doorbell, hesitated, and then pushed it. One of the crows flew off of the tree branch, and a piece of fruit fell and hit the ground, startling Nicole. Then her eyes widened as the big brown door creaked open, and revealed a tall, skinny man who had white hair, and was wearing a dress shirt and black pants. The man spoke with a French accent. "May I help you?"

"Yes, I need to see Dr. Dopum."

"And who shall I say is calling?"

"My name is," she paused, suddenly confused about giving her true identity, "My name is Nicole."

"And are you a patient of his?"

"No, absolutely not. I am...tell him it's Nicole Jensen."

The butler, who had heard of her but never seen her, gave her a look of surprise. Then he shut the door as he told Nicole he'd get right back to her.

Nicole folded her arms tightly and paced around on the circular landing of the front porch steps. Another crow flew by, and unlike the other silent ones on the tree, squawked loudly. Several moments went by, and as Nicole turned and stared at the black Mercedes in the driveway, she wondered what Lester's response would be when the servant told him of her unannounced visit.

Nicole had her back to the door. She heard it open and jumped as she turned around and faced the butler.

"Miss Jensen, please do come in," he said. She cautiously followed behind him as he led her toward the den. Nicole glanced around, sensing an eeriness in the mansion as she walked along. A large crystal chandelier, the size of which she'd only seen once before, was perfectly still as it hung high above her. Hanging on one of the large, white walls she noticed an oil painting of a man, with a smile on his face, standing with his arm around a boy. This portrait seemed to have more life in it than anything else in the gloomy room. There was a title on it that said "Father and Son." She noticed the signature of the artist on the bottom of the painting. It read, "Troy Dopum." Nicole had had no idea that Troy, whom she'd never met, only heard about, was such a good painter.

Every second seemed like an hour as Nicole got closer and closer to the room where Lester awaited her arrival. When her guide led her into the den, she didn't even remember to thank him, but, rather, just let him silently walk off as she stood and faced "the ogre." The tension in the room mounted as Nicole and Lester quietly eyed one another like a couple of animals who circle one another before making a major attack. There was something horrifying about Nicole that Lester couldn't put his finger on.

Lester sat behind a desk and slyly spoke to his uninvited victim, "Miss Jensen, I can't believe you have actually dared to enter my home. Have you come alone, or do you have an army of artists outside of my home waiting to shoot me?"

"I don't operate that way. I'm alone." she said. Lester turned and looked out of his window to make sure.

"Then I assume my butler Pierre was telling me the truth when he said you were here by yourself. And I suppose that thanks to my beloved ex-wife, you were given the directions to get here. Is that so?"

"Perhaps," Nicole said, and swallowed, trying to say as little as possible at first.

Lester opened a small plastic bottle and took out a little white pill and popped it into his mouth. Then he shakily reached for a goblet of water and chased it down his throat. "Care for one?" he asked.

"No, thanks."

"Why, of course you wouldn't. Thanks to you and your friends, more and more people are depriving themselves of the benefits of these barbiturates," he said resentfully as he lifted up the small bottle of pills and clutched it tightly. Then he gently put it back down on his desk. Lester noticed that Nicole was still standing a comfortable distance away from him, "How rude of me. I didn't even offer you a seat. Why don't you come here and sit on this couch. Don't worry, I won't shoot you," he paused and said, "yet" softly under his breath.

"Even if you did, it wouldn't stop me. I'd just come back next lifetime and continue my crusade."

"Ms. Jensen, do you really think you can outsmart the most brilliant group of all?" he said, and laughed wickedly. "It's now no secret that I'm the one who has been wanting to get revenge on you for what you did to me and other respectable members of my association! My acts are completely justified, given all the trouble you have caused!"

As Lester spoke, Nicole gasped in astonishment at his first sentence and his familiar laugh, then went slightly unconscious. She barely heard the rest of what he said, but instantly felt a sharp pain in her back, while looking at the man in front of her who spoke words that were identical to those that Libol had said to her! "My God, it's him. That's what drove me here," she thought so loudly that it was almost audible.

"Well, by the look on your face, it appears to me that you are now suffering a guilt complex. Maybe you'll come to your senses and start to realize the extent of your evil deeds."

Nicole became enraged, "There's nothing wrong with my senses, and my perceptions tell me that you've been chasing me for a long, long time. I was running away from you. Now it's your turn to run! You can try to keep denying the extent of the chaos you've inflicted, but people are now aware of your crimes and the destruction that you've caused."

Hot flashes of both fear and anger swelled up within Lester. He was experiencing a disturbance in his mind, the likes of which he couldn't grasp the cause of. Names of several psychological disorders that were possibly wrong with him leaped through his mind - psycho-paranoia, pre-natal hysteria. "Why? What is it about you that makes me hate you beyond reason?"

"We have played this game before! We go back several lifetimes, Libol!"

"Stop! What are you doing to me? Where did you come up with that name?"

"You've libeled me all right. Not only that, but you helped separate a powerful group of artists in the past with your lies and pretensions of wanting to help! It's my duty to see that you and your group are stopped in your tracks from not only obliterating artists, but everyone else on the planet!"

Lester worked hard to fight back at Nicole's words. Although deep inside he knew they were true, he didn't want to allow them to permanently seep into his mind, as this could cause an admission of guilt. He got hysterical and frantically pulled open a sticky desk drawer and put his hand on an object that he was not yet ready to show Nicole. Instead, he just laughed wickedly, feeling both a sense of insecurity and power. "Once again, you've stepped beyond your bounds. How dare you come intruding into my household, thinking that you can whip me into shape with your words? Your weapon is one that merely makes sound waves by hitting the air without creating any physical impact. I'm afraid that in order to handle you, I'm forced to use the only weapon that will shut you up forever," he said, nervously revealing a small silver pistol.

Nicole's eyes grew wider as she attempted to remain still and fully confront the gun that she knew had the power to put an end to her life.

Lester stood up, holding the weapon in his shaky hand. Then he walked towards Nicole. Confusion overcame him as he thought of his choices. Either kill Nicole and possibly spend the rest of his life in jail, or keep her alive and experience more death of his power and his profession. Then an idea came to him as he approached her. Nicole had the stillness of a statue as she sat on the couch, knowing that if at any moment she stopped fully confronting Lester, she could be doomed. He held the gun up to her and then gently rubbed it on the back of her neck, as if seducing her with an appendage to his own hand. Then he stroked her cheek, "I must say, I hate to admit it, but you are a pretty one. I tell you what? I'll be kind and not just blow you away. I'll give you a choice. Give up on your crusade and publicly apologize for all the slander you've wreaked upon my field. Then come and work with me to re-build the reputation of the group that rules the minds on this planet. Use your art for a 'better' cause. Your other choice is simply to undergo a painful death."

Nicole sat still unmoving for a couple of minutes, as Lester took the gun away from her neck and started to pull back on the trigger.

"I'd rather die than have anything to do with forwarding the goals of your group," she said and then closed her eyes.

Then, for several seconds, time stood still as Lester remained nearly as motionless as Nicole, perspiring as he contemplated following through with the choice Nicole had chosen. He felt a tug of war going on inside his mind, with one side saying "shoot her, come on," and another nudging on his conscience by saying "Don't do it, it's wrong. You're the one that should be punished." He let go of the trigger when he listened to his conscience and then cocked it again when he listened to the other side. Back and forth his uneasy finger went, while Nicole spent every agonizing second bravely sitting in the most perilous position she'd ever put herself into this lifetime.

Then, just as Lester was getting dizzy with confusion and uncertainty, he swiftly pulled the trigger into the cocked position and as he did, much to his surprise, a shot went off! Startled and shocked, he dropped the pistol. He saw that it hadn't fired, and that Nicole was sitting still and unharmed. Nicole, whose life flashed before her eyes, jumped as she opened her eyes that had tightly closed at the sound of the shot. Lester's terror and amazement caused him to drop to the floor where the gun had fallen. He picked up the pistol and examined it, trying to make sense out of how merely cocking a gun produced the sound of a live shot. He saw the bullet, unmoved, in its proper place.

It was as if he'd nearly forgotten about Nicole and was more interested in what had just occurred than in carrying out his murder. Nicole was so stunned and perplexed that she took advantage of Lester's preoccupation with the gun, and ran out of the den, down the long hallway toward the front door. Lester didn't even bother to go after her.

On her dash to the front door Nicole heard a scream, and then a woman's voice shouting desperately from one of the upper floors of the house, "Dr. Dopum! Dr. Dopum! Come quick!" the housekeeper said as she bounded down the stairs from the third floor. Nicole froze in her tracks and turned around and saw the housekeeper run to the doorway of the den.

"What is it, Hilda?" asked Lester.

Hilda was practically in tears, "Dr. Dopum, it's Troy. He's shot himself!"

"NO!" he shouted as he suddenly realized where the mysterious gunshot had come from. Lester leaped up off of the floor and ran like an Olympic athlete, bounding up the long stairway.

Nicole walked to the front door and opened it, and as she did she saw Pam's car pulling into the driveway. Nicole ran towards the car and noticed that Chris was in the front seat with her. Both of them quickly got out of the car. Nicole, about to collapse, raced to Chris and fell into his arms. He held her limp body up as she shivered with remnants of the fear she worked so hard to abate while Lester held the gun to her head.

"Nicole, are you okay? What did that beast do to you?" asked Pam.

"I'm okay. Please don't worry about me now. I'll tell you later."

"Oh, Nicole, we're just glad to see you alive. I couldn't live with the fact that I let you come over here unguarded," said Chris.

"And I couldn't forgive myself for giving you this address. I know you wanted to confront him alone, but we feared for your life too much to leave you here by yourself," Pam said, as two police cars drove up into the driveway and parked behind Pam's car.

"You called the police."

"Yeah, we wanted to protect you from a possible murder attempt," said Chris.

"Oh Pam, he tried, but other than my willingness to confront him, one of the things that may have stopped him might have been..." Nicole looked at Pam's wrinkled brow.

"May have been what?"

"May have been the shot that went off when Troy fired a gun at himself."

"Oh my God! My son! No!" Pam screamed and ran into the house. The housekeeper heard her shouting and told her that Troy was in his room. Pam then leapt up the stairs at a pace that nearly matched Lester's.

As she stood at the edge of the doorway of her son's room, she looked in and saw Troy lying on his back on the bed. Lester was sitting next to him. His head was on Troy's chest as he held him while listening to the silence in his chest that had once pulsated with a heartbeat. Pam then rushed over to the other side of the bed, across from Lester and sat down and looked at her lifeless son. Lester didn't even notice her, until she spoke, "What have you done to him?!"

Lester jumped up off of Troy's body and faced Pam as tears from a very old, deep well inside of him covered his coarse cheeks. After the shock of the death set in, Pam cried loudly as she leaned down and took her turn holding her son. Her white blouse sleeve became covered with some of the blood that oozed from the wound in Troy's head where he'd shot himself. "My baby! Oh my God, Troy! So young! Such a waste of a life!" Pam said and then sat up and gave Lester a look that was aimed to kill, "You murderer, damn you! I knew that something might happen to him! Haven't you learned that your drugs are the cause of this sort of thing! That boy had so much potential, and you killed it! He's dead, dead! It's all your fault!"

Lester said nothing, just sat with eyes blurred and the taste of salty water in his mouth. For the first time in ages, he started feeling real guilt as he flashed back to the time Troy saved his life at the beach. Pam's words battered hard at him, along with the memory of all the things Nicole had recently said in his office. "God, what have I done? What have I done? My only friend. My God. What am I going to do?" he cried. The death of his own son was the final straw that shook him up enough to finally wake up and start to open his eyes to some of his sinful deeds. The tough membrane of his evil character had finally cracked enough for him to see that he actually had a heart. He felt more lost and alone than he had in years and he didn't know where to turn.

Chapter 17

After Troy's death, Pam decided to press charges against Lester for the excessive drugging of their child. Gossip about this incident traveled around the city and made its way to the front page of a large newspaper publication. Pam was at home looking at the headlines of the paper which read, "Son of American Psychiatric Association Executive Commits Suicide." She went on to read the article, which also gave accurate mention of many of Lester's other crimes which Pam had revealed to a reporter who was thirsty for any juicy information he could get his hands on. Pam knew that the only good thing that came out of Troy's death was that Lester's true deeds were finally being revealed to the public at large.

* * * *

Lester was at home in his office looking at the piece of paper from Miss Noos, which Pam wanted him to sign. He took out his monogrammed pen with the letters LSD on it, nervously clicked it several times, and then signed the disapproval line. He made this decision although Pam had gone ahead and ruined his reputation already. He was scared that he might dig himself into a deeper hole than he was already in if he didn't do it and partly because he feared the possible loss of his other son.

Nicole's reputation was stronger than ever, as several articles were done exposing the fact that Lester was behind the libelous articles written on her, and also was the source of her attack two years ago. Because of these articles, and the interview done by Pam, more and more support was obtained for the Get High on Art Campaign.

Nicole and other members of her group planned a large event to reveal the abuses of psychiatry to the public.

Gina came back and confronted Nicole and told her that she wanted to make up the damage she'd done for failing to carry out her promotional duties. She told Nicole that she'd had some realizations after talking to Danny Jordan. Nicole knew that Gina was a real pro at advertising and that she'd been a big help to the group in the past, so decided to give Gina another chance. Because of the problems Gina had caused with the group, Nicole told her that she would not allow her to perform at this particular event, but when she made up the damage, she would consider her for future shows. Gina humbly agreed. The day of the event arrived, and several thousand people filled a large Los Angeles coliseum. Attendees included officials and celebrities from around the United States who wanted to be informed as to the true nature of the age old profession which had been entrusted with authority in many areas of life.

Nicole and the other artists and event personnel were backstage and could hear the overlapping voices of all the people in the audience. As more people entered the coliseum, the roar of sounds got louder and louder. Nicole looked at her watch and saw that it was time to quiet the crowd by starting the show. She walked to the center of the stage and looked out upon one of the largest audiences she'd ever addressed. Conversations started to die out as the eyes of the people turned to Nicole.

"Good afternoon," Nicole said into a microphone, and was then welcomed by enthusiastic cheers and whistles. "Thank you. It gives me great pleasure to be here today. I am honored to have the support of so many great people, who have helped me in my crusade to create a better world. I have found that in order to make positive changes in society, we must know who the foes are that would try to prevent such changes from occurring. Today, our production company will be revealing to you the truth about psychiatry, one of the biggest enemies that has ever existed. You will also hear from a few speakers who will share some enlightening facts," she said. Several television and video cameras zoomed in on Nicole to capture her words. She spoke briefly to the crowd and then announced Pam, who was the first speaker of the day.

Pam came out and told her story of what her life was like while living with Lester. At the end of her speech she made a special announcement, "As I mentioned to you, my teenage boy recently committed suicide. My younger son Peter has written a special poem as a tribute to Troy and the many other children whose lives have ended prematurely and unnecessarily. I'd now like to have Peter come out and share his words with you," she said as Peter bashfully walked up to the front of the stage where Pam stood. Pam lowered the mike for him.

Peter looked out to the audience nervously as he held a piece of paper in his hands. Then he swallowed and read his poem. "It's called, 'Behind the Drugged Eyes of a Child,'"

"I had hope down in my heart
that someday I'd fill the world with art.
I was young and alive and bright,
but then something happened to block my sight.
The drugs you gave me robbed my sanity.
I felt like I was in a jail without a key.
I tried to progress, but I was just too insane.
So I pulled a trigger and blew out my brains.
My dreams died along with my body,
all because you wouldn't let me be."

Peter stepped back from the mike, his body trembling from the after effects of stage fright. Hearts in the crowd were touched by the moving words of the eleven-year-old boy.

Nicole came back out on stage, and Pam and Peter exited. Nicole then proceeded to introduce Dale's wife Lori. Lori had gotten revitalized as a painter after going to one of Nicole's performances several months ago, and came up with a painting that suited the theme of the event. Lori walked up to the mike, followed by two stagehands who carried the large painting that she had recently completed. Cameras focused in on the artwork and displayed her picture on screens in the coliseum that gave all members of the audience good views of the piece. Lori explained how the picture was inspired by having worked for a law firm for many years. It was a painting of a courtroom where a defense lawyer was at the stand, along with a psychiatrist. The criminal that was being defended had a sign around his neck that read "mass murderer." The psychiatrist pointed to the murderer while the words "Temporary stress syndrome" where shown coming from him. The jury members looked to one another as thoughts of "not guilty" were written above their heads.

Lori went on to explain how she'd seen numerous cases where criminals were dismissed from their crimes due to reasons similar to the one she'd depicted in her painting.

After Lori was done, the event continued, with several more performers and speakers. The final act for the day was Nicole's band, who played a few songs and then ended with a gripping piece, with lyrics written by Pam Dopum, called "The Enemy of Man", a true story about one of Lester's patients.

"Young Johnny was on the beach
with his friends in a game of play.
They were laughing and talking about
what they wanted to be someday.
Someday when they grew older
Suzy wanted to be a housewife.
 Danny wanted to be a doctor and live a comfortable life.
As the sand slipped through Johnny's hand
he said I want to do the best I can.
I want a job where I can make people smile,
take away their pain for a while, make em smile
In school Johnny was popular. He made people laugh.
He was very bright.
But school soon became confusing.
No education. No wrong from right.
The teacher noticed how often Johnny
would be squirming in his seat.
She said there's a school psychiatrist
I want you and your mom to meet.
The doctor convinced Johnny's mom he was hyperactive.
Something's wrong with his brain.
He needs to be on Ritalin to keep him in line,
to make him sane.
They held out a helping hand. It was a TRAP...
 set by the enemy of man......"

Chapter 18

Renee, twenty-five-year old daughter of the President, was alone in her father's office in the White House. As she rocked back and forth on a swivel chair near his large desk, she looked at a copy of the poem that Peter Dopum had read to the audience at the event. She reached into her sweater pocket and pulled out a tape with some of Nicole's songs on it, including the one entitled "The Enemy of Man". Two weeks ago, Renee had insisted on going backstage after the show and meeting Nicole and some of the other artists. She was so inspired about their cause that the first thing she decided to do was inform her father of the necessity to put an end to psychiatric abuse. She only hoped that her father, who would be coming into the office at any moment to meet with her, would be as moved as she was with the words of Nicole and Peter.

Renee placed Nicole's tape into a cassette recorder. She fast forwarded it to the Enemy of Man song, and pressed the play button while making adjustments to the volume and balance of the sound. Then, unbeknownst to her, the President stepped into the office while her back was to him. Hit by the powerful words of the song, he stopped in his tracks for a moment and listened to the intensity of the communication. Then he cleared his throat and made his presence known as he walked into the stately room and took his proper place behind his desk. He knew the subject matter his daughter wanted to talk about, but wasn't aware that she'd brought any music to help relay her point.

Renee pushed the "pause" button on the recorder when her father sat down. He insisted that she rewind the song and start it over so that he could hear it from the beginning. Renee gladly complied, and glued her eyes to her father's face, careful not to miss any expression that reflected his feelings. When the song was over, the President was silent. He rubbed his chin and Renee knew that this was a sign that he was still absorbing the message. Although his eyes had been somewhat closed to the problems of psychiatry, the song got him to open them slightly, though he was not quite willing to admit the extent of harm caused by this government funded "elite" group. He had heard about the Get High on Art Group and was aware that they were making a dent in the amount of drugs consumed by citizens of the country. He knew psychiatry was becoming less popular, but, because of other office duties, he hadn't paid that much attention to Nicole and her crusade.

Renee zealously went on to tell her father about the performances and speakers at the event and he patiently listened to her words. He hadn't been over-eager about the meeting with Renee that day, as he had much more pressing issues on his mind, such as what to do about the declining illiteracy level in the country. But out of love and respect for his daughter, he was willing to hear what she had to say. When Renee informed him of some of the things Pam had said in her speech regarding the effect of psychiatry on the educational system, his ears perked up with interest, as some of his criticism melted away. One of his pet peeves had been the lack of motivation and industriousness displayed by the young people these days. He had a hard time believing that the mental health authorities were really the ones that were behind this dilemma, but considered the possibility.

As Renee continued, the president looked at his watch, realizing he'd have to leave soon, as he had a meeting with the Vice President and Secretary of State. Although he was somewhat swayed by Renee and Nicole's song, he was not at the stage where he wanted to consider taking serious actions to put an end to any of the activities of psychiatry.

Some of Renee's hopes had waned, after trying to persuade her father to become unfixed from his conservative position and take a look at the facts she was exposing. She had pressed the fact that if government funding was cut, then the very lifeline of this treacherous group would be severed, and the country would be better off. He was not quite ready for such a drastic move. But Renee was not willing to give up, as she knew that in the long run, he'd have to see the truth. Just as the President once again looked at his watch, and was about to leave, Renee unfolded Peter's poem and insisted that he read it before going. He complied, and although he tried to suppress it, he experienced a feeling of sadness and grief. Renee then quickly told him the story behind it and how Peter had dedicated it to Troy and the many other children who had lost their lives.

The president got up and told Renee that he was late for the meeting, but that he was interested in getting back with her about this issue, which he was now starting to see from a more realistic angle. Renee's hopes rose again, and she was happy to hear that so much of a change had been produced in her father's views. She knew how stubborn he could be at times, and she considered what she'd done so far a good accomplishment. However, it was not nearly enough, and she knew that in order to make enough of an impact on him, something more dramatic would have to be done. Four days had passed since Renee met with her father.

* * * *

It was now three months since the death of Troy Dopum, and the anniversary of his birthday. Pam had gone to Troy's gravesite to reminisce about her son. She stood with her right arm wrapped tightly around Peter's shoulder. In her left hand she held a handkerchief that she used to sporadically dab away her tears.

Lester also arrived at the site. He was immersed in guilt, which had recently turned from a puddle in his mind, to a deep pool.

Peter went over read him the poem that he wrote as a tribute to Troy. This was the final blow for Lester, who was now preoccupied with feelings of self-abasement. He wondered how he could ever make amends for what he'd done.

Pam, who hadn't talked to Lester at all yet, now approached him. "Hello, Lester," she said with a muffled tone of resentment.

"Hello," he replied, his eyes fleeting around her, not quite able to look at her.

Pam reached into her purse and pulled out an envelope as Lester suspiciously wondered about her actions. She put a black gloved hand into the envelope and took out a letter.

"What's that?" Lester asked, slightly paranoid.

"A letter from the daughter of the President of the United States."

Lester gave Pam a defensive look. "Does she know about me or something?"

"Yes, and not in a favorable light. But I'd like to see her change that.

She badly needs your help right now."

"My help, Pam? Are you being delusive? According to all your accusations, I'm the one who destroys everything he touches."

"Lester, please hear me out for once."

"I've heard you a lot lately."

"Good, then let me explain," Pam said as she went on to tell him about Rene's plan to help eliminate the abuses of psychiatry in the country by getting their funding cut. Lester cringed, and at first found himself resisting her words. Then he contemplated them more seriously as she pleaded with him to reveal his own crimes and those of his cohorts to the president himself. He knew that he was now under close scrutiny by the public, that he was about to face his own trial, and that this move could help his reputation. Lester knew that there had been psychiatrists who had turned against their own field, but he never dreamed that he'd ever be in this position, not in a million years. It had been so far from his mind that it was inconceivable, and now here he was batting the idea around like a ping-pong ball. "Do it, don't do it, do it, don't do it," raced through his mind and made him dizzy.

"Do it, please Lester, for your son and all the others!"

"Why don't you go? You're the one who seems to be doing all the exposé lately."

"It would make a much bigger impact coming from you."

Lester couldn't stand it any longer. He put his hand to his forehead and shut his eyes. All he could see was the coffin where Troy's young body lay. He knew that soon his young tender flesh would be rotting. He removed his hand from his perspiring brow, and wept for the second time in many years. "My son is dead, and now I'm faced with making the choice of putting another nail in

Psychiatry's casket. What's come over me? Why do I actually feel like this is the right thing to do?"

"Because it is."

Chapter 19

P am acted as the liaison between Renee and Lester. She got Lester's agreement to meet with the President and his Congress as soon as Renee could set up a meeting. Nicole, who had also gotten a letter from Renee urging her to come to the White House once approval was gotten, had also agreed to such a visit. Renee wanted Nicole to talk about her group, as well as give a special private performance for the President and his staff.

It was seven a.m. and Lester was at home in his mansion. He tied his bathrobe belt around his waist and walked to the kitchen and fixed himself a bowl of cereal. He sat at the kitchen table in a pit of emptiness that was only filled by the ghost of Troy, who haunted his memory. Lester normally had Muriel, the housekeeper, fix him a big breakfast, but he'd given her the day off.

When he was done with his Wheaties, he climbed up three flights of stairs with the voice of his housekeeper screaming through his mind, "Dr. Dopum, Dr. Dopum, come quick!" He forced himself to put aside this memory, which seemed as if it was occurring right then and there.

Lester went to his room and got dressed, combed his rumpled hair, and walked down the stairway towards the front door. He got into his car and made his way to his nearby office. When he got to the office building, he didn't even hear the cordial hello given to him by the receptionist, but just walked past her into the large room where he'd spent a good part of his life. He looked on his desk and saw a pile of letters, and thumbed through them. He could tell they were mostly regarding psychiatric conferences and issues. Instead of his usual fiery interest in such things, he was rather indifferent

Sitting at his desk, he went through the mail piece by piece. He briefly glanced at the letters and then stuffed them into a pending basket. The last envelope he opened was from the head of the American Psychiatric Association, who resided in Chicago. He pulled out a letter, unfolded it, and discovered a large government check inside. He looked at the $500,000.00 figure and was shocked to see this amount, which was larger than the usual monthly checks he'd received at his office. He wondered why the APA head was sending so much money.

"Dear Lester,

"We must act with urgency in the continued implementation of our various programs. As you are aware, another enemy has been encroaching upon our territory, attempting to throw us out of business. Yes, I am referring to the 'Get High on Art' group which you have sought to warn me about. Of course, if you hadn't botched the attack on Nicole Jensen a couple of years ago, perhaps we'd be in better shape. Instead, I'm afraid we're faced with the dilemma of having to wage war with a bunch of artists afflicted with 'prima donna' syndrome who think they know better than you and me about how to handle the pitiful humans in this society.

"Part of this check is to cover the campaign I have initiated regarding educational control programs. This will include non-mandatory parental consent for the prescribing of drugs to children. The teachers will be allowed to enforce which kids are to be put on Ritalin and other necessary substances. The first step to get legal approval for such a plan is to flood the public with articles that state the urgency of such a move. This will give parents the truth about the importance of such an undertaking, and should serve to keep them from attacking us unnecessarily for our helpful actions. Then we must get the final approval from our friends in the White House, who have still been giving us a portion of our operating funds." The letter also mentioned other areas that were to be covered with the check. Much of it was to be used for newspaper and magazine articles to flood the public regarding various issues, such as "The need for psychiatric counseling;" "The therapeutic effects of shock therapy;" "The importance of drugs in enhancing Creativity;" "The eradication of old-fashioned societal moral codes;" etc. A portion of the check was also payment to Lester for the work he'd be doing to get this major publicity for the APA.

Lester put down the letter and picked up the check and stared at it in a much different manner than he had in the past when he'd received such payments.

Renee had managed to get her father's agreement to see both Nicole and Lester, and arrangements had been made to have both of them fly out to the White House at separate times. Nicole went first, and gave a special solo performance to the President and Congress. Then she explained about her group and the successes they had in helping many thousands of people to lead better lives. She gave examples of the people who had gotten off drugs and had channeled their energies into artistic activities. Because of the large number of people who were now achieving goals in the arts and various other areas of life, the crime rate had diminished in several cities. Many people were once again recognizing the importance of morals and how they were vital in keeping a society from ruin. Nicole's performance and speech shook up members of Congress, and they started taking a serious look at the fact that they'd intentionally been kept blinded as to who this enemy of society had been.

A few days after Nicole's visit, Lester arrived at the capital of the United States, at first apprehensive about following through with his trip. He forced himself to walk through the doors of the ominous White House.

Lester could hardly believe that he was actually sitting in a room with the President of the United States and his Congress, something that he never dreamed he'd be doing. He fidgeted with the arm of his chair as he turned and faced the head of the nation, who looked at him with stern eyes. Lester could hardly bear to look at the captive audience of Senators and members of the House of Representatives.

"Dr. Dopum, I understand that you have decided to put yourself in the vulnerable position of confessing your crimes and those of your profession," said the President.

Lester gulped and tensed up, "Yes, sir," he said and paused, whirling with confusion and last minute regrets.

"I hear that the death of your son was one of the traumas which helped to turn the tide for you regarding your stance on your field."

"Yes," he squeaked, and forced himself to speak, "I can no longer allow the drugging of innocent children to continue," Lester said and continued to spill out some of the horrors he'd been involved with over the years. Then he revealed some shocking truths about the head of the APA, and the felonies that were committed by him, making Lester's own deeds look like misdemeanors. The President sat practically unmoving as he listened with amazement at what he was hearing. He couldn't believe that he'd been so unaware of the atrocities of psychiatry. But now he was hearing truths revealed to him right out of one of the horse's mouths.

Lester's last move was to show the President the letter and check the head of the APA had sent that to him. After the President read the letter aloud, he questioned Lester as to what his reply was going to be.

Lester held the check with his left hand. Then he paused for a moment and swallowed again. He demonstrated his response by slowly ripping it in half. Then he tore it again and again. "Do something more useful with the money of the tax paying citizens. I can't accept this," he said after making the move that pushed the President and many others over the edge as far as their decision about what to do with government funding of mental health programs.

Although Congress made a practically unanimous decision to cut the funds of psychiatry, there were soon desperate pleas by members of the National Institute of Mental Health not to follow through with the decision. This group, which had been responsible for coercing the government into supporting psychiatry, didn't want to stop receiving its large checks that funded their vested interests in controlling the population. The head of the Institute spent several days writing a document urging the President and Congress to repeal their decision. He dug up as many reasons as he could find regarding the importance of psychiatry, and why this funding should not be allowed to be cut. Congress met once again, and reviewed the document, and even arranged to meet with the Institute head to ask him some questions about his document. After listening to this man, members of Congress observed that he couldn't adequately prove the necessity of psychiatry. A few days after Lester's meeting at the White House, papers throughout the U.S. publicly announced the verdict. Headlines made such statements as "Executive of APA Helps Sway Congress to Cut Government Funding of Psychiatry," and "APA Executive Rips up Large Check from Government." The articles went on to expose damages done by this profession.

More and more people started waking up to the treacherous ways of those to whom they'd entrusted their minds. Citizens who read the papers were happy to see that their money was no longer filling the coffers of the men in white coats. There was one person, however, who wasn't filled with joy at the decision.

The head of the APA was at home in the morning when he picked up the paper outside on his front porch. Much to his unsuspecting horror, he looked at the headlines, and then went on to read an article.

"That traitor! That bastard!" he said, along with several profane words directed at Lester. Then he rolled up the paper and smacked his pet Collie with it. The dog yelped and whimpered away.

He immediately rushed to his phone and dialed Lester's home phone number. He knew that it was only six a.m. in Beverly Hills, but the last thing he cared about was waking Lester and causing him to lose some beauty rest.

Lester had been sleeping more soundly than he had in several years. While deep into a dream, the loud ringing of his phone rudely awakened him. He jumped out of his slumber and listened to the ringing for a few seconds and then, while still half asleep, picked up the receiver.

"Hello."

"Lester, you God damn son of a bitch! You are a traitor to me and your profession!" blasted so loudly, that he instantly woke fully. He suspected that he'd be receiving an infliction of wrath from his boss, but he didn't think it would be so early in the morning. "I never expected such behavior from someone who I thought was a devout member of the most prestigious group on Earth! You are afflicted with the most deadly mental illness of all, compulsive-destruction syndrome! You are bringing down your own kind!"

Normally, Lester would have been extremely perturbed by such accusations. Instead, because of some newfound mental soundness, he remained unscathed by his words. "So, what are you going to do about it?"

"The one thing that will put you out of business for good."

"What's that?"

"Fire you!"

"Thank you. You've helped to put an end to my miseries!" he said and then slammed down the phone and pulled the cord out of the wall so he wouldn't be bothered again.

Chapter 20

I t had been one year since the President of the United States publicly announced that the National Institute of Mental Health was no longer to receive government money to fund psychiatric programs. Lester had gone to trial and testified to his crimes. Although he would have normally served several years in prison for his acts, he was put on probation due to the noble deed he did when he visited the White House. Lester made further amends by helping with an investigation of the president of the APA as well as his entire field. After investigations were done, it was found that psychiatry was not in fact qualified to be the mental health authority of the nation.

Nicole and Chris, who had been going nonstop doing numerous media interviews, along with various performances and events, decided to take a break one weekend and spend some time alone. Jeremy was staying at a friends' house.

Chris was glued to the TV set. "Nicky, come here quick," he said.

Nicole turned off the kitchen faucet, put down a dish she was washing, and ran over to him, "What's the urgency?" Without waiting for a reply, she got her answer by listening to the Newscaster on station KGOOD.

"Yes, that's right, since the Get High on Art campaign was started two years ago we have seen some remarkable changes throughout the U.S. To tell you about some of the improvements, I'd like to introduce you to Dr. Newborn, a reformed psychiatrist who will inform you of some of the progress made since the disbanding of IB Dilly."

"Thank you, Chuck," said the bearded man in the white jacket who sat next to the newscaster. "One of our biggest improvements is in the educational arena. Since children throughout the country are no longer subject to the detrimental effects of Ritalin and Prozac, there is far less violence in our schools. There are still a small percentage of parents who feel that drugs are the only solution for their unruly children, but because of numerous campus lectures being done by myself and my colleagues, more and more parents are becoming disillusioned of this idea. They are seeing that there are other ways to handle their children."

"Dr. Newbern, that's quite an accomplishment. I'd like to bring up the fact that school test scores are going back up to what they used to be fifty years ago. To what do you attribute this?"

"Yes, Chuck, many young people are once again becoming educated with real knowledge. Instead of channeling all their energies into emotional therapy programs, they are learning how to think."

"That's great, and I also hear that many schools, from elementary on up to college level, are now being given grants which support creative arts programs. What are the results of this?" "For the first time in many years, the number of young people pursuing artistic careers is on the rise," he said and chuckled. "Why, I've been so inspired by some of these kids, that I recently pulled my old tuba out of the closet to see if I still remembered how to play."

Chuck smiled, "So now I suppose you're going to join a high school marching band."

"I was thinking about it. But enough of me. I'd like to show you further results by showing you a short clip of a new child prodigy in a low-income school district who was able to pursue classical piano because of a large grant given to his school. His school had no music programs prior to this, and thanks to the help of Uncle Sam, the school was able to purchase several pianos and hire some music teachers."

A video was shown of a ten-year-old child who was sitting at a grand piano playing a complex piece of music by Chopin.

"So, there you have it, a child who might never have gotten the chance to touch a keyboard if it wasn't for this new program," said Dr. Newborn.

Chuck thanked Dr. Newborn for being his guest and then went on to mention some of the other nationwide statistics that had been improving over the past year.

"Crime rates are at an all time low, with a decrease of 60% over last year at this time. This is directly related to the decline of drug abuse, which has dropped by 65% throughout the country.

"This wraps up our Good News broadcast for the evening. Be sure and stay tuned for the upcoming documentary entitled 'Morals Revisited', which will air tonight at nine p.m."

Chris turned off the TV and he and Nicole talked about how proud they were of all the accomplishments of their group.

"I'm kind of thirsty, Nicky. I'm going to get some apple juice. You want any?"

"Sure, sounds good."

Chris went to the kitchen and got a couple of glasses of ice cold juice and sat down next to Nicole, who was flipping through a photo album. He handed her a drink and she thanked him by giving him an affectionate kiss on his cheek. Chris' eyes were drawn to one of the photos on the open page. It was a picture of Gina standing in front of a group of teenagers, teaching them various singing techniques.

"Now she's one person that has really amazed me. I never expected her to come back and join us, let alone be the tremendous asset that she is," said Chris.

"We can thank Danny Jordan for that one."

"Yeah, that's true. I guess it takes being ruined before some people wake up enough to see that they've been heading in the wrong direction."

"That's true," Nicole said as she turned a page and pointed to another picture of Gina, who was smiling while holding up a copy of her own CD. "It's great to see that she finally got what she wanted."

Chris and Nicole went on to amuse themselves with the pictures. Nicole told Chris that she was especially happy to hear from artists in other countries who often consulted her about problems in their nations. She had informed them as to how to start up their own Get High on Art campaigns, which many were now successfully doing.

"It's good to see that so many artists have been cured of their Dream Demise," said Chris.

"That's true. Unfortunately, this planet still has a way to go before it compares with Athena, but things are certainly starting to turn around nicely."

"Speaking of Athena, do you have any idea what ever happened there after you left?"

"No, this is a question that has often silently plagued me ever since my vision, Nicole said. She and Chris were silently contemplative about this matter for a while. Then the unique singing of a bird, one that sang a different tune than Nicole's two pets interrupted them. The intensity of the other bird's tune was so strong that they did nothing but listen to this mysterious creature. Then a smile leapt upon Nicole's face, as she recognized a familiarity in the voice of the outdoor bird.

Chris looked at her in awe and disbelief, "Nicole you're not going to tell me that the bird out there actually flew here all the way from Athena."

"I..." before Nicole could answer there was a knock on the front door, "Just a minute, let me go see who this is."

Nicole looked through the peephole in the door, and stepped back in shock, and then looked again, hardly able to believe her own eyes. She opened the door and blurted out the name of the woman who helped to change her life, "Devon, you're back!"

"Hello, Nicole," said Devon, who was dressed in a green Athenian gown, and wore golden sandals on her feet. The mystery bird that had been flying around outside of the house came and landed on Devon's shoulder.

Chris, who barely had time to formulate doubts about the bird, put his doubts to rest. While Nicole led Devon and the bird into the house, he quickly stood up.

Nicole introduced Devon to Chris. He was speechless as he looked at the stunningly beautiful alien with the bright turquoise eyes.

Nicole offered Devon a seat, while she and Chris sat down and looked at her in awe.

"So, you really are from Athena?" Chris asked, while trying to break through the shock of seeing Devon.

"Yes, I am."

Nicole thanked her for giving her the vision awhile back, and then asked why Devon had returned.

"I have come as a messenger from the Empress. She wanted me to give you a special acknowledgment for all that you and your fellow artists have done," she said as she reached into a pocket in her gown and pulled out a small golden plaque and handed it to Nicole. On it was the engraved picture of a girl riding a winged horse. She held up a torch in her right hand. An inscription read, "Your group carry's the torch that helps light the way to a better world."

Nicole clutched it tightly, as both she and Chris admired it. "Thank you Devon, but how did the Empress know what had occurred here on Earth?"

She told Nicole about the code light in the galactic map room, and how the color for Earth had recently changed to a less dangerous color. Devon went on to explain about Zeena's perceptic abilities and said that after she saw the light, she tuned in on Nicole and sensed the impact she and the others had been creating. "Devon, that's incredible. I'm so happy to hear that the Empress cares about Earth. And I'm glad to see that you're all right. I was so worried about you after you came to visit me last year. You seemed so ill."

Devon smiled. "That was just because unfortunately, my system cannot tolerate the toxins in your planet's atmosphere. I had to use my body sparingly, and I almost destroyed it by overuse."

"What do you mean?" Nicole asked, as Devon went on to explain what she meant, as well as tell her about the process of de-molecularization.

"Devon, there is another question that has been haunting me, ever since my visit to Athena."

"Oh, what is that?"

"What exactly happened when I left, after the Knight invasion?"

Devon smiled warmly, "The Empress was aware that you may be asking such a question, and this was one of the pieces of the puzzle she didn't want to leave out for you. In order to give you an answer, I have brought a special message from the Empress herself," she said as she put her hand into another pocket and pulled out a tiny silver box, "This is a recording device, similar to what is known on Earth as a cassette recorder. The difference is that it uses no tapes or compact discs. One simply pushes a button and speaks as their vocals get directly recorded onto a tiny metallic chip inside the machine. In this case, although the Empress is speaking in Athenian, a translation has been programmed into the machine, telling it to recite her words in English. She pushed a button to activate the message.

A chill ran down Nicole's spine as she listened to the voice of the Empress, "My dear Rhianna, thank you for alerting me to the invasion of the Knights. I heeded your warning, and after observing the franticness of Vaadra and Libol at your home in North Valley, I knew that there was chaos on the planet. I returned immediately to arrange a meeting with my staff and warned them that there was severe trouble within the palace and on Athena. I informed them that the Knights had infiltrated the creative conference. Some were unwilling to confront the insidiousness of the evil around them, and it took much work on my part to get them to see the whole picture. They were so wrapped up in palace affairs that they weren't aware of what was happening. To make matters worse, it turned out that Jirmak and some of the other staff were willfully betraying me behind my back and intentionally aiding the enemy. These traitors were exiled from Athena.

Then I interviewed all officials from other planets that were residing in Etherea, and discovered which ones were in fact Knights. They were transported back to Trod, where Kilbor had them ostracized to a dark corner of their own planet for failing to bring Athena under their control. Libol and Slandor had long since gone on to attempt to create trouble in other sectors of the galaxy before I arrived.

"I telecommed all artists on Athena and informed them as to what had been occurring on the planet during the time that I was away. Unfortunately, the damage was so extensive that many Athenians were unwilling to stand up for their land and re-unite as a team. Some had given up on the creation of their favorite art forms.

"Many of the artists who were shuttled away to other planets decided not to return home, because of rumors they'd heard about impending dangers still lurking on Athena.

"A group of disaffected Athenians was discovered right here in our own land, and even with my return, it took a long while to discover who they were. Refusing to reform and insisting on dissension, they too were exiled.

"After many, many years, I was able to assemble together the most dedicated Athenians, who were still willing to stand up for their home. We planned a large 'Crusade for Creative Freedom,' whereby artists went out to key spots on the planet and created together without restriction. Artists contributed and helped one another, and demonstrated to any in doubt that artistic expression was one of the most important, inherent traits of a spiritual being.

"It took many years to heal the war wound that was suffered during the Knight invasion. The team has just recently been revitalized. We are once again united, although not quite as strong as before the tragedy.

The population on Athena at this time is smaller than it was when you were here.

Like yourself, many of the team have traveled elsewhere in the galaxy. Some still have the devotion and purpose that they had when on Athena. Others have long since forgotten their role as artists. You and those on your team, of course, fit into the former category and are highly commended for undying dedication. The challenge you face on Earth, in healing the wounds inflicted by the group that has destroyed many a great civilization, is no small task. Your planet was in far worse shape than many that I know of. You and the other artists have succeeded to demonstrate that it is possible to join together and make a difference. You have my deepest love and admiration. Carry on!"

The tape ended and Devon turned off the device. The golden bird, which had been resting on Devon's shoulder, flew over to the cage where Nicole's two pets resided and perched on top of it. The two creatures inside looked at this unusual bird. The

Athenian bird turned his head back and forth as he looked from one bird to the other.

Nicole and Chris were speechless after hearing the tape. Then Nicole spoke, "Devon, can I record a message for the Empress?"

"Sure, let me just press a couple of buttons here. All right, go ahead and speak whenever you're ready."

"Thank you so much for caring about me and helping me get my strength back. I'd like to assure you that my team of artists is more invincible than ever. We're well aware of the vital importance of the mission of the artist. You have my deepest love and respect."

Devon turned off the little machine when Nicole was done and put it back into her gown pocket. She talked with Chris and Nicole a while longer and then told them that it was time for her to leave. Nicole hugged her tightly. The golden bird alighted upon Devon's shoulder. Devon asked Nicole's permission to exit her home differently than the way she'd entered. Nicole told her that she'd had people disappear on her before, but not the same way that Devon wanted to. Devon smiled. Nicole led her to a bathroom. She used it as her own private undressing room for herself and her bird. Devon had told Nicole she'd be gone in a couple of minutes. She laughed to herself about how much easier this was than having to pop in and out of large trash receptacles. Then she saddened a bit as she thought about the fact that most Earthlings weren't at a point where they could easily believe that anyone could actually perform such a simple procedure as de-molecularization. "Oh, well, maybe someday," she thought, as the last traces of Devon's gown became invisible.

"Nicole, I'm now convinced that there's probably nothing you could tell me that I wouldn't believe," Chris said, still astounded by the fact that they had just been visited by an actual Athenian.

"Well, thanks for your trust," she said as she punched his arm playfully.

Chris picked up the gold plaque that was resting on the coffee table and inspected it carefully, "What do we do for our next number to handle this planet?"

"Oh, I don't know. How about helping to create world peace?"

"Hmm, such a small game. Don't you want a bigger challenge?"

"Actually, it's smaller than it used to appear to me."

"What do you mean?"

"I've learned that many of the foolish battles on the planet have been instigated by our dear friends in white coats."

"Oh, really?"

"Yeah, for example in Bosnia, the Serbs were convinced by a psychiatrist that they were a superior breed and should indulge in ethnic cleansing. This led them to the murder of the Croatians. This has been a strategy like the one used by Hitler. I understand that Hitler wasn't thrilled about the idea of killing all those Jews at first. He was coerced by Dr. Ernst Rudin, a Professor of Psychiatry at Munich University."

"My god, when will those guys ever quit?"

"I don't know, but I suppose the more people are truly willing to confront the evils on this planet, the faster the job can get done."

"There's no shortage of things to handle here."

"Hey Chris?"

"Yes, honey?"

"Wasn't this supposed to be our day off?"

Chris laughed, then hugged her, "Yeah, it was."

THE END

About the Author

Barbara Joy Cordova has been a songwriter for many years. She has also produced numerous events, which have included a variety of talent. Years ago, after studying the works of L. Ron Hubbard, she was motivated to write this story.

Barbara is also the founder of Artists for a Better World, a group of artists who have united to change conditions in society for the better. Visit their web site at:

www.artistsforabetterworld.com

~~~~~~~~~~

A selection of songs (lyrics & music) from the novel brought these responses:

"I loved the tape! It was full of passion and new ideas. It made me want to read the book. The songs were uplifting and inspiring and appealed to a purpose I have to join together with other artists and make a better world."

Becky Mate, Writer/Executive Director of Creative Artists Forum for Expansion (CAFE)

* * * *

"Very unique. It was different than everything out there: a pleasant surprise. I wanted to share it with others. Great sound! Excellent job!"

Santi, Singer/songwriter - On the top 10 charts on Latin stations

* * * *

"Very original. The songs took me right into the story and I enjoyed that. Excellent music! It was fun!"

Phylis Forsch, Legal Assistant

Order Form

Name _____ Phone (___)_____

Address _____

City _____ State _____ Zip _____-_____

e-mail _____

Products for Sale:

Cassette: $11.00 (includes tax)
plus $2 shipping & handling = **$13.00 total**

Book: $13.95 (includes tax)
plus $3 shipping & handling = **$16.95 total**

Cassette: Quantity_____ Total Cost_____

Book: Quantity_____ Total Cost_____

Send payment to:
Artists for a Better World
PO Box 11081
Glendale, CA 91226